FEB 2012

Y0-CBI-139

The Dark

Before Dawn

Laurie Stevens

Copyright © 2011 Laurie Price
All rights reserved

ISBN: 1456450115
ISBN-13: 9781456450113
LCCN: 2010918623

This book, or parts thereof, may not be reproduced in
any form without permission.

Published by Follow Your Dreams Productions
19411 Londelius Street
Northridge, CA 91324

This book is work of fiction. Names, characters, places,
and incidents are used fictitiously or are a product of
the author's imagination and any resemblance to actual
persons, living or dead, business establishments, events,
or locales is entirely coincidental.

Your support of the author's rights is appreciated. Please
purchase only authorized electronic editions of this book.

ACKNOWLEDGMENTS

The author gratefully acknowledges the following people whose expertise made possible the writing of this book: Sergeant Dan Taylor, Homicide, Los Angeles County Sheriff's Department; Captain James Bird, Los Angeles Fire Department, Elizabeth Harris, Ph.D, Leslie Kurtz, Ph.D. Colleen Kelly, William Carter, Esquire, Shelley Berman, Martin Retting, Inc., Culver City Modern & Antique Firearms. Thanks also to Kathy Magallanes and Jody Hepps for their keen eyes.

DEDICATION:

For Steven, Jonathan and Alanna
And to Grandma Dena
for believing in "big dreams and a little luck"

PROLOGUE

The motorcycle cop stood along Malibu Canyon Road leveling his radar gun at the passing motorists. The morning sun was already warm enough to cause sweat to gleam under the brim of his helmet and dampen his moustache. Some cars hit the brakes upon spotting the policeman; others flew by, truly speeding. The cop didn't care. The radar gun was a fake.

Whoever was meant to come along would appear, of that the cop was sure. A beach breeze wafted through the canyon and cooled him off. This was totally meant to be. Even the pink wildflowers capering at his feet were cheering his progress. Keeping the radar gun pointed westward, the policeman pretended to look serious under his dark sunglasses.

He finally waved over a white pickup truck. A phone number and the word "handyman" were printed on the long bed.

The cop went to the driver's side window.

"May I see your driver's license and registration, please?"

"Was I speeding?" The handyman had a sparse brown beard, friendly eyes and seemed to be in his late-twenties.

The policeman ignored the question and inspected the handyman's identification.

"You're Ted Brody? This is your truck— your business?"

"Well, yes." The friendly eyes became apprehensive.

"I didn't realize I was speeding, Officer."

The policeman paused a moment, thinking. Finally, he pocketed the handyman's ID and went over to a stretching oak tree where a moped was parked.

"Are you going to give me a ticket?" The handyman asked, trying to be polite.

The policeman didn't reply. Instead, he hoisted the moped into the bed of the pickup truck.

"What are you doing?" the handyman cried.

The policeman reappeared on the passenger side of the pickup with a backpack in one hand and a gun in the other.

"Let's drive, Ted."

He instructed the handyman to drive over a winding canyon road and onto one of the fire roads that crisscrossed the Santa Monica Mountains north of Los Angeles.

The cop calmly answered the endless stream of questions. No, he wasn't commandeering the vehicle. He wasn't a thief or a carjacker. No, he didn't want the handyman's money either. The cop simply wanted them to get to a more remote spot.

When they reached a satisfactory destination, the cop opened the backpack and pulled out a trench knife.

"W-What," the handyman stammered. "W-why?"

Catching him by surprise, the cop furiously rammed the knife into the handyman's throat and dragged the blade horizontally. An arc of arterial blood instantly splattered the windshield, the dashboard, and the cop's uniform. The cop stabbed the handyman again and again, until the struggling stopped.

When silence permeated the truck's cab, thick as the spreading blood, the policeman sat back and looked at the dead man.

"One down, six more to go. But you, my friend, have no idea how much you've helped me today. I will not forget you, Ted. Now, if you don't mind—" The policeman parted the handyman's legs and went to work with the knife again.

When his task was complete, the cop unzipped his own pants and rubbed the velvety red warmth against himself until he gripped the dashboard in ecstasy.

"Thank you," he whispered harshly, still shuddering. The cop sat back once more, breathing heavily. After a moment he zipped up his pants and reached into the backpack. He pulled out a can of gasoline and put it aside. He then pulled a damp towel from a plastic bag and wiped off his hands. Once they were moderately clean, he took a folded newspaper clipping from a pocket in the backpack.

"Do you believe in divine intervention?" The cop looked at the still-warm corpse next to him. "No, I guess you wouldn't. But I do." He gently spread out the newspaper and read the headline: "Sheriff's Detective Gabriel McRay under Investigation for Brutality." The cop giggled as he pocketed the clipping, unsnapped his helmet and pulled off his fake moustache. "It doesn't get any better than this."

CHAPTER 1

A large black fly buzzed inside the window that overlooked the grassy area bordering the headquarters unit of the Los Angeles County Sheriff's Department, seeking a way outside. Dr. Raymond Berkowitz, the departmental psychiatrist, observed Gabriel McRay looking wistfully at the fly, and he knew his patient felt trapped, wishing also for escape.

"I asked you a question, Gabe."

The detective shifted in his seat and cleared his throat. He looked squarely at Dr. B. "I'm sorry," he said, "Say again?"

"Are you still having the nightmares?"

"Yes."

"And the headaches?"

"Yes."

The psychiatrist regarded Gabriel through his wire-rim glasses. Dr. B could gain insight into a patient's personality by noting his posture. Gabriel sat rigidly, his ankles and arms crossed in front of him. He assumed a defensive pose, defensive and protective. An invisible calamity burdened Gabriel's psyche, and Dr. B was supposed to help lift that weight off his patient. So far, Gabriel was resisting his assistance.

"I received the test results from your physician, Gabe, and the results of the MRI are negative. I think I'm justified in saying that your headaches—"

"Are all in my head."

"I didn't—"

"No pun intended," Gabriel finished and cracked a smile, which faded in an instant.

Dr. B continued. "I'm ninety-nine percent sure your problems don't stem from anything neurological, Gabe, so give me something to work with."

"What do you want from me? What do you want me to say to you?" Gabriel asked.

"Well, do you have anything to say about why you're here?"

"I was just doing my job."

"You don't think you were a tad hyper vigilant?"

Gabriel licked his lips and smiled again. This time the smile stayed. "All right, you've got me. I'm impressed. Hyper vigilant. A-plus, Raymond."

"Okay." Dr. B grinned through a pebbly, dark beard salted with a generous amount of gray. He was a lean and bony man who moved with a calm grace that kept him from appearing gangly. His wire rim glasses constantly dropped down his nose in a rather eccentric manner. Like the consummate nutty professor, Dr. B was just too preoccupied to get them adjusted. Perhaps the doctor's most notable feature was his eyes – a rich chocolate brown that could take a person apart and gently piece him back together. Above the bearded grin, those eyes regarded Gabriel earnestly. "Plain English, Gabe. We both know you don't want to be here. We both know Internal Affairs ordered you here. But I cannot help you until you take some responsibility for –"

"I'm not going to be the fall guy," Gabriel interrupted. "LAPD has this department running scared ever since the

Rodney King and Rampart deals went down. I am not going to be the Sheriff Department's scapegoat."

Dr. B held back a sigh and peeled off his glasses. He rubbed tired eyes. Gabriel was not taking responsibility. Without taking responsibility, progress would not be made. Rubbing his eyes gave Dr. B time to think.

He was trained in the school of Adlerian psychology, so he took a friendly, encouraging approach to his patients. Alfred Adler, a peer of Freud's, envisioned a teacher/pupil relationship between physician and patient, rather than the more mechanized approach used by Freud, where the psychiatrist demanded absolute servility from his patient.

Instead of lying on a couch, Gabriel sat in a comfortable chair beside Dr. B so they could be equals. So they could be friends.

Dr. B sniffed and repositioned his glasses atop his nose. "This last case you were on – you assaulted a grandmother."

"Her grandson is a person of interest in a homicide I'm investigating."

"No one questioned that."

"Grandma had a twelve-gauge shotgun lying on a table in plain view from the front door. Her drug-pushing grandson lives with the old lady and was a known gang-banger. Grandma was very agitated with me. Now, what am I supposed to think?"

Dr. B chose his words carefully. "But did you think first, Gabe? When you pushed her, she fell and broke her hip. She's an eighty-year old African-American grandmother. She is claiming racism and is suing the city. The shotgun you're referring to belongs to her other grandson who is a hunter with all the right permits. The dope dealing gang-banger had moved out the week before."

Gabriel didn't comment.

"In a separate case two weeks ago," Dr. B said, "you nearly throttled a fifteen- year-old boy."

"That kid threatened me with a knife. I had the Department's politics in mind when I didn't shoot him."

"You choked him. Excessive force, Gabriel. Bad press. What do these words mean to you?"

Gabriel looked away and said nothing. A large-faced wooden clock sat on Dr. B's desk and ticked off the minutes.

"Okay," Dr. B said carefully. "Then let's talk about the young man who was shot at that Halloween party you responded to when you were in uniform."

"Let's not."

The sigh Dr. B had been holding back finally escaped him and he said, "They want to suspend you, Gabe. The Department doesn't need this kind of publicity, you know that." The psychiatrist clasped his slender hands in front of him, as if he were about to utter a prayer. "You've got a good track record for solving homicides, but a proven track record may not be enough to save your job. Now, tell me Gabe, what's going on?"

"Nothing."

From down the hall, a shout broke the stillness in the room, someone calling happily to someone else. Dr. B removed his wire-rims and cleaned them on the sleeve of his shirt. The clock ticked off a couple minutes more and finally Dr. B said to Gabriel, "Lieutenant Ramirez wants to see you."

Gabriel sat in traffic on the Santa Monica Freeway. His aging Toyota Celica was trapped between a Kenworth Truck and a convertible that was blowing rap music into the stratosphere. The truck in front of Gabriel blocked the breeze which was a bummer because Gabriel's air conditioner was broken. Gabriel reached over and opened his glove box. He fished for a bottle of aspirin and dropped two into his mouth.

Ever since the earthquake of 1994, when the Hall of Justice building was condemned, the police divisions had split up and settled in various areas around the metropolis. Headquarters Unit, where Gabriel had been today with Dr. B, handled administration and was located in Monterey Park. The city of Commerce, Gabriel's home away from home, handled homicide and arson. The Whittier Bureau handled such cases as child abuse, kidnap for ransom, and terrorism. Various other stations scattered throughout Los Angeles and its contract cities housed their own detectives for robbery, domestic violence and misdemeanor crimes. LAPD handled Los Angeles proper. From Dr. B's office Gabriel drove to Commerce to see his Team Lieutenant. Navigating freeways was simply a way of life in Los Angeles.

Finally at the end of his busy day, Gabriel headed home to his apartment in Santa Monica. His first stop was the supermarket. Gabriel exited the freeway at Fourth Street and pulled into the parking lot of Ralph's Market.

He could now feel the sea breeze ruffling his hair, moving his shirt, refreshing him. He took off his tie, tossed it on the passenger seat, and headed into the market. Gabriel walked slowly up the aisles, weary from the traffic and his workday. Although colors splashed at him from every angle, and the box covers and bags begged for attention, Gabriel found the effect strangely numbing. He didn't lose himself completely, and concentrated on selecting the few items needed for tonight's dinner. Cooking was Gabriel's relaxation and kept him busy at night. He needed to be busy.

At his apartment, Gabriel neatly laid out the items on the white tile countertop crisscrossed by aging grout. He had been lucky enough to get one of the last rent-controlled apartments on Bay Street, and while the building possessed an old Los Angeles Spanish charm — the place was still old. His ex-wife, Sheryl, had gotten the house in Culver City as part of their settlement. Gabriel had gotten the stereo.

He couldn't see the ocean from his place, but he could walk to it. The carefree, bohemian lifestyle of Santa Monica and Venice attracted him the way any opposite would attract. Gabriel never joined the rollerblading, artistic cafe crowds, but he did like being close to them, like a gopher hiding in a hole in a beautiful garden. The constant temperate weather was a friend to him; never too hot and never too cold. He experienced enough extremes in his line of work.

Gabriel pulled a bottle of Dos Equis out of his refrigerator and swilled down half. The beer would taste great with his recipe of choice tonight: beef stew with dill and artichokes. Gabriel put Ben Webster on the stereo, and then set to work. He dredged cubes of stewing beef in a mixture of flour, salt, and pepper. From the stove, the heady aroma of sautéed garlic and onion meandered through the small rooms.

Gabriel liked food, which was why he kept up his gym membership; but he liked cooking even more than eating. Whenever Gabriel measured and kneaded; sautéed and baked, he left the stress of the world behind and relaxed.

Gabriel poured some burgundy into a measuring cup and some beef stock into another. Although he was trying his best to unwind, the conversation Gabriel had had with his team lieutenant earlier played in his head like a bad movie.

"So?" Lieutenant Ramirez had asked, standing squarely in front of Gabriel, catching him in the hallway in front of his office and smelling of cigarette smoke.

"So?" Gabriel had echoed, looking down on the man. Gabriel may not have hit six feet, but Ramirez didn't even reach Gabriel's chin.

"What's up with you?" Ramirez said with a heavy Chicano accent. He had risen from one of the poorest, gang-infested barrios in east L.A., and had climbed the ladder of the Sheriff's Department, rung by difficult rung; encountering the

Southland's strange blend of bohemian tolerance and abject bigotry. On his way up, Miguel Ramirez had collected both his hard-won promotions and a huge chip on his shoulder. Ramirez relished putting people on the spot and then gauging their reactions. He felt this made him an extraordinary cop.

"Nothing," Gabriel told him.

"Nothing." The lieutenant nodded. "Well, you made front page news again, Star." Ramirez shoved a newspaper in front of Gabriel's face. "What did the shrink say? Can you work or not?"

"Of course, I can work," Gabriel answered and walked down the hall, making a beeline for the exit.

"Really?" Ramirez remarked; his voice tinged with sarcasm. "There's a Grandma laying flat on her ass crying 'police brutality' to any reporter who'll listen and she's suing us for a cool five million." Ramirez peered into Gabriel's face. "I need to know if you've completely lost it."

Gabriel stopped in his tracks and stared at his lieutenant with blazing eyes. "There's nothing wrong with me. The whole thing was a mistake."

"I think this one cost you," Ramirez muttered and allowed Gabriel to pass.

Now Gabriel stared at the simmering pot on his stove and realized it would still be about two hours before he would eat. Good thing he had lost his appetite. He moved away and stood with his arms crossed, gazing into the little courtyard that separated his apartment from an alley. Fuchsia tufts of bougainvillea fell over a stucco wall and draped into a lion's head wall fountain, now dry and broken. A white plastic patio table and two chairs collected dust. One of the chairs had fallen over long ago and lay on its back like a dead bug. Gabriel finished off the beer. Could he continue working?

Lately he had been experiencing anxiety attacks, panicking when he should be under control. If the tension in a given situation ran high, a blossoming rage would begin to boil. Gabriel tried to keep a lid on his temper, but sometimes, despite his effort, the rage escaped.

He would never forget the look on the fifteen-year-old boy's face nor would he forget the pressure of his hands around the boy's neck. Gabriel's partner, Dash, had pulled him off. The two detectives never spoke about the incident, but it was the first time Gabriel's name had made the newspapers.

As if being a human pressure cooker wasn't enough, something else worried Gabriel. Something worse... He suffered from memory lapses once in a while.

These bouts of amnesia didn't last too long, but Gabriel worried about their increasing frequency. Blanking out frightened him more than anything. He would be at the supermarket picking out choice tomatoes for his favorite ratatouille, and then suddenly find himself holding a carton of milk in the dairy section. Peering warily into his cart, Gabriel would see the neatly bagged tomatoes, plus a host of other groceries he didn't remember collecting. People would pass by him, mothers with babies, bagboys on breaks, a cyclist stopping for bottled water — none of them would notice the lone man staring at a milk carton held out at arm's length, quaking in his shoes despite the badge in his wallet.

Dr. B had told him there were no tumors in his brain. Then what was going on?

Gabriel walked back inside and grabbed another Dos Equis beer. Could he work? His work provided him sanity. He had better be able to work.

CHAPTER 2

Two hikers trudged past a field of mustard flowers surrounding a grove of Coast Live Oak trees. The hikers, Emma and Marie, were about to graduate Calabasas High School and talked earnestly about the future. The Santa Monica Mountains that separated the San Fernando Valley from the beach had always been a refuge and the girls were feeling nostalgic. When they heard the puttering of an engine, they frowned at each other, not wishing an intruder to spoil their walk down memory lane. Happily, the puttering faded into the distance.

Emma and Marie walked through a stand of wild oats and emerged onto a fire road. Checking for ticks along their pant legs, they suddenly noticed a white pickup truck facing them; parked about two hundred feet away.

The girls exchanged glances, annoyed again. They moved forward, intending to march right on by. But as they approached the vehicle, the two girls noticed something strange. Red whirls and loops were painted all over the windshield. They could now smell the faint odor of something burning and through the paint they made out a human form seated inside.

"Do you think it's some crackhead?" Marie whispered to Emma. She was worried that a junkie might get crazy on them.

"I don't know. Let's just walk faster."

About ten feet from the truck, the girls could make out letters and odd symbols, painted on the inside glass; scrawled all over, still wet and dripping in places. The air was thick inside the truck – moving. Curious now, the girls slowed down and came around to the driver's side. A man leaned against the window. Through the dripping red scrawls, his eyes stared in surprise and his mouth hung open in a wide "O." The burning smell was stronger now and the car seemed alive with heat. Emma stepped back in fear, but Marie put her face against the window.

The man's neck and shirtfront were drenched in red. The lap of his khaki pants held a puddle of blood. Marie let loose a squeal that sent Emma blurting, "What is it?"

The car seat was on fire. Marie stared dumbstruck for another moment as the fire grew and caught the man's shirt. Gray smoke billowed around the man and soon all Marie could see was his frozen, horror-stricken face floating amid the smoke and the melting letters. Having seen enough, Marie screamed and ran back toward her friend. At that moment, the car erupted into flames.

✹　✹　✹

Gabriel had to pick up some reports on the case of the dope-dealing grandson from the coroner's office at Los Angeles County hospital in east L.A. The hospital was a large beige complex, visible from the freeway. Surrounded by a clutch of Hispanic shops and old Craftsman style houses, L.A. County General was also the home of the city morgue, bringing in the dead from as far as Lancaster, more than seventy miles away.

Serving a sprawling metropolis such as Los Angeles kept the hospital ER staff and the morgue attendants continually busy. Visitors were obliged to pass through metal detectors on their way inside.

Gabriel decided to lunch at the hospital cafeteria since he had brought with him his leftover stew. Going about business as usual helped him to forget that his job was on the line. He was pleasantly surprised to see Ming Li enter the green and brown painted room. He waved at her.

"What are you doing in my neck of the woods?" she called out cheerfully. As Chief Medical Examiner of Los Angeles County, Ming was one of the busiest pathologists in the country. Her thoroughness had helped her rise through the ranks of other more political professionals and had won her widespread respect. However, that was not the only reason Los Angeles detectives liked working with Ming Li. They liked her looks.

Her father was Chinese and her mother was Mexican, giving Ming's features an exotic blend. Her long, thick hair curled at the ends and her mocha skin was as smooth as cocoa butter. The quick retorts and straight-shooting words that popped out of her full, sensuous lips often took people by surprise. Gabriel liked straight shooters. He liked Ming.

She nodded at his savory beef stew. "Good idea to bring your own. You can't get anything that smells that good around here."

"Have some. I have plenty."

"Are you sure?" Ming surveyed the room. "I mean, were you meeting someone?"

"Yeah," Gabriel grinned, holding the stew out to her. "You."

Ming raised her finely arched eyebrows and matched his grin. "My good luck then. Let me grab a paper plate."

Gabriel watched her body as she made her way across the cafeteria floor. The surgical greens she wore could not hide her curves. A moment later, she was settled across from Gabriel, helping herself to his lunch.

"Hmmm," she murmured, taking a bite. "It's delicious!"

"Well, it's not so good microwaved, but it does taste better the next day."

"I love it. You're quite the chef."

"It's nothing more than a hobby, really."

"Anytime you have leftovers, count me in," Ming said, and then her eyes narrowed curiously at him. "Do I have something on my face?"

Gabriel realized he was staring at her. "No. I'm sorry," he said, looking away in embarrassment. "I was just thinking that I always have leftovers."

"Bring 'em over," Ming said, chewing.

Gabriel said nothing. He always had leftovers because he never cooked for anyone but himself. Once in a while he had Dash and his wife Eve over for dinner, but most of the time, he dined alone.

"Are you there?" Ming asked, and Gabriel widened his eyes in fear, wondering if he had spaced out amid the clattering of cutlery and conversation. He then realized she was smiling and nothing had changed.

"Right here." He smiled back. Gabriel would have liked to tell Ming that she need not wait for leftovers. He would have liked to invite her over for dinner. Though her skin was creamy and tempted him and her almond eyes sparkled with interest when he talked, Gabriel made no attempt at intimacy. Sheryl had called him an icicle man, untouchable, impenetrable. Marriage isn't a surface situation, his ex-wife had said to him, and she'd been crying when she'd said it. Ming and Gabriel had a nice working relationship. Better keep it that way.

"How is your case going?" she asked.

"Oh, wrapping it up," he said casually, digging into his lunch. *Keep your mouth full and then you won't have to talk.* Once this case was finished so was his career.

Ming's pager went off. She glanced at the clock on the wall. "Oh, hell, I've gotta go. I've got an exam waiting."

Gabriel nodded and slid the plastic container toward her. "Take this and finish it."

"You sure?" Ming said with obvious glee. "Thank you so much." She tucked the plastic under her arm and walked toward the exit. "Whatever it was, it tasted great!" she called back to him.

He nodded again and leaned back; taking the opportunity to admire her trim figure once more.

Ming Li rode the elevator to the second floor and walked through two steel doors. She readied herself for the autopsy and, with the help of two coroner's attendants, began examining the body which was newly arrived from a crime scene.

The badly burned corpse lay on a steel table equipped with holes to allow water and fluids to drain. A dissection table stood nearby, along with tanks, scales, and machine grinders to grind down bones for samples. A diamond bladed saw, used to cut sections of bones and teeth for later examination under microscopes, sat on a long counter with a small anvil, a saw, and an assortment of screwdrivers and wrenches – mostly there to be matched up against wounds.

The detective on this particular case was named Rick Frasier, a baby-faced blonde with a penchant for Ralph Lauren shirts and other preppie attire.

"Well, Rick," Ming said. "It's a male in case you were wondering."

"The skull is thicker," Rick told her with confidence. He was brand new to Homicide and seemed determined to prove his investigative prowess. She had heard a rumor that the yuppie detective had a problem with professional women.

"You get an A for effort, Rick," Ming said. "It's quite true. The male skull is thicker than the female's. However, I haven't examined the cranium yet." Ming pointed to the blackened groin area. "His penis is intact."

The detective blushed. Ming grinned satisfactorily and continued working.

"Rather amazing thing about fires. They seem to have a mind of their own. Barely singe one thing then burn another to a crisp." She moved to the head and inspected the mouth of the victim. "Dental gold has a high melting point. Way higher than a thousand degrees Fahrenheit. This one's had some work. We'll be able to identify him, no problem."

Ming saw the detective roll his eyes.

Maybe I should just shut up and serve him tea, Ming thought derisively. Maybe the only Mexican women Mr. Polo can tolerate are maids. Too damn bad, Ming decided. She'd seen enough peacocks strut their stuff. She didn't need to play a weak, easily impressed woman to make a man feel at home. She never had problems with Gabriel McRay. He always seemed to accept her on her own level.

"The pickup is registered to a Ted Brody," Rick Frasier offered indifferently. "His address with the DMV isn't current, but I think we'll find where he's been living."

He held his speech as Ming talked into a tape recorder, making verbal notes on the few external markings she could see that the fire had not destroyed. Finally, she flipped off the recorder and said to the corpse, "Ted, is it you?"

Again, the detective rolled his eyes. "Can you just tell me what killed him?"

"His throat was slit," Ming said plainly. "But I don't know if that was the first wound."

"The witness, Marie Engstrom, said there was a lot of blood on his shirt."

"That helps." Ming examined the dead man's hands. Bone was breaking through at places, but a lot of charred flesh still remained. Damaged flesh revealed more secrets than bone.

Rick Frasier leaned closer and gagged on the smell. He backed up.

"You know, Rick," Ming said, still holding the charred hand. "The more you avoid the smell, the worse it is. A smooth-edged blade was used – an inch in width. I'm not sure of the length yet."

A deputy coroner entered and at Ming's signal, turned on the tape recorder once again. She talked as she pried at the space between the fingers and carefully examined the palms. "Defensive wounds on the hands are not apparent. He must have been caught by surprise."

She took up her scalpel and cut from the shoulders to the sternum. Then she made a midline incision down the entire length of the abdomen to the pubis. She exposed the breastplate. Ming raised her eyebrows toward the detective, coyly inviting him to witness the gaping "Y" incision. Rick took a step back.

Ming continued along the body. Some parts were only slightly burned depending how protected the flesh was. "No soot is found in the windpipe so your boy was dead before the car burned. I don't see any other stab wounds so–"

Ming stopped talking. At the base of the spine, between the anus and genitals, a deep hole was gouged. Her brows furrowed in curiosity. "Now here's something." She spoke into the recorder as she measured the wound. "Appears to be cut with the same blade used on the other wounds. Looks very purposeful and appears to have been made postmortem." She used special tweezers and pulled a fiber from the wound. She stepped back, allowing the deputy coroner to snap pictures and the detective to get a better look.

Meanwhile, she dropped the fiber onto a slide and checked it under a microscope. "I believe this came from the victim's own pants." To make sure, she carefully inspected the remnants of the burned slacks from the evidence bag and checked the crotch area. The fabric was slashed. "He was wearing his pants when he was stabbed."

"The witness said that she saw blood down there," Rick said, more animated now. "She remembers him wearing clothes."

Ming surveyed the body. The neck wound was vicious and deep. The assailant had wanted the man to die quickly. Then there was that specially carved hole. She measured the depth of the cut. "Nearly four inches in length. Interesting. A sex crime would have been my first thought, but that would have made more sense if he had been naked."

The detective rolled his eyes again. "No offense, Ming, just stick to the pathology and we'll handle the rest."

Ming raised her finely arched eyebrows indignantly. "That's Dr. Li to you."

The city of Commerce lay just east of downtown Los Angeles. The Homicide Bureau of the Sheriff's office was located in a low building in a bleak industrial area. Since Homicide was not open to the public, not much attention had been paid to making the place attractive. The investigators sat in a large L-shaped room lined with desks. The only private areas were the interviewing rooms and the secretaries' cubicles. Although the investigators themselves typed the bulk of the reports, the secretaries were often heard clacking away at their own computer keyboards; taking dictation from tape recordings.

Sitting at his desk, Gabriel neatly compiled all of the reports on his last case together with those of the medical examiner. He took his time, knowing that this may be the last time he sat in this room.

A few of his peers passed by and grunted out greetings in low voices. One of the detectives dropped two Dodger tickets on Gabriel's desk.

"Hey Pal," he said quickly, "Go ahead, take 'em and enjoy yourself."

Before Gabriel could even utter thanks, the detective had slid past like a ghost. Gabriel had to chuckle. *I ought to be wearing a scarlet letter – "P" for Pariah,*

People were afraid to get near him. For all intents and purposes, Gabriel was a drowning man. The others were afraid he would pull them under with him. Only Dash had remained a friend.

Gabriel logged into his e-mail and immediately stopped chuckling. A message from his sister Janet waited in the inbox. With a heavy heart, he read it. Janet wanted to have a family reunion. She wanted him to speak to his parents, who had left San Francisco for Seattle to be closer to Janet and her family. She reminded Gabriel that their folks were getting older and they desired a relationship with their only son.

Gabriel swallowed and typed in his usual two-word reply. "Not now."

He pressed 'send' and the message disappeared into cyberspace. Afterwards, he deleted Janet's message.

Absently, he felt for the bottle of aspirin in his jacket pocket and pulled it out. It was empty. He sighed, tossed the bottle into the trashcan and put his head into his hands.

In his mind, he heard a woman berating him, her words skinning him like a hunting knife on an animal hide. "You're an evil, evil man! How could you do that to a child?"

CHAPTER 3

Ming and Gabriel sat in the mustard colored seats of the field level between home plate and first base. Palm trees poked over the top of the bleachers, illuminated by stadium lights glowing in the balmy night sky. Gabriel had not invited Ming over to his apartment for dinner but he had mustered up enough courage to ask her to the Dodger game.

Vendors strolled up and down the aisles hawking sodas and bags of blue and pink cotton candy. The irresistible aroma of French fries, hot dogs, and onions made Gabriel's mouth water. He and Ming started out with Dodger Dogs and ate their way through the innings with peanuts, pizza, cotton candy, and beer.

"Take him out!" Gabriel shouted as the crowd booed the pitcher. He had allowed four hits in one inning and two runs. "Can you believe this guy?" Gabriel plopped down beside Ming.

She took a swig of beer and shook her head. "Well, it's late in the game. Maybe he's beat."

Gabriel smiled secretly and thought how cute Ming looked with a baseball cap crowning her wavy black hair. Though she wore a simple t-shirt and Levis, Gabriel could make out her well-formed breasts underneath the shirt, and as for the jeans, they hugged her in all the right places. He'd never seen her out of a white lab coat or surgical greens.

The crowd roared again, this time with approval. Another pitcher was making his way onto the field from the bullpen. Rock music, geared to incite the crowd, blasted from the speakers.

"You've heard about the case off Kanan road, haven't you? You know Rick Frasier? He's handling it," Ming said.

Gabriel shrugged. "I've heard about it. Rick's a good guy."

"Oh," Ming said, nodding innocently. "I guess you don't know him."

Gabriel laughed and eyed her. "Was he hassling you?"

"I let it run off my shoulders." She looked at her watch. "Well, we've given him one minute's worth of attention — too long in my book. Now let's talk about something else."

"Just running off your shoulders, eh?" Gabriel winked at Ming and then said, "Okay, tell me what you found." He couldn't resist learning about the case. He liked his work. Ming related her findings on the victim, Ted Brody.

Gabriel reflected for a moment and said, "Knives are usually women's weapons. Maybe it was a lover's spat."

"If she was going to mutilate his parts, why not go for his penis?"

A blue-haired lady, biting a hot dog and sitting in the seat in front of them, turned around and scowled at Ming.

"Maybe she was in a passionate frenzy, not thinking."

Ming shook her head. "You need to see the pictures, Gabriel. I'll show them to you. There was something very definitive about that wound and his scrotum was untouched."

The blue haired lady swiveled in her seat, giving Ming a dirty look as she slowly chewed her hot dog. Ming smiled genially and the elderly lady turned back around. Ming continued, saying, "When we made a positive ID on Ted Brody, Rick Frasier interviewed his live-in girlfriend."

"Yeah, and what's her alibi? What do they say about her?" Gabriel asked.

"She's 'hotter than a red-headed whore in a cayenne pepper patch.' That's what they say about her. Regarding her alibi? She says she was at the mall around the time of death, but doesn't have any receipts or anything to prove it." Ming shrugged. "I couldn't get much more out of Rick. I think he's a little tongue-tied around professional women."

Gabriel cocked his head and gave Ming a sideways smile. "Ah, the gender gap."

"Always a problem for me." She tossed her black hair over her shoulders and sighed. "I just can't seem to please men. They think I'm too forward. But I have to be! I mean, I didn't get where I am by being meek and mild. It's odd. Men like that I'm a professional, but they want me to be subservient too. When I come home from work, I want someone to rub my feet."

I'll rub your feet, Gabriel thought, that and more. He must have gazed at her too long, for her prominent cheekbones colored and a Mona Lisa smile played on her face. She reached out and gripped his hand.

Gabriel squeezed her hand in return then released it. "Don't worry about what other people think."

Ming adjusted her baseball cap, and said, "Rick told me that neighbors and friends said Ted Brody and his girlfriend seemed to be a happy couple. So it's unlikely that she's a suspect."

Gabriel gazed pensively at the field. "Yeah, well, what passes for happy on the outside doesn't mean happy on the inside."

"No, of course not." Ming watched the new pitcher strike out the man at bat.

"Then again, I'm no expert on happy couples," Gabriel offered.

"Are you friends with your ex?"

He shook his head and reached into an open bag of peanuts. "Not really. I think Sheryl's pretty happy I'm not shading her life anymore."

"Shading?" Ming dug into the peanuts as well. "You think of yourself as a shadow?"

"Maybe."

"Do I sense some self-pity going on here? You know, when you pout, Sergeant McRay, it's damned attractive. Feeling sorry for yourself quite becomes you."

Gabriel broke into a smile. "You are a straight-shooter. I don't feel sorry for myself, Ming; but I was responsible for the breakup." Gabriel's smile faded into a poker face as he stared at the field. He decided to shoot straight as well. "I had some problems with violence."

Ming swiveled her eyes toward the field and took a nervous swallow of beer. "Was–was that what broke you two up?" She tried to sound casual.

"No. I made sure we didn't get close enough for me to hurt her." Gabriel broke a peanut in half and picked at the shell. "Don't get the wrong idea. I don't hit women. I never have. I never would." Even as he said it, the memory of pushing over the grandmother crashed down on him.

"May I ask what 'problems' you _have_ had with violence? I'm assuming this means more than the incident with the boy."

She knows. It's embarrassing. "That kid with the steak knife. Oh, yeah." Gabriel rose from his seat and brushed peanut shells from his lap. Any chance he'd had with Ming was already blown. _Nice work, Pariah._

"It's all good now, Ming. I'm working it out. I guess it's no secret that I'm in therapy." He forced a smile. "I could use a Krispy Kreme donut right about now. How about you?"

Ming stared at him and nodded warily. "Sure. Why not?"

Out in the bleachers, some people were starting a wave.

"911. What is your emergency?"

"I'd like to report a fire."

"Hold, I'll put you through to the Fire Department."

"Hot damn! She put me on hold!"

"L.A. County Fire. Operator 86."

"Hi, I'm on a car phone–"

"Are you reporting a fire?"

"Yes!"

"Where are you located?"

"I'm on Topanga Canyon going south toward the beach. Near the Theatric—Botanic – whatever."

"You see flames in the brush?"

"No, I see only smoke. It's not on the road–"

"Hold please."

"Hot damn! She put me on hold again!"

"I'm back. What color is the smoke?"

"Good thing I'm not being murdered right now. Good thing I'm not about to jump off a frigging building. How can 911 put people on hold?"

"I'm sorry. What color is the smoke?"

"What color is it? I don't know! It's black, I guess."

"Can you see an automobile? Can you please stay on the line?"

"Are you putting me on hold again!? Hello? Hello? Hot damn!"

Due to the wooded location of the fire, the dispatch operator called in a Brush Response. Within five minutes, two helicopters were in the air and circling above the blaze. On the ground, five fire trucks, three engines, and a stocky battalion chief named Phil Panzram raced to contain the half-acre brush fire before it developed into something more serious. Luckily, the day was not windy.

When the smoke cleared, Phil Panzram and a lanky, soot-stained engine captain named Desmond Gein walked down the blackened hillside hoping to find the cause of the fire. Down the hill, they spotted a smoking minivan. It lay crushed on one side where it had rolled into the ravine. Also apparent were the car's tracks where it had made its descent.

"A car fire? Strange place to find a minivan," Panzram remarked to Gein. "What's that shit on the windows?"

"Beats the hell out of me. There's someone inside," Gein said, and yelled up at the other firefighters posted on the hilltop, "Get the jaws!"

Panzram, a stocky man with a nose reddened from a past desire for booze and the present heat, looked into the van through a window smeared with melted red streaks. "Forget the jaws. This one's cooked." He could see the corpse crushed between the driver's seat and the windshield. "See how bad this burn is? Not your ordinary car fire." He yelled up the hill, "Call Arson."

The seasoned battalion chief yanked off his hat, peering closely at the corpse's neck. He could make out a vivid gash along the black, leathery flesh. "While you're at it," he said morosely, "call Homicide."

❧ ❧ ❧

A couple of days after the firemen discovered the burned out minivan, Gabriel McRay and his partner Dash, joined an arson investigator, Paul Vacher, at Edwards in the city of Commerce. The Victorian themed restaurant was a local favorite; a true meat and potatoes eatery.

"How is your fish cooked?" Dash asked the waitress. Dash's real name was Michael Starkweather and he and Gabriel had been partners for ten years. Dash had inherited the appellation not because he was quick on his feet, but because he constantly carried around the salt-free seasoning Mrs. Dash in his pocket. Heart disease ran rampant in his family and Dash was careful to the extreme. Going to a restaurant was a test of endurance, both for Dash and his fellow diners because he drove the waiters crazy with his special requests.

The waitress wore a neat little cap and a black apron over her long, white skirt.

"Our fish is sautéed in a little white wine sauce with capers." Her tough, tanned face and diesel engine voice betrayed the prim Victorian outfit.

"Okay, I'd like the fish, but with no sauce. Just plain, okay?"

"Just plain. Broiled?"

"Fine." Dash pulled the Mrs. Dash seasoning from his pocket and displayed it on the table. "What does it come with?"

The waitress looked bored and started rattling off, "You can get mashed potatoes, rice pilaf, steamed vegetables or—"

"What's in the rice pilaf?"

"Rice."

"I mean, what else?"

The waitress glanced away thoughtfully. "I guess some veggies."

"Don't you know? Can you ask the chef?"

"Would you like a baked potato instead? Baked potatoes are our specialty."

"No, I want to know what exactly is in the rice pilaf."

The waitress glowered at Dash, and said, "I'll check." She turned on her heel, slapping the pad against her thigh, and strode back toward the kitchen. The long dress rustled in her wake.

"I'm starved, Dash," Vacher said, complaining. "You got rid of her before we could order."

"She'll be back; don't worry." Dash changed the subject. "So Paul, did you get the lab results regarding the fire?"

Vacher was a tall, carrot-topped investigator with a fine mesh of freckles covering his face. "Yep. Gasoline. Just like the other one. This time the vic was a woman, Tania Dankowski. Housewife and mother of one." He shook his head at the loss.

"I understand she was also cut," Dash said, sliding a forefinger across his neck.

Gabriel broke a hot roll in two and took a bite. "Think we have a repeater on our hands?"

"I don't know," Vacher said. "But he plays with matches and I don't have to tell you that we are coming into one very hot and dry season."

"How can this guy do it?" Dash asked. "He's got to be in good shape. First, he stabs someone to death, must be a struggle, right? Then he gets on a bike and peddles away."

"A bicycle?" Gabriel asked.

Vacher shrugged. "Some kind of mountain bike. Treads are bigger than a regular bike anyhow. We picked up another tire track up the hill from the Dankowski car which matches the first track we found."

"Do we have a make on it yet?" Dash asked.

Vacher shook his head. "Not yet."

"I hear the witnesses said they saw something on the windows of the first car," Dash said. "Some doodling written in blood."

"They found blood residue on the windshield," Vacher said.

"Did they run DNA?" Gabriel asked.

"From what I understand it's the victim's blood," Vacher said. "But because of the heat, the DNA samples are totally screwed up, not viable."

A busboy dressed in a dirty tuxedo arrived with their drinks and placed them around the table.

Gabriel waited for the busboy to leave, and then said, "What were the doodles?"

"I don't know offhand. Some circles and slashes. Could be letters, who knows? Figuring it out is your department."

Gabriel made no reply. It was no longer his department. Another article about Gabriel had made this morning's Los Angeles Times.

As if reading Gabriel's mind, Dash pulled a folded newspaper from his jacket. "See this morning's paper?"

Gabriel's heart dropped and he looked at his partner in shock.

Vacher went for his own bread roll. "I try not to read the news."

"Well," Dash told him, "If you did, you'd see that the press already has the buzz on these two killings. So, let's hope we don't have a repeater on our hands." He tossed the paper over to the arson investigator who grabbed and read it.

Gabriel felt a little nauseated and pushed away his bread. Next to the article about the killings was a larger article featuring Gabriel's outbursts and his suspension, and how, unlike the LAPD, the Sheriff's Department cleaned up its messes right off the bat. No need for government intervention. No need for investigations. No need to keep Gabriel McRay around.

Gabriel shifted in his seat. Vacher had to be reading the article if he hadn't done so already.

"Thank God there's not a whole lot of press on this yet," Vacher said, reading the newsprint. "It could cause the killer to change his tactics out of fear and loosen any leads we might get." He glanced at Gabriel over the paper then quickly looked away.

The waitress stomped over angrily.

Dash ignored her and said, "The article says Tania Dankowski was a very charitable and friendly woman; a take-charge PTA president type who was liked by all. And so was Ted Brody; everybody's favorite handyman. Come out at midnight if a customer needed him. I guess Rick's gonna be hard-pressed to find enemies for these two. Not the same friends. Not the same interests."

The waitress bristled in her skirts and squared her shoulders at Dash. "The rice pilaf has nothing in it but rice. Plain rice. Okay?" She readied her pad and pencil to take down his order.

"Thanks. I'll have the steamed vegetables."

Gabriel guffawed and smiled. Paul Vacher put his head in his hands.

Ming hovered above the autopsy table, carefully examining the body of Tania Dankowski. She worked as she always did, with a quiet thoroughness. Today, however, she was less focused than usual. She couldn't help thinking about Gabriel McRay.

She remembered him winking at her at the ballgame. His eyes were such a deep blue; looking into them was like jumping into a cobalt lake. Alone, Gabriel's features may not have been called handsome – his nose was slightly crooked and his lips were too thin, but put together... Ming smiled. Put together, Gabriel was one very attractive man. Conversations with him so ignited her that Ming imagined she threw off sparks when they were together. Yet when he made that confession to her regarding his issues with violence, she was really thrown. She could not figure out why he would admit such a thing. Then again, maybe she should be grateful that he did. Suddenly, Dr. Ming Li didn't feel so sure of herself.

Throughout her childhood and into adulthood, Ming had known how to cultivate a safe environment. Her Chinese father, who felt he carried the superior genes in the family, downplayed Ming's Mexican heritage. Ming always knew that this hurt her mother, but instead of sympathizing, she sided with her father, vowing to make him proud and win his approval. Ming had been pressed into piano and violin lessons, private schools, team sports, and community service – anything that would expand her intellect and get her into a fine university.

Ming never played pretend games with friends, jumped on trampolines, or roller-skated down the street. When she left for college, a part of her wanted to cut loose in her new found freedom, but her father's influence gripped her strongly and Ming wrapped herself in her studies. She continued hiding in her residency, and then in her work, like a caterpillar asleep in her chrysalis. Sometimes when Ming drove the freeway and approached her off-ramp, she longed to pass it by and continue driving; going wherever the road took her – somewhere far from the smell of formaldehyde. She never had the guts to do it.

Being with Gabriel McRay was like driving through unchartered territory. He challenged her space of security. Looking at Tania Dankowski's silenced, stiffened features, a random thought occurred to Ming. She suddenly empathized with battered women because she could now see what made those women stay with men who hurt them. Ming Li, always the professional, would never have considered a date with damaged goods, and yet she was clearly attracted to Gabriel. Was he dangerous like he thought he was?

She cleared her throat and spoke into a microphone hooked to her green surgical shirt. "Right earlobe has been excised. There is a small, gold hoop in the left earlobe." This factor did not present much of a mystery. After having performed countless exams on unfortunate murder victims, Ming had acquired a detective's insight for clues. She figured that the killer had used his smooth-handled blade to cut off the earlobe and earring to take as a trophy. Not a good sign. Trophy-takers usually didn't stop with one victim.

She made a note for Rick the WASP. He should ask Ted Brody's fiancé if Ted was minus a piece of jewelry or some other personal item.

Ming continued her examination. The breasts were burned but other than that, appeared untouched. To make sure, she inspected the tissue underneath. She found no traces of blood, which would have been a telltale sign of bruising. The breast tissue was undamaged.

Ming was mystified. The detectives felt that the Ted Brody killing had been a sex crime. It would follow that this would be the same. Yet sex crimes involving women almost always included some injury to the breasts.

She continued her trek down the body, fully expecting to see the gouged out area near the base of the spine. What she discovered instead sent chills through her. A group of stab wounds marked the flesh in a vicious, ragged line, starting at the lower abdomen and extending to the vulva.

Ming stared at the gruesome cuts for a long time, a shocked witness to the knowledge that someone very sick had done this to a child's mother. Ming again weighed the idea of a sex crime, but as she continued her examination, Ming discovered a track of XXX branded onto the beef jerky skin of the victim's thigh. The stitching from Tania's jeans pockets had fused to her flesh.

She had died with her clothes on, Ming decided, just like Ted Brody, which made it unlikely that she was raped. Her assailant could have dressed her again, but to what purpose?

And those cuts – the vagina was damaged, but not any more so than the lower abdomen.

Gauging blood loss was next to impossible due to the burned out interior of the van, but Ming determined that the wound at the poor woman's neck was the fatal one, which meant the other wounds were made postmortem. Ming carefully measured the wounds and their depth and concluded that the killer had alternately twisted and plunged the knife.

Finding it hard to breathe, Ming stepped back and removed her surgical mask. As her eyes roamed over the incredible damage inflicted upon the corpse, she asked herself, "What is this guy doing?"

Trying to dig.

The thought surfaced involuntarily and Dr. Ming Li shuddered despite her professionalism.

"...It seems to be that all our human culture is based upon feelings of inferiority... men are the weakest of all creatures."

Alfred Adler 1931

CHAPTER 4

Gabriel tried to not make his departure obvious, but everyone noticed just the same. The decision had come down that morning that suspension would not be enough and Gabriel McRay would be laid off his job. Dash dragged a chair over and sat down, watching him.

"This is shit," he muttered dolefully.

Gabriel shrugged and Dash said, "I just want you to know, I talked to the lieutenant and told him this is shit. You know what he said? He said it had to be done. That means it had to be done to appease the political assholes that need appeasing." Dash watched Gabriel put his things in a cardboard box and cracked his knuckles. "He said he knows you're good. He says there are plenty of other jurisdictions that would be glad to..." Dash's voice tapered off.

"Some hick town in no man's land, I presume," Gabriel said in a low voice, not meeting his partner's eyes.

Dash looked down at his knuckles. "Well, that's what he said. It looks like the city is settling with that old lady."

"I know."

The surprised look on Dash's face gave Gabriel a sense of satisfaction. "I called her. I wanted to know how her hip was."

"Really? What did she say?"

"She hung up on me."

Dash nodded and looked away awkwardly.

Rick Frasier, wearing his yuppie clothes and blow-dried blond hair, approached them and knocked softly on Gabriel's desk. "Gabe, can I talk to you a moment?" He held a manila envelope in one hand.

Dash rose from the chair, eyeing Rick curiously, and said, "I'll catch you later, Partner. Let's go out tonight."

"Yeah. Thanks." Gabriel turned to Rick, who didn't speak until Dash was out of earshot.

"I know this is a strange time to ask you…" Rick cleared his throat nervously and looked at Gabriel with puppy eyes.

"What's up?" Gabriel hoped it wasn't about his layoff. He didn't want anyone's sympathy.

Rick's young face was drawn and tired. "It's this case I'm working on. I'm following all the protocols and I — I've just got no gut feeling with this one. Nothing's jumping out at me and I thought that, well, since you've handled a lot of caseloads, maybe…" He flapped the envelope nervously back and forth.

"Sit down," Gabriel said, calmly. "Show me what you've got."

Rick sat quickly in the seat Dash had vacated. "The press has dubbed him the Malibu Canyon Murderer." Rick pulled an artist's rendering from the envelope. He carefully handed it to Gabriel.

"What is this?" Gabriel looked at a grouping of lines and circles, which appeared as bits and pieces of letters. Also pictured was an "O" with a "V" inside and a couple of odd lines.

"It's a witness description, what she could remember anyhow, that was written in blood on the windows of Ted Brody's car. He was the first vic."

"I remember." Gabriel traced the fragmented letters with his finger.

"I was wondering if you'd ever come across something like this before."

Gabriel looked pensively at the bulletin board on the far wall with its pictures of homicide victims. He had come across a lot in his twenty years with the department. He had been a star rookie, showing a keen instinct for getting into the criminal mind; to sense a killer's next move. This talent had been instrumental to him over and over again. In the past, many more pictures had hung on that wall. There were fewer photos now thanks to Gabriel. At one time in his life, he actually believed he could be a hero.

Every hero has a tragic flaw. Even when Gabriel was in uniform, he had sensed his flawed character. An incident occurred when he was out on a disturbance call one Halloween night. He arrived at a home where a party had turned loud and the neighbors were complaining. The costumed partiers were mostly drunk, but Gabriel saw cocaine residue on their noses and smelled the sweet scent of pot. He stood at the door asking them to turn their music down, and they nodded their agreement through glassy eyes and slack mouths.

One fellow, dressed as a cop, came to the front door. "Whatever yer selling, asshole," he shouted drunkenly, "we don' wan' any!"

He sauntered up to Gabriel, chuckling in his face, and Gabriel could smell his foul breath, as if the man had just puked. Gabriel had fought with Sheryl earlier in the day and his patience was running thin. The man started to bellow and curse, telling Gabriel where he could stick his complaint.

Gabriel had felt the anger rising and he threatened the costumed cop with the option of cooling down in a county holding cell.

To this, the man had responded by pulling out a gun, pointing it in Gabriel's face, and shouting, "Let's blow this dude's head off."

Gabriel had shot him twice. The man died, holding a plastic toy gun.

Nobody blamed Gabriel. A few eyebrows were raised and he was put on probation for awhile, but even the people at the party had to admit that their intoxicated friend had acted stupidly. But Gabriel blamed the anger for not allowing him a moment's hesitation. If he had hesitated he would have seen the black muted plastic of the toy pistol.

Then, only recently, that fifteen-year-old druggie with a history of petty theft lunged toward him with a steak knife. Gabriel had been surprised and a little amused. The kid was a short little waif. Gabriel only meant to subdue the kid, but somehow his amusement had escalated into anger. Somehow his hands had found the boy's slender neck and squeezed tightly, feeling the life pulse under his fingertips. The rage urged his thumbs to press harder, wanting to crush the smug look off the boy's face; and Gabriel would have obeyed the rage if Dash hadn't pulled him off. The boy lost consciousness, and the bruises on his neck stood out in a mottled purple and yellow as he lay at Gabriel's feet like a wilted flower.

Where the rage sprouted from, Gabriel didn't know. His bursts of temper came unbidden, and Gabriel was frightened that he could lose control so easily. The boy's parents, who up until then had played a very passive role in the rearing of their offspring, lunged at the Department with legal knives. Because the boy had been threatening with a weapon, Gabriel had only been given probation again and a stern warning about police brutality. Even today, he wasn't the only cop in the department guilty of excessive force, but he was the one who was going down for it. Since he was a teenager, when the rage first reared its ugly head, Gabriel knew it would bring about his downfall.

"So, have you ever come across something like this?" Rick asked, shaking Gabriel from his reverie.

"No," Gabriel said slowly, gazing sadly at the snapshots of the murder victims. "I've never come across anything like this." He pushed the paper back toward Rick. The younger detective made no move to retrieve it.

"How 'bout sleeping on it?" Rick stood up, shuffling in his loafers. "Maybe something will ring a bell. Is that okay?"

Gabriel looked at Rick. The younger cop was nervous. Maybe he was afraid Gabriel would grip <u>his</u> neck.

"Sure," Gabriel said dispiritedly. "Leave it."

Rick made his goodbyes, knocking on the desk again in a good-'ol-boy way. Gabriel tossed the rendering into the cardboard box and continued packing.

Dr. B hung up the phone and waited for his patient. The caller had been Isaac, his twenty-one year old son who was about to graduate UCLA and was taking the GMAT this summer. Isaac was a bright student but did not always test well and he was nervous. The call gave Dr. B a warm feeling. Isaac still needed his dad, and Dad was still able to provide comfort.

My father was so different, Dr. B thought to himself. His father had been a university professor and a perfectionist. Young Dr. B would never have called his father to express worry. He'd be too concerned that the elder Dr. Berkowitz would think him imperfect. Police work had fascinated Dr. B, but his father had been dead-set against his son becoming a cop. So Dr. B had studied psychiatry, attracted to the Adler School of Individual Psychology. Unlike Freud and Jung, Alfred Adler was concerned with crime and delinquency and their prevention and treatment. Dr. B had profiled criminals for the FBI for a while, and then decided to get out of the criminal mind and into the mind of the crime fighters. So now he sat in his office, waiting for Sergeant Gabriel McRay to arrive.

Dad wasn't around anymore to complain, but sometimes Dr. B felt an invisible judge looking over his shoulder. He knew if he could see the judge's face, it would be that of his father.

A bony forefinger pushed up the wire rims that were perpetually sliding down his nose. Dr. B chuckled and thought, psychiatrists don't just become psychiatrists to treat others; they do it to treat themselves as well. And don't kid yourself about that, Raymond Berkowitz.

That's why Adler's School of Individual Psychology had appealed to him so much. He dealt with his own issues of power and inadequacy. Adler wrote about feelings of inferiority and how an individual compensated for them. Dr. B always likened this theory to physical ailments. If a man breaks his leg and neglects the injury, he is going to limp. He will compensate for it one way or another. He'll find a crutch, but he will always experience pain. Soon, he won't even realize something is damaged inside of him and the crutch becomes a natural part of his life. A mind can fracture like a bone. Left untreated, that person compensates for his injury by establishing patterns that help him to live with the pain. Those patterns dictate how he lives his life. Dr. B never forgot a phrase from one of his college textbooks, "The better the adaptation to pain, the greater is the maladjustment."

The door creaked open and Gabriel hesitantly poked his head inside the office.

"Are you ready for me? Should I have knocked?"

"Yeah, could you please go back out, close the door, and knock?"

Gabriel shook his head and entered the room. "To the moon, Alice, to the moon. Go easy, okay? I've just sat in bumper to bumper traffic; I'm feeling pretty raw."

"Oh, then it will be easy to dig right in. Sit down, by all means; sit down."

Dr. B came from behind his desk, shook Gabriel's hand in greeting and took a seat in the comfortable armchair next to his patient.

"So, what do you want to talk about today?"

Gabriel acquiesced, giving the psychiatrist a cursory overview of the day, his packing, and of Rick's request for assistance.

"Are you offended by that?" Dr. B asked.

"No. Though I think it's a moot point. I mean, I'm outta there, so what's he want from me?"

"Your expertise."

Gabriel shrugged. "Whatever. I can take a look at it, I guess."

Gabriel was acting sketchy, not wanting to reveal his deeper feelings as usual. Dr. B, however, was determined to get somewhere with his patient today and he was going to try a new tact. He maneuvered back to the subjects of Gabriel's headaches and nightmares.

"You know, Gabe, I feel you are in denial of something and cannot remember what it is. You once told me you experienced anorgasmia, sexual avoidance. I wonder why."

"Couldn't help you there," Gabriel said, and stretched out his arms, yawning. "I just want to get home, lie down on the couch, and become a vegetating slave to the TV."

"You can rot your brain in forty minutes. Until then, it's mine." Dr. B told him. "Numbness or emotional constriction is all part of denial."

Gabriel shook his head. "I don't feel I'm in denial."

Change the direction. Throw him for a loop. Dr. B leaned closer to his patient. "I encourage you to formulate an emotional relationship, Gabe. That would certainly help you. Are you seeing anyone now?"

The sudden warmth in Gabriel's eyes told Dr. B that his patient was indeed visualizing someone meaningful, but then Gabriel shook his head, "No."

Dr. B paused for a moment and then said, "What is really puzzling me is your symptoms of PTSD."

"My what?" Gabriel squinted at him tiredly.

"PTSD. Post-traumatic stress disorder."

"You're impressing me again, Raymond." This time there was true malice behind the statement. "Is this supposed to catch me off guard?"

"Never," Dr. B responded. "You're never off your guard, Gabe. Post-Traumatic Stress Disorder is a condition common to people who have experienced a traumatic event in their lives. Did something happen to you?"

"Like what?"

"You tell me."

"I don't know." Gabriel shrugged. "Nothing."

"Something your parents did, maybe?"

Gabriel flinched and said too quickly, "My parents were normal everyday people." He caught himself and made an effort to joke. "I don't have PMS or PST, or whatever you're saying."

Dr. B stared seriously at Gabriel and would not be thwarted. "Well, you seem to have the symptoms of it. The fact that you don't remember something in your past that could have been traumatic—"

"What don't I remember?" Gabriel scowled. "Hey, don't put words in my mouth."

"It's called selective amnesia."

"Or thoughts in my head!"

Dr. B sighed. "I'm just trying to help you solve the riddles inside you."

"How poetic."

"Gabe,"

"You guys are all the same. I think you get into this job because of your own head problems."

Very astute, thought Dr. B. "Why are we angry, Gabe?"

"Why are <u>we</u> angry?" Gabriel mocked. "Don't talk to me like I'm seven."

"What's so special about a seven-year-old?" Dr. B honed in. "Did you talk to a therapist when you were seven?"

"Shut up!" Gabriel rose to his feet and fought for composure. "Look, I'm tired."

"Post-Traumatic Stress Disorder," Dr. B pressed, undaunted. "Nightmares, chronic headaches, memory lapses. What happened, Gabe?"

"Nothing, dammit!"

"The longer you deny, the longer the road to recovery."

"There isn't anything wrong with me!" Gabriel shouted, and then gathering himself together, he added tightly, "Are we done?"

"Go home and get some rest."

"No, I mean, are we <u>done?</u> I'm not coming anymore. I don't have a goddam job here, remember?"

"Lieutenant Ramirez has agreed to let the department pay for a few more sessions."

"How generous. Only, I'm not coming anymore."

"That would be a mistake," Dr. B replied, "Look, you're highly agitated—"

"I'm through."

"Then I'll have to recommend to Internal Affairs—"

"You'll have…" Gabriel stepped closer, hovering above Dr. B, and growled, "Are you blackmailing me? Are you holding my future for ransom? You want to destroy my career altogether?" Gabriel's nose was in his face and Dr. B saw beads of sweat forming there. Gabriel wasn't a tall man, but he was fit and strong. He could easily be menacing. Dr. B sensed the anger coursing through his patient like water down rapids.

"I want to help you and your career." He clasped his pale, long fingers together and met Gabriel's eyes, watching the waters of rage slowly recede.

Finally, Gabriel's shoulders slumped and he backed off, looking deflated. He moved to the door and eyed Dr. B momentarily. "I'll see you next week," he muttered and walked out.

Dr. B let out a long, tense breath and pushed his glasses back up his nose. He felt the invisible judge looking over his shoulder, shaking his head at a job poorly done. No, I did right in pushing the envelope. At least Gabriel jumped out of his clamshell for a minute; something about being seven-years-old…

Dr. B grabbed a pen and wrote in Gabriel's file. "Refuses to talk about early recollections – does he have any? Claims to have "normal parents." Yeah, well, there's a new one. He was sure that Gabriel was living what Adler would have called the "faulty style of life." Gabriel was running around in patterns set long ago, set by Gabriel himself. He had found a way to survive through something, but what? Dr. B would flush it out.

An Adlerian psychologist was nothing if not optimistic.

When Gabriel returned home, he set the cardboard box that held his work items on the middle of his living room carpet.

He grabbed a Dos Equis from the kitchen and then took a seat on his worn leather couch. He took a swill of beer and stared at the box, thinking how an entire career could end up in one lonely box.

I shouldn't have been so tough on Dr. B, Gabriel thought, ashamed. He had felt the anger again. It had taken an immeasurable amount of willpower not to crush in the good doctor's skull. That's what Gabriel had been itching for, what he felt compelled to do. It would have felt good to do it, too; that was the worst thing of all. That was the most frightening thing of all. The anger was a cave where he could hide. Nothing hurt him when he was in the anger. He was strong in the anger.

Gabriel took another swallow of beer. Intellectually, he knew Dr. B was trying to help him. Instinctively, he knew Dr. B was a warm and caring soul. If Gabriel could keep his mind on those conscious thoughts, he could control himself. But the rage waited in the wings of his mind, coiled like a rattlesnake, looking for an opportunity to strike. Perhaps he did suffer from PT – whatever the doctor had said, but he wouldn't look at that now. He would look instead at the box and think about what the hell he was going to do with the rest of his life.

Gabriel got up and crouched down on the carpet, setting down his beer. He opened the box and pulled out his dog-eared, spiral notepad and a geode paperweight Dash's wife had given him one Christmas. He then withdrew the drawing of the witness's description and studied it for a moment.

He had no idea what the O with a V inside might be. Possibly a symbol? Was it complete? He focused on a line of three letters. The first two were "DY" that much was clear. The third resembled a "W" but something was odd about it. The last letter was the fragment, a line attached to another line that slanted – a "V" maybe? Were these initials? Did they stand for a name or words?

Gabriel rubbed his eyes. Why was he doing this? He was officially an ex-homicide detective. He analyzed the last letter again. Was it part of an "R?"

Leave it to an eyewitness. Eyewitness accounts were totally unreliable. How could the girl not recognize most of a word two feet in front of her? Gabriel reached for the beer and halted. He looked at the word again. Maybe she did catch the word, but she was trying to read it in <u>English.</u>

Gabriel took the rendering to his laptop and logged onto the Internet. He went to one of his favorite bookmarks, a foreign language website that showed the alphabets of many major languages.

Excited, he scrolled through different tongues and then stopped. He looked at the letters on the monitor and smiled.

The letters were Russian. Okay, so what's the word? Gabriel typed an e-mail to the site's administrator asking for help. They had been electronic pen pals for some time and Gabriel knew he would get a quick response. He wanted to know what the last letter could be and what word would finally materialize.

He went to page Rick Frasier and then hesitated. Why should he offer his expertise? Let them figure it out on their own. Wasn't he the departmental scapegoat? He owed them nothing.

But Gabriel paged Rick anyways. He left a message on Rick's voicemail informing him that the letters were Russian. He finished off his beer and returned to his laptop. No reply yet.

Gabriel closed up the cardboard box and tucked it far back into his bedroom closet. He heard the phone ring, knowing it was Rick.

"It's Russian! Why didn't we think of that?" Rick said. "I knew you could help, Gabriel. How can I thank you?"

Gabriel walked back to his laptop. "You don't have to." He sat down and pecked at the keyboard, retrieving his e-mail messages.

"Listen, Gabriel, for all it's worth, I think the department is losing a solid detective. I'm sorry."

Gabriel received one message; the one he'd been waiting for. He read the reply, and was instantly drawn in. He hooked the phone underneath his chin, enabling him to cross his arms in contemplation.

"Gabriel? Are you there?" Rick said over the phone.

"Yeah, I'm here." Gabriel continued to stare at the word on the screen. "I think I know what our unsub spelled out."

Rick's voice tensed in excitement. "What is it? What's he spelling?"

"Souls,'" Gabriel said simply. "He wrote 'souls' in blood on the window."

CHAPTER 5

The Malibu Canyon murderer sat in the backseat of an expensive Mercedes Benz and moved in his seat to the music on the stereo. He wore a fake piercing in his lip and left nostril and a black wig. Deep slashes of black pencil shadowed his eyes and he had used a touch of white pancake makeup to make his skin appear pale. Although the evening carried the weight of the day's heat he wore black leather pants and boots. A leather vest with no shirt underneath draped his shoulders. He looked every bit the emo-whore.

"So why were you hanging out in front of my beach house? What did you expect to find there?" the fat one in the front asked him. The fat one winked at the driver of the Mercedes.

"I told you," the Malibu Canyon Murderer said, "I'm just One looking for Fun. If you're not interested in fun, let me out and I'll find someone else to party with."

"Oh I'm interested in fun, alright," the fat one told him. "It's just that you sort of popped up out of nowhere."

"I heard the famous producer liked to party with boys, so here I am."

The fat one smiled and shook his head at the driver. The driver, a young man wearing designer clothes, leered at the Malibu Canyon Murderer through the rearview mirror. "Here you are," repeated the younger man.

The Malibu Canyon Murderer danced to the music in the backseat, loving the way the two men up front thought they were playing him. Their condescending manner excited him to no end.

The driving younger man looked up at the mirror again. "You want something to get you in the mood, Sweetheart?"

Sweetheart? God love them, they were going to have such fun tonight.

"Oh, no thanks," the Murderer replied. "I'm high on life and I am already in the mood, trust me. Tell you what, why don't we go into the mountains – off the beaten path. Let's find a lookout point of our own."

The fat one shook his head. "Not in this car."

The Malibu Canyon Murderer frowned, stopped dancing, and reached for his back pack. "Gentlemen, I'm afraid I have to insist on it."

Later, when the moon rose high and illuminated the quiet Mercedes sitting on a deserted fire road, the silence was so palpable and thick he imagined he could pick it up and squeeze it like Jell-O.

He looked out the window at the cold, bone-white moon. Funny how a gun could wipe the smirk off their faces. Funny how a gun made them so docile. They didn't start screaming until he had brought out the knife. He didn't like screaming. It was uncivilized.

As he leaned against the car seat, the Malibu Canyon Murderer thought of a time when he was in another car many years ago. His family had taken a drive to Reno for a vacation when he was about twelve.

Mom was driving and she let him sit in the front seat while his sisters sat in back. She told him he was the man of the family and had been from the time Daddy had abandoned them.

He remembered feeling an alien sense of pride, which was rare when it came to interactions with mother. When he glanced at her driving he saw an odd smile twisting her lips. He did not like that smile. I *do not like that smile, Sam I am.* Bad things happened when she smiled like that.

Mom had stopped at a liquor store to buy a bottle of stout Polish potato vodka for herself. He saw her exit the store with a brown paper bag. She returned to the car and put on her Jackie O sunglasses that would eventually hide her booze-red eyes. She also had some spearmint gum on hand in case a cop decided to pull her over for weaving on the road.

"Guess what I have?" she said, smiling. This time, the smile was genuine.

"Candy!" the kids cried out in unison.

"That's right. For my special angels!"

Mom turned around and handed both of his sisters a big Butterfinger candy bar. He smiled, waiting for his.

His mother started the car and pulled out of the parking lot. He swallowed, still waiting, afraid to say anything.

Mom pulled out on the road. Once comfortably settled there, she reached into the brown paper bag. He readied a "thank you" smile.

She pulled out her vodka and cranked off the cap. She took a deep slug and tossed her dirty blonde hair in a careless gesture.

"Mom?" he said with hesitation.

She took another swallow and said, "Hmm?"

In the back seat, his sisters were chomping noisily on their chocolate.

"Is mine still in the bag?"

His mother swiveled her face toward him. Those round, black sunglasses gave her the detached, callous look of an insect.

"You don't need one."

He didn't know what to say. He could only stare at his reflection cowering in her sunglasses.

She turned her gaze back to the road and drank more vodka. "You're the 'man' of the family, remember? So man up!"

That seemed to be a joke, because a laugh bubbled out of her, but it didn't last long. Soon, it was drowned in another swallow of booze.

Now, as he sat in this fancy car, he felt completely at peace. The famous one, the fat one, had just aided him immensely.

The murderer dipped his fingers into the solar plexus of the fat one, the powerful one, and withdrew them, gazing at the redness there. He unzipped his pants and rubbed his fingers against himself until he forgot about his mother.

"Thank you," he whispered harshly. Now he would have more energy, more spontaneity. His power was growing.

He dipped his other hand once more into the man's abdomen and drew a red circle on the windshield. He finished it off by inserting an upside down triangle inside. He then wrote the words he had memorized long ago.

The metallic scent of spilled blood filled the car. He needed to clean up, put things in order. This time, however, his plans had a slightly different angle. He carefully cleaned the knife and tucked it safely in the bag at his feet. He pulled out a plastic sandwich bag that contained a single envelope. His heart leapt with joy. Surely, his time in the sun had now come. Everything he ever dreamed of was finally falling into place.

Gabriel stared at himself in the bathroom mirror. The light was off, but the hall light illuminated him from behind. His eyes rolled toward the bathroom window, where a wedge of white moon hung in an indigo sky. The last time he was himself, it had been morning.

He was naked. He was an angel with the halo of light surrounding his head and body, although he felt anything but holy. Tears of perspiration coursed down his face and his blue-black hair curled wetly against his forehead. His muscles ached as if from some strenuous exercise. He was incredibly thirsty.

Where have I been?

When did he come into the bathroom to stare at his reflection? Why was he naked? Panic swept through him and Gabriel shut his eyes, hearing only the pounding of his heart – threatening to break through his chest. Gradually Gabriel became more focused and he realized the pounding sounded from outside his body. He made out a distant voice – Dash calling his name and knocking heavily on the front door.

Gabriel opened his eyes and looked around like a man lost. His hands were tightly gripping the porcelain edge of the sink, knuckles white. He detached them, shocked to find his fingers tingling from a lack of circulation. He shook out his hands, staring at them as if they were diseased. The pounding outside – he had to move; do something.

Gabriel turned and twisted the knobs on the shower; they slipped in his sweaty palms. He grabbed a towel from the rack and carefully wrapped it around his waist. The pounding was stronger now, more persistent; or was he imagining that?

"All right..." he muttered. "All right!" he called more loudly toward the front door.

Gabriel wiped a hand across his brow and hurried to the front door. Dash tumbled inside, bristling with unwelcome electricity.

"What's going on? I've been standing outside knocking on your door – I was about to kick it in. Ramirez has been paging you–"

Gabriel shook his head, "I was in the shower. I'm sorry."

Dash regarded Gabriel curiously. "Are you okay?"

Gabriel shrugged. "Sure. I'm fine." He went to the refrigerator. "Want a soda? Beer?"

"No, thanks." Dash was obviously agitated. "I've actually come to get you. We've got another one."

Gabriel paused. "Another –"

"Another burned-out car with a stiff in it. This time two stiffs found in the trunk."

"Shit."

"Same guy. It's got to be. They found another tire track."

"I don't understand what this has to do with me?"

Dash headed to the door. "A piece of evidence was found on one of the bodies."

Gabriel put the cold water bottle to his forehead. "Yeah, so?"

"Look, Lieutenant Ramirez says I'm supposed to bring you over there."

Gabriel was annoyed with his partner's enigmatic answers. "Over where? What the hell are you talking about?"

"You're supposed to come with me to the crime scene. That's all I was told."

"And as usual, the good boy's just following orders."

Dash reddened with anger. "What's that supposed to mean?"

Gabriel caught himself, knowing he had spoken out of line. He felt himself shrink beneath his skin. "Look, you caught me at a bad time."

"I don't give a shit. I don't deserve that and you know it."

"No, of course you don't." Gabriel stood silently for a moment. "I'm sorry."

Dash's complexion returned to its normal peach again. "It's okay. But we've got to get over there."

Gabriel nodded and headed toward his bedroom.

"Maybe you should turn off your shower," Dash said.

"Oh, yeah." Gabriel walked unsteadily back toward the bathroom.

"You sure you're alright?"

Gabriel didn't answer. He didn't want to lie. Instead he moved to his bedroom and searched his closet for his favorite tan Dockers. The slacks were nowhere to be found. Annoyed, Gabriel pulled on some jeans instead.

The crime scene was chaotic. The press had gotten word of the killings from their police band radios, and newspaper and television reporters choked the narrow fire road with their vans and equipment. Curious drivers, crawling along a clogged Malibu Canyon Road, had followed the news vans and helicopters and were now talking excitedly, watching the play unfold before them. Patrol officers pushed the swarm back, using bullhorns and muscle, and managed to keep outsiders clear of the tape surrounding the burn area and the charred Mercedes sedan sitting in the middle.

The smell of fried electric wires and gasoline permeated the night air. Bright lights danced in concentric patterns, beaming down from noisy helicopters circling in the sky above.

Engine captain Desmond Gein, joined by Lieutenant Ramirez, approached Gabriel and Dash.

"Hello, McRay," Ramirez said loudly above the din.

"Lieutenant."

"Thanks for coming," Ramirez said, refusing to meet his eyes.

Gabriel got the distinct impression they had been waiting for him all along. A couple of the uniforms loitering nearby looked at him suspiciously.

What did I do now?

The three men advanced on the car.

The engine captain spoke. "The coroner's men have been working here already. They pulled something interesting out of–" Gein glanced at Ramirez, who quieted him with a sharp look.

Dash asked Gein, "Do we have an ID on the car?"

"Damn, do we have an ID," Gein said. "It belongs to Brian Goldfield."

"Brian Goldfield." Dash paused. "Why do I know that name?" Suddenly, his eyes widened. "Oh, he's a movie producer, isn't he?"

Ramirez lit a cigarette. "That's right. Guy is one powerful sucker."

Dash frowned. "This is going to become a circus."

The Mercedes sedan sat stoically on a plot of bare earth. Under the beams of artificial light the exterior hardly appeared damaged. The interior however, was black as pitch and emitted a bitter, charred odor. Moving closer, Gabriel smelled something underneath the burned leather, a chemical odor, and something else – something more animal. Gabriel aimed his flashlight inside and noticed a couple of rips in the leather back of the passenger seat. He passed the light over the windshield and the blotchy, streaks in the glass. He could barely make out the letters as everything had run together, but they were there.

Gabriel stepped back and looked at Ramirez, surprised to see his lieutenant staring directly at him. Gabriel had no clue as to why he was summoned to this macabre scene. A warm Santa Ana breeze kicked up with the breaking dawn, carrying with it the stink of the car and the promise of a difficult summer.

Rick Frasier appeared behind Gabriel like a blond ghost. "Hey, Gabe."

Gabriel gave him a cursory nod as Rick sidled up alongside. "I think you ought to check back there in the trunk." The younger detective motioned Gabriel toward the rear of the Mercedes.

Gabriel gagged from the odor of cooked flesh that hit him when he reached the open trunk. Slumped together were two men. Gabriel panned his flashlight over the first body – a young man, no more than twenty-five. A diamond stud in the young man's ear winked brightly under Gabriel's meager light. Lying next to the young man was an older gentleman, graying sideburns, loose jowls, and tubby stomach: Brian Goldfield, the movie mogul.

Clothes that were once hip and finely tailored now lay in a mangled, brown mess due to the complete and hideous violation to the man's torso. His chest had been hacked so religiously Gabriel could only liken it to raw hamburger meat. Gabriel leaned closer, fighting the smell, and shined his flashlight deep into the trunk's interior, noting very little blood had spilled.

He wasn't stabbed in the trunk. Gabriel remembered the rips in the seat back. The real action had taken place inside the car.

Gabriel straightened up. To his left, he saw a Mobile Crime Scene Unit photographer regarding him coolly as he changed the film of his camera. To Gabriel's right stood two latex-gloved deputy coroners, staring at him as well.

Gabriel looked from Ramirez to Rick Frasier and back again. He had the unpleasant feeling he was being set up for one of Ramirez's little power-plays. He might as well bite.

"Nice spot for a campfire," Gabriel said. "Now, what the fuck am I doing here?"

"Look at the fat guy's chest, McRay," Ramirez told him.

"I did."

"Look again."

Gabriel took up the latex gloves that Rick proffered and snapped them on. He reached down and sifted through the shreds of clothing that were stiffening in the breeze with drying blood. His fingers touched something that crunched. Repelled but curious, Gabriel grasped the object firmly and pulled it out.

In his hands he held a plastic Ziploc sandwich bag. He looked at Dash, Gein, Rick, and Ramirez. "This is the first time the victims have been trunked, am I right?"

"Yeah," Ramirez answered evenly. "This time the perp planted something he didn't want burned. We put it back for you just the way we found it."

Dash took Gabriel's flashlight and steadied the beam on the baggie. Inside was a folded piece of white paper. Typed on one side in neat computer font, was "Gabriel McRay."

Mice ran down Gabriel's spine and he looked at the other men in surprise.

"You know something about this?" Ramirez asked.

Gabriel shook his head.

"Open it."

The other men huddled close, craning to see what would appear.

Gabriel carefully pulled out the note, and unfolded it slowly.

"What's it say, McRay?"

Gabriel shook his head in disbelief and his voice creaked like a haunted house when he spoke, "We are one."

"Everyone is like the moon and has a dark side."

Mark Twain

CHAPTER 6

Gabriel waded through a throng of reporters as he made his way to the entrance of headquarters in Monterey Park. A group of citizens held up anti-police brutality posters and heckled Gabriel as he approached the entrance. The reporters stuck microphones in his face and although the cacophony of the mixed voices made his ears ring some questions filtered through.

"Detective McRay, how do you feel about being back on the force?"

"Detective McRay, is it true you'll be handling the Malibu Canyon Murder case?"

"Do you have any leads on who killed Brian Goldfield?"

"Is there a serial killer stalking the canyons, Detective McRay? Was Tania Dankowski having an affair with Brian Goldfield?"

Gabriel pushed a microphone out of his face and turned on them. He spoke calmly, "There is no reason for anyone to panic.

You can be assured the L.A. County Sheriff's Department is working hard to bring–"

"Blah, blah, blah!" shouted a chunky male onlooker with a pug nose. He held a sign that depicted a pig in a cop's hat sitting on an African-American child. "Hey, weren't you supposed to be fired?"

Gabriel glared at the heckler. A hawk-eyed reporter took up the cue, and quickly asked, "Yes, can you tell us, Detective McRay, why exactly did the department decide to reverse your termination?"

How about fuck you? Before Gabriel could voice what he truly wanted to say, he abruptly turned on his heel and strode inside the building.

Ramirez was right on top of him in the lobby. The Latino lieutenant stuck his chin under Gabriel's nose. "Why didn't you answer the question? Why did you walk away like that?"

"I didn't know what to say. You don't want them knowing about the note," Gabriel said in a low voice, aware that other officers had stopped what they were doing to watch their comrade get dressed down. "I'm not a PR person. What the hell am I supposed to say – Sir?"

Ramirez smiled evilly. "Don't you fuck with me, McRay. You are still a walking disease in this Department." Ramirez' eyes moved past Gabriel to the reporters milling outside. The shorter man straightened his jacket and darted into the limelight.

Gabriel let out a tense breath, watching the nosy cops pretending not to stare. Uncomfortable, Gabriel retreated down the hall to the conference room.

Waiting for him inside were Dash, arson investigator Paul Vacher, Ming, Rick Frasier, and Dr. B. Gabriel took a seat between Dash and Ming.

"How are you doing, Gabriel?" Dr. B asked warmly.

Hanging by a noose.

"Hanging in there."

Gabriel offered Ming a brief smile. Her ebony eyes gazed at him wistfully. Instead of returning the smile, Ming mindlessly shuffled through some papers stacked in front of her. *I'm the pariah again,* Gabriel thought and pretended to read through his crime scene notes.

Ramirez burst into the room, fired up from his press interviews. "Okay, People, let's get started. I might as well tell you, there were no fingerprints on that note. It was printed off a laser jet printer in a font called 'Arial'. That's what they tell me, and that's what I've got. Now, what have you got?"

Paul Vacher spoke first. "What we've got is a Santa Ana condition. If this firebug continues on this track, it spells real trouble from my standpoint."

"Thanks for the weather report," Ramirez nodded. "Now, tell me what you know about his fires."

"Oh, si, Jefe," Vacher said, acquiescing. "Gasoline is the accelerant. That much we know. There's no evidence of siphoning, the Mercedes had a full tank, so the Torch must bring the fuel with him somehow."

Rick Frasier chimed in. "We've searched for discarded gas cans but never have found any."

"So he takes it home with him," Vacher said. "He's careful."

"He hauls it around on a bike?" Dash said.

"Why not?" Vacher replied. "Maybe he lives in the mountains somewhere."

Ramirez nodded in agreement as he pulled out a pack of Winstons. "We've got to continue interviewing residents and businesses along Malibu Canyon, Topanga, Kanan Road – all through the hills." The team lieutenant shifted gears and turned toward Gabriel. "Any idea why this killer would say 'we are one' to you?"

Gabriel had been asking himself that same question since he read the eerie message. He had no clue as to why the killer focused on him so he offered the only reason he could come up with.

"He's seen my name in the papers. He's interested in me."

"Why do you think?" Ramirez prodded gently.

"Gently" was completely out of his superior's character and suspicious hairs on the back of Gabriel's neck stood at attention. He answered carefully, "I don't know."

"You know of any family, friends, anybody you've run into that—"

"Wait a minute," Gabriel interrupted. "Are you implying that someone I know is doing this? A family member, for God's sake?"

Ramirez said nothing, only peered at Gabriel as he lit his cigarette. The tension began building in the room like a smoking volcano.

Ming cleared her throat. "Like Gabriel said, he has gotten a lot of press."

"A lot of _bad_ press," Dash added.

"And the killer has honed in on him," Ming finished.

Ramirez continued to study Gabriel as if he were a bacterium on a glass slide. "You know why you are back on the force?"

Gabriel said nothing.

"I'll tell you why," Ramirez continued in his best barrio twang. "You are being put on this case because the Chief, the mayor and the press are up my ass like a high-speed dildo."

Dash held back laughter and Ramirez swiveled in his chair to look at him. "Something funny about that Señor Spiceless?" Dash swallowed his smile. Ramirez swiveled back, exhaled smoke into the room, and leaned across the table toward Gabriel. "Personally, I wouldn't have let you back through the door, much less on a high-profile case. The movie producer's family is putting on a funeral the likes this city has never seen. Like fucking Michael Jackson. Everyone is eager to catch this guy, and the powers that be feel that if this dude has some connection to you, then maybe you can be of help."

Gabriel reddened. "Like bait. Twenty odd years working the streets as a detective count for nothing, I suppose."

"This perpetrator has succeeded in saving a job for you that you fucked up. If you can manage to bring in this asshole you just may salvage your reputation, McRay."

"And yours," Gabriel said pointedly.

Ramirez glared at him. "Behave yourself, Vato."

Gabriel sat stiffly in his chair, ordering himself to remain calm.

Dr. B intervened, saying, "This is totally unproductive. We have a serial killer out there, and I think we all have the same goal. We want to catch him. Gabriel has a proven track record, and besides, he's already contributed something useful to the investigation."

"Yeah, I know," Ramirez said, waving his hand in the air. "We've got a Russian on our hands."

"Not necessarily," Dash said. "He wrote 'souls' in Russian. I don't think we should jump to any conclusions and focus on any one group of people."

Ramirez took a puff. "Doc, any hunches? Can you profile this creep?"

"I'll try." Dr. B took off his glasses and regarded the present company. "All the victims have been Caucasian so far. Since most killers usually prey upon their own race, I'd have to assume the Malibu Canyon Murderer is white. Most likely a white male, between the ages of twenty to thirty-five." Dr. B turned to Ming. "Tell me something of the victims and how they were killed."

Ming obliged, saying, "All were killed prior to the burning of the cars. All but one were stabbed numerous times with the same non-serrated blade of one inch in width and at least six inches in length."

"The one that wasn't stabbed, who was he and what was he killed with?" Dr. B asked.

"That was Adam Parraco," Ming said.

"Parraco was Brian Goldfield's lover," Rick added.

"So the producer was gay," Ramirez said, extinguishing his cigarette. "Maybe a past love interest – make sure that's checked out."

Ming continued calmly, "Parraco was shot one time at close range with a 7.62 caliber bullet. Ballistics is working to identify the gun. Because the flesh heated in the car trunk, I couldn't make out any gunpowder tattoos, but the gunshot wound, which was against the sternum of the chest, was in a ragged star pattern."

"The gun gives us something new to work with. That's good," Ramirez said. "¿Qué más?"

Ming did a double take. "What?"

"Don't you speak Spanish?"

"No."

"Aren't you Mexican?"

Ming's eyes dropped to her lap. Gabriel wanted to club his lieutenant across the back. Ramirez waved Ming away, "Never mind, continue."

Ming frowned at Ramirez and then said, "Star patterns result from a contact entrance wound. The explosive gasses from a direct contact expand between the bone and the skin and burst the flesh apart in a star pattern. Parraco had no defense wounds. In fact, he wasn't stabbed at all."

Gabriel gazed thoughtfully at Ming. "Sounds like the killer wanted to get him out of the way."

"Maybe," Ming replied. "Because he sure took his time with Goldfield. He was stabbed nineteen times. At least ten were fatal, and most all the wounds that weren't defensive cuts were centered between the navel and the base of the sternum."

"Were most of the wounds made before or after death?" Dr. B asked.

"The fact that the bodies were not burned this time gave me a lot more to work with. I can tell you that the first wound, which bled the most, was a direct hit in the abdomen. The killer seemed to concentrate around that area. Brian Goldfield was stabbed as he was expiring and after death."

Dr. B reflected a moment, "Hmmm. Our friend is not showing a particular rage toward either sex. That makes things a little more complicated."

"How so?" Ramirez asked.

Dr. B shrugged. "Well, for one, he's not going to be so obvious. Tell me, Dr. Li, was the woman raped? Were the men, for that matter?"

"Very hard to tell with a burned body like Tania's. Any tears or abrasions would be obliterated. But I believe that all the victims died with their clothes on."

"Why do you believe that?" Gabriel asked.

"Well, no apparel fibers were found off the bodies and the stitching on Tania Dankowski's jeans fused into her body. They were quite clear. I've got pictures." Ming reached for a file on the desk in front of her and pulled out some colored 8 x 10 photographs.

Everyone could decipher the "XXX" shaped stitches branded onto the flesh. Gabriel glanced at Dash, who looked a bit green.

"I don't believe Tania was raped," Ming said. "At first, I thought the perpetrator may have had some sort of reason to rape and redress her, but I don't think that was his focus. Rick, show them the pictures of her body in situ."

Rick Frasier shook back a shock of blond hair, and pushed some photos lying on the table toward the rest of the party. Ming took a pencil and pointed at the picture.

"Notice how Tania's body is sprawled. Look at her head, cocked back, out of the way."

Gabriel caught Ming's drift. "Right. It looks as if he cut her throat to get to the business at hand – that of mutilating her lower abdomen."

"Ted Brody was found in an unusual position too," Dash said. "It looks like he was propped so the slasher could get at his crotch easier."

They inspected the crime scene pictures. Sure enough, Gabriel thought, Ted was slightly on his side, facing the driver's side window, with his backside facing the killer.

"It looks like he's making a trek up their bodies," Gabriel said.

Ming nodded. "I thought the same thing myself."

Vacher tossed the picture back to Ming. "We've got a real psycho, don't we?"

"Probably not a psychotic," Dr. B said, his brown eyes sparkling with interest. "A psychotic personality tends to hear voices, have hallucinations–"

"How do you know this one doesn't?" Ramirez quipped.

"I don't. Not for sure," Dr. B said. "But a psychotic tends to react rather than act. By this I mean, that a psychotic who is haunted by voices, frightening delusions, and the like, tends to react to them. If he kills, he does so in what he believes is self-preservation. Although there are certainly exceptions to the rule, most psychotics kill people they have relationships with, if they kill at all. And most psychotics leave a trail of mental illness throughout their lives that is apparent to those who know them."

"Well," Vacher argued, "this creep probably has a freak reputation plus a sheet."

Dr. B remained undaunted. "Usually, a psychotic killer is disorganized. Sloppy. He's too busy battling his demons to worry about neatness. Your boy, on the other hand, is organized. In my opinion, that makes him a sociopath. These killings are serving him, and he doesn't give a damn for his victims. He's driven by what he feels is a higher power, but what is really an impulse-control problem."

"An impulse-control problem?" Dash made a face. "You call slashing and burning four people an impulse-control problem?"

"As light as that may sound, Detective, that's exactly what it is. It has ugly roots, I'm sure. Most sociopaths have inflated egos. Overcompensation for what really is a total lack of self-worth. Maybe homosexuality had something to do with why the movie producer was interested in the killer, but it had little to do with why the killer wanted him. This man revolves in his own world. Like I said, he's organized. He covers up his deeds with fires that not only destroy evidence, but create a dazzling display for him. He probably enjoys watching the panic ensue."

Gabriel spoke up. "You say he enjoys watching. Could he be sticking around?"

"He's not going to hide in burning brush," Vacher argued.

"But who's been looking?" Dash admitted.

"Yeah," Ming said, "that could be part of his thrill."

Ramirez stood up. "Okay, hold on, People, please. I got a headache from all this shit."

Rick sighed. "We've talked to family, friends, and co-workers of each victim. With the exception of Parraco and Goldfield, none of the victims have had a common link."

"They may seem to be random victims to you," Dr. B stated, "but they fall into his game plan somehow."

Gabriel turned to Dr. B. "Let's say he is a stranger to them, why do you think they let him into their cars?"

"No one in L.A. picks up hitchhikers anymore," Vacher piped up. "He's probably meeting them somewhere – in a bar, maybe."

"Tania Dankowski in a bar?" Dash said. "Not likely."

"Obviously, he's not arousing anyone's suspicions," Dr. B said. "You're not going to find him drooling in the street with body parts dangling from his hands. I'll bet our boy puts on a neat appearance. He's very careful, and that makes him dangerous."

"Speaking of body parts," Ming said brightly, and all of the men frowned at her. "He did take an earlobe from Tania Dankowski, which I believed came equipped with an earring."

"Trophies." Dr. B regarded the pathologist. "He hopes to recapture the feelings of power and dominance that he experienced by holding onto something of theirs."

"You know," Rick said, flipping through his spiral pad of notes, "Gloria Lusk, Ted Brody's fiancé, said Ted always wore a diamond promise ring that matched her own. We never found that."

"What's your take on him writing 'souls' on the window?" Gabriel asked Dr. B.

The psychiatrist shrugged. "The word has a special meaning somehow. He could be summoning up a past experience by using it. He could be performing a ritual that has a specific purpose for him. He could have religious issues, maybe performing some sort of pagan sacrifice. Who knows?"

"I'm not discounting the sex crime angle," Ramirez told them.

"We've used the Luminol, despite the burn," Rick said, "but we couldn't find any traces of semen."

"But how is he getting in their cars?" Dash repeated Gabriel's earlier question.

"That, I'm afraid, is something you gentlemen will have to figure out," Dr. B answered.

Ramirez looked at Rick Frasier. "What else have you got so far?"

"A tire track."

"A tire track?" Ramirez repeated. "That's it?"

Rick nodded, looking like a puppy. Gabriel felt sorry for him.

"Do you have a make on it?" Ramirez asked.

Rick shook his head, "Working on that one."

Ramirez sighed heavily and suddenly looked tired. "A tire track, souls, and wounds moving up the body."

"Let's not forget his note," Gabriel added.

"Oh, don't worry." Ramirez kept his eyes pinned on Gabriel. "No one's forgetting that."

�֍ �֍ ✖

We are one. We are one. We are one.

The words beat a tattoo against Gabriel's brain, threatening to give him a headache. Night had fallen and Gabriel sat at his desk, which was now devoid of all his personal items. His cubicle seemed sterile and cold. *We are one.* What had Gabriel done to warrant being compared to a serial killer?

Don't do this to yourself, Gabriel thought, or you'll come apart at the seams and lose again the one thing that's kept you together all these years – your job. Gabriel popped some aspirin into his mouth and walked to the water fountain. The floor was nearly empty, save for a couple of officers working at their desks. The air conditioner blew icy drafts down the hallway, reminding Gabriel of yearning ghosts.

Dash had gone to get some Chinese take-out since the two of them would be working late. Being newly assigned to the case, they needed to catch up. Tomorrow the newspapers would let everyone know that Gabriel McRay would be taking charge of the Malibu Canyon Murder investigation.

In an objective way, Gabriel had to admire Ramirez for taking such a political risk. The Sheriff's Department was not plagued with scandal like the LAPD. If its one problem child could redeem himself, the whole department would appear sparkling clean again. Gabriel was their problem child.

Gabriel returned to his desk and accessed the CII, which was short for Criminal Information Index, a computer network that allowed an investigator to check for similar crimes in other cities. The National Crime Information Computer, or NCIC, furnished information from other states.

Rick Frasier had done a check already, but only over the past five years. Gabriel wanted to be more thorough and ran a search over the past ten years.

We are one.

Gabriel rubbed his temples, trying to rid himself of the headache. In his mind's eye he saw the costumed cop falling to the floor with two of Gabriel's slugs in his chest. He saw the expression of surprise on the fifteen-year-old boy's face as Gabriel's thumbs dug into his flesh. He saw his arm shoot out like a bullet and swat the old woman off her feet. And farther away, he heard another woman's caustic voice, drilling into him, "How could you do that to a child? You're an evil, evil man."

The hydraulic whoosh of the door blocked out other sounds and Gabriel looked up to see his partner striding toward him.

"Hey," Gabriel murmured, and stared back at the blinking cursor of his monitor in an exhausted half-daze.

"Ready to eat?" Dash asked merrily, plopping down four white cartons onto Gabriel's desk.

Gabriel suddenly grimaced at Dash. "Oh, I forgot. You got the food. Is it edible?"

Dash clucked his tongue. "Now would I give a gourmet like you pig slop? I got you kung pao chicken – burn your frigging mouth off."

"What'd you get?"

"Steamed chicken and veggies. No sauce."

Gabriel opened up his own carton, inhaling the mouthwatering spices.

"There's also plain rice and vegetable pan fried noodles, so dig in."

"How much do I owe you?" Gabriel said, reaching for some chopsticks.

Dash waved him away and opened up a carton. His desk was right next to Gabriel's and he hunkered into his own chair. "Not a red cent. How many times have you had Eve and me to dinner? Besides, we're celebrating, aren't we?"

"Are we?"

"Yes, indeed, Partner. We're celebrating your return to the bump and grind."

Gabriel smiled. Dash was as light as Gabriel was dark.

They both heard a "beep" and exchanged glances. The computer had found a match. The two detectives edged in front of Gabriel's monitor.

"Unbelievable. 2001," Dash said.

"Victim, Thomas Welby," Gabriel read. "Found stabbed in the throat near the Sunset District in San Francisco…" His voice trailed off.

Dash took up the slack. "Body found in the driver's seat of the victim's car. Both car and body were victims of arson. The arson investigators say that gasoline may have started the fire. No other evidence was found. The case went cold. Well, what about the blade used?" Dash sighed in frustration. "Oh, here. Coroner's report. One wound made by a smooth-edged, non-serrated blade of at least five inches in length. Other than that, they couldn't garner much from the burned body."

A flash of pain rammed its way into Gabriel's head and he winced. He turned away from the screen and closed his eyes.

Dash returned to his desk and made some notes. "I'll call San Francisco PD tomorrow and see what they've got. I'll bet you ten to one that blade belongs to our guy. But shit, this happened nearly ten years ago!" He finally noticed Gabriel. "Something a matter?"

Gabriel couldn't speak until the pain subsided somewhat. He ran a trembling hand through his dark hair. "Nothing, I'm just tired." He looked up to see Dash's concerned expression. "Actually, it's a weird coincidence."

"What is?"

Gabriel regarded his partner over the cartons of steaming food, and said, "I'm from the Sunset District in San Francisco."

CHAPTER 7

Los Angeles Times, July 1

"Troubled Detective to Solve Troubling Case.
Four people, including movie producer
Brian Goldfield and his live-in
lover, have now perished in the Santa
Monica Mountains. While the police
have not released any details surrounding
the murders, sources say that the killings
are similar in nature and might be the work
of one perpetrator. Detective Gabriel McRay
is leading the investigation. Sources reveal
that McRay is under a psychiatrist's care and
was recently terminated. His problematic
behavior sent one eighty-year old
pensioner to the hospital. That case has settled
out of court for an undisclosed amount.
Lieutenant Miguel Ramirez stands by McRay's
past exceptional record and is quoted as saying,
"I have every confidence that Sergeant McRay
will bring this criminal to justice."

Gabriel and Dash split up, investigating different areas of the Santa Monica Mountains. The murders had taken place at various times, so the killer was not chained to a schedule. Gabriel considered the fact that perhaps he was unemployed.

At one point, Gabriel stood visibly at the side of the road and stuck out his thumb. The cars sped by, ignoring him. Vacher is right, Gabriel thought as he inhaled exhaust; no one stops for hitchhikers anymore. Then how did the suspect enter their cars? He had a gun. Perhaps he carjacked them; but he had to get them to stop first.

Gabriel's cell phone vibrated in the late afternoon and displayed Dash's number. Gabriel pulled into the parking lot of a restaurant called the Inn of the Seventh Ray. Here, diners sat creek side amid a grotto-like atmosphere and munched on holistic fare such as lentil loaf and barley pilaf. In a store called The Spiral Staircase, which abutted the restaurant, Gabriel returned his partner's call.

"Hey," Gabriel said into his cell phone. "Where are you?"

"The Taco Bell on Malibu Canyon near the freeway. Can you hear it?"

"I only hear chimes and mantras."

"What?"

"I'm kidding, but only about the mantras." Gabriel glanced behind him. A profusion of wind chimes hung from the ceiling. Also displayed for purchase were incense and crystals. "Have you got anything?"

"I've got cottonmouth from talking so much. Couple o' people had bikes, but nothing that aroused my suspicions. Nobody seems to know someone athletic who has a penchant for knives."

"Speaking of knives," Gabriel said, "we need to visit Sam."

Sam Stanton was the proprietor of the Knife Trader, an army surplus store in the northern town of Camarillo.

"Good idea," Dash agreed. "Ballistics left a message on my voicemail. They got something on that gun that did Parraco."

"Yeah?"

"They said you may want to see for yourself. Geez, I gotta get outta here. Just the smell is going to send me into cardiac arrest."

"What, no greasy tacos, Dash? I'll bet you're a closet junk food junkie."

"Ha ha," Dash said tiredly. "Why don't we call it a day?"

Gabriel wanted to get over to Ballistics but he decided to let Dash off the hook. "Okay. I can't have Eve blaming me for overworking you." Gabriel reached out a finger and touched a wind chime which tinkled pleasantly. "Hey, why don't you two come over for dinner tonight? You can tell her I'm serving charcoal-broiled salmon en brochette with lemon rice."

Dash laughed. "How're you gonna cook a fancy dinner now?"

"That's just gourmet talk for barbecued salmon on skewers. I'll have time. What do you say?"

"Sounds great," Dash said. "Why don't you ask Ming to join us?"

Gabriel went silent. He could hear Dash catch his breath, probably wanting to kick himself for butting in.

It's not your fault, Dash.

"What kind of wine should I bring?" Dash asked, trying to sound casual. "White?"

"That'd work fine."

Gabriel tucked his phone away. Behind him, the wind chimes tinkled and the heady fragrance of sandalwood incense drifted into his nose. A dark-haired saleslady, dressed like a gypsy in flowing silks and beads and sporting a nose ring, smiled at him from the cash register. Gabriel nodded back.

His throat was tight, and he felt an odd sense of shame. Thinking of Ming without her lab coat should have produced a welcomed heat in Gabriel, but he wished only to close up like a clam in frigid water. When Gabriel had made love to Sheryl, he'd gone through the motions, detaching himself from the act because he felt fearful and ashamed. What did Dr. B call it? *Sexual avoidance.*

Gabriel didn't know why he had felt ashamed; maybe he had been fearful of becoming emotionally dependant on his wife. He hated being vulnerable. Gabriel thought his emotional non-commitment would go unnoticed but Sheryl could not ignore his acting jobs in the bedroom. She had begged him to see a marriage counselor, but Gabriel refused, insisting there was nothing wrong. After a year of playing charades, they both gave up and divorced.

Maybe this was something he and the killer had in common; Gabriel thought as he shook out two aspirin and chewed them, comforted by the chalky, bitter taste. Both he and the killer were disconnected from the real world.

Gabriel began thumbing absently through the self-help books. Whatever happened, Gabriel was determined to prevent his personal demons from interfering with his work. He would catch this slasher and earn some feel-good time. Then maybe he could ask Ming out. Then maybe he wouldn't feel like a ghost of himself.

"Can I help you find something?" The gypsy asked from her post behind the counter.

"No thanks." Gabriel headed toward the door, brushing against the wind chimes as he went.

Something caught the corner of his eye and he paused. Gabriel moved to a small poster hanging on the wall, depicting a serene figure, sitting cross-legged in an East Indian style, hands on knees, palms upraised. The figure didn't interest

Gabriel much, but the vertical line of circles marking various points down the body did.

Gabriel inspected the picture. The heading at the top read "The Chakras." One circle was positioned at the bottom where the ankles crossed, the next was at the crotch area, and the one above that was at the navel area and so on, all the way to the top of the skull. Gabriel counted seven in all.

"Excuse me," he said to the gypsy saleslady. "What are these circles?"

The dark-haired woman moved like a dancer, calm and graceful. She floated over to Gabriel with her intense green eyes and a strong scent of patchouli oil.

"Those are the positions of the seven chakras," she told him.

"What are chakras?"

"Chakras operate like valves that channel the current of the universal life force into the body."

Of course; and too many wind chimes can drive a person insane.

"I'm afraid I don't understand."

She waved her tapering black fingernails at the circles, and said, "Each chakra has a glandular connection, a body part that is associated with it. You can actually heal your physical self by nurturing your chakras."

"Okay." Gabriel studied the poster. "I see that they make a track down the body."

"Up the body, would be more like it," she said looking at the picture. "The bottom chakra is Chakra One; it is associated with the earth and physical identity. It's essential to one's sense of grounding and is located at the base of the spine."

Gabriel's heart beat faster. "Go on."

"Chakra Two is water or emotional identity. It's also related to sexual identity. It connects you to others." She winked at Gabriel and he caught a whiff of patchouli.

"It's located near the sex organs and the lower abdomen," the saleslady continued. "Chakra Three is associated with fire and is known as the power chakra. It's located at—"

"In the solar plexus, between your belly button and chest."

The gypsy's full red lips drew back in a broader smile. "Why, yes. You understand more about chakras than you thought."

Gabriel grinned, saying. "I'm beginning to." He strolled over to the self-help books. "Can you find me some material on this?"

Her emerald eyes found his, and she said seductively, "It would be my pleasure."

The pleasure is all mine, Gabriel thought, but not because of the invitation in the saleslady's eyes. He had a hunch he'd stumbled onto the killer's disconnected fantasy.

With an armful of books in hand, Gabriel exited the store for a second time, waving amicably at the gypsy, who had slipped her business card into one of the books. If she'd been truly psychic, she wouldn't have bothered with him.

Balancing the books in one arm, Gabriel moved to open the car door. When he grabbed the door handle a flash of pain hit his hand and Gabriel leaped back, spilling the books onto the pavement.

Gabriel held his throbbing hand and gaped at his dented Celica. His palm burned as if he'd taken a blowtorch to it. Swallowing, he turned his palm up, fully expecting to see redness and blisters; but his flesh was smooth and undamaged. Gabriel looked quizzically at his car and reached out a quavering finger to touch the door handle. The metal was warm, but not hot.

Gabriel carefully opened the car door, wondering if his face would be met with a furnace blast. The temperature inside the car was normal for a summer's day.

He crouched down and collected the fallen books, thinking that now would be a most inopportune time to lose his mind. Again Gabriel was reminded of the suspect's cryptic statement, 'we are one.'

No, Gabriel thought as he sat in the driver's seat, we are not. And I am not losing my mind. Even as he thought it and placed his hands on the steering wheel, Gabriel felt a ghostly aching in his palm.

"My bout with depression lasted five chambers."

Raymond Pettibon

CHAPTER 8

Under the penetrating eye of the microscope, the firearms expert studied an arrangement of spiral lines on the bullet that had killed Adam Parraco.

Gabriel stood over his shoulder and yawned, tired from the traffic, and absently rubbed his palm.

"Bored, Sergeant?" the expert said. He was a dark-haired Italian named DeSalvo who had transferred from the NYPD and had brought his Brooklyn accent with him.

"Not bored, you geek, just beat from traveling to hell and back." Gabriel knew DeSalvo and liked him.

"I thought hell started here," DeSalvo said, taking a break from the microscope to eyeball Gabriel. "This bullet was quite a find, my friend."

"How so?"

"Take a look."

Gabriel inspected the bullet. Inside the barrel of every gun are lands and grooves, a rising and falling of the surface metal. Every brand has its own distinct pattern. When the gun discharges the bullet, the intense heat and friction brand the lands and grooves onto the slug. As long as the slug is fairly undamaged, the ballistics expert can determine the make and model of the gun that fired the bullet. Ming had provided them with the impact velocity or speed the bullet had been traveling when it hit, basing her findings on the wound, the trajectory, and where the bullet had finally ended up. Ballistics had done the rest.

"Pricey ammo. 7.62 Nagant cartridge," DeSalvo said.

"Did you say Nagant?"

"I did indeed. I had to consult my ammunitions manual from the Forties to be sure, though."

"No kidding."

DeSalvo shook his head genially. "No kidding. This had to be fired from a Nagant revolver. Interesting little piece – believed to be the weapon that assassinated Czar Nicholas and his family."

"A Russian made gun," Gabriel said, his mind flickering at the Russian word for 'souls.'

"Righty-O," DeSalvo said, mimicking Felix the Cat. "First adapted by the Russian army in 1895. Known as the M1895 or just plain M95, whichever you prefer. The Nagant is a seven shot design, with a barrel length of four and a half inches. They produced them both in single action and double action. Here, I've got a picture for you."

DeSalvo walked over to a desk cluttered with gun parts and papers. He handed Gabriel a few stapled sheets.

Gabriel shook his head in disbelief. "He's offing people with an antique gun? Well, that helps us. It's unusual enough to be noticed by somebody, somewhere."

"The design of the Nagant is unique due to the fact that its cylinder moves forward into the rear of the barrel when it is cocked, creating a 'gas seal' effect," DeSalvo explained. "This causes all of the force of the exploding gunpowder to propel the bullet out of the barrel without losing energy at the flash gap, perhaps adding several hundred feet per second to the round. Quite an achievement for one hundred years ago, seeing that even to this day, this 'gas leak' happens with all modern revolvers."

"The manual says this gun was used as late as World War II."

"That's right. Even though the Russian army had other guns available, the troops liked this one for two reasons: first, it could fit in the firing slits of tanks and second, it was easily repaired if damaged. They stopped producing them after 1945, but you can pick one up just about anywhere for one hundred dollars or so."

Gabriel studied the photos of the gun. The grip was diamond checkered and made out of a light tan wood. Up close, he could make out little manufacturing symbols etched in the hammer and the cylinder.

The killer couldn't be an actual veteran, unless he was a superman senior citizen, but the killer could know a Russian WWII vet. Something caught the edge of Gabriel's memory and the picture beneath his eyes began to wave and blur. He focused his blue eyes on the linoleum, searching his mind, knowing that his transient thought was important. But then it was gone.

Gabriel felt a slight sick feeling in his gut, in his third chakra, and he looked back at the picture of the Russian Nagant. He left ballistics with the feeling that he'd forgotten something worth remembering.

※ ※ ※

Gabriel trekked back across the freeway during rush hour. The summer sun, still high in the sky, relentlessly baked his car. He nervously tapped his steering wheel; willing the line of cars to move faster, knowing he had dinner guests coming.

"Come on…" Gabriel muttered as the perspiration rolled down his face. He should have fixed his air conditioner. Repairs were on hold, like everything else in his life. Gabriel kept one eye on the Celica's temperature gauge because the old car had overheated many times before.

A shiny black Corvette blaring loud music shimmied behind him and crept right on Gabriel's tail. Gabriel gave him a dirty look in his rearview mirror. The teenager behind the wheel wore sunglasses and was knocking back a Coke. The Corvette wavered impatiently, tail-gaiting Gabriel.

Gabriel tapped his brakes, a clear signal to back off. The Corvette jumped back, and Gabriel could see the frown on the kid's face below the dark shades.

Probably spilled his coke, Gabriel thought with satisfaction.

A space momentarily opened in the lane next to them and the Corvette slipped in. The traffic slowed to a crawl. As the teenager pulled alongside Gabriel's Celica, the kid lowered the window, raised his middle finger, and yelled, "Fuck you!"

The rage leaped up and squeezed Gabriel from the inside out. With one hand on the wheel, he grabbed his badge.

By this time, the cars had completely stopped. Hundreds of motorists sat in their metal cars, like sardines cooking in tin cans, as the sun danced, liberated in the sky. An inner voice pleaded with Gabriel to leave things alone, but he jumped out of his paralyzed car and shoved his badge in the teenager's face.

"Taking daddy's car for a little joyride?" he asked and stepped back. "Get out."

"I didn't do anything."

"I didn't ask you to talk," Gabriel opened the Corvette's door, grabbed the kid by the collar of his surfer shirt, and hauled him out, shoving him against the door of the car. The designer sunglasses fell to the asphalt and broke.

The rubbernecks in the nearby cars leaned out their windows to get a better view, hoping the action would assuage their boredom.

"You want to repeat what you just said to me a minute ago?" Gabriel said, still tightly gripping the kid's collar.

The teen looked at Gabriel with frightened hazel eyes. He couldn't be any more than eighteen, Gabriel thought. Acne sprouted on his chin and forehead like a haphazard garden. The kid's nose was dirty and his shirtfront was drenched in soda.

Leave him alone. Leave him alone.

"You want to tell me to fuck off again?" Gabriel was tempted to smash the kid's forehead against his dad's fancy car.

Leave him be. Gabriel felt the boy trembling under his clenched hand and heard the woman's grating voice, "You're an evil, evil man."

Flinching, Gabriel loosened his grasp and backed away from the quaking teen.

"Don't be so flippant when it comes to strangers," Gabriel told him. "You never know what kind of crazy person you're gonna insult."

The teen stared at Gabriel in mute fright as Gabriel tucked his badge away and returned to his car. The line of cars slowly began inching forward and Gabriel started his car and moved into traffic.

Later, while the rice bubbled on the stove, Gabriel sat on the couch and skimmed through some of the new age books he had purchased. He wanted to get his mind off the scene on the freeway. *But you can't stop thinking about it, can you?*

He read that the seven chakras corresponded exactly to the seven main nerve ganglia, which emanated from the spinal column. He perused the guided meditations for each chakra that guaranteed to heal and energize a suffering person. He read about incorporating chakra energy into group rituals and being something called "chakra intensive." Gabriel, for all his reading, understood nothing.

I'm the wrong person for this, he thought. I'm so out of touch with anything spiritual. *I should have left that kid alone.* Gabriel continued reading, searching for something that would jump out and grab him.

He was grabbed on the third book.

His attention was drawn to a picture depicting a line of circles traversing down the human body, only this time particular symbols sat within the circles. Quickly, Gabriel searched his desk for the witness' rendering of the writings on Ted Brody's car. He found it, pulled it into view, and compared the symbols to the artist's sketch. Ted Brody had had a hole carved between his scrotum and anus. Chakra One was located at the base of the spine. Close enough, Gabriel thought.

He studied the symbol for Chakra One, which depicted a circle with a square inside. Inside the square floated a triangle. The witness drawings showed an "O" with a "V" inside and a couple of other lines alongside the "V." It had to be the same, but how could Gabriel be sure? What if he was totally off base with this theory? He needed to talk to someone, Ming maybe, or Dash.

Gabriel heard a strange hissing noise from the front of the apartment and his eyes widened in alarm. "Oh, shit!" He had completely forgotten that Dash and Eve were coming over and that he was preparing dinner.

He ran into the kitchen and turned the fire off the rice, which had bubbled out all over the stove. He grabbed the pot handle and it sizzled in his hand. "Ouch!" The saucepan abruptly dropped back onto the stove with a loud clatter.

Gabriel shook out his reddening hand. He heard the gravel crunching outside and then car headlights shone through the kitchen window. His guests had arrived. Gabriel leaned over the stove, eyeing the mess. All he wanted to do was forget the day and find solace in sleep.

Sleep offered Gabriel no shelter that night. He dreamed of being pursued by a man. Gabriel could not see the man, but knew in the strange way people know things in their dreams, that his pursuer's only goal was to destroy him. Gabriel scrambled over fields of boulders and rocky outcroppings that seemed never-ending. The more he fled, the more tired he became. His pursuer was gaining on him. Gabriel could feel his body slowing down, every muscle aching with exhaustion. Finally, he laid himself down at the feet of the murderer. The man did not hesitate. He began slashing Gabriel with a knife, in a frenzy of hate. Gabriel heard his flesh ripping and watched the bright red blood fly out of his own body. He seemed too paralyzed to protect himself in any way. He knew he was going to die.

Gabriel clutched the edge of the nightstand near his bed and managed to pull himself upright. His breath caught in his throat and his head reeled. The bedroom was dark, but the digital clock beside Gabriel glowed with the red numbers, three-thirty. Gabriel buried his head in his hands.

He was losing control. The fact that he had forgotten dinner signaled that. Sure, Dash and Eve had laughed it off and the three of them ended up going to a cafe on Pico Boulevard. But Gabriel wasn't laughing. His symptoms were getting worse and now this nightmare had wormed its way into his psyche. Gabriel wondered if he was heading toward a nervous breakdown. This wasn't his first nightmare, but it won the award for being the most violent. Gabriel slowly lay back in the sheets. After work, he needed to see Dr. B.

The canyons that weave through the Santa Monica Mountains have seen their fair share of personalities. The whole mountain range had been under water at one time, and the rocks were filled with the fossils of sea creatures. The waters receded and the mountains grew and the trees and caves sheltered Native Americans. When the Spanish missionaries arrived, searching for gold and converts, they rode their horses along the winding Sepulveda Pass and marked a simple dirt trail that would become one of the busiest freeways in the world.

Today, an entirely different breed of people inhabited the hills. Some residents lived in dried out campers lying on biers of firewood. Gabriel spent his day maneuvering paths choked with weeds and rusted cars to get to the front doors. Other people lived on expensive view lots and Gabriel would speak to them through intercoms bolted to their locked wrought iron gates. Some folks were friendly and some were frightened; most looked upon Gabriel's badge with a slight air of contempt.

After their interviews, Gabriel and Dash sat down to compare notes at Malibu Cliffs Park – a small, grassy baseball diamond positioned over the ocean. Across the Pacific Coast Highway rolled the green hills of Pepperdine University.

"You want to go to an early dinner?" Dash asked his partner.

"Sure, but we have a little time to kill. Ming is meeting us out here."

Dash's cream complexion went rosy. "Really? Do you two want to go somewhere by yourselves?"

"No. You're coming with us."

"No, no, no." Dash waved his hand in a dismissive gesture. "I actually brought my trunks in the car and I'm gonna sit out on the beach for a while. Tell me that doesn't look inviting." He gave a nod toward the broad ocean.

Gabriel eyed his partner. Dash feared skin cancer as much as heart attacks. "That's a crock of shit."

"I'm serious," Dash said cheerily. "I'm catching whatever sun is left."

Gabriel didn't believe it, not for a minute, but he shrugged and said, "Have at it."

"We could meet after dinner," Dash suggested. "Eve's got a Pan game going."

Gabriel rocked back and forth on the bench and gazed at the water. "Nah, tonight's no good. I have an appointment."

"Where?"

Gabriel paused. "With Dr. B."

Dash pretended to study the ocean. "Everything okay?"

"Like normal."

"Damn."

Gabriel had to smile. He rose from the bench and said, "Have a great tan. I'm gonna burn some time across the street and check out the college."

Set above the Pacific on waves of green lawn, Pepperdine University glittered like a coastal jewel. It was a private college and richly endowed. Gabriel strolled around, impressed by the vivacity of youth, the kids with their backpacks full of books, talking animatedly to each other, the whole world ahead of them.

Even though it was summertime, a lot of students were in attendance. Gabriel spoke with counselors, departmental deans, and a few students. He covered the math/science buildings and then went to the Department of History, hoping to get a lead on any WWII aficionados. The late afternoon sun beat down and Gabriel envied the kids who whizzed by on mopeds. Vacher was right. The summer promised to be long and hot.

Gabriel stopped at the Fine Arts Department, happy to take a breather in the air-conditioned building. A broad woman wearing a colorful geometric patterned shirt and sporting a double chin filed papers in a cabinet. She met his badge with a smile and told him that she would call a student counselor who would take him on a tour. Gabriel, dizzy from her Mondrian-styled shirt, nodded and waited patiently on a bench. Soon a lithe young man with red hair waltzed up and quickly tapped Gabriel on the shoulder.

"Sergeant?" He said with a distinctly female inflection. The counselor wore a flowing white shirt reminiscent of a medieval minstrel performer that undulated like the ocean whenever he moved rapidly, which seemed to be all the time. "I'm Damien."

Gabriel introduced himself and asked the usual run of questions: "Have you heard anything from students regarding the crimes? Any reports of unusually violent or suspicious behavior lately? Do you know of anyone who has a penchant for collecting army and navy surplus, particularly WWII weapons? Can you tell me about any Russian students in this department or students that may have knowledge of the Russian language?"

Damien gave him one Russian student's name, a freshman that Gabriel soon discounted because the boy had arrived in the country just two weeks prior.

That done, the redheaded counselor gently pulled Gabriel's jacket sleeve and proceeded to give him a tour of the department. Their first stop was the costume shop. Here, Damien informed him, you could find anything from false eyelashes to wigs, witch's hats to waitress uniforms. You could pick any era and be dressed to go, be it a fifties sock hop or a thirteenth century joust. And if you couldn't find the right apparel, Damien told him, the students could sew costumes. The counselor swept his arm proudly over a row of vacated sewing machines.

"Things are a little quieter during the summer, but not much," Damien said. "Many students use the summer quarter to complete their units; that way they don't have to do a fifth year, although some kids do like to stay in school."

"I'd stay here," Gabriel said, looking around. "Who doesn't like the beach?"

"My feelings exactly." Damien nodded emphatically and swished down the hall. His shirt rustled and danced with him. "This is our scenic shop."

He led Gabriel into a huge room complete with all the materials needed to build professional sets: skill saws, band saws, drill presses, crosscut and steel saws, welding torches, and stacks of plywood. In a square of chain link fence covered by color-splashed tarpaulin stood the painting cage.

"Each student goes through a whole regime of classes, taking turns at each craft, hoping to find his niche. They take acting, writing; they direct. They compose or perform music. We have classes on sound, lighting, set design, set construction, and prop handling. Students can be stage managers and call cues or they might like working on the sound or light boards instead."

"Impressive," Gabriel said, running his hand along the silent skill saw.

Damien pulled at his sleeve again. "Come, let me show you the property room."

He opened the door and Gabriel walked under a gothic archway, bordered by classical Greek columns, and entered a world of the mythical and the grotesque. Rows of masks watched Gabriel from either side. Misshapen monster faces and feathered masquerade masks hung on false walls of brick and stone.

Gabriel maneuvered around a large boulder, hollowed out TVs, and phony computers. On the many shelves he saw an array of false books, telephones, crutches, leg casts, swords, shields, and many other whimsical items, all designed to support the magical illusion of the theater.

Gabriel touched a very real looking gun.

Whatever yer selling, asshole, we don' wan' any!

He pushed the image of the costumed cop from his mind; turning his back on the prop gun.

"Everything in the Department is state of the art," Damien continued. "Take the vacuform machine, for instance." He made a sweeping gesture, which reminded Gabriel of a game show host, over a large, squat machine that looked like some sort of press. "This puppy creates things like roof tiles and boulders that weigh less than a paperback book. Afterwards, we paint on the finishing touches and no one can tell the real item from the fake. See?"

He hefted the large boulder onto his shoulders and then hurled it at Gabriel, who instinctively ducked. The boulder flew over his head and bounced on the linoleum floor. Gabriel retrieved it, finding the boulder light as a rubber ball.

"Amazing."

"Come on," Damien said, walking toward the door. "I'll show you an even bigger example."

He led Gabriel to the theater, which was quite large and replete with all the accouterments of a Broadway venue. Gabriel stood in the darkened seats. On stage was a dark and gloomy set. Dungeon-like medieval catacombs were filled with bones, skulls and dusty wine bottles.

"Good, huh?" Damien remarked.

"I can almost smell the rot and damp," Gabriel told him.

A few actors, dressed in middle-age garb were hanging out on the stage.

"What's the production?" Gabriel asked.

"A student adaptation of Poe's 'The Cask of Amontillado," Damien replied. "It's dress rehearsal."

He motioned Gabriel down the aisle toward the stage.

High above the gloomy set crisscrossed the narrow catwalks. Long metal cords hung, swaying slightly from the air conditioning.

"What are all those wires for?" Gabriel asked, tilting his head back. The catwalks were impossibly high.

"We fly stage sets in on those," explained Damien, and suddenly he clapped his hands. "Oh, kids! Sergeant McRay here wants to ask a few questions."

Certainly not kids, Gabriel thought as he approached the stage, most of them were taller than he.

"I'm sorry to interrupt your rehearsal. I'm sure you are aware of the murders that have taken place nearby and I'd like to know if any of you have heard anything or have any tips for us."

"Too close for comfort," said an ingénue who wore a medieval headdress and an elaborate velvet gown.

"I know. That's why I'm here."

Gabriel told them to drive with awareness, avoid picking up hitchhikers, and to let the police know if they hear of anything suspicious. Sensing their discomfort, he changed the subject. "When is the performance?"

"Next Monday," stated the ingénue.

"I'll try to catch it," he lied.

One man wearing parti-colored tights and a jester's conical cap complete with tinkling bells, asked, "Do you like the theater, Sergeant?"

"I haven't given myself much exposure to it, but yeah, I like plays." Gabriel regarded the jester. "And who might you be?"

"I'm Fortunato."

"Oh yeah?" Gabriel shrugged indifferently, and said, "I guess I should brush up on my Poe."

"He's the one that's always taunting Montressor."

Gabriel grinned at the others. "If you say so."

"Got any leads, Detective?" the jester asked.

"Some," Gabriel said, caught off guard. The bells tinkled. Gabriel handed out his cards to the assembled cast. "Let your fellow students know I'm around and–" he smiled. "Break a leg."

"Who's the jester?" Gabriel asked Damien as they walked away.

"Oh, that's Bill. He's a graduate student." The counselor leaned his red head close to Gabriel and whispered conspiratorially, "And one of those I mentioned that enjoys staying in school. But Gawd, is he talented! And not bad-looking either, right?"

Gabriel's stomach grumbled, reminding him of his dinner date. He thanked the counselor and walked back to his car, knowing he still had more ground to cover at Pepperdine.

He met Ming at Froggy's, a neat little spot off Topanga Canyon that served up barbecued meats and fresh fish. They walked with their meals to the outside patio and chose a cozy table at the railing overlooking Malibu Creek.

"So," Gabriel began, "how are you?"

"I worked late last night," Ming said, "and was up at the crack of dawn today, so I think, unless the murder rate goes up in the next twelve hours, I'm taking the rest of the night off. I'm all yours."

Ming looked good. Her hair was pinned up casually and she wore a dress that showed off her long, tanned legs.

"I like your –" Gabriel shifted uncomfortably. "I like you in a dress."

Ming raised an eyebrow at him.

"Please don't take it the wrong way," Gabriel explained. "I know we work together. I shouldn't have made a comment about the way you look. Don't sue, okay?"

Ming chewed a piece of fish as she calmly studied him. "Wow. Now that that's done... Can I say, thanks for the compliment?"

They regarded each other for a moment and then Gabriel reached for his fork. "Dig in. I hear the barbeque sauce is really good."

They ate silently for a minute and then Ming cleared her throat and said, "I wasn't sure if you knew but when a body burns the bones shrink and compress between twenty to twenty-five percent."

Gabriel gave Ming a curious look.

"In figuring out how tall a burned skeleton is, I have to take that into account." She paused and munched on a French fry. "Bones that are burned as bones react differently than bones which are encased in tissue, you know, with high fat content and other fluids. This different reaction tells me how long a body was dead before being burned. Now take your victims for example. They were all burned right after death."

"Ming, could we talk about something else?" Gabriel asked, and pointed down to his plate of pork ribs.

"Oh. Sorry," she apologized. "I won't talk shop anymore."

Gabriel went back to eating, swallowing uncomfortably. "So, tell me about all the men in your life. Enquiring minds want to know." He winked at her in a weak attempt at being jovial.

Ming shrugged her shoulders. "The only men in my life right now are ones with maggots on them."

Gabriel broke out into laughter. "You're nuts!" He took a swallow of his beer and warmly regarded her. "I like nuts."

"My good luck then," Ming said, cheerful again.

Across the creek, a rabbit hopped around in the underbrush. "Gabriel?"

"Yes?" Gabriel took another sip as he watched the rabbit.

"It's okay," Ming said and her eyes seemed a little sad. "I don't have to be your responsibility for the night. I don't want us to be awkward around each other."

Gabriel slowly put down his drink, feeling like a fool. He tried to say something but couldn't find the right words.

Ming saved him by speaking, "Why don't you tell me how your studies of eastern practices are coming along."

"You mean in regards to the chakras?" Gabriel said, grateful for the break.

Ming nodded, sipping at her white wine.

Gabriel wiped his sauce-covered hands on a napkin and said, "I'm not one for believing all that crap but—"

"How do you know its crap?"

"You don't believe in it, do you?"

"I may practice western medicine, but eastern philosophies are in my background. For treatment of a problem, I don't think much beats western medicine. But we western doctors are absolutely negligent when it comes to preventative medicine. Eastern medicine incorporates treatment of a problem and prevention. So, I guess I wouldn't completely discount the power of the chakras. And you better not either, because your killer believes in it."

"If this guy is killing people and following the course of the chakras—"

"Then he's only at Chakra Three," Ming finished. "He's got four more to go."

Gabriel looked back at the creek. Suddenly, a rush of spraying leaves broke the stillness and a coyote flew out of the brush. In an instant, he caught the rabbit in his jaws and raced away. Gabriel stared, astonished, at the spot where the rabbit had stood only moments before.

Four more to go.

"Truth has no special time of its own. Its hour is now—always"

Albert Schweitzer (1875-1965)

CHAPTER 9

"You're not paying attention."

Gabriel was sitting in his usual chair next to Dr. B who was holding a small red light in his eyes.

"I need you to concentrate and relax. For God's sake, relax."

"This isn't going to work," Gabriel announced.

"Yes, it will."

"No, it won't."

"Shut up and watch the light, and listen to my voice."

Gabriel sat back and began to listen. He tried to relax.

"Try taking a deep breath," Dr. B suggested. "Think of this light as a beacon. A beacon on a vast ocean. Bobbing up and down – up and down. You're floating there, on that ocean, and you are completely at ease."

Gabriel inhaled slowly. He tried to think about Ming, but that only frustrated him. Sometimes, he longed for nothing more than to run his fingers through her hair – that veil of black silk and put his lips upon her smooth skin. Well, he thought sourly, he'd had that opportunity and had blown it, plain and simple. Distracted, he tried to focus on the red light and oceans. Soon the psychiatrist's voice was actually lulling him.

"Gabriel."

Yes?

"Gabriel, look at me."

Yes?

"Gabriel, look at me when I'm talking to you."

Yes, Mother?

"Put down your spoon and look at me."

No more Captain Crunch cereal. Okay, Mother.

"Gabriel, you soiled your sheets again! There's shit all over your bed."

Someone's giggling. Stop laughing at me. Stop looking at me.

"Stop laughing at your brother! Gabriel, what is going on with you? Wetting your bed like a little baby. And now this... now this!"

Please, don't throw the sheets at me, Mommy; I know what I did.

"I can't deal with this, Gabriel, I work every day! You are a big boy, and I shouldn't have to deal with this."

I'm sorry. I know you're busy.

"I don't have time for this! I changed your sheets yesterday. Dammit, Gabriel!"

Sorry, Mother. So sorry.

"What did you say? Quit whispering! Oh, forget it, I have to go to work."

"Sheet-shitter, sheet-shitter, baby little Gabey–"

Stop laughing at me. Some more Captain Crunch. The little yellow bouncing balls in the rich, white, milk. Little yellow crunch balls with cherry red crunch berries bobbing up and down, up and down, up and down...

"Gabriel."

What now?

"Yes?" Was that <u>his</u> voice?

"How do you feel?"

Gabriel opened his eyes and blinked, focusing on Dr. B's face. He swallowed and looked around the room.

"I feel okay. Did it work?"

"Yes, it did."

Gabriel guffawed, and said, "Amazing."

Dr. B eyed Gabriel suspiciously. "The way this works is that you're supposed to remember what you've talked about. Do you remember?"

Gabriel paused a moment, then reluctantly nodded. He was sure Dr. B was going to ask why he soiled his sheets. For the life of him Gabriel couldn't remember why he did.

Instead Dr. B said, "Were you a latch-key kid?"

Gabriel could clearly see his neighborhood; the pastel colored houses lined up one after the other, each with their patch of lawn and single car garage–an ordinary middle-class neighborhood. He could remember how the fog crept in from the ocean and wreaked havoc on the wood trims and the automobile paint.

"One of the first," he told Dr. B.

"I doubt that," Dr. B said, "but being one is never easy. Did you miss your mom when she worked?"

"Of course."

"I've had patients who were somewhat relieved when their parents were away. Were you somewhat relieved when your parents were gone?"

Gabriel thought a moment. "No," he admitted. "I missed them. I'd have a million things I'd want to tell my mom about what happened at school; if some kid and I had it out, or if I'd made something in art class, got a good test grade, that kind of thing. I just remember always waiting; like standing in line. I always had to wait until my mom came home, got settled, got dinner going, and then we could talk."

"Did you resent her for working?"

"Sure. I'd rather have had her with me."

Dr. B made some notes, and then regarded Gabriel thoughtfully for a moment.

"On the other hand," Gabriel continued, "as I got older, I kind of liked having nobody to bother me when I got home."

"Let's concentrate on when you were of sweetened cereal-eating age."

Gabriel laughed. "I was always that age."

"Okay," Dr. B said, "then let us concentrate on when you were say, about seven years old."

Gabriel's laugh faded and he focused on Dr. B. "Why that age?"

"Seven seems to be a pivotal age for you. You became quite agitated when I mentioned the age once before."

Gabriel stared at the fingers folded in his lap and said nothing.

"Keep telling me about your seventh year."

Gabriel shrugged. "I was an ordinary kid. My parents worked and I was alone. There weren't any kids my age to play with on my block, so I watched a lot of television." He grinned. "When you're a kid, you don't mind that too much." Gabriel paused. "My parents were good parents. On weekends, they made special efforts to do fun things with me." He shrugged again, and smiled at Dr. B.

The psychiatrist smiled back. "And you were a chronic bed wetter, too."

Gabriel's smile disappeared and Dr. B said, "Excuse me, Gabe, but I don't believe everything was as merry in Mayberry as you're putting out."

"What do you want me to say then?"

"Just tell me what happened to you in your seventh year?"

"Nothing, really."

"Nothing?"

Gabriel's eyes surveyed the room and then settled back on Dr. B. "Nothing out of the ordinary." He glanced at his wrist-watch, his inexpensive Seiko. "Whoa, look at the time. I'm beat. I'm sure you are too." Gabriel rose out of his seat like a phantom. He looked back at Dr. B. The psychiatrist's normally warm expression appeared chilled.

"What?" Gabriel asked him pointedly. The tick-tock of the doctor's desk clock was quite audible.

Dr. B seemed to be mulling over something. "Just keep thinking on what was revealed tonight. And go home and get a good night's sleep, okay?"

❧ ❧ ❧

Patrick Funston drove his black Honda Civic home from a music club in the San Fernando Valley. He was heading south along the dark and winding Malibu Canyon Road toward Pepperdine, where he was completing summer school. He would be a sophomore in September and his studies were already grueling. He had dallied at the nightclub too long – one of his friends was in the band, and they had hung out after the set, drinking and talking. With luck, Patrick might make it home in time to cram for his exam tomorrow and still get in a few hours of shut-eye.

Patrick was running over some equations in his mind when he saw a black figure holding a backpack trying to hail the scant cars that sped by. Patrick's Honda slowly went past, but

Patrick could still make out the figure through his rear view mirror.

The boy pulled over and backed the car up. The figure approached the Honda's driver's side window. Under the moonlight, Patrick clearly saw the Pepperdine University sweatshirt and felt no apprehension.

"Do you need a lift?" Patrick offered.

"Yeah," the figure said, "I do."

The figure entered the Honda and asked Patrick where he was heading.

"Back to school. Aren't you?" Patrick answered, putting his car into drive.

"Of course." his passenger said, settling in. "What is your major?"

"Physics."

"Good. A smart guy," the passenger remarked and beamed at Patrick.

❧ ❧ ❧

Blood, like the tentacles of a thin red squid, crawled from the wound at his groin, down his legs, giving him the sensation of having urinated on himself. His hands were crossed protectively over his crotch, but he knew he had to look. Slowly, he uncrossed his hands and looked down.

A black hole was there and Gabriel bent his head closer. Something pulsed inside, something dark and slick. He peered even closer, wondering if he should touch it. The pulsing mass seemed to be breathing, alive. It seemed to be waiting.

Suddenly, a jet of blood sprayed out from the hole and soaked Gabriel's face, his hair, and his chest. The red torrent spewed from the hole, hitting his mouth, prying it open, forcing apart his clenched teeth. Gabriel couldn't move his head; he was choking on the spray, fighting for breath, suffocating–

Gabriel awoke with a gasp just as his alarm clock began ringing. As the alarm drummed shrilly through his head, his eyes traveled down the length of his naked body.

No gaping wound at his groin. No blood. No pulsing monster where his penis should be. Nothing. Thank God. Nothing.

Later, after he had showered, shaved, and dressed – a normal routine for a normal man, Gabriel went to his closet to get the tie he wore the day before. He could not find it. He searched his apartment, trying to stay calm and clinging to the hope that this would be a normal man's morning. With an eye on the clock, Gabriel gave up and chose another tie, wondering why all his clothes were disappearing.

❦ ❦ ❦

He drove north along Pacific Coast Highway, hoping to finish his vetting of Pepperdine University. Although it was still morning, the temperature was already climbing into the eighties.

He paged Dr. B and held the cell phone in his hand, waiting for the doctor to return his call.

Gabriel's Celica passed the turning Ferris wheel and the carnival booths of the Santa Monica Pier. He passed Gladstones 4 Fish where diners sat watching the white-capped waves.

His cell phone chirped – the display reading "Raymond Berkowitz" and Gabriel quickly answered the call. "It's Gabriel. I'm sorry to disturb you, but I had one hell of a nightmare last night."

Gabriel recounted his dream of the night before, and then told Dr. B about the nightmare in which the knife-wielding assailant chased him.

"Most dreams of being hunted or chased signify a feeling of not being able to overcome life's problems, of having limited abilities."

"And what about the other dream?"

"The blood flowing out of the groin area may symbolize ejaculation. Anything ring a bell when it's put in that light?"

"Not really. I mean, I've had my troubles with emotional commitments, but I've never had a problem, you know, with that. Can't you just give me a pill or something?"

"I can prescribe some sleeping aids if you like, but the only way to truly get rid of these dreams is to address the source of your problems."

Gabriel gazed out at the sun-dappled water and said, "I just want to be happy."

"Robert Louis Stevenson said, 'There is no such duty we underrate as the duty of being happy.' People usually think we're born happy. No one realizes it takes effort. My mentor, Alfred Adler, is quoted as saying, 'every human being can do everything,' and I have to believe that if happiness is what you want, you will find a way to achieve it."

"Thanks for my morning's quotation ration."

"Sorry," Dr. B said amicably. "It's a habit of mine."

"Better than some. I may take you up on those pills."

"Just let me know."

Gabriel hung up the phone and rubbed his temples. He had a stiff neck and pain in his shoulders. His dream had left him tense and worn out.

As he drove PCH under the Greek facade of the old J. Paul Getty museum, a large fire truck passed him, sirens wailing. Gabriel watched it go by, and then saw in his rearview mirror, two additional engines bearing down on him. He pulled right to let them pass and they raced by with whirling red lights and a loud shrieking. An ambulance and three police squad cars followed fast and an ominous feeling enveloped Gabriel.

He stepped on the gas, scanning the horizon for trouble. As he swung past Topanga Canyon, Gabriel saw the smoke billowing in the hills and his heart sank.

He followed the fire department's strike team. Two black-and-white units from his own department sped passed him, sirens also screaming.

It's something else, he told himself. A careless smoker tossed a match. Some kids played with mom's Bic lighter. Sure, why not? Spontaneous combustion; an aerosol can exploded in the summer sun.

All plausible explanations, but Gabriel knew the smoke was caused from none of these. As he drove into the hills, he saw the fire. The Santa Ana winds had arrived, and were doing what they do so well – fanning the flames.

Two helicopters were making runs into the heart of the fire from the sky. Gabriel quickly negotiated with embattled firefighters who were screaming at him to get lost. He drove where they directed him, parked in a hot spot of black, smoking chaparral, and grabbed his notepad, pen, and camera.

Gabriel located Desmond Gein and caught him by the sleeve of his brush gear. The engine captain turned to him, his face covered by a fire-resistant Nomex hood. A fire shroud hung over his ears and neck. Backed by the red air and clouds of gray smoke, he looked like an alien. Gein was out of breath and motioned Gabriel to follow him. He led him to Phil Panzram, the battalion chief, who was covered in chemicals, soot, and sweat.

"Have you got it contained?" Gabriel yelled amid the helicopter's buzz.

Panzram shouted back, "It's about eighty-percent contained! A few more hours and we'll have it." Panzram hawked and spit on the ground. "That is, if this wind doesn't get any stronger."

"What?" Gabriel said, leaning closer.

Panzram shook his head, never mind. He pointed his finger past rows of skeletal trees.

"That's where it started!"

Gabriel followed his finger. He couldn't see anything through the smoke. "I want to go in!" he yelled to Panzram.

"Sorry, you'll have to wait!"

Gabriel shook his head. His quarry could be hiding in that smoke.

"You're crazy!" Panzram shouted, reading his mind. "This fire started hours ago! No one's in there now!"

Gabriel stood his ground and the firefighter gave in.

"Go ahead then," Panzram said, gesturing wearily. "But be careful. Everything's hot!" Panzram trudged off in the direction of the still-burning flames like a man entering hell.

Gabriel moved through the smoke, coughing and wondering if he should wait it out. Then the fickle Santa Anas changed direction and the smoke cleared. Gabriel found himself surrounded by a desolate no-man's land. Smelling worse than a barbecue gone bad, the air had a suffocating quality to it and burned his eyes. Hot, blackened trees reached up in frozen supplication toward the heavens, their leaves burned off. The ground was a black blanket.

Gabriel's shoes crunched on the crisp soil and he shook his head at the destruction. What had been green and verdant was now a smoking wasteland. What kind of person enjoyed doing such damage?

There was only one reason Phil Panzram would allow Gabriel to walk into a heated burn area. Rounding the bend of a small hill, Gabriel saw the smoking car. It appeared to be a Honda Civic.

Gabriel saw a fire engine sitting stoically in the distance, but no one was manning her. He stood alone with the small, burnt car amid the shadowy landscape. Above him, the sky was thick and gray.

Gabriel's eyes itched and watered. He paged Dash and Ramirez. His partner was probably in the vicinity interviewing residents. No doubt Dash had already seen the smoke and was heading this way.

Gabriel thought he heard a twig crunch and his blue eyes jerked left. Smoke still rose seductively from the barren trees, curling like the arms of a dancing harem girl.

"Phil?" he called out.

From out of the Honda, Gabriel smelled something raw and metallic. He walked toward the front of the car, fully expecting to see a twisted, charred corpse behind the wheel – but the interior was unoccupied.

Gabriel headed toward the trunk. Firefighters following standard procedure usually opened the trunks, but these good men and women were too busy dousing the flames. Gabriel pressed the button to pop the trunk and immediately retracted his hand. The metal was burning hot.

Inwardly, Gabriel cursed his stupidity as he wiped tender fingers along his pants, and then he shuddered, remembering how his own car had burned him with a ghostly heat.

Get a grip, he thought, and using his jacket sleeve as a mitt, he tried the button again, and the trunk flew up.

Immediately the smell of cooked flesh assailed his nostrils. Gabriel covered his mouth with his sleeve and peered inside. Something resembling a man was in the car. While the brush had caught fire, the trunk had protected its inhabitant – somewhat. His dead eyes stared at the detective through steaming blood. The body was red, swollen with heat but not burned. Gabriel gagged. A giant hole gaped where the heart should have been. The organ itself lay on the dead man's stomach. Peeking out from under the man's heart was a plastic baggie.

Fighting the urge to retch, Gabriel shook out two latex gloves from his pocket and pulled them on. A police siren sounded from the distance, approaching him. Gabriel took up his camera and snapped a few photos. Then, he carefully lifted the corpse slightly to reach into the pant's pocket for identification. He found no wallet.

Gabriel stared at the corpse and the pulpy, slick heart. He remembered his dream of the night before and felt his knees weakening.

I should wait until the MCU people arrive. I know I should.

But curiosity got the better of him, and Gabriel gently pulled out the plastic sandwich bag. He laid the baggie on the viscera and took pictures of it. Using a tissue, he wiped the baggie clear of blood.

His name was clearly typed on the paper within.

Gabriel stared at the plastic bag, transfixed. Eventually, he looked over his shoulder. No one was coming. In the sky, the helicopters were moving away. The Santa Ana winds ruffled his dark hair and the acrid smoke made his nose run.

Gabriel quickly unzipped the baggie and pulled out the paper. He unfolded it and read: "You are a great pretender. Take heart, I know who you really are."

Gabriel shut his eyes and steadied himself, dizzy from the heat and the stench. *You are a great pretender. Take heart, I know who you really are.*

He opened his eyes and met those of the dead man.

"What'cha got?"

Gabriel jumped as Dash stepped up behind him.

"Don't you sneak up on me like that," Gabriel growled.

"What's your problem, Man?"

"What were you doing, creeping around?" Gabriel dropped his hand, hiding the note.

"I didn't want to disturb what was obviously a crime scene so I parked over there." Dash gestured to the smoke behind him. "I was looking for tire tracks. Geez, I didn't mean to scare you."

"Fat chance of finding any tracks on this toasted ground," Gabriel said, angrily cocking his head at the charred landscape.

"Take it easy, Partner. We're under a lot of pressure to haul in this suspect, so I'm not taking anything for granted." Dash eyed him quizzically and said, "What's with you?"

Gabriel nervously wiped his nose, his brow; and stepped aside, "Look."

Dash made a face upon seeing the body. "Jesus."

"This makes five."

"This time he made a real mess, didn't he?" Dash grimaced at the wound. "God, is that his <u>heart</u>?"

"That's not all."

Dash looked at his partner curiously.

"There's also this." Gabriel held up the note for his partner to see. The paper rustled and flapped, pushed by the relentless warm wind.

"The truth is often a terrible weapon of aggression. It is possible to lie, and even to murder with the truth."

Alfred Adler (1870-1937)

CHAPTER

Lieutenant Ramirez studied the note over the fingerprint examiner's shoulder. "Any special impressions? Anything?" he asked anxiously.

"The suspect used common eight-and-a-half by eleven copier quality paper. It was printed off a laser jet printer. We've seen the font before with this suspect: Arial."

"What else?"

"Patience, Lieutenant, patience. Paper is really easy to lift prints off of, if there are any."

Ramirez watched the officer use an aerosol spray solution on the paper that contained a chemical called ninhydrin, which emitted a strong, unpleasant odor. If the document did indeed contain fingerprints, the ninhydrin would work on the amino acids left by perspiration and would appear as pink to purple prints.

"Now we have to wait."

"Ahhh." Ramirez turned away with a complaining whine.

"Tomorrow something should show up," the examiner assured him.

"Unless he used gloves," Ramirez replied. "Any prints off the body?"

"Nope. Too much blood from the victim; not to mention the heat."

Ramirez nodded, frowning.

The examiner moved to a sink and attempted to wash the chemical from his hands. It was a vain effort as his hands were blotched with permanent stains. "I did put some silver nitrate plates on the wrists and palms, but unfortunately nothing came up."

"Page me as soon as you know something."

"Will do."

Ramirez nodded a frustrated good-bye and exited. He walked down the halls of the lab and went out the doors of the Monterey Park headquarters.

Outside in the fresh air, away from the chemical smell, Ramirez blinked in the sunlight. He spied Dash exiting his car in the parking lot.

"Señor Spiceless," Ramirez called enthusiastically and walked over to him.

"You wanted to talk, Sir?"

"Yeah, I do; a little heart-to-heart." Ramirez steered Dash toward the intersection of the boulevard. "There's a little Chinese place I thought we'd hit. You know that Monterey Park is the new Chinatown, don't you? No shit. They got great restaurants around here."

"Well, I don't know if I've got a lot of time for lunch, Sir. Gabriel and I have been really busting our butts out in Malibu. I think I've spoken to every Russian person that lives–"

"I know, I know. And that's why I thought you'd update me on everything going on. There's that place I was telling you about." Ramirez stuck out his chin toward a little slot in a strip mall. Carcasses of pigs and ducks hung in the window.

"Hungry?" Ramirez asked.

"Well, I…"

"You eat duck?"

"Well, not–"

Ramirez slapped him on the back as they entered the restaurant. "¡Venga! "

They took their seats and a waiter wearing a stained white apron came over. Dash pulled out his Mrs. Dash seasonings bottle and looked evenly at the waiter.

"Do you use MSG in your–"

"Fuck that," Ramirez said, and turned to the waiter, "Give us a plate of garlic cod filet; pan fried noodles with pork, fried rice with extra egg, and two cokes. Make mine a diet." He turned and smiled at Dash. "Wait'll you taste this food."

Dash timidly slid the Mrs. Dash bottle back into his jacket pocket. "I was thinking that maybe Gabriel should be here. He's really the lead investiga–"

"Egg rolls!" Ramirez yelled, leaping from his seat. He rolled his eyes at Dash. "Stupid me. I forgot the egg rolls. Spring rolls I think they call them here. Uh, could we have an order of spring rolls?" He sat back down. "Speaking of Sergeant McRay, how did he take that latest note?"

"Well, he's naturally shook up, Sir. I mean, this guy's got it in for him."

Ramirez nodded, brows furrowed in concentration. "Yeah, we've got one sick dude on our hands, don't we?" He looked into Dash's eyes. "I mean the killer, of course."

Dash gaped at his lieutenant for a moment and then looked down awkwardly at his napkin. "Lieutenant, this is just, you know a weird thing that's going on. It's like we said before, the suspect has seen Gabriel's name in the media and he's jumping on the bandwagon."

"But wouldn't you agree that Sergeant McRay has a problem controlling his temper?"

"He gets stressed out a little more than most, I suppose, but everyone's got problems."

"Tell me about his."

The waiter returned and set down their drinks. Dash shifted uncomfortably, and said, "Sir, you're barking up the wrong tree."

"You just leave the barking to me," Ramirez assured him and popped a straw into his soda. "Tell me about his problems."

"Gabriel McRay is a good, decent person and a top-of-the-line investigator. He doesn't deserve this."

"But something is wrong with him, right? You can tell; I can see it in your eyes. What's on your mind?"

Dash shook his head, reaching for his Coke. "This is... It's nothing. Look, I probably shouldn't even say this. No, it's ridiculous."

"Say what?"

"Gabriel once mentioned to me that he lived in San Francisco – now I don't know when or—"

Ramirez sat back in surprise and said, "Where that Welby murder took place? That wasn't in your report, Starkweather!"

"It had nothing to do with the case, Sir."

"When a damn suspect writes 'we are one' on a note addressed to one of our investigators and that investigator just happens to be from the same city where a similar crime took place, you put that in your damn report, Sergeant!"

"Look, I didn't want to say anything; I mean, big deal! I've been to San Francisco hundreds of times. It doesn't mean I committed a murder there."

"No, it doesn't mean you committed a murder there," Ramirez mimicked him.

The waiter returned balancing steaming platters. He set down the food and handed the two officers chopsticks.

Ramirez began heaping globs of rice onto his place. "I want you keep a close eye on your partner. That's an order. I want to know who he sees, what he does and why he does it."

"But I'm his friend. He trusts me."

"Perfect."

"I don't feel right about this. Not at all. Why are you pursuing this?"

"Why?" Ramirez repeated with a hint of sarcasm. "Among other things, such as notes that say 'we are one' and a cop with head problems, it's because of a question you yourself asked, Señor Spiceless. How does he get in their cars?" Ramirez put down the rice and leaned close to Dash. "There's only one kind of person I can think of, that people would trust enough, or possibly be forced to, allow into their cars – and that's a cop with a badge."

Stunned, Dash was silent.

"The man is identified as Patrick Funston. He was a sophomore at Pepperdine U," Ming said, shaking her head at the body on the steel table. "Too young."

Gabriel nodded sympathetically. Ming wore her surgical greens and latex gloves. The lower half of her face was concealed behind a gauze mask and her hair was tucked under a cap. Next to Gabriel stood Dash. They hovered over the body of an athletic young man, with a pitifully wide hole in his chest and other rust-brown lines crisscrossing his flesh.

Looking at the man's strong thigh muscles made Gabriel question again how the killer got them by surprise every time. How did he get in their cars and get them off the road? The

Highway Patrol and L.A. Sheriff's Department had stepped up security in the canyons and were warning motorists against picking up hitchhikers. Gabriel and his partner could find no common link between the victims.

Was there some tavern or business they all frequented? Was there one person they all knew and trusted? An employee, a fellow patron, a friend – someone they would give a lift to somewhere? If they had all been surfers he could explore the beaches. If they had all been entertainment people he could explore the rich enclaves of Malibu. The killer bounced around, not operating in any pattern of hours or days. The suspect was like a ghost.

But he's not a ghost, Gabriel told himself. He's flesh and blood and he's zoning in on me, making it personal. But why? If he wants attention, why write me? Why not write the newspapers?

Seeing his name yet again along with the inscription "take heart" threatened to push Gabriel's frail emotions over the edge. He forced himself to concentrate on what Ming was saying, fighting the impulse to bolt from the room, dig a hole somewhere, and bury his head like an ostrich.

"Because the body wasn't burned," Ming said, "I could get a better look at those wounds. See this?" Ming pointed to a dark line about an inch long against the gray, waxy skin. "He literally dug out the heart. No easy task, considering the amount of bone in the way. The job was not done cleanly, so I'd assume he's no medical expert or surgeon. He stabbed the boy here and here very hard. The knife went in until the hilt. These first two were enough to kill the victim."

"Looks like he wanted to get down to business quickly again," Dash said.

"My thought exactly," Ming agreed. "But check out these wounds. Notice the small mark at the left side of the wound, almost parallel to it? Do you see?"

The two detectives peered closer.

"That small indentation. There's a small bruise surrounding the mark."

"Yeah," Dash said.

"I see it," Gabriel affirmed.

"On the other one—" she moved her gloved hand once more, "the delivering blow was not as forceful, but you can still make it out, can't you?"

Gabriel saw a very faint scratch to the left of the wound.

"I've measured the distance from the edge of the left side of the blade to the mark. All the details will be put in the report." Ming held up the corpse's left palm and pointed to staggered but parallel cuts, stretching from the little finger to the wrist. "See these? They're defensive wounds. This young man was not taken by surprise. He had the chance to fight. Now, look at his right palm." Ming gently picked up the right hand. "He was right-handed, I can tell by the wear of his nails. See the wounds on this hand?"

The detectives could make out gashes on the insides of the middle and pointer fingers and the thumb.

"I'm going to call these 'offensive' wounds, if you'll pardon my own terminology. What I read from these is that Patrick succeeded at grabbing the blade at one point and pulling it – see the small mark here? Unfortunately, he lost the tug-of-war."

Dash shook his head. "Like I've said before, this guy has to be built. He has to be strong."

Gabriel caught Dash eyeing him oddly and Gabriel raised his own eyebrows as if to say, "What?" But Dash looked away from him.

Gabriel turned to Ming, "Did the lab find anything else? Any hairs or fibers on the clothes?"

Ming pulled off her mask. Her high cheekbones and beautiful brown eyes once again struck Gabriel. "We've got the suspect's DNA."

"That's great," Gabriel told her. "What was the speciman? His blood?"

"No," Ming answered. "We found a smudge of semen on the victim's pant leg. There is no evidence that the victim was raped. Again, the victim was found fully clothed."

"So, what do you think?" Dash asked her innocently.

"I think he's masturbating, Dash," Ming said with a hint of amusement. "Anyhow, Anthony Hamilton at the lab is working on it. Let's hope the sample isn't degenerated by the heat."

Gabriel nodded and thought someday there should be a databank with every newborn baby's DNA listed. All a detective would have to do, if indeed he had a DNA sample, is log onto a computer to identify his suspect.

"Any trinkets or trophies taken that we know of?" Gabriel asked Ming.

"I found something that may be of interest." Ming went to a small, steel bowl and drew out a broken gold chain. The necklace had already been tested for prints and fibers and Ming handed it over to the detectives. Dash examined the chain and gave it to Gabriel.

"I think some sort of pendant hung on it." Ming said. "From the look of that broken link, it was probably torn away."

Gabriel fingered the gold links. Suddenly, the necklace became very heavy in his hand and he fought the urge to hurl it at the wall. From somewhere deep within his brain, the steel drum of a headache began beating; the hammering getting louder and louder.

"We found remnants of his wallet," Dash said. "Unfortunately, it was left in the front seat of the car and it's pretty much a charcoal briquette now."

"Anything else in the car?" Ming asked him.

Dash shook his head. "Sunglasses. Some other personal items of the victim, burnt to a crisp."

Gabriel began to sweat from the pounding in his brain. He looked over at the body on the table and the young man suddenly sat up, the rust-brown hole gaping in his white flesh. Patrick's eyes, just turning a milky blue, searched for Gabriel and found him. The corpse opened a dried mouth with a shriveled tongue and croaked, *"Take heart, I know who you really are."*

From far away, Gabriel heard Ming ask if he was okay, but Gabriel was frozen, staring into the dead man's accusing eyes. He heard a woman's voice saying, "How could you do that to a child? You're an evil, evil man."

Gabriel forced his eyes to drop down to the gold chain, which lay coiled in his hand like a viper ready to strike. Behind the hammering in his head Gabriel heard the rumble of a car engine.

"Gabe?" Dash asked, "You okay?"

Gabriel's body flinched as he stared trance-like at the necklace.

"What's wrong, Man?" Dash put a hand on his partner's shoulder.

Ming walked over to him. "Gabriel?"

The headache exploded full force and Gabriel's hands went numb. The necklace fell to the floor. Gabriel reached out to support himself on the steel sink. The stench of formaldehyde and death enveloped him in a putrid cocoon and he felt himself falling —watching the floor tiles soaring upwards to meet his skull.

And then everything went black.

Someone was going to perform surgery on him. A bomb was going to be surgically implanted in his chest, and if he told the secret, the bomb would explode and his insides would spew out in a million pieces.

Gabriel sat up with a start and was shocked to find four pairs of eyes staring at him. They belonged to Ming, Dr. B,

Dash, and Lieutenant Ramirez. His own eyes darted around. White walls. A bed. A hospital room. Had he been shot or something?

"Hello, Gabe," Dr. B said.

"Why am I here? What happened?"

"You passed out," Dash answered.

"Shit." Gabriel put a hand to his brow. Attached to his arm was an IV. "What's this?"

"A slight anticoagulant," Ming said, taking a seat on the bed. "We were worried about the possibility of a stroke."

Gabriel looked at Ramirez for comment. For once the Lieutenant was silent, just sitting in a chair and eyeing him.

"How do you feel?" Ming asked with genuine concern.

"Fine, I guess," Gabriel said.

Ming cleared her throat. "I examined you, I hope you don't mind. Just an EEG–while you were out of it. I, we were very concerned," she added quickly.

Gabriel looked around again. "How long have I been – out?"

"Four hours," Dr. B answered.

"Four–" Gabriel stuttered. "Four hours?"

"Your physical tests were normal," Dr. B said. "It seems you went into some sort of fugue state."

"Why?" Ramirez addressed Dr. B but looked straight at Gabriel, who glared back at him, not liking the lieutenant's suspicious tone. "Why does someone go into a fugue state, Doc?"

Dr. B frowned at Ramirez, and said, "That's something Detective McRay and I will discuss – at another time."

"Discuss it now," Ramirez said and rose up from his seat. "Don't worry. I got to get back to work. I've got a killer to catch." Ramirez gave Gabriel one last withering glance and then turned to Dash. "You coming?"

Dash nodded, smiled quickly at Gabriel, and then exited alongside Ramirez, closing the door behind them.

Gabriel moved to get up. "I've got to get out of here."

Ming put a restraining hand on his shoulder. "Not just yet." She looked at Dr. B, who was pulling his chair closer to Gabriel.

"The lieutenant wants you to take some time off." Dr. B said in an assuring voice.

"I'm not gonna do that," Gabriel argued. "I'm fine."

Ming looked down uncomfortably and Gabriel silently admonished himself.

"I'm sorry," he said quietly. "I blew it."

"You didn't blow anything," Ming said. "You scared us; that's all."

"This has happened before, hasn't it?" Dr. B asked him. "Not just memory lapses, but dissociative fugue states."

Gabriel nodded.

"How often?"

Gabriel was about to recount a figure but then sighed. "I'm not sure. I think a lot. What is a fugue state?"

"A psychological disturbance, really. Usually, you don't remember your actions when you wake up again." Dr. B said. "In most cases, it's a symptom of post-traumatic stress disorder."

"We're back to that again," Gabriel stated tiredly.

"Yes, we're back to that again."

Ming stood up, and said, "I've got to get back to my office." She smiled gently at Gabriel. "I'll check on you later."

Gabriel nodded, "Thanks."

The two men watched her leave and then regarded each other.

"How sick am I?"

"I don't know if you're sick at all, Gabe," Dr. B answered. "But I think you're hiding something inside that's giving you a lot of pain. That pain is causing you all kinds of problems. Do you want to tell me anything now?"

Gabriel shook his head, fell silent for a moment, and then said, "When I was in uniform, I put myself in the line of fire everyday. I had twelve-year-old kids taking potshots at me from apartment windows. I broke up domestic battles, held the hands of kids whose parents were being hauled off to jail. I've dealt with more drug-addicted idiots than I'd like to remember but I've never dealt with anything like this. You don't think this all stems from that guy I shot, do you?"

"The 'cop' with the toy gun?" Dr. B shook his head. "I'll admit that you're feeling guilty and guilt can cause a lot of pain. But your symptoms scream suppressed memory. And you're very much aware of that man's death and you're not afraid to talk about it." Dr. B paused a moment, thinking, and then said, "Sometimes, the oddest things can trigger a suppressed memory. Something about a gold chain, maybe?"

Gabriel shook his head. "Gold chains mean nothing to me."

"Would you be willing to undergo more hypnosis to support that claim?"

"If I said yes, could I get out of here right now?"

"I'm scheduling an appointment for you." Dr. B pressed the call button for the nurse. "You've got to be committed to this, Gabe."

"I am. I swear."

Ramirez waited patiently while the forensic scientist worked with his ampoules of liquid. The scientist was a good-looking African-American man named Anthony Hamilton who possessed a sharp wit he especially liked to use against the short-tempered lieutenant.

"Now we just have to wait," Hamilton said. Ramirez continued to loiter. Hamilton's world was a whitewashed sterile lab, filled with whirring centrifuges, incubators, and printers, all spitting out data, graphs, and chains of chromosome bands.

On the wall hung a chart of DNA strands, looking like twisting ladders upon whose rungs hung the prototypes of human beings. Hamilton, adorned from head to toe in a white gown, looked at Ramirez with pretend annoyance. "Anything else, Lieutenant?"

Ramirez glared at Hamilton as if he were stupid. "No, I'm waiting."

Hamilton rolled his eyes. "Feel free. But the floor's going to seem awfully hard after two weeks."

"I don' have time to wait two weeks," Ramirez said, purposely accentuating his Spanish accent for effect. "I need answers. Now. Today."

Hamilton feigned a pained expression until Ramirez began bristling. "Okay," he said, "enough torture for one afternoon. Let me tell you what's up. You have given me degraded DNA. It's been cooked, it's merely a swab, and it certainly doesn't have the value of RFLP–"

"What?" Ramirez barked with annoyance.

"R-F-L-P. Remember that from DNA-101?"

"Shut up, Tony. That's your end of the business." Ramirez plopped himself in a chair and sighed. "I've got the chief and the mayor riding my back. You can't imagine how heavy that is on mi espalda."

"Pobrecito."

Ramirez frowned at him and the scientist relented. "RFLP, restriction fragment length polymorphisms, is the most reliable and accepted type of DNA evidence used by the courts today. It's highly discriminating and the match probabilities are greater than a million to one. Now, your specimen, as I said, has been degraded, but it's still suitable for PCR, or polymerase chain reaction analysis."

Ramirez' pained look was genuine. "Just tell me in English–or Spanish."

"This is a newer method and is popular because it's less expensive and it's fast. PCR is just sensitive enough to take a beat-to-hell sample like yours and tell us certain things. While it can't be considered reliable enough to 'fingerprint' a suspect, it can certainly <u>exclude</u> someone as a suspect."

Ramirez looked thoughtful. "That's good enough. When can you give me something?"

"I'll have some info to you in a week, week and a half tops. That okay?"

Ramirez nodded to the forensic scientist and said, "The sooner the better. Someone's life is depending on it."

CHAPTER 11

The sharp knife went easily into the white part of the leek and Gabriel sliced one cup's worth. The onion was strong and stung his eyes, but he didn't care. The stinging centered him; reminded Gabriel that he was present and in control. He tossed the onion in a three-quart saucepan along with the leeks and some parsley. Now came the arduous task of peeling and cubing one and a half pounds of potatoes for his crab vichyssoise. His hands worked and his mind kept busy. He wouldn't think about fugue states and the future appointments he had with a psychiatrist. He would instead mull over his mental list of leads on the Malibu Canyon murder case.

He planned on taking Ming's report on the victim's wounds to Sam the Knife Trader tomorrow. Gabriel was sure he could glean some information there. Dash was covering the tire track lead. Next week they should have DNA test results. So far, the Russian angle had left them cold. They had checked out the pasts of Russian students attending Pepperdine and had interviewed many Russian area residents. Nothing had made Gabriel's spine tingle and his gut told him it was a wrong turn. But there must be some connection, Gabriel thought as he ran the peeler down a potato, regarding the Russian military revolver and the Russian word.

That left him thinking about the chakras. The victims had to be tied somehow to the killer's notion about chakras. From what Gabriel had garnered from his new age books, he knew that Chakra One represented physical identity and self-preservation, a sense of grounding to the physical plane. Each chakra was assigned an element or natural substance, such as earth, air, fire, and water. Chakra one's element was earth. Ted Brody had been butchered with this chakra in mind. Who was Ted Brody? He was a handyman with a fiancé.

Emotional identity and self-gratification, along with feelings of sexual fulfillment, fluidity, and change, were characterized by chakra two. Water was its element. Tania Dankowski, wife and mother, charity worker, and volunteer had been tied to chakra two.

Chakra three was symbolized by ego identity and self-definition. Its element was fire. Brian Goldfield was divorced, recently out of the "closet", and a movie producer – a power player.

Chakra four was represented by creative identity and self-acceptance with air as an element. Feelings of love, compassion, and peace were connected with chakra four. What had drawn the killer to Patrick Funston? He was a young college student, good-looking and athletic. Adam Parraco had been young and good-looking. Why had he been dispatched so quickly and neatly when Funston had been brutally carved up?

Gabriel put the potatoes in the saucepan and threw in some broth and a bay leaf. He stirred the mix thoughtfully then lowered the flame.

The fact that the killer chose to execute Adam Parraco but leave his body intact bothered Gabriel. Who was Adam? From what Gabriel could gather he was a gold-digger. A hanger-on who liked the rich and powerful. He had no real hobbies of note and no career. He was financially supported by Goldfield.

The phone ringing interrupted Gabriel's pondering.

"Hi, Gabe," Ming said.

"Hey."

"I wanted to see how you are doing?"

"Much better, thanks."

"What are you doing right now?"

He held the phone in the crook of his neck and continued cutting more potatoes. "Cooking. What are you doing?"

"Starving."

Gabriel smiled. "Where are you?"

"I'm in your neighborhood. I had to drop off a wedding gift to a friend who lives on Fourth."

"Hmmm… I guess I can't let you become skin and bones. Where do you want to meet?"

An awkward pause came between them, and then Ming said, "You pick."

"Third Street Promenade?"

"Okay."

"Feel like a steak? The Gaucho Grill makes one hell of a garlic ribeye."

"I'll see you there," Ming agreed. "In twenty minutes or so?"

Gabriel surveyed his kitchen mess. "Yeah, I can do that."

"Okay, bye." And she was gone.

Gabriel could tell Ming was disappointed. He knew she wanted to come over, but he could not risk getting close to her. It was bad enough that Ming had witnessed his "psychological disturbance;" bad enough that she had seen him in a hospital room accompanied by his psychiatrist.

In his own home Gabriel was even more vulnerable and exposed. Ming's inquisitive mind would be searching the myriad little clues lying around that furnished insight into Gabriel's personality – and what's more, his problems. He didn't buy her "wedding gift" excuse either. Ming wanted to check up on him.

Gabriel turned off the fire under the saucepan and stored his meal in the refrigerator. After he changed clothes, he grabbed his wallet, pager, and car keys and walked out his front door.

The night carried the beach scent and the sky was marked with a round, bright moon. Gabriel inhaled the salty air and walked toward his car. Halfway there, the hairs on the back of his neck stood on end and Gabriel slowed his pace.

He glanced from side to side. A layer of dew had formed on the parked cars and on the asphalt. Moths skittered around the yellow street lamps. Gabriel heard their wings flutter in the otherwise quiet neighborhood.

Something is out here, Gabriel thought, his eyes scanning the darkened street. Gabriel never ignored his instincts. Nature equipped mankind with an immune system to defy invading germs and she had also provided an instinct to ward off impending danger. As a cop in uniform, Gabriel had learned to trust that prickly feeling on the back of his neck. It usually spelled trouble.

Someone was watching him. He was sure of it. Gabriel whistled to bolster his confidence as he strode to his car, unlocked it and sat himself down. In a moment he spied an unmarked cop car parked across the street and down a ways. It was the only car that the evening moisture hadn't settled upon.

Did they think he would not recognize an unmarked? Hadn't he staked out suspects in similar cars countless times? The word 'suspect' rang in his brain. *Suspect.*

Angry, but determined to keep the rage under tight wraps, Gabriel started his car and drove off.

Over savory garlic steaks and empanadas, Ming and Gabriel discussed the case, carefully avoiding the subject of Gabriel's fugue states. They sat outside on the Gaucho Grill's patio where they could enjoy a view of the promenade. Gabriel tried not to be obvious as he alternately glanced over his shoulder and then looked past Ming's head, searching for the comrades who were tailing him.

"Dr. B told me that many killers have an inner desire to reveal themselves and then get caught. Is that your experience?" she asked him.

"It isn't my experience with this one."

Ming took a sip of red wine. "He left notes for you. He obviously wants you to follow through, don't you think?"

Gabriel sawed through his meat with a steak knife. "If he wanted follow-through, he would have left his prints."

Ming grinned and said, "That makes things a little too easy, Detective."

Gabriel shrugged and glanced over his shoulder again. "I wanna catch this guy, Ming. I hate that he's calling attention to me. I've had enough negative attention." Gabriel turned back to Ming and once more was struck by her simple beauty. She wore a black sheath and strappy sandals. Her dark hair fell long and wavy down her back. Sitting there, she looked less like a pathologist and more like an exotic model.

You should have come over to my place.

"Okay, I'll say it. You look beautiful."

Ming observed the pedestrians browsing the shops and a small smile played at her lips. "Aren't you worried I'll sue?"

"What the fuck? I have enough problems. What's one more?"

Ming laughed; perfectly white teeth and full lips.

"I should have invited you over–" he began.

"Stop!" Ming poured more wine for the two of them.

Gabriel nodded. After an uncomfortable moment, he said, "I was thinking about the chakra thing. I don't really know where to go with it."

"You ought to talk to a holistic expert."

"Only in Los Angeles would you need to consult psychics to solve a homicide," Gabriel said dourly, shoving a forkful of beef into his mouth.

"For someone from L.A. that's an awfully cynical thing to say." Ming chewed on her lip. "But then again, you're from San Francisco."

Gabriel swallowed his mouthful and met her eyes. "How did you know that?"

"I heard Ramirez talking about it."

"How does he know? Wait… never mind." Gabriel paused a moment. "You know, they're following me."

Ming's dark eyes widened. "Who's following you?" She craned her neck, eyeing each passerby.

"My fellow officers," he answered, and waved his hand at her efforts. "Don't bother."

"They suspect you? Oh my God…" Ming set down her fork, shaking her head. "Why don't you confront them? Why don't you go to Ramirez and tell him he's being ridiculous!"

"Is it ridiculous? Look at it from his angle. I've got issues, right? Our suspect is claiming that 'we're one,' and that I'm a "great pretender." Ramirez knows I'm from San Francisco, where a crime similar to these murders took place."

"But did you live there during that time?"

"No, but what does that matter?" Gabriel resumed eating. "Go ahead; finish your steak. Why waste a good one?"

"I'm going to say something," Ming told him.

"No, don't."

"Why not?"

Because something is wrong with me. Aloud Gabriel said, "I'm not giving up. I'm not quitting."

Ming took a large gulp of wine. Gabriel watched her.

"Why do you bother with me?" he asked quietly.

"Because I think it's worth it."

"What if it's not?"

Ming sighed uneasily. "I think the chakras are supposed to be something like the seven windows of the soul."

Gabriel gazed at her, surprised and grateful. No other woman would have changed the subject. Still, an aura of tension surrounded Ming that hadn't been there before. Her dark eyes darted around and the edges of her mouth were tight.

"He did write the word 'soul' in Russian. That much we know." Gabriel waited a beat. "Ming?"

She regarded him with a poker face and raised her eyebrows. "Hmm?"

"Thank you."

Ming studied her plate, no longer eating. "Tell me your thoughts about the victims," she said.

Gabriel carefully poured more wine. "He couldn't have picked more random victims: a handyman, a mother – none of them frequenting the same places. They lived in different parts of the city, except for Funston, who lived at the university and Goldfield who lived on Broad Beach."

Ming pulled her gaze from the plate, picked up her glass, and watched the red liquid swirl inside. "He's obviously not looking for one particular type of person. If he's hitching rides, he doesn't have a choice of who picks him up. He's going to get a variety."

Gabriel paused over a bite of steak. "Variety," he said, putting down his fork. "Here I've been knocking my head against the wall, trying to see what tied the victims together, but it's never been about that. It's what they don't have in common that turns him on."

Ming shook her head, saying, "You're losing me."

Gabriel began counting off on his fingers. "A handyman, a mother, a student, a producer. A fat man, a woman, a young man – he likes that they're different."

"What about Adam Parraco?" Ming asked, "He was someone different. There are seven chakras. Why wasn't he tagged with one of them?"

Gabriel hesitated, absorbing her words, and then said, "I'll tell you why. Because Parraco couldn't give the killer what he wanted. Parraco was in the way." Gabriel regarded his half-eaten dinner, thinking. "Parraco. What did he do? He was a party boy who lived off powerful people. Chakra three is self-definition. Maybe the killer knew that Parraco didn't fit his perfect picture."

"How could he find out about his victims in such a short time?"

"Maybe he asks the pertinent questions right off the bat. What's the first question people ask each other? What do you do? He didn't like what he heard from Parraco, but he liked what he learned about Goldfield enough to kill them both."

Ming shook her head. "I don't buy it."

"I can prove it."

"How?"

"I'll bet he's been picked up by other people and he let them get away."

"Oh, yeah, sure," Ming said, guffawing. "We would have heard. If someone picked up a creep, they'd come forward in light of all this press."

"Who said he's a creep? Like Dr. B said, the killer probably appears totally harmless."

"He's sure taking his chances, isn't he?"

"That could be a turn on for him as well."

"It's a stretch, Gabe."

"When you're looking inside the mind of a madman, do you think you're going to find much that smacks of normal?"

Gabriel was surprised to see Ming give him a cautious look. She then turned her attention back to the Third Street Promenade.

The following day, Gabriel posted flyers along the canyon roads asking for people to come forward if they'd had a chance encounter with any and all hitchhikers in the vicinity. He was betting on a long shot, he knew, but Gabriel had nothing to lose.

His venture took most of the day, and it was late afternoon by the time he made the drive north along the coast highway up to Camarillo.

The sleepy agricultural farming town bordered by acres of flowers and vegetables had been home to a population of middle-income whites and Mexican immigrants. Now Camarillo was turning a new leaf with tony golf resorts and retirement villages. Even its one claim to infamy, the Camarillo State Hospital for the mentally ill, had become a college.

Gabriel pulled into the lot of the Knife Trader in old town Camarillo, located between a cozy Mexican restaurant with a blinking red neon sign and an antique store. Across the street he saw the mission, proudly stuccoed and serene, lit by the balmy orange light of the setting sun.

Dash was waiting for him in the parking lot. Gabriel grabbed his folder of papers and the two detectives entered the dim store at the hail of a jingling bell hung above the door. Gabriel had been a visitor here on many occasions.

Only the whirring of an electric fan and the creaking of a wooden chair that the proprietor was sitting in broke the calmness inside. Sam Stanton was a burly veteran of the Korean War. He sat, tipped back, with his feet resting on the top of a glass counter, a newspaper perched on his ample belly.

Sam's store was dark and packed from floor to ceiling with war mementos. Military green helmets hung above coats and uniforms and looked like rows of sleeping soldiers. Racks of rifles, bayonets, revolvers and other guns stood side by side in a modern and antique weaponry section. A cabinet stocked with hundreds of war medals, stood next to another with pins. And under the glass counters, there existed one of the best collections of knives this side of the Rockies.

"How's it going, Sam?" Gabriel asked.

"It's going," Sam answered. "You two?"

"Same as always," Dash said, giving a small salute.

"I was wondering when you guys were gonna wander in," the Knife Trader said and put his chair upright again. "Seeing as how your fire-bug likes using knives." He tossed the front page of the Los Angeles Times their way and the two detectives glanced at the newsprint.

The small, square pictures of Ted Brody, Adam Parraco, Brian Goldfield, Tania Dankowski, and Patrick Funston stared out at the world in black and white under the heading, "Malibu Canyon Murderer Still at Large."

Gabriel had read the article. So far the press knew nothing of the notes or the clues they had. Nor did the press know about the lead investigator's lapse into the world of fugue states.

"We're hoping you can shed some light on the weapon. We have some information for you," Gabriel said.

"I'll try." Sam stood and hitched up his pants. "What'cha got?"

"This is between us and the wall, right?" Dash added.

Sam shrugged. "Why not?" He eyed the manila envelope Gabriel held under his arm. "Something for me?"

Gabriel began pulling eight-by-ten photos out of the envelope. They were enlargements of the wounds that Ming had pointed out on Patrick Funston's body.

"The ME wanted us to ask you what causes that mark to the left of the actual wound. The measurements are consistent with each wound."

"They would be," Sam commented, studying the pictures. "It looks like part of the guard. What are the wound's dimensions?"

"One inch by six-and-a-half," Dash replied.

Sam Stanton whistled absently and began thumbing through a large manual laying on the credenza behind his desk. After a moment he frowned and said, "Nah." His whistling resumed as he flipped through another equally thick volume. "Uh-huh," he grunted and brought the book over to the two detectives.

"A knife with a guard and a blade of those dimensions is most likely a military knife – like these. Now that particular mark you were talking about looks like it was caused by the quillon hitting the skin when the knife went up to the hilt. Your guy must pack a wallop."

"What's a kwee-yon?" Dash asked.

"A quillon is part of the guard that sort of dips down parallel to the blade. It's not on every knife, but it is on a lot of military knives. Here, see for yourself."

Sam went to another case and grabbed a lethal-looking blade with a twisted leather grip. A portion of the black metal guard dipped slightly downward parallel with the blade.

"This is a Kabar. Good weapon. Soldiers are trained to hold a knife properly so's it can't be pulled out of their hands. Like this, see?"

Sam Stanton wrapped his hand around the grip and looped one finger over the quillon. "During the World Wars there was a lot of hand-to-hand combat in the trenches. By using the quillon, no one can pull the knife from my hands. If there are marks from the quillon on the body, I can tell you, your boy is no military man. He doesn't know how to hold a knife."

"The ME said the victim was nearly able to pull the knife from the assailant."

"Case in point. He wasn't using the quillion properly. Guy didn't have military training."

"Well, he's been pretty effective with the knife so far," Gabriel muttered. "Now you're sure it's some sort of military issue?" Gabriel exchanged looks with Dash. "And that it could have been used during World War Two?"

Sam Stanton shrugged. "Sure."

"Any pictures of Soviet knives?" Gabriel asked.

The knife trader shook his head. "The Russians used daggers mostly, and a dagger doesn't fit the picture from what you've told me about the knife in question."

"But a trench knife is kind of large, isn't it?" Dash said. "I mean – to conceal it from the victims?"

Gabriel nodded his concern, scribbling in his spiral notepad.

Sam said, "You can always conceal it in a boot or a jacket."

When the two detectives left the spooky, calm darkness of the Knife Trader and stepped out into the twilight, Dash turned to his partner.

"Are we looking for a Russian vet?"

"Not according to Sam," Gabriel answered. "Our guy is a collector of second world war weapons. Not necessarily Russian. Doesn't help much." Something again caught the edge of Gabriel's subconscious and he furrowed his dark brows in concentration, tapping his notebook against his leg. "I feel liked I've overlooked something. What have I forgotten?"

Dash thought a moment. "We've followed up on everything."

The two detectives walked toward Gabriel's Celica.

"Tire mark?"

"Guys at the lab are still not sure." Dash stepped in front of Gabriel and hung his head awkwardly, "Hey, have you given any thought to um, all that stuff the suspect is writing in his notes to you?"

Gabriel halted and faced his partner, "No. I think he's just trying to fuck with me, that's all."

Dash cleared his throat. "Well, did you ever think that maybe he knew you. I mean, if he did kill that guy in San Francisco and you're from there, maybe he knew you. Or knows you. Did you ever think of that?"

"My circle of friends doesn't include serial killers."

"How would you know? It's usually the guy-next-door, type of thing, isn't it?"

Gabriel crossed his arms, saying, "And who do you think the guy next door is, Dash? Me?"

His partner's complexion reddened and he held up a defensive hand. "I didn't say that. But maybe it is someone you know. Or it could be someone you nailed a few years back. Don't you think it's worth checking out to see who's been paroled recently?"

Dash had a point. Gabriel tucked his notepad and pencil into his pocket, and said, "All right. I'll check it out."

"I'll do it for you," Dash offered.

Gabriel frowned. "I think I'm capable of handling it."

"Sorry."

The two men regarded each other. Finally Gabriel softened. "I know. I must really freak you out, don't I?"

"Hey, everyone cracks once in a while," Dash assured him, shuffling his feet. Then he focused on Gabriel. "You crack a lot."

Gabriel smiled, "Don't worry about me, okay?"

"Sure," Dash nodded, grinning sheepishly.

Gabriel entered his car and looked back at Dash, "So, are your buddies somewhere around or are <u>you</u> following me home tonight?"

"Uh…"

"That's what I thought," Gabriel nodded and closed the car door.

CHAPTER

The red light shone like a bright garnet, a jewel. Other than the red light, Gabriel saw the Pacific Ocean, broad and undulating, as welcome as a warm, fleshy woman. He sat back in his chair across from Dr. B and breathed deeply. In a moment, he found himself sitting on the front porch of his family's home in San Francisco.

I haven't been here for years.

But there he was — sitting just like he used to, waiting on the granite steps for the familiar hum of his mom's Chevrolet that would soon turn the corner of his street. His teacher had given him an "outstanding" on his math test and he couldn't wait to tell his mom.

Gabriel sat on the steps, amazed that he was back. Things were as they always had been. A quiet neighborhood near Golden Gate Park with lots of pastel-colored homes with granite steps. He wanted to run to the park, but Mom always said, "Wait until I come home–that's the rule." There could be bad people at the park and it wasn't safe for a young boy to go alone.

Gabriel sat and watched the sun turn orange and dip down. Other than the sound of the trolley cars rumbling along the main boulevard, the afternoon was quiet.

Soon he heard the sound of an approaching vehicle, but it wasn't the purring of his mom's car. This engine made a loud, chugging sound. Andrew Pierce and his Pinto rounded the street corner. Andrew was seventeen and lived across the street from the McRay's.

Gabriel often saw him working on his car, tooling around the garage. But he was an older boy, practically a man, and didn't want much to do with little boys like Gabriel.

This time Andrew noticed the young boy sitting on the front porch with his arms hugging his knees up to his chin. "Hey, Gabe!" he called out from his Pinto.

"Hey, Andrew," Gabriel called back.

"What are you doing all alone there?"

"Waiting for my mom."

"Oh."

And that was that. Andrew Pierce pulled his car into his driveway, hopped out with the motor running and the exhaust belching smoke, and hoisted up the garage door. Then he jumped back into his car and drove in. Next thing Gabriel knew, Andrew had disappeared inside his house. Gabriel smiled as he watched the sun go down behind the row of houses. The big boy had said "Hi" to him. That was totally cool. Andrew Pierce was now his friend.

The following day, Gabriel was walking to the TG&Y to get some candy. He had been home alone and had gotten frustrated with the television. After spending an hour feeling sorry for himself, he went into his mom's bra drawer and searched for the little envelope of cash he knew she hid there among the underwire and cotton. His mom called the money "bread-and-butter." Gabriel pulled out a five-dollar bread and butter bill and tucked it into his jeans. He pulled on his San Francisco

Giants windbreaker and made his way toward Irving Street and the shops.

Gabriel gorged himself on five dollars worth of candy and then headed home. The walk back seemed much longer and his side was hurting him. The sky around him darkened and Gabriel was astonished to see that the sun was already setting behind patches of incoming fog. A rush of panic went through him and he forced his tired legs to jog. Oh, no, he thought, Mom is probably home by now. She's going to be so worried. She's going to be so mad. Gabriel felt tears well up behind his eyes.

Just then, Andrew Pierce pulled up next to him in his growling car. "Hey, Gabe."

Gabriel looked down and quickly wiped the tears from his eyes with the back of his sleeve. Only babies cried.

"You gonna walk all the way home by yourself?" Andrew asked.

"Yeah," Gabriel answered, trying to sound tough.

Andrew Pierce looked at him for a moment and then smiled, stopping his car. "Come on; get in. I'll drive you home."

"Can I?" Gabriel asked hopefully. It was unbelievable that the big boy would want to spend even a minute with him.

Andrew laughed, leaned over and opened the passenger-side door. Gabriel hopped inside and off they went.

Wow, Gabriel thought. This is more than cool. I'm in Andrew's bitchen car. I can hang with the big guys.

Andrew let him out in front of his house. His mom's car was not there. Gabriel breathed a sigh of relief.

"Well, see ya, Gabe."

"See ya, Andrew."

Imagine him, hanging out with a seventeen-year-old. Andrew pulled into his own driveway just when Gabriel saw his mom's car turning the corner of their street.

What luck! Gabriel thought. And he owed it all to Andrew Pierce.

That night he decided against telling his parents about his ride with Andrew. If he did he would have to admit he went to the TG&Y. And that would mean he'd have to tell where he'd gotten his candy money. Gabriel would be skewered on both counts. Besides, his mom didn't talk nice about Andrew Pierce. She called him a dropout. She said he wasn't going anywhere in his life. How could his mother say such a thing when that fine car of Andrew's could take him anywhere he wanted to go?

The following afternoon, Gabriel took his place on the porch much earlier this time and was happy to see Andrew working on his car. He secretly hoped Andrew would talk to him, maybe even give him another ride in his cool car, but Andrew disappeared inside the house.

Dejectedly, Gabriel stood up to go into his own home and make himself a peanut butter and banana sandwich, when he heard Andrew calling his name.

"Hey! How much time do you have before your ma gets home?"

Gabriel shrugged, hands in pockets. "Couple of hours, I guess."

"Well," Andrew called from across the street, "You wanna see a movie at the Melody Theater? I'm going."

Gabriel couldn't believe his ears. "Really?" He bounced on his feet. "Umm, wait a minute, okay? I just – I gotta get some money."

Andrew waved him away. "Don't sweat it. It's my treat."

"Cool!"

On the way to the theater, Gabriel stole a glance at the bigger boy who was kicking back and driving with one hand, while his other arm rested on the open window. The wind ruffled his long, auburn hair. Andrew Pierce – spending time with little Gabe McRay. Well, he wasn't so little now, was he?

Gabriel looked up, expecting to see Andrew's teenage face, but instead saw Dr. B. The session had reached its conclusion.

"What are you feeling?" Dr. B asked.

Gabriel took a deep breath and fell silent, thinking. Finally, he looked up at the psychiatrist. "Nothing bad. I remember how proud I was to have this bigger boy as my friend. I was so incredibly lonely at that time of my life. I really remember that now. I was lonely and alone. Andrew was like a savior to me. Here was this big kid, giving me the time of day. Treating me to movies and candy."

Gabriel leaned his head on the back of the chair and closed his eyes. "Sometimes we had hot dogs in the theater and popcorn. My mom would be cross because I couldn't finish my dinner."

"You never told your mom about your afternoon outings?"

"She never asked."

Dr. B smirked. "Now you're talking like a young boy."

Gabriel grinned, and said, "I guess I am."

"This is very good. I want you to remain on that track. I wouldn't be surprised if you act a bit like a seven-year-old for the next few hours. Please page me, if you have any problems."

Gabriel frowned at the psychiatrist. "Why do you say that? I actually feel pretty rejuvenated right now."

"Well, we're drudging up the past, a past that has been dormant in your mind for many years. We now know what's behind door number one. Door number two is still a mystery, but it could open at any time."

Gabriel felt a ball of fright roll through him, but couldn't place the origin of his fear. "Couldn't we just stop now at door number one?"

"No. I'm afraid stopping now wouldn't help you at all."

Gabriel watched the second hand smoothly glide around the wooden clock on Dr. B's desk, and said, "You know, I've been thinking about that last note the suspect left for me. He said that he knows who I really am. I don't even know what's going on inside of me, how could he?"

Dr. B gathered his notes together, straightening his desk. "Don't let the workings of a disturbed individual's mind affect you. He's messing with you; that's all."

"But what if he does know something about me? What if he's door number two?"

"What are you getting at? Please, Gabriel, tell me if you're hiding something; anything. I can't help you if you aren't straight with me."

Again, Gabriel heard the woman's voice, harsh and accusing, *"How could you do this to a child? You are an evil, evil man."*

"Gabriel, tell me what's on your mind. Are you thinking this man, Andrew Pierce, may be connected to these killings somehow?"

Gabriel jerked his blue eyes up to meet Dr. B's inquisitive brown ones. "I didn't even think of that," he said in surprise. "Jesus, it's a possibility."

The killer took out his metal fishing tackle box, left over from the time his dad was still in the house. It was the only thing his dad left him – and that had been quite by accident. Dad had forgotten to take it. Nope, he'd never gone fishing with Dad, but he had dad's tackle box. It was a heavy thing, and when it was opened, all these little drawers popped out like an accordion. The killer had used all the fishing lures and flies a long time ago. Now new treasures took their place.

He picked up the earring, still with its piece of dried brown flesh attached, and rolled it around in his palm. He knew that his emotions could be balanced simply by touching what was the woman's – and here was her flesh! He pinched it between his thumb and forefinger. Careful, don't ruin it, he told himself.

He gently replaced the earlobe and earring in its rightful drawer and picked up a diamond ring. He could make out the inscription etched inside the gold band: Gloria loves Ted.

All mine, he thought. Gloria and Ted, ears and earrings – everything of theirs and everything they are belong to me.

He replaced the ring in the ring drawer and as he did so, his knee bumped the box. He heard something jingle. Curious, he searched through his belongings and pulled out an old, blue cat's collar with a bell. He flicked the bell with his finger, enjoying the pleasant jingle. The tag on the collar read: "Duffy. Please call 929-3570."

Now that brought back memories, reminding him of what he did with Dad's fishing hooks.

School had let out and he had gone hunting in Golden Gate Park. He could walk to the park by himself because he was thirteen and Mom didn't give a damn anyhow because she was at work. He did okay in school; mostly kept to himself. Some of the girls thought he was cute, but he had other interests.

Golden Gate Park was a secret world of draping trees overlooking calm ponds where ducks quacked and flocked to the people bringing them crusts of bread. The fresh, salty air mingled with the fragrance of spruce and pine trees. Joggers, lovers, and mothers with strollers walked the pathways to hidden oases. The Japanese Tea Gardens served tea and cookies. As a kid he would study the fish in the ponds, admire the pagodas, and delight in running across the arching bridges. Under a canopy of green, the huge park beckoned children with its countless hiding places.

One time he had found a cat. A fluffy gray cat with blue eyes, with a metal tag on the collar, which read: "Duffy, please call 929-3570." He took Duffy home with him and once inside the shed, the killer gently removed the collar and went to work, opening his daddy's tackle box.

The animals always knew what was coming. They had more sense than people most of the time. One day he might take a hammer and smash a foot. Another day he might take a battery operated drill and see what it was like to drill their eyes out to the other side of their heads. Or maybe he would just burn their sexual organs with a Bic lighter. The first time an animal had screamed he'd dropped it, jumping back; sure the creature would break free and kill him. But of course, that never happened. In fact, if the animal were conscious, it would just look at him, whimpering and shaking. A feeling would overpower the killer, empower him, and he would just pick up where he had left off.

There was a look in their eyes that he found quite interesting. First expressions of despair, and then, realizing their fate was sealed, the animals would get this glazed, defeated look in their eyes. The killer had seen this look in some of the library books he checked out from time to time. Victims of medical experiments during WWII had this bland stare on their faces – like the photo of the concentration camp victim sitting in a tub of ice water for countless hours. The killer had been particularly interested in that one. The organized Nazi doctors had been leaning over the man, checking his vital signs, while the guy just sat there, obviously beyond hysteria, frightened beyond movement; or perhaps merely freezing to death. Whatever it was, the killer saw the same look on the animals he tortured right before they died. He liked that look because it confirmed his role as the conqueror. The incredible power over and life and death was his.

The excitement over Duffy's struggles and cries had been apparent in his pants. On that long ago day, he had freed himself from his jeans and let his nakedness hang. Then he had cut Duffy open, letting the blood gush warmly over his erection. He had masturbated, pretending the flowing blood was the soul of the cat flowing into him. The soul of the cat would give him catlike quickness and the ability to see in the dark. It would probably afford him nine lives – or at least some luck in that area. His grandma had often told him about the power behind the souls of the dead.

Outside the dim shed, the birds had chirped, enjoying the sunshine. Inside the shed, the killer became a cat.

The killer replaced Duffy's tag in the tackle box. Duffy wasn't the first animal he had experimented on, but he had been the last. The animals had begun to bore him.

He replaced the tackle box in its corner near the bureau and went to his computer, pulling on latex gloves as he took his seat. The killer put fresh paper in the printer tray, started his word processing program, and began to type.

Gabriel paid a visit to Kolbe Honda in the San Fernando Valley. Kolbe was a motorcycle super-store and he felt he could gather some useful information from the salespeople. He was here because the lab had finally given him the identity of the vehicle the suspect was using.

Gabriel parked near the service area and walked over to the polished chrome and glass building that showcased the motorcycles. He displayed his badge and the manager promptly assisted him.

"You've got dirt bikes that use Dunlops," Gabriel said, glancing at the lab's report. "Dunlop dual-purpose tires for a Two-twenty-five CC?"

"Sure, I've got them."

"I'm not much interested in the tires, but the dirt bikes they go with. My guys believe the tire in question came off a Yamaha XT 225. It's a combination dirt bike and moped."

"That's right. Unfortunately, I don't have any Yamaha XT 225 dirt bikes on the lot, but I've got some catalog pictures you could copy, if that would help."

"That would do."

The two men walked over to the manager's office, where they thumbed through catalogs until they found the Yamaha.

"That bike is a relatively new model, maybe a year old," the manager stated. "It's very light and similar to a moped, but has off-road tires. Good for handling dirt roads and such. 225's are more popular than mopeds because they're more versatile."

"Popular with whom?" Gabriel asked, busy writing in his spiral pad.

The manager shrugged. "Anyone who wants to have some fun on a trail; anyone who wants a motorcycle feel, without driving the real thing. You know, teenagers, weekend warriors, little old ladies from Pasadena..."

Gabriel grinned a little as he wrote. "Ha, ha. I have yet to see a grandma on a Harley."

"You'd be surprised," the manager replied.

"Maybe I would at that," Gabriel mused as he studied his notes. Biking off road was a popular recreational trend these days. Too popular. Gabriel wished there was some way he could narrow down his search for the killer. He proceeded to collect the names of some competitors that sold the same bike. He asked the salesman to compile a list of every sale of motorized dirt bikes made in the last two years from his store. The competitors would be asked to do the same.

The manager walked Gabriel to his Celica. "Sure you're not interested in trading this in for a bike, Detective?"

"No, thanks," Gabriel answered, and noticed for the first time that the manager wore a slick dark suit with a stylish white shirt. Not quite the attire Gabriel would have expected for pushing iron horses. A black leather jacket and jeans would have surprised him less.

Gabriel thanked the snappy dresser for his help and slid into his car, which was hot as an oven. He wiped his brow of perspiration, when something struck him.

He remembered standing under the hot sun at Pepperdine and envying the kids whizzing by on mopeds; bikes just like the Yamaha.

He leaned out his car and called to the sales manager, "Students buy this type of bike, don't they?"

"Absolutely. College kids know that to maneuver around campus, motor scooters beat a regular bike any day."

Gabriel nodded, waved goodbye and got back into his car. He pulled out his spiral pad once more and began scribbling some notes when a loud drilling suddenly punctuated the air around him. Gabriel swiveled in his seat to see a mechanic repairing a motorcycle in the service center.

The creeping fingers of discomfort inched through his body, leaving the hairs on the back of his neck standing on end. A wave of nausea coursed through him in an unwelcome tide. Gabriel gripped the steering wheel and closed his eyes.

What is it? Gabriel remembered how his palm burned with imaginary fire. He thought of Andrew Pierce and his forays into amateur auto repair. *What is it?* Suddenly, Gabriel glimpsed a flash of memory, something strange and disconnected. He saw the dime store in San Francisco where he used to buy candy as a boy and heard the theme song from the Gilligan's Island television show of the late sixties playing over and over; something about a fateful trip...

The headache crashed down on him with thundering impact – locking Gabriel's skull in a vice-like grip. The sheer suddenness of the pain caused his stomach to revolt, and Gabriel quickly leaned out the window to puke. Nothing came up.

When he could focus again, Gabriel fumbled for his aspirin bottle, and chucked three into his mouth. His stomach rebelled again and this time he yanked open his car door and vomited onto the pavement.

Time to call Dr. B, Gabriel thought miserably as he wiped his mouth, but instead he called Ming.

"I'm getting worse."

"You're not."

"Look, you've always been level-headed. You've always gotten straight to the point with me. You're a smart woman. Do you think – do you think I should go away somewhere and quit this case?"

Ming stared at Gabriel as she sat on his couch. She finally pursed her lips together in mock seriousness, and said, "Yes, Gabriel; I think that you should."

Gabriel blinked at her in surprise.

Ming had meant to surprise him, because she didn't like being toyed with. Gabriel lived for his work and she knew it. He knew it too.

She hated being a cliché, but as soon as he had called, she had come running. Halfway to his apartment, she'd berated herself. Turn around, go back! But had she listened to her own advice? No.

He said that he needed her. That's all it took.

"I brought whiskey," Ming said, reaching into her oversized handbag. She came out with a bottle of Glenfiddich.

"Nice," Gabriel said appreciatively.

"Any hitchhikers call you?"

"No." Gabriel shook his head and then quickly added, "Not yet."

"Since you're quitting the case anyhow, it doesn't matter."

"I'm not quitting, Ming. But you should have seen what happened today."

"What happened today?"

Gabriel looked like he was about to fess up when he swallowed his words. He walked to his kitchen and brought glasses down from the shelves. "Guess what?" he said. "It turns out the vehicle the suspect uses is part moped, part dirt bike. Perfect for off-roading and perfect for getting around a campus."

"Campus?" Ming asked. "You mean a campus like Pepperdine?"

"Well, it's a college in the vicinity, isn't it?" He set the glasses on the coffee table.

"That's wonderful. You've got a concrete lead to follow," Ming said, regarding him carefully. "But that's not all that 'happened today,' am I right?

Gabriel sighed. "You shouldn't be burdened with this."

"Burden me!"

"What are you, a welcome mat?" Gabriel said, looking away. "You deserve better."

"Gabriel, this self-pitying shit is getting old."

He sat next to her with a grin. "And I thought you liked my pout."

Ming smiled and took his hand. She stroked his fingers. He had beautifully sculpted hands.

"I didn't have a chance to shower," Gabriel admitted, watching her fingers touch his own. "Should I run into the bathroom and clean up?"

"If you're asking me if you stink, the answer is no."

He looked at her with his deep blue eyes and she wanted nothing more than to have him continue looking at her. Why were mystery men so attractive?

Ming toughened her expression and opened the whiskey bottle, pouring the amber liquid into the glasses without spilling a drop.

"Salud," she said, clinking his glass. "Where did you get the beautiful crystal? Did you split it down the middle with your ex-wife?"

"No, I gave everything to Sheryl except for my stereo. The glasses are from my mother."

There was a hard edge to the word "mother" and Ming thought it better to not push the subject.

"You want something for dinner?" Gabriel asked. "My stomach's a little – empty."

"I don't want to put you out."

"It's my form of relaxation."

"Personally, I prefer massages; but if you want to cook, please do!"

"I'll whip something up."

Dinner turned out to be penne pasta with a sun-dried tomato and caper sauce that Gabriel put together from ingredients in his pantry. Ming had made a salad. The two of them working together in the kitchen and talking non-stop gave Gabriel the alien feeling of contentment.

There is joy in this life, he thought, as he stirred the boiling pot of noodles and bit the celery stick that Ming stuck in his face.

She's so comfortable with herself, Gabriel observed as he watched her. She makes me comfortable being around her.

Things did not go badly until after dinner.

The table was littered with cloth napkins, plates and crumbs, burning candles at half-mast, and a near-empty whiskey bottle.

Gabriel and Ming went back to the leather couch, glasses of whiskey teetering on their knees. Skip Heller, a local LA jazz artist, played alluringly on the stereo and crooned about the things that were "rough" since his "last affair..."

"Here's to dinner," Ming said, hiking her glass into the air. The whiskey sloshed inside, almost spilling. "Oops."

Gabriel nodded, raised his glass, and looked at Ming through slightly blurred eyes. "Here's to great company and women who don't mince words."

Ming took another swig. "Dinner was delicious. I don't know how you do it."

"I'm getting old. Too much hunkering over a pot tweaks my shoulders."

Ming promptly set down her glass on the coffee table, and moved closer to Gabriel. "Here; turn around; I'll give you a massage."

Gabriel hesitated slightly, and then did as he was told, facing the opposite way. He felt fingers, light as butterflies, dancing on his shoulder blades. A calm rush swept over him and on the heels of that, a deep sexual tension in his groin. He hadn't been touched in so long.

"Do you like a harder massage or light pressure?" Ming asked.

Gabriel moved his neck back and forth under the signal of her hands. The whiskey was loosening him up. He mumbled something and then realized his speech was incoherent. Gabriel's mouth quickly picked up the slack and he said, "Whatever you're doing now feels great."

The compact disc ended and the stereo was silent. Outside, the city seemed to be asleep. Only the sound of their breathing and the rustle of his shirt being manipulated by Ming's slender fingers broke the quiet of the apartment.

She edged closer to him, smelling of fresh soap and a subtle spice.

Gabriel reached up, gently stilling her hands. He turned to face her and, before his fear could metastasize, he pulled her to him and kissed her. She tasted of whiskey and her tongue was soft and smooth. Her clothes, having become rumpled as the night wore on, afforded him a wonderful view of her cleavage, and he desired nothing more than to free her small, round breasts.

Ming's busy fingers were already loosening his tie, and heading for his shirt buttons. Under his own heated excitement he sensed a longing flowing from her, an unbridled passion. He could tell she had wanted this for a long time.

And it bothered him.

As Gabriel fervently wished his petty annoyances gone, they cooled his passion, overriding every exploring stroke of his tongue, preventing him from doing what he'd like to do – ripping Ming's clothes off her body.

This was Gabriel's pattern, of course. Searching for all the negatives in an intimate situation. Finding something about her to criticize. Gabriel pulled away from her and stilled her roving hands once more. He couldn't meet her eyes.

"What is it?" Ming whispered.

Gabriel heard the ice in his voice as he said, "I don't think this is a good idea." He let go of her hands and sat back, away from her.

"It's a good idea if we both want it," she said gently.

"It complicates everything." Gabriel reached for his whiskey glass.

"If you're thinking that maybe I'll expect something more from you because we– we go to bed together, then don't worry."

"Every woman says that," Gabriel countered, taking a large swallow of the liquor.

"I'm not every woman," Ming said, adjusting her blouse. She glanced wistfully at Gabriel, and then covered her expression with a brief smile. "The last thing I want to bring out in you is discomfort." She gave him a peck on the cheek and whispered, "Thanks for everything. It was a great evening."

Ming rose and reached for her purse. Gabriel grabbed her hand. "I'm really no good for you, Ming."

"I'm not a teenager, Detective McRay. I don't need anyone telling me who's good for me and who's not."

She pulled her hand away and headed for the door.

His eyes closed at the sound of the door shutting. Gabriel sat in the hush of his one-bedroom apartment, finally alone with the demons that could now feast off his wasted lust.

"Does not the history of the world show that there would have been romance in life if there had been no risks?"

Mohandas K. Gandhi (1869-1948)

CHAPTER 13

The following day Gabriel sat at his own laptop in Commerce, compiling his notes on the case. On his desk sat the latest Los Angeles Times article. Relatives of the murder victims were forming a support group that would be spearheaded by Brian Goldfield's ex-wife, who was living in Beverly Hills and, in Gabriel's opinion, wanted some media attention. *What else is new in Los Angeles?* He tossed the newspaper into his wastebasket.

Five people murdered, four chakras used, three chakras to go. Gabriel thought about the significance of the fifth chakra. This one related to self-expression and creative identity. Gabriel rubbed his forehead, contemplating what sort of person would fit the killer's idea of creative identity.

He reviewed his notes on the laptop monitor but Ming's face kept springing up in his mind's eye. *Think about something else.*

Teams of investigators were scouring antique weapons stores, trying to grab a lead on collectors of Russian military relics. The DNA test results were still not ready, but they would be helpful. Gabriel had directed an undercover team to hang around the university and ask questions. And then there were the notes to Gabriel.

Something should have rung a bell in my head with those notes, Gabriel thought. Something should have stood out. If he had some sort of blocked memory as Dr. B insisted he did, then Gabriel needed to get unblocked before someone else got killed.

Gabriel considered what he knew about the suspect. The suspect rode a Yamaha dirt bike, owned antique military weapons, and was possibly a student. Gabriel had no students in his circle of friends nor did he know anybody who collected vintage weapons.

Why did you blow it with Ming?

"Sergeant McRay?"

Gabriel looked up from his laptop to see a secretary standing at his desk.

"There's a witness in the interrogation room. Headquarters sent her here to talk with you and Lieutenant Ramirez."

"What witness?"

"She says she's responding to the flyers you posted. She had a strange hitchhiking experience."

The chair Gabriel had been sitting in fell backwards as he sprang out of his seat. The secretary, watching Gabriel's hasty exit, shrugged her shoulders and righted the overturned chair.

❧ ❧ ❧

Gabriel entered the interrogation room to find a thin, young woman with fine, honey colored hair. Her pale green eyes looked apprehensively at Gabriel. At her side sat Ramirez.

She introduced herself as Megan Farley and upon Ramirez's cue, she began speaking.

"I was driving along Decker Road, right before it dumps out into Westlake Village."

Ramirez and Gabriel shared worried glances. The killings had not occurred that far north, and if the suspect were looking for potential victims, then he was widening his territory.

"I saw someone flagging me down and I pulled over, thinking someone needed help, but then I saw it was this man wearing a shoulder holster and a gun."

The two cops eyed each other once more.

"If you saw a man with a gun, why did you stop?" Gabriel asked.

"I didn't think, I mean... I didn't really see the gun until I had already pulled up."

"Did the man take the gun out and coerce you with it?" Ramirez asked.

"Not at all. He showed me his badge. He said he was a detective with L.A. Sheriff – with you guys."

With a thumping heart but a level voice, Gabriel asked, "This man claimed to be an investigator? Did he identify himself? Did he give you a name?"

"He said his name was Detective McRay."

Gabriel regarded the girl silently for a moment. *He won't get away with it. Keep calm and ignore that look Ramirez is giving you.*

Gabriel calmly pulled the chair out from under the conference table and took a seat in it. He carefully clasped his hands together in a decent imitation of Dr. B.

"Miss Farley, I am Detective McRay."

The girl quickly looked Gabriel up and down, and after a moment, said, "Oh... Oh, I didn't know."

"Tell me what this 'detective' looked like, Miss Farley," Gabriel said with a tremor in his voice.

Again, the girl studied Gabriel with her pale eyes. "Well, it was really dark on the road, but he had black hair," she waveringly touched her own blond strands. "Like yours; and he seemed about your height. Maybe taller. He was wearing a baseball cap."

"What team?" Gabriel asked.

"Excuse me?"

"Did you catch an emblem or team name on the cap? A city maybe?"

"I think it was a Dodgers cap. I can't remember. The brim was pulled down low. He was pretty agitated, saying he was investigating the murders, and his car had broken down. He'd been walking for a couple of miles. He wanted to know if I could give him a lift into Westlake where his cell phone would work."

"Was he alone?"

"As far as I could tell."

"Anything else around him? Do you remember him carrying anything with him?"

"He had a briefcase."

Good thing her green eyes never got a look into that thing. Gabriel glanced at Ramirez, but the lieutenant was fixated on the witness. Gabriel turned to the girl and said, "Megan, look at me carefully. Am I really the man you saw at the side of the road?"

She swallowed, nervously studying his face, and said, "I don't think so. It was really dark, and I wanted to get outta there. Honestly, I couldn't make out much under his cap. I really didn't want to look at him."

She's scared, Gabriel thought, and pressured. He knew the minute he left the room Ramirez would press her into identifying Gabriel as the killer.

"What happened next?" Ramirez said.

"I didn't say yes or no, and he asked where I was going. I said I was on my way to work. He wanted to know where I work."

"And you said...?" Ramirez lowered his chin, allowing her to finish.

"I told him I'm a bartender at the Westlake Grill."

"And what did he say to that?" Gabriel asked, anxious to know. "Tell me Megan, what was his exact reaction as you remember?"

The girl picked at a speck of lint on her pant leg. "He just looked at me for minute – which I thought was kinda weird. I remember putting my car into drive, because you know, it was dark and I've been watching the news."

"What did he say?"

"He asked me how far I thought it was before civilization. That's how he put it: civilization. And I told him just a mile or so. He backed away from my car and said, 'That's okay, I'll walk.' He told me thanks anyway."

"When was this?"

"The night before last."

"What made you come in and tell us?"

"I saw the flyer posted on a telephone pole a few days ago. But I thought, him being a detective and everything – nothing was really the matter."

Ramirez wouldn't meet Gabriel's eyes. "Thank you, Sergeant McRay. Please wait for me in my office. I'll take it from here."

Gabriel nodded slowly, bade the girl with the pale green eyes goodbye, and walked out of the room, numb.

A day later, Gabriel sat in the interrogation room, only this time, he wasn't asking the questions; Rick Frasier was interrogating him. Rick wanted to know what he had been doing three nights ago. He wanted to know if Gabriel owned a dirt bike and certain antique weapons.

Ming entered the room followed by Anthony Hamilton. Rick kept firing questions at Gabriel but Gabriel kept one eye on Ming. After a quiet discourse between her and Anthony, the DNA tech retreated from the room. With halting steps, Ming approached Gabriel and asked if she could take a blood sample. They wanted his DNA to match up against the suspect's DNA. Lab results from the suspect's specimen were due any day.

Dr. B watched the goings-on through a one-way glass partition in frustration. Ramirez stood next to Dr. B; arms crossed as he watched the interrogation unfold.

"Wasn't Gabriel under surveillance three nights ago?" Dr. B asked.

Ramirez pulled a pack of Winstons from his jacket pocket and shook out a cigarette. "Two guys were on detail and they swore his car stayed put all night."

"Then why this?"

"McRay's apartment is next to an alley. He could have hopped the fence and took off. Who knows?"

"But he doesn't own a dirt bike, does he?" Dr. B argued. "And he doesn't have a collection of Russian weapons."

Ramirez turned toward the psychiatrist. "So maybe he has a secret stash."

"Miguel, it's not Gabriel and you know it."

"I don't know that, Doc. He's got major head problems, we've got notes that tell us he and the perp are 'one'–."

"You trust me as a forensic profiler, right?"

"You're not God, Berkowitz."

Stung, Dr. B pushed his glasses up his nose and crossed his arms as well. Defensive posture, he knew, but he couldn't help himself. "Gabriel suffers from an inferiority complex caused by a trauma he's unable to remember. Your suspect has <u>superiority</u>

complex, embodying the false belief that he's above other people. Basically, a superiority complex is nothing more than an overwhelming inferiority complex disguised."

"You know what's complex?" Ramirez asked, turning to Dr. B. "The mumbo jumbo that comes out of your mouth. I've got a witness, the only <u>live</u> witness in this case I might add; who put a positive ID on Gabriel as the same dude that thumbed a ride."

"What color were the hitcher's eyes?"

Ramirez' mouth hung open a notch. A second later he said, "It was dark and she couldn't tell."

"Could she read the badge clearly? What did the badge say?"

"She didn't mention it."

"She wasn't asked," Dr. B said, irritated. "You're in a rush to end this, Miguel. I know you've taken a lot of heat about this case; but for God's sake, taking one girl's testimony as proof of a man's guilt..." Dr. B chewed his lip for a moment, wondering if he should risk it. Patient/Doctor confidentiality was paramount. Dr. B watched Gabriel in desperation and then decided to take a chance. "Gabriel mentioned a name to me once; an Andrew Pierce."

"Andrew Pierce? From here or San Francisco?"

"Up north," Dr. B said, and could hear his father telling him he would never cut it as a therapist. "I can't give you any more details, Miguel, but it may be worth looking into."

"Don't worry, I'll check into Andrew Pierce," Ramirez assured him and brought his lighter up to the Winston dangling from his mouth.

"And will you promise not to take Gabriel off the case?"

The lighter's flame froze an inch from its target. "You're as crazy as he is."

"I do think Gabriel and the suspect are connected. But if you pull Gabriel off the case, he won't get any closer to remembering his past and the killer is in his past."

Ramirez regarded Gabriel for a moment through the glass. "I don't know. I don't like the idea of a detective following clues that may lead right to his own door."

"Trust me, Miguel."

Ramirez grunted and lit his cigarette.

Ming Li held the sample of Gabriel's blood in her hand as she exited the Homicide building and walked briskly to her car. Anthony Hamilton was waiting for her at the downtown lab, only Ming was melting like the watered down witch in The Wizard of Oz. She wanted to drop the vials of dark red onto the asphalt. Taking the DNA sample from Gabriel was torturous – both for her and for Gabriel. When she heard Anthony Hamilton had been dispatched to draw blood from Gabriel, Ming had intervened. She hoped that her presence would lessen Gabriel's ordeal, but instead, her being there had made the situation worse – much worse. Bad enough Gabriel had to be questioned by Rick the Rookie, but it must have completely crushed him to see her walk through the door, all business, and ask for a sample of his DNA.

Ming passed an industrial sized trash bin and she licked her lips. I could toss the sample in there, she thought wildly. Then she berated herself for thinking something so imbecilic.

I could replace this sample with the blood of someone else. Ming eyed the tubes in her hand. *I could do it before Anthony Hamilton ever saw the specimen.* No one would know the difference. The suspect's sample would be different than Gabriel's, that's all. Simple. Over and done with.

Ming entered her car, placed her hands on the steering wheel, and looked at the building where Gabriel was sitting under fire. How could she consider lying?

Gabriel doesn't need protection, Ming told herself, because he's not the killer. His DNA is going to be different than the suspect's, so why worry?

But she was worried. She was worried that the DNA would be a match.

Ming glanced wistfully again at the trash bin, and then quickly started her car and headed toward the lab.

CHAPTER 14

The traffic buffered him. Seeing nothing but the red brake lights of thousands of automobiles on the Santa Monica Freeway lulled Gabriel, allowing him to retreat into a private area where nothing mattered except avoiding fender-benders.

When he arrived at his apartment on Bay Street, Gabriel immediately went to the fridge and grabbed a bottle of beer. He uncapped it, put it to his lips, and then suddenly flung it across the room. The glass crashed mightily and the amber liquid made a frothy trail down the wall, quickly descending to the carpet. His cooking pots sat neatly on the stove in anticipation of his next culinary adventure. With one fell swoop of his arm, Gabriel sent them all clanging to the floor.

He trekked back to his bedroom looking for something else to destroy but, finding nothing; he collapsed upon his bed, wondering if maybe he should destroy himself. Gabriel ripped the Band-Aid from his muscular arm, staring at the small hole and feeling humiliated that Ming had witnessed his interrogation. He wondered if this was the intention of the killer – to torture Gabriel. But who was it and what had Gabriel done to warrant this vendetta? *I can't remember. Nothing and nobody comes to mind!*

Gabriel had researched the lives of recent parolees from his past cases but they were easily accounted for, and he discounted them as persons of interest. The other convicted perpetrators were still safely ensconced in prison.

Gabriel let his mind wander to Andrew Pierce for a moment. In retrospect, he could see that Andrew was exactly what Gabriel's mother had labeled him: a high school drop-out living off his parents, with no direction and nothing to do except tinker with his dump of a car. Thinking about Andrew fixing his car caused a black flower to bloom in Gabriel's chest, a blossom with unfurling petals that gave promise of a hideous scent. Gabriel abruptly flipped over in bed, turning away from the memories of Andrew Pierce.

He concentrated instead on his current predicament. Frankly, he was surprised Ramirez was keeping him on the case. Gabriel knew he would be watched very carefully. He wondered if his phone was tapped.

I could quit, he told himself, but what good would that do? If he quit they'd still watch him. If Gabriel could bring the true killer to justice, the Department would owe him much more than an apology.

Tomorrow he was scheduled to attend the victim's support group meeting in Beverly Hills. He could just imagine what those relatives of the victims would say if they found out that the main investigator of their case was also the main suspect.

❧ ❧ ❧

Brian Goldfield's ex-wife was a dyed blond skinny mix-ture of plastic surgery and diet pills. Imogene Goldfield's large Beverly Hills home, bought with the considerable settle-ment she had received from her late ex-husband, was fabricated in glass and mirror; the masterpiece of an expensive interior decorator.

Gabriel spoke at the meeting and brought the support group up to date; allowing them access to the few leads which could be made public. He kept the members ignorant of the typewritten notes and his own hunch about college students.

Gloria Lusk, the leggy, redheaded fiancée of Ted Brody, sat stirring a martini that Imogene Goldfield had dropped in her hand earlier. She didn't say much, just stared sadly into the clear vodka. The parents of Patrick Funston and Adam Parraco sat on opposite sides of Imogene's spacious living room; each pair telling a different story. Patrick's parents, standing next to a large Lalique crystal figurine, bemoaned the loss of a beloved son who had had a bright future. Mr. and Mrs. Parraco, leaning against a display case of Imogene's collection of crystal shoes, dolefully shook their heads, blaming Adam for the way he died; never having approved of his lifestyle.

Imogene herself sauntered around like the quintessential hostess, ignoring the solemnity of the meeting and entertaining as if for a party. A hired bartender served drinks and a caterer passed canapés. When it was her turn to ask questions, she stood up, the granddame, sniffling and claiming that the loss of Brian Goldfield was a detriment to society in general; that the world could possibly be heading toward apocalypse now that her husband's contribution to filmmaking was over.

Gabriel patiently weathered her monologue, recalling that by all accounts the Goldfield's divorce had been a particularly brutal war.

After a general discussion of investigative procedures, Gabriel and Dash wandered from person to person, attempting to answer questions on a more personal basis. Gabriel left Dash to engage Gloria Lusk in conversation and he continued working the room. At last Gabriel found himself standing above Tania Dankowski's son.

He was a big boy of nine or ten, with a moon face topped by a sandy crew cut. He stood near his father, a sad hulking man who had taken root in an armchair. The boy held his head sorrowfully and was quiet. Looking at him, Gabriel felt incredible empathy and a strange sense of desolation.

He crouched down in front of the boy. "Want to see a trick they taught me in magic school?"

The boy regarded Gabriel for a moment, and then slowly nodded.

Gabriel bent his thumb, pretending it was only half a digit. He bent a finger from his other hand and then put them both together in such a way that it appeared he was pulling away half his finger.

The boy smiled and asked how the trick was done. Gabriel obliged and showed him. He took hold of the boy's hands and manipulated his fingers.

How could you do that to a child? You're an evil, evil man!

Gabriel abruptly let go of the boy's fingers and stepped back.

"Like this?" Tania's son asked him.

Gabriel composed himself and nodded to the boy. He moved away and went into Imogene's oversized kitchen. He helped himself to a glass of water and hoped a headache wouldn't ensue.

Gabriel closed his eyes and leaned against the granite counter. Tania's son was tainted now. Tainted with tragedy that would affect him in such a way that he could never be the boy he was two months ago. Someday he would sit across from a therapist – spilling his guts to a stranger instead of living a happy life.

Gabriel opened his eyes to see Dash staring at him in concern.

"Are you okay?"

Gabriel pulled away from the counter and headed back toward the living room. "Aren't you getting tired of asking that question?"

Later, Gabriel and Dash went to Pepperdine to interview more students. Gabriel found quite a lot of moped/dirt bikes being utilized, and he was determined to question every owner.

He spent most of his day at the History and Russian Language Departments, but he did not find any clues that related to the murders. As he was talking to a counselor, he noticed a case filled with Russian medals. Again, his memory sparked for a brief moment—something in his youth. He knew something was there that had to do with Russian military artifacts... but what was it?

The evening brought another appointment with Dr. B. Gabriel sat in the armchair and for once, welcomed the opportunity for therapy. He desperately wanted to crack open his own shell.

"Ramirez thinks I did it," Gabriel told Dr. B.

"If he truly believed that, you'd be in custody."

"The DNA from the suspect has come in. Did you know that? White male. They're processing my blood now. They're waiting to see the match."

Dr. B pushed his glasses up the ridge of his nose. "You say 'the match,' not the results. Tell me, Gabe, do you think the two samples are going to match?"

Gabriel swallowed, surprised at the Freudian slip. He dug in his pocket for his aspirin bottle, and put a tablet into his mouth. "Everyone else thinks they'll match."

"I asked if you do."

Gabriel rested his elbow on the arm of the chair and rubbed his chin. "I'm not going to lie to you, I am worried. Where do I go when I'm in those fugue states?

"Somewhere comfortable I imagine. Some event triggers the suppressed memory, but before it can surface you check out – you go away from it before it can hurt you. Going on a killing spree is highly doubtful."

"How can you know for sure?"

I'm not sure, Dr. B thought, and felt the invisible presence of his dad frowning over his shoulder.

"Because you're not a killer, Gabe," Dr. B said. "Now let's talk about today. You went this morning to a victim's support group where this child had a profound effect on you."

"Yeah, I was touching his hands, showing him a trick, and um, I got this feeling."

"What kind of feeling?"

"Of being ashamed."

"Shame usually means guilt. What is it that you feel guilty about?"

Gabriel inhaled deeply and drummed his finger in an obscure beat along the arm of the chair. "I can't think of anything offhand."

Dr. B studied him. Gabriel studied the roving second hand of the wooden clock. In his head, he heard the voice of a harpy, assuring him he was an evil, evil man.

"Something I never told anyone," Gabriel admitted quietly, not taking his eyes off the ticking hands of the clock. "When I shot that guy at that Halloween party, I really did think he was going to shoot me, he was so drunk and belligerent. But right as I pulled the trigger for the second shot, I saw there was something wrong with the gun he had. I fired anyhow."

Dr. B said nothing and Gabriel continued, "I asked the ME back then to determine which shot killed him, the first or second; and he told me it was my first shot. It didn't matter. I still shot him a second time. And that kid with the knife and that old lady. Something burned inside of me which I couldn't control."

Gabriel smiled and continued. "Everyone thinks that old lady was some grandmotherly type." He chuckled without mirth and said, "She was a real sweet old lady that one. You know what she said when I showed her my identification? 'Get off my doorstep you cop-pig mother fucker before I put a cap in your ass."

Gabriel glanced quickly at Dr. B and continued, "Anyhow, you get the picture. When I saw that shotgun laying in plain view on the table behind her as she was riding me, I felt this rage swell up out of nowhere. I've always had this incredible anger brewing inside me. It's like carrying a demon around in my pocket."

Dr. B clasped his hands in front of him, and asked, "When did you first notice this 'incredible anger?'"

Gabriel reached for his aspirin bottle again and shook out another white pill. "When I was a teenager."

"What happened?"

"It's so fuc—frigging scary, you know?"

Dr. B nodded, understanding, but remained silent.

Gabriel continued, saying, "I was in charge of watching this kid when I was about seventeen. A babysitting job for some kid down the street. My sister took swimming lessons at his mother's swim school. You don't think of people hanging out by pools in San Francisco, but, hey, kids need to learn to swim and her school was the only one for miles. My mother volunteered me for the job. The boy was about six or seven. I think he had it bad in his house. I never knew what exactly went on there, you know, I was a stupid teen, what did I know or care? But I got the feeling things weren't very kosher in his house."

"The child told you he had it bad?"

"Never. I'd just catch the tail end of something. Anyhow, this kid really looked up to me, almost too much, like I was his savior or something. I liked it. He was a smart little guy, and I used to take him to Golden Gate Park where we would take the boats to the island. We would find hideouts and do all the things that boys like to do."

"Then why the rage?"

"I don't know," Gabriel said in almost a whisper, and he shook his head. "I don't know what happened. One day, I looked at him and I wanted to hurt him. It wasn't anything he did necessarily, I just went off. I was in a bad mood to start with that day and I resented having to watch him, and I..." Gabriel picked at his fingernails nervously. "I beat him up. I beat him up. I punched him in the stomach. I can't believe it."

A tear escaped Gabriel's eye and he quickly wiped it away. "I threw him against the wall. Jesus, I don't know why I did it."

"He told his parents."

"No, that's the thing; this kid loved me so much he didn't tell. I don't know. I can't remember how it all went down. I think I've blocked it, but – oh, I don't know."

"No, Gabriel, listen to me, please go with this; don't block it." Dr. B edged forward in his seat. "Please tell me. He didn't tell his folks, but what happened?"

"I guess his mom must have seen the bruises or something, because–I'll never forget it as long as I live."

"Forget what?"

"She spat at me and called me an evil man. I remember thinking it was weird to be called a man, because I'd never thought of myself as a man before that. She asked me how I could have done such a thing to a child."

Dr. B swallowed. "You left San Francisco when you were a teen, didn't you?"

"Yeah, soon after that."

"Was this why?"

"I don't know. I don't think she ever told my mother, but you can bet I never went there again."

"You never told your parents."

"No, I didn't."

"What about now?"

"I don't speak much to them."

"Why not?"

Gabriel studied Dr. B's wooden clock again. "I don't care much for them."

"Why not?"

"I was a latch key kid, remember? They didn't have much to do with me when I was a kid, I don't have to have much to do with me now that I'm grown."

Dr. B nodded and rubbed his lips with a bony finger, lost in thought.

"Where do you think the rage comes from?" Gabriel asked.

Dr. B answered with a question. "Tell me Gabriel, was the beating of this boy the memory that pains you so much you've blocked it?"

"No. I wish I could block this memory. I've remembered his face since the day it happened. I just couldn't tell you, Raymond. I'm sorry. I've never told anyone."

"Then the rage originates from something else. Door number two."

Gabriel blew out a breath, looking away. "God, I wish this was all over. I want to remember, I do!"

"Then let's continue with hypnosis next session. I should warn you though; this was a great revelation today."

"Why is that a warning?"

"Because door number two is about to swing open, I think. You're right next to it with your hand on the doorknob. You were able to confess something today that you've hidden forever. You are less afraid now; less afraid means being ready to open that door."

"Should I quit the case?"

"On the contrary," Dr. B told him. "You said yourself this case is bringing you closer to closure."

"But how and why?"

Dr. B sat back in his chair. "That, my friend, is something you're going to tell me."

Gabriel returned home that night, his brain feeling like a stuffed sausage. He had been given so much to think about. To get his mind off the events of the day, Gabriel turned to the chakra books. As he hoisted the first one onto his lap, the raven-haired saleslady's card fluttered out. Gabriel was bending to retrieve it from the carpet when everything went black.

CHAPTER

Meredith Hall flipped up the cosmetic mirror in disdain and looked at her husband, Ronald, who was driving. His graying hair and sun-baked complexion was only making him look more distinguished. It's certainly a man's world, she thought unhappily, turning her gaze out the window.

They were taking their newly purchased Lexus for a drive to meet some friends for a late dinner at Geoffrey's, a beachfront establishment with a penchant for attracting movie stars. They passed Tapia Park. Seeing the rocky hills encrusted with chaparral made Meredith a bit melancholy. Once upon a time, she had hiked these hills without a moment's thought as to how her nails looked or if her eyeliner was on straight. Now, she wouldn't be caught dead going outside without makeup. When did manicures and facials go from sporadic luxuries to weekly rituals? She was a slave to the beauty salons and had a retinue of stylists, facialists, personal trainers, and nutritionists.

Meredith studied her fingernails in the sunlight streaming in from the open sunroof. They weren't her nails, not really. They were acrylic overlays that needed constant care. Her jewelry, however, wouldn't look good on hands with stubby fingers.

Society put unfair pressure on women, Meredith complained silently. She was constantly fighting – fighting to keep weight off, fighting the gray hair, fighting wrinkles and sagging skin. Meredith gazed out the window again, scanning the moonlit peaks and the dark crevices of caves. The hills hadn't changed, but she had. She had gone from a cheerful, natural beauty to a high-maintenance mannequin, striving for life out of a magazine ad. Once upon a time she had been a painter, an artist. She still painted, but no one took her seriously. She had sold a painting once, to a man who later committed suicide. She liked to think that the passionate strokes of her paintbrush had driven the man to interminable frustration.

She glanced back at Ronald. He never said anything, but after twenty-five years of marriage, Meredith knew what he was thinking. He had a plastic wife, not the freewheeling artist to whom he was first attracted. Would a younger, more natural woman attract him someday?

Ronald caught his wife looking at him and winked at her.

She smiled gratefully. Maybe he wasn't thinking badly about her at all.

As they rounded a curve in the road they saw, up ahead at a dirt turnout, an old man; his hair white and wild in the moonlight, blown by the Santa Ana winds. He seemed to be wandering dementedly, talking to himself, and clutching a bulging grocery bag to his chest.

"Is he crazy?" Ronald asked his wife. "What's that guy doing out here?"

Ronald slowed a bit and Meredith stared at him. "You're not stopping, are you?"

"Well, don't you think we ought to? We can offer our cell phone."

"It doesn't work in the canyons," Meredith told him dryly.

The car slowly passed by the agitated old man. Ronald pulled the Lexus into the dirt turnout, and said, "Are you okay?"

The old man wouldn't look at them; he seemed to be waiting impatiently for something. Finally, he said in weak voice, "My nephew Alan, my nephew Alan – he was supposed to meet me here and take me to his house tonight."

Ronald exchanged curious glances with his wife, and said, "Your nephew was supposed to pick you up <u>here</u>? How did you get here? Did you walk?"

The man waved Ronald away, still scanning the passing cars.

"Do you live around here?" Ronald pressed.

"Yeah, I live – I live off that street," the old man said, pointing toward a one-lane road that wound its way into the mountain.

"Why don't we take you back home? It's late and you shouldn't be standing out here in the dark."

The old man shook his head, and said, coughing, "I told Alan I would meet him right here and here I have to stay!"

"Okay," Meredith said, acquiescing.

Ronald shot her a disapproving look. "What time did your nephew say he was picking you up?"

"He told me two nights." He coughed again. "In two nights he would pick me up."

Again, the Halls exchanged glances. Ronald put the Lexus in park and got out. "Look, you can call Alan at your home and tell him to pick you up there."

"You think so?" the old man asked weakly.

"I know so," Ronald said, "Here, let me help you in the car."

"No!" the old man cried, avoiding his touch. "I can walk myself."

The old man entered the car tightly clutching his paper grocery bag, as Ronald shrugged, winking at his wife.

"Were you going to stay with your nephew for awhile?" Meredith asked.

The old man nodded, saying, "Yes. Just for a night to visit with his kids."

Ronald got back in the Lexus and rolled onto Malibu Canyon Road. He drove toward the tree-bordered entrance of the side street the old man had indicated.

Meredith glanced at their passenger in the rearview mirror. The old man seemed nervous. Well, he'd been waiting on a dangerous road for a pickup. That could cause anyone to become nervous.

The Lexus hummed genially beneath them.

"Just ahead?" Ronald asked.

"Yes, right up this street – at the top," the old man wheezed.

"You walked from up there?" Meredith asked.

"I need my exercise," the old man said.

Meredith studied him in the rearview mirror. A field of gray stubble grew on his cheeks and his nose was bent, his earlobes elongated with age.

"Such a nice car," the man said.

"It's brand new," Ronald told him.

"You must do well. What do you do for a living?"

"I'm in advertising."

Meredith smiled at Ronald's modesty. He was CEO of a very large advertising firm. She was still smiling when the old man asked her what her job was.

"I'm an artist," she said, gazing at the star-studded sky winking through the sunroof.

The old man quieted down for a moment, seeming to take everything in, and then blurted, "How nice!"

An uneasy feeling swept over Meredith. There was something odd about the old man, something not quite right. She could have rationalized his strangeness as senile dementia, but she had a queer hunch that he wasn't senile at all.

Ronald, who was usually gregarious with strangers, kept strangely silent. Meredith thought maybe he was getting the same peculiar vibe.

"Why would your nephew let you walk alone at night like that?" Meredith asked the old man.

"Meredith," Ronald said, admonishing her.

"Well, he could have been hit by a car!" She turned to face their back-seat passenger and found him staring at her with alert blue eyes.

Something's wrong, Meredith knew it intuitively. And there was something else becoming apparent, a strong, pungent odor. What was it?

Ronald must smell it too, Meredith thought, for now he was scanning the front panel of the Lexus, looking for a warning light.

"Do you smell gasoline?" he finally asked.

Gasoline, Meredith thought. Of course, but where was it coming from? She turned back to the old man, who was digging through his grocery bag.

"Just up a little further," the old man said.

Something's wrong, Meredith thought again, watching the old man rifling through his bag. Fright suddenly bloomed in her stomach, and Meredith wished, truly wished, they hadn't stopped their car.

"I can't turn here," Ronald remarked. "This is a dirt road. There aren't any more houses up there."

"Turn anyways," the old man said, and pulled out a gun. He smiled, showing off strong, white teeth.

His grandfather used to push him on the swing as long as the Malibu Canyon Murderer wanted (and it was always a long time), and his grandfather would listen to everything the little boy said. He marveled at how sensitive and creative his grandson was. He would smile at every word and never berate the boy or tell him he was stupid. In fact, his grandpa often complimented him. They would play tag, and hide-and-go-seek and all the games he never played at home. Grandpa was perfect.

He often asked his grandfather if he could come live with him as they strolled the paths of the park, hand in hand.

"Dedushka, can I go home with you?"

The old man would fall silent, and then explain that the killer's parents would be very angry if he took him away. "Vnuk," he would say, "this way is better."

But he could see the old man's eyes mist and knew his grandpa didn't mean it.

The elderly man would take off his hat, sadly wipe his brow, and explain to his grandson that Grandma was a very sick woman. Not sick in her body, but sick in her mind. He didn't think she could raise a boy properly.

The killer didn't know if "being raised properly" meant the beatings that he endured when his father was draped in booze or the cold that radiated from his mother. For his part, the killer never talked badly about his parents. They were, after all, the gods of his existence.

Grandpa had been an artisan and made little sculptures out of brass. On one Easter he gave the killer an intricately scrolled brass egg. Looping around the perimeter of the egg was the word "dedushka," which meant Grandfather. The egg opened like a box and inside the killer had found candy.

"Thank you, Dedushka," he had said politely, looking up at his grandfather.

The old man bent over and planted a kiss on his grandson's head. "So, you always have something of your Grandpa, yes?"

"Always." The killer nodded and reached up to hug the old man.

One Christmas his grandfather gave the killer a little brass tree that opened the same way and was filled with treats, and on a Valentine's Day one year he was presented with a box that had two entwined hearts on the lid. Each heart had an engraved inscription: "Dorogoy" which meant Dear and "Vnuk," meaning Grandson.

The days at the park didn't last too long. His grandfather passed away, leaving to the killer all his war medals, uniforms, a Red Army issue gun, and a Camillus M3 military knife that Grandpa had gotten by trading with an American soldier. Grandpa had treasured that knife because it was from America – the land of the free and the brave. The knife was manufactured by the Camillus Cutlery Company in New York around 1943 and measured six and a half by one inch. It had a black blade, a grip composed of leather washers cut with six grooves, and a metal tip on the end – a real beauty.

In special deference to his grandfather, the killer made good use of the knife. Grandpa's knife was helping him to better himself. And even though Mom had hated Grandma, when the old woman came to live with them, she became the source of his education regarding souls in search of homes.

With that thought in mind, the killer dipped his fingers in Meredith's blood, and began writing on the windshield.

The houses built on the small canyon roads pay a king's ransom for fire insurance every year. The insurance companies insist on rooftop sprinklers, fireproof roof tiles, and brush clearance around a large perimeter of the house, all at the owner's expense. Residents know how vulnerable they are to the sweeping hand of flames. But living in the serene mountains, while being conveniently close to a large metropolis, is more than enough reason for many of them to take the risk.

Sy Epstein had lived in his house for ten years. He finally saved enough money after years of running his own jewelry store to build the house of his dreams at the top of a curving, one-lane road. No one bothered him and he didn't bother anyone. He just lived with his wife, Linda, and their poodle, Jimmy. They kept Jimmy indoors at night because of the coyotes and the cougars, but other than that, the hills were a blessing to a man who had made his fortune in the hectic world. Life was good.

Sy had just come out to his balcony, which had an incredible view of the mountains, to sit down to an early breakfast. Suddenly Linda, wearing a bathrobe and following right behind him, said, "I smell fire."

Sy sniffed the air. He put his breakfast plate on a glass-topped wrought-iron table and scanned the pink, hushed Santa Monica Mountains with careful eyes. He didn't see anything.

"Look there!" Linda called, and pointed at a plume of smoke issuing from the other side of their house. Sy raced through the house, flung the front door open and ran into his front yard.

Sure enough, he saw flames coming from behind a large stand of coastal oak that grew right beyond the dead-end sign at the top of his street. Sy ran over and immediately saw a car on fire behind the brush.

"Linda!" he yelled back to his waiting wife. "Call the firemen!"

Being prepared for this, Sy turned on the sprinklers surrounding his landscape and unwound a long hose. He turned the water on full blast, the spray barely reaching the burning car.

"Goddamn people," he muttered, shaking his head as he turned the force of the water between the car, the brush, and his own roof. "When I find out who left their shitty car there, I'm gonna kill them."

The press had found Gabriel's apartment and were gathered at his door. Gabriel was in no mood to talk to them. He ignored their pleas for an interview and their incessant knocking.

Outside, a merry afternoon sun beamed down on them. A few people whizzed by on roller blades, unfazed by the clutch of reporters haunting the apartment building. The day was too nice and the beach called.

Inside, the phone was ringing, but Gabriel was unable to answer it. He was too busy staring at his clothes. The last time he was conscious of anything was yesterday. These weren't the clothes he remembered wearing yesterday. In fact, the shirt, pair of pants, and windbreaker he wore had completely disappeared. He had no recollection of the night before or this morning.

"Detective McRay," he heard, muted, through his front door. "Can you please give us a little more on the Malibu Canyon Murderer?"

"Leave me alone," he whispered, and fingered the buckle on his belt. Who had clasped this belt? And when?

Gabriel slid onto his couch and buried his face in his hands. He wondered if death wouldn't somehow be better than this dark space he was living in.

"Detective McRay," a reporter called, thrumming his fingers on the door, "has anything new developed?"

"I'm developing a breakdown," Gabriel muttered, as he rose and walked into his bedroom. He picked up his ringing phone, hung it up, then lifted the receiver and dialed Dr. B's phone number.

The doctor's voicemail answered and Gabriel said, "Emergency session needed." Gabriel hung up. The phone immediately rang again. Gabriel picked it up.

"Hi, Sergeant McRay? This is Gary at Gold's Gym. I just wanted to ask you—"

"Fuck you," Gabriel said simply, and replaced the receiver. He went to his bureau, grabbed the aspirin bottle resting on top, and gulped down a couple of white tablets. The phone rang again, and he picked it up.

"Fuck you," he repeated.

"Fuck me?" Ramirez barked.

Gabriel's shoulders tensed. "Sorry, Lieutenant—"

"No, fuck you, fuckhead," Ramirez told him in his Spanish-accented baritone. "You fucking lame fucking turkey. We've got two more dead fucking fucks out there in fucking Malibu Canyon and the Captain's tearing a new hole in my fucking—"

Gabriel hung up and ran through his apartment, grabbing his notepad, pager, phone, and briefcase, which contained a camera, a small tape measure, and his evidence collection kit. He threw open his front door to the surprise of the reporters standing there and ran past them, into his car.

Gabriel slid under the yellow tape wound around the crime scene, looking for his partner. The Mobile Crime Scene Unit was already there, taking pictures and lifting prints. Three fire trucks were there as well, although the brush, thankfully, had not caught fire.

He spotted Dash standing near a quieted fire engine. His partner looked angry upon seeing Gabriel.

"Where were you? We've been calling you; we've been paging you," Dash said, striding over to him.

"I didn't even check my pager," Gabriel confessed.

"Obviously," Dash said. "Where were you?"

Gabriel shook his head. *Not now.* He nodded to the burned Lexus. "Is this from our guy? Was there a victim?"

"There are two of them," Dash answered, staring fixedly at Gabriel. "But the meat wagon is long gone."

Gabriel looked around. The crime scene was being cleaned up. He had missed the action.

"Gabe," Dash began, exasperated, "where <u>were</u> you last night and this morning?"

Gabriel glanced at his partner. "Couldn't your boys tell you?"

"I'm asking you," Dash said, searching Gabriel's eyes.

"I was at home."

"Your car was there, but you weren't." .

"I went to sleep early and I slept late," Gabriel lied, and added sarcastically, "Things have been a little stressful lately."

"You left sometime last night. They saw you hop into the alley, but they lost you."

Gabriel looked toward the charred and blackened car, shuddering, trying to remember. He had jumped over the wall? Where had he been going?

Dash took a deep breath and came close to Gabriel. "You and me have known each other a long time. We've been through a lot of shit together. What—" he paused and then whispered, "For Christ's sake, Gabriel, did you do this?"

Gabriel wiped the sweat from his brow with the back of his hand. "I couldn't have. But—it's crazy..." he shook his head, and then sighed at his partner. "I blanked out again."

Dash viewed the mountains dotted with oak and chaparral and made no comment.

"I spaced out and I don't know what happened to me." Gabriel pulled at his clothes. "See these pants? This shirt? I don't remember putting them on."

185

Two MCU officers passed them, toting fingerprint kits and cameras. The detectives were silent.

"I didn't do this, Dash," Gabriel said in a low, desperate voice when the others were gone. "God, you know I didn't kill these people."

"I'm with you, okay?" Dash assured him. "Can you handle this today?"

Gabriel nodded. He had to appear as normal as possible.

The two partners gazed at the Lexus. Odors hung in the air, a fried electrical smell and a sickening, meaty stench. Finally, Dash recited, "I arrived on the scene as the fire department was dousing the flames. We didn't find any bodies in the car's interior. The fire department opened the trunk and we found the two victims. The victims were identified as Ronald and Meredith Hall, who reside in the Victory Estates area.

"Were there any notes on them?"

Dash shrugged and then motioned Gabriel over to a patch of dirt near the coastal oaks. "Come over here."

Gabriel crouched down and studied the dirt. "The Yamaha track."

"Yep."

The Mobile Crime Scene Unit was setting up to photograph the track. They brought out a special camera, mounted on a frame that pointed directly downward. This ensured that the photo could reproduce the exact size of the original track later at the lab. An officer then sprayed the track's surface with a fixative similar to shellac.

A frame of wood was placed around the section of track, and then, working with extreme care, the officers poured plaster into the frame.

Gabriel volunteered to search for twigs and grass from the surrounding soil to be used as reinforcement for the plaster. Later, he would use a twig to carve in his initials and the date into the drying plaster. Then the cast would be lifted out and placed in a cardboard box, providing the lab with the track plus the associated earth and twigs from the crime scene, in case a forensic botanist was called in.

As Gabriel sifted through the dirt closest to the tire track, he noticed some white flecks in the soil. Curious, he rolled the flecks in his fingers. They were miniscule pebbles of some hard white substance.

Gabriel fished an evidence tube out of his briefcase, and dropped the white flecks inside.

"Make sure you collect soil samples of this whole area," Gabriel told the MCU officers. "And I want to see any reports from previous soil pickups."

Gabriel stood up, wiping dirt off his hands, and noticed Dash talking to an elderly, but fit-looking man who was gesticulating wildly toward the burned out Lexus. Gabriel walked over to them.

"Detective Gabriel McRay," he said to the older man, extending his hand.

The man shook it heartily, and said in a raspy voice. "Sy Epstein. This is my house. I saw the fire. I can't believe there were really dead bodies in that car!"

"I'm afraid there were," Dash told him.

"Can you beat that? A man can't even move into the mountains to escape urban decay."

Dash turned to Gabriel, and said, "I'm going to talk to Mr. Epstein awhile longer. Can you go downtown? I know Ming will start the examinations on the Hall couple right away."

"Sure, I've got a soil sample I want to get to the lab anyhow," Gabriel said.

"What did you find?"

"I'm not sure. Something different though. I'll keep you posted."

"Hang in there," Dash told him.

As Gabriel descended the private road and headed toward the coast highway, he could see the unmarked car trailing him.

CHAPTER 16

"**W**e've got two more?"

Ming looked up at Gabriel as he entered the autopsy room. Her gloved hands hovered over the bodies of a man and woman, a husband and wife.

"Where have you been?" she asked worriedly. She already knew that Gabriel's stakeout team had witnessed him leave his apartment on foot.

"I was tied up," he said, pulling on latex gloves.

Ming surveyed Gabriel's appearance. He looked sweaty and haggard, like he had been up all night.

A deputy coroner shot photographs of the bodies laid out before them on identical steel tables. The snapping sound of his shutter echoed loudly in the sterile room.

Gabriel stood tensely above the autopsy tables, his blue eyes fixated on the bodies. "Let's see what he left for me this time," he told Ming.

Ming felt her insides caving. While she was sure that the Department's suspicions of Gabriel had no basis in fact, his midnight adventures chipped at the foundation of her belief.

He had crept out late last night and two bodies had surfaced this morning.

He's not a murderer. You would never be attracted to someone who could commit such atrocities, Ming assured herself. She obediently moved to the steel counter and pulled the two plastic sandwich bags off a metal tray. Using tweezers, she carefully extracted the notes folded within the bags, and looked once more at Gabriel.

Gabriel reached out his hand and took the first note from her. He read out loud: "You are moving away from everything you know." Ming watched him digest the words for a moment and then Gabriel returned the first note to her and took the second note.

Gabriel stood motionless, reading the second note silently, and then out of nowhere he began crushing the paper in his fist.

Surprised, Ming grappled for the note, yelling, "What are you doing? Ident hasn't seen this yet!"

"It doesn't matter!"

"Gabriel!" Ming succeeded at pulling the paper from Gabriel's shaking hands without tearing it. She gaped at him and then her eyes dropped to the macabre words printed on the page: "These two tempted me. The young ones tempt you, don't they?"

She swallowed, jerked her eyes at Gabriel, and said desperately, "What's he talking about? You can tell me!"

Gabriel made no reply. He only gazed wistfully at the dead couple. The deputy coroner took his photographs, apparently trying to ignore the drama in the room. The snapping shutter noises caused Ming to jump, as if he fired a gun.

Gabriel moved away and leaned against the stainless steel tubs.

Ming pulled off her mask and gloves and placed her hands on his shoulders. His muscles were hard and twisted with tension. Tentatively, she leaned her head against his back. He didn't move.

Being close to him, feeling the breath within his body, created a longing in her she could barely contain. "Everything will work out, Gabriel," she told him. "You'll see; it will all work out."

"Please Ming, leave me alone."

Ming felt coldness radiating from Gabriel, not only in the tone of his voice but also off his rigid body. She slowly lifted her head and removed her hands from his shoulders. She gazed at him as she backed away. She then regarded the murdered couple laid out on her exam tables and thought of doomed unions.

"Could I have done this?" Gabriel sat across from Dr. B and looked at the psychiatrist with a defeated expression and lonely eyes. "Under these 'fugue states'," Gabriel continued slowly, "could I have butchered these people?" A tear escaped his eye. He quickly wiped it away, embarrassed at how raw his emotions had become. He cleared his throat and sat up straighter, a parody of a man composed. "When I—when I'm myself again, I'm wearing different clothes. What if I've killed these people and then I clean up and change clothes. This guy is supposedly white, athletic... Am I a murderer?"

"Are you?"

"Don't hand that clinical bullshit to me," Gabriel told him squarely, and then his shoulders slumped. "Please, I'm begging you."

Dr. B asked, "Do you own the weapons used?"

Whenever thoughts of the Russian Nagant and the military knife surfaced, Gabriel couldn't help but feel that he'd forgotten something important.

"Maybe my 'other half' owns the weapons."

"Your other half?" Dr. B questioned. "I said I feel you suffer from fugue states. I never said anything about multiple personality disorder. No, Gabriel, I don't think you become someone else, someone homicidal in your fugue states."

"You don't think," Gabriel echoed hollowly.

"That's right."

"Thinking isn't good enough. People are dying. There's a monster out there." His voice lowered to a whisper. "Is it me?"

"I think the sooner this case is solved—"

Gabriel guffawed, and said sarcastically, "Solve the case." He stood up brusquely, gathered his things, and looked soberly at Dr. B. "Maybe the guys tailing me should chain me up at night, like those mythical peasants did with people they thought were werewolves. Has Ramirez told you he has 'probable cause' to make my arrest yet?"

"Wait a minute, wait a minute –" Dr. B said, waving at him to sit down. "Whatever is happening with these notes seems to be making your condition worse. In my opinion, that gets you closer to solving your problems."

"If it's making me worse, how can I be solving my problems?"

"Door number two, remember? You're coming closer to what you fear the most," Dr. B explained. "That's why your mental system is on overload. I can tell you, Gabriel that you will not recover from PTSD until you feel safe. If you continue to avoid the dark spaces – the fear, you will not get cured. 'Reconsideration involves an ability to confront the trauma, and then become a survivor who can integrate the catastrophe into his or her life history, and use it as a source of strength.' Figley said that."

Gabriel frowned. "Who the hell is Figley? And what the hell did you just say?"

"Figley is someone knowledgeable in this field who wrote something worthwhile. The most important thing you need to remember is to go forward. Try not to identify too much with the mind games this suspect is playing on you, but stick with this case even if it causes you pain. Even if it causes you to fall into a fugue state again."

"That's easy for you to say."

"You're still up for hypnosis, right?"

"I guess so," Gabriel answered pensively.

"I think it will definitely speed up the process."

Gabriel stood pondering for moment, and then slowly sank back into the chair. "Say it's not me that's doing these things. You said the suspect and I were connected somehow. Who is he and why is he doing this to me?"

"Look Gabriel, he could be just a stranger, some deranged individual who has targeted you because of your media attention and by mere chance is able to push your buttons." Dr. B paused, pushing his glasses up on his nose. "Then again, he could be someone who knows you—someone who knows something about you. In your quest to find him, you've been finding things out about yourself."

"He's right about me, you know," Gabriel said.

Dr. B cocked his head. "How so?"

"He said I'm moving away from everything I know. I couldn't have put it better myself. I feel divorced from everything normal." Gabriel looked away.

Dr. B shook his head. "You're not though. Like I told you, you're stepping closer to what you fear, that's all. You're exploring new territory. Fear is a defense mechanism. We think somehow our fear protects us, but really it's no good. Once you confront the trauma, the fear will dissipate and so will all the symptoms. Don't be afraid. This is the time to jump in."

The following day, Gabriel sat on the expansive lawn at Pepperdine University facing the ocean and watching the waves break. The beach was crowded with sunbathers; brightly colored umbrellas decorated the sand. A hurricane in Mexico had sent moist gray clouds north, and Gabriel could feel the humidity under his jacket. He was tired.

Gabriel had trekked through one college department after another, sure his quarry lurked somewhere on campus. He had interviewed students, professors, and employees– anyone even remotely associated with Russian artifacts, military or otherwise – and had come up empty-handed.

The young ones tempt you.

A headache was buzzing around Gabriel's brain, searching for a place to nest. *The young ones tempt you.*

Gabriel flashed on the fifteen-year-old boy's face as he choked him—the kid's bulging eyes, his protruding tongue; the harshness of his partner's hands as Dash grabbed Gabriel's shirt, yanking him off the boy.

The young ones tempt you.

You're identifying with this creep, Gabriel told himself, just like Dr. B warned. The suspect is playing mind-games, and you're listening with baited breath.

The young ones tempt you, the young ones tempt you, the young ones tempt you—

He saw Tania Dankowski's big boy. *The young ones tempt you, the young ones tempt you...*

Feeling burned out, Gabriel fished for aspirin, took two, and headed for his car. He had to get to Monterey Park for a meeting with the rest of the investigative team to compare notes.

His cell phone rang as he crept along the Santa Monica Freeway.

"Am I bugging you?" Ming asked.

"Not at all," he answered into the phone. As soon as he heard her voice he felt a troubled mix of relief, excitement, and shame. He had to be on the alert. Gabriel was used to walking away at this point. Ming was so compassionate, and he kept snapping at her helping hands like a rabid dog.

"I wanted to see how you are doing?" he heard her say. Ming sounded unsure of herself. Why did it repulse him when other people were insecure? Was Gabriel the only one who had sole rights to being messed up?

"I've been an idiot," he blurted before the ice could freeze his mouth. "I keep pushing you away when—"

"I'm the idiot," Ming said. "I come on too strong. I push too hard—"

"You were trying to help me and I was a jerk."

"You're under terrible pressure. Look, Gabriel, just because things are not going to work out <u>that</u> way, we can still be friends—"

"Wait a minute," Gabriel interrupted. "You don't think things will work out?"

He heard Ming catch her breath and could imagine her raised eyebrows. "I assumed—"

"Don't assume." A driver quickly cut into Gabriel's lane. "Hey, shithead!"

"What?" Ming cried.

"I'm sorry," Gabriel said into the phone. "I'm on the freeway. Listen, don't you know what happens to someone when he assumes?"

There was silence on the other end, and then he heard some gaiety in Ming's voice as she asked with feigned innocence, "He becomes a shithead?"

"No, he becomes an ass," Gabriel told her, smiling in his car.

"You certainly have a way with women, Gabe."

"I'm horrible with women. But you hang in there, Doctor Li, okay?"

He heard no reply.

"Ming?"

"I promise," she said. "Am I coming on too strong if I ask you out to the theater this Saturday night?"

Keep the warmth in your voice, Gabriel commanded himself, and said aloud, "This Saturday night I expect you to come on to me real strong."

"I'll take that weak attempt at a one-liner as a 'yes.' See you at the meeting."

Gabriel hung up and, for the first time in a long while, felt his shoulders relax.

"The lab called regarding the tire track area," Ramirez said, slapping a file of reports down on the conference table.

Dr. B sat next to Ming, who sat next to Gabriel. Dash sat opposite, lodged between Paul Vacher and Rick Frasier.

Dash spoke up proudly. "We're checking out all the area dirt bike dealerships and their Yamaha customers of the past two years. We've narrowed it down to about ninety individuals that fit the profile that Dr. B has provided, and Gabriel has vigilantly been tackling the student-as-suspect angle."

Ramirez stared at him long and hard. Finally he sneered, "Here's your fucking gold star, Señor Spiceless. That's not what I was going to talk about."

"Oh," Dash said, turning pink. "Sorry for interrupting."

Ramirez rolled his eyes in exasperation and turned to Gabriel. "The lab called and told me they've identified that plastic residue you found in the soil at the Hall scene. Now, it's definitely not indigenous to the area, which means the substance could have come off the bike itself, could have been left there previously by someone else, or could have come off the suspect."

"Could it have come off the victims?" Dash asked.

Vacher shook his head, saying, "We combed that Lexus inside and out. The interior was pretty shot from the fire but we checked the carpeting thoroughly and we didn't find any traces of a similar plastic."

"Nor did we, anywhere else around the crime scene," Rick said. "Except of course near the bike track."

"And no substance like that was found on either victim," Ming added, acknowledging Dr. B.

"What type of plastic is it?" Gabriel asked, getting to the point.

"It's a chemical called styrene," Ramirez said, and looked over his crew. "Hey, anybody want coffee and donuts?"

"Styrene?" Dash echoed. "What is styrene?"

Ramirez picked up a paper and read from the report, "The compound is as follows: $C_6H_5CH:CH_2$. Styrene: a colorless or sometimes yellowish aromatic liquid, easily polymerized, from the storax family."

"What's it used for?" Gabriel asked.

"It's 'used in organic synthesis'," Ramirez quoted from the report. "Particularly in the manufacturing of synthetic rubber and plastics." He tossed the report to Gabriel and whistled toward the conference room door. A clerk entered, carrying a tray of paper cups filled with coffee, an assortment of sugar and non-dairy creamer packets, and a large pink box of donuts. "See? I'm not such an asshole. I provide refreshments. At least I didn't ask the one mujere here to do it."

"You know, Miguel," Ming said, twirling a pen in the corner of her mouth, "Your thoughtfulness astounds me."

"Gracias," Ramirez said in Spanish for Ming's benefit. "Now let's take a look at the two latest notes the suspect left for McRay. 'The young ones tempt you, don't they?'" Ramirez looked directly at Gabriel. "Any idea what he's talking about?"

Gabriel reddened. "I can't imagine what he's talking about." Gabriel exchanged a look with Dr. B and Ramirez caught it.

"Are you sure about that?" Ramirez asked. "I swear to you, McRay, if you are holding back something to prevent us from—"

"I'm not holding anything back."

"Then tell me what he means by saying the young ones tempt you! What the fuck does that mean?"

"How do I know? He's crazy!"

"And so are you!"

Dr. B waved a hand in the air. "That's enough."

Dash shifted uncomfortably, and Ming took a shaky sip of coffee. Dr. B frowned at the lieutenant. Rick narrowed his eyes suspiciously at Gabriel.

"I don't know what he meant by it," Gabriel said, glaring at his superior.

Ramirez reached for a donut. Gazing intently at Gabriel, he took a big bite out of one filled with grape jelly, which promptly dribbled down his chin. The atmosphere in the room thickened with tension.

Dash cleared his throat, and said warily, "Maybe we can use this in some way. Maybe Gabriel could lure him in."

"I doubt it," Dr. B told him. "He's taunting Gabriel. He's never once hinted in his notes that he wants to meet with Gabriel."

Gabriel stood up, clenched his teeth, and said, "Why don't you all go to hell? This asshole has nothing to do with me!"

"Shut up and sit down!" Ramirez commanded.

"You shut up, you short piece of shit!" Gabriel yelled back.

Ramirez slammed down his donut, squishing grape jelly out on the table. "That's it, you're done, give me your badge and your piece, McRay."

Dr. B stood up, saying, "Please, Miguel..."

"I already have probable cause to arrest your crazy ass, so don't—"

"Miguel," Dr. B continued, "Gabriel is under intense pressure. I mean, look what's happening here. Gabriel, Miguel, sit down. Please both of you just sit down."

Gabriel's head pounded as he reached behind, pulled his chair forward, and slumped down.

"Miguel," Dr. B said, "Could we break this meeting right now. Could we meet again on Monday?"

Ramirez rubbed a napkin angrily against his chin and eyed the psychiatrist.

Please," Dr. B pressed. "Everyone knows what they should be doing."

The lieutenant picked up his coffee. "Alright, everyone continues following the track he's on." He slurped his coffee. "I want an apology from you first, McRay."

Gabriel stared at a spot on the table. He was worn out. "How can you really suspect me, Lieutenant?"

A look of surprise passed over Ramirez' face and his eyes scanned the room. With his coffee cup in tow, Ramirez left the room without another word. Rick followed on his heels like an obedient pet.

Paul Vacher exhaled in relief and put his head in his hands. Dash gave Gabriel a heavy-lidded, guilty look as he walked out the door, muttering, "Hang in there, Pal."

Ming sat motionless. Gabriel looked at her, trying to read the expression in her eyes, but she seemed distant and afraid.

"I'm outta here," Vacher finally announced and squeezed Gabriel's shoulder as he exited.

Finally, Ming rose, touching Gabriel's elbow – a touch so light, he felt as if a feather brushed him. "Call me," she whispered, and then she too was gone. Only Dr. B remained, still seated.

Gabriel ignored him. Instead, he gazed at the white messages on the Formica table in front of him. He picked up the latest note and re-read the last line. The young ones tempt you, don't they?

Gabriel closed his eyes, still holding the note.

"I'd like to suggest," Dr. B began, "that we have a hypnosis session."

"Okay. Next week?"

"Right now."

CHAPTER 17

Gabriel had come down with the flu and was out of school. His mother was upset because she had to stay home with him. They don't give sick pay if your kids are sick. Mommy lied on the second day of his flu and told her work that <u>she</u> was sick. That way she wouldn't miss her pay. She sat downstairs, watching soap operas, eating a long lunch, and talking on the phone to her friends who didn't work.

Gabriel walked down the stairs holding his blanket from his bed. The blanket had kept him company since he was two-years-old and hung in tatters, but no one dared take it from him.

"Mommy, will you play Operation with me?"

"In a minute, Gabe. Mommy's on the phone."

"Will you play Operation with me instead?"

"Gabriel, I'm on the phone!"

Gabriel sat on the stairs with a feverish head, twiddling the worn fabric of his blanket, and daydreamed of going to the theater with Andrew Pierce.

The next afternoon he was better but not well enough to go to school. His mother, however, couldn't miss any more work, so Gabriel sat on his front porch like usual, awaiting her return. He heard a rusty metal clanging and saw the garage door of the Pierce house open. Andrew appeared from the shadows. He opened the hood of his car and leaned over the engine. The bigger boy spied Gabriel sitting across the street and smiled.

"Where have you been, Little Buddy?"

Gabriel giggled. That's what the Skipper called Gilligan on Gilligan's Island; one of Gabriel's favorite reruns.

"I've been sick."

"You want to come over?"

"Sure, Andrew!"

"Call me Skipper."

"Okay, Skipper."

Gabriel raced across the street to Andrew's house. First Andrew showed him all the tools he used to make his car run faster. Then they entered Andrew's house.

Nobody was home. Andrew's house had a stuffy feel and smelled like cooked cereal. In a kitchen with a pink and white tiled floor, Andrew made Gabriel a plate of cheese and crackers and handed him a glass of chocolate milk. They sat on the overstuffed couch in the family room, turned on cartoons, and began watching television.

The Skipper stroked Gabriel's dark, silky hair. "You're my Little Buddy."

Gabriel rested his head on Andrew's shoulder. "You're my Skipper."

Andrew put his hand on Gabriel's pants, between his legs. After a moment, he undid Gabriel's pants, wrapping his fingers around Gabriel's penis.

"That tickles." Gabriel squirmed, embarrassed. He was always told to keep his hands out of his pants.

"Call me Skipper." Andrew's voice was a little breathy and too close.

Gabriel giggled. Andrew's breath tickled the soft skin of his face, and the little boy curled up, laughing.

Then Andrew tried to put his fingers where the poo-poo comes out and Gabriel jerked away.

"Don't. That's icky."

"Don't worry, Little Buddy," Andrew said, breathing hard. His eyes were shining with an intensity that frightened Gabriel.

Gabriel made to move away to the other side of the couch, when, to his shock, Skipper grabbed his pants and yanked them to his ankles. Gabriel tripped onto the floor, nearly hitting the coffee table. His underwear was caught, twisted. Gabriel yelped.

Andrew Pierce was no longer the Skipper, but someone fierce and angry. He clamped a hand over Gabriel's mouth and suddenly Gabriel was scared and he couldn't breathe and *how did this happen?* Something terrible was happening! He choked for air as unbelievable pain shot through him. Why was this happening to the Skipper and his little buddy? The only sound, besides his own yelping, was the sound of the gold chain Andrew always wore thumping in rhythm against the older boy's neck.

Later that night, Gabriel locked himself in the bathroom. He was bleeding and it hurt so badly that he cried. His father stood outside the door, asking him what the matter was. Gabriel didn't answer. He was too busy trying to shut out the memory, shut out the gasping for air, and the incredible burning pain that seared his lower half and the blood on the carpet. Andrew Pierce had cleaned up the blood as Gabriel cried in the corner, and he eyed the little boy carefully.

"This is our little secret," he told Gabriel. "The Skipper and Gilligan share things they'd never tell Ginger or Mary Ann. I'm your only friend, aren't I? I'm the only one who takes you to the Melody Theater and buys you treats. Not your ma or pa, that's for sure. Me. The Skipper. And if you do tell, I'll drown your ma and pa and sister in my pool. I can do that you know. Then you'll go into a foster home and nobody will talk to you. They'll know you told a secret that caused your family to die. And I, your only friend, will never speak to you again. So, you'd better keep our secret, Little Buddy."

Gabriel sat in the armchair across from Dr. B in his Monterey Park office.

"You knew, didn't you?" Gabriel asked, feeling numb.

"I had a hunch in the beginning," Dr. B said. "Sometimes, certain behavioral patterns give you clues."

"How come you didn't tell me?"

"It's something you needed to discover yourself. You probably wouldn't have believed me. Remember, you've hid this memory from yourself for years." Dr. B clasped his hand together, regarding Gabriel gently. "You never told your parents?"

"I guess I didn't. I guess I didn't tell anybody."

"Gabriel do you think Andrew Pierce could be involved somehow? I mean, the subject of the last note – the young ones tempt you, well, young ones certainly tempted him."

"Andrew Pierce? Involved in this case? I don't think so. He'd be a little older than the profiling age range, wouldn't he?"

"True," Dr. B said and paused, looking embarrassed. "Gabriel, I had Lieutenant Ramirez check him out."

Shocked, Gabriel jerked his head up at the psychologist. "You told Ramirez about Andrew Pierce?"

"Just his name. Remember, I've only just found out that he abused you."

He abused me.

Gabriel forgot all about Ramirez momentarily. He had been a victim. No, Gabriel argued silently. My childhood was a good childhood. I wasn't abused. *It didn't happen. Not to me.*

Dr. B continued, "Lieutenant Ramirez was about to pull you off the case and I gave him something other than you to chew on. He's still convinced that you and the suspect are—"

"Are one?"

"Are connected," Dr. B finished.

Gabriel rubbed his temples, wondering how soon he would be plagued by a headache. Strangely enough, the revelation about his trauma didn't pain him; it simply left him feeling like a hollowed-out gourd. "What did you find about Andrew?"

"He served a two year sentence in San Quentin."

Gabriel swallowed, and asked tentatively, "A child molestation charge?"

"Yes, actually," Dr. B said. "However, he drops out of sight after his parole. Lieutenant Ramirez is tracking him. How are you feeling, Gabriel?"

Gabriel felt something crumbling inside of him, but he shoved dense mental material in front of it and the broken pieces of his soul were hidden away. He cleared his throat and nodded at the doctor, saying, "How could I block a memory like that?"

Dr. B took a deep breath, and said, "Because it happened more than once."

Gabriel stared at him, astonished.

"Your parents weren't aware that a pedophile lived across the street. Andrew probably got at you more than once. Perhaps it was a regular occurrence in your childhood."

Gabriel shook his head, not believing. "I couldn't have shut it out if it kept happening."

"When a child is exposed to repeated trauma, it's often too horrifying for the mind to take, so a defense mechanism comes into play. During the actual trauma, many children, and adults for that matter, check out and enter a fantasy world where the trauma isn't happening. In some cases, they develop multiple personalities. But you didn't have those symptoms. You simply locked it away. It didn't happen to you. The power of thought is truly a power. But the trauma never went away and because you never accepted it, never dealt with it, the trauma looms as large to you now as when it was occurring. You mentioned Andrew wore a gold chain when he raped you."

I was raped.

"Now we can see why Patrick Funston's necklace brought out the emotional break in you," Dr. B continued. "Your work on this case has been bringing up the suppressed memory right and left, forcing open that locked door. The headaches and the nightmares all stem from post-traumatic stress disorder."

"And what about the fugue states?" Gabriel asked. "We still haven't found out if I… Where I go."

Gabriel caught the look of concern passing over Dr. B's expressive brown eyes. Between them, the wooden clocked ticked.

"What are you thinking, Raymond?" Gabriel asked.

"I'm thinking you might have beat that child when you were a teenager because of symptoms associated with this suppressed memory. When one has been traumatized, one can suffer from perpetration issues."

"Explain," Gabriel said calmly.

"You deal to another what was done to you."

Gabriel swallowed, listening to the clock. "Then it's possible that I could be hurting people."

"I'm going to say this once again: you do not fit the profile of the Malibu Canyon murder suspect, Gabe."

"But you can't be positive, can you?"

"Yes, I'm positive."

Gabriel stood up as the clock began to chime. "Funny, I've never heard it chime before."

"Are you okay? Do you understand what Andrew did to you? Do you want to talk about it?"

Gabriel managed a small smile. "Gabriel McRay, you've just found out you were molested as a boy! What are you going to do? Hey, there's always Disneyland!"

Dr. B stared soberly at him for a moment, and then said, "This is really big growth. You may feel destroyed inside, but you will become better from this. You've got to believe that."

Gabriel's smile dropped. "Sure."

At that moment, the office door flew open and a young man entered, breathless and excited.

"Dad, guess what I scored on the GMAT? I—" He froze upon seeing Gabriel hovering like a shadow against the wall. "Oh, I'm sorry, Dad. I didn't know you were with a patient – I mean, someone."

Dr. B's cheeks went rosy as he stood and greeted his son. "Don't worry. Gabe, this is my son, Isaac. Isaac, this is Detective Sergeant Gabriel McRay."

The two shook hands.

"Nice to meet you," Gabriel said, taking his leave.

As Gabriel walked out the door, he looked behind him to see Dr. B coming around the chair with a huge smile; gathering his son in his arms.

For someone surrounded by crackpots, Gabriel thought wistfully, Dr. B sure knew how to keep his private life wholesome.

Gabriel made his way through the darkened parking lot to his worn car, alone at last with the burden of his memories.

✴︎ ✴︎ ✴︎

The fluorescent lights in the ceiling above the desks in the Homicide Bureau in Commerce flickered rapidly. They didn't bother Gabriel, whose fingers busily tapped the keys of his laptop computer. It was dark outside, past ten in the evening, but Gabriel wasn't budging.

His phone beeped, signaling that he had messages on his voicemail. Gabriel ignored the phone. He was too intent on accessing the NCIC, his network to national crimes, looking for any information on Andrew Pierce. Andrew had pleaded nolo contendere in the case he had been convicted. The maximum he received was twenty-two months in jail plus five years probation with therapy.

Except that he got off for good behavior.

Gabriel glared at the information on the website. Of course he had good behavior in prison. No children were around to tempt him.

The young ones tempt you, don't they?

"I didn't turn into him," Gabriel said loudly, his voice echoing along the walls. Ashamed, he quickly looked around. Nobody was there to hear him. Everyone had gone home.

His only company was the pictures of the homicide victims on the bulletin board. Only the flickering fluorescent lights and the quiet hum of the computers reminded Gabriel that he wasn't dying.

The young ones tempt you, don't they?

Gabriel closed his eyes and took a deep breath. Steady, steady. Don't let the words of a maniac press you into believing something that isn't true.

Gabriel kept his eyes glued to the computer screen, researching the psychiatric report on Andrew Pierce. He was considered a "fixated" molester, someone who was exclusively attracted to children, as opposed to someone who was "regressed." Regressed molesters were attracted to their own peers, but used children as sexual substitutes whenever they were under pressure or stress.

Yes, Andrew had certainly been fixated, Gabriel thought derisively.

A wave of nausea swept through him and he brought his papers up to his mouth. As suddenly as the nausea appeared, it was gone, and Gabriel wondered if he should call it a night. The phone beeped again, Gabriel jumped.

Gabriel closed the file in the computer and pushed his chair back. Again, he felt nauseous, his heart pumping wildly – what was happening to him? I've got to go home, he thought, I should call it a night. But it was too late.

Memories floated to the churning surface of his mind like bloated corpses, reaching swollen hands out to him and begging Gabriel to look, to listen.

The young ones tempt you, don't they?

Gabriel groaned, put his hands to his head, and whispered, "Damn you."

Door Number Two swung wide open and there in the darkness... Bedknobs and Broomsticks. Sitting with Andrew Pierce at the Melody Theater watching Bedknobs and Broomsticks. Some older folks smiled at them. An older boy taking a young boy under his wing, buying him Black Cows and popcorn. It made a wholesome picture.

The Skipper would smile at them, winning them over with his braces-straight teeth, but little Gabriel never smiled.

He'd sit on his sore rump and stare as the credits rolled. He'd watch other little kids running freely down the aisles, laughing, throwing candy at each other.

The Skipper would lean over very close, a hint of licorice on his breath, and whisper in Gabriel's ear, "Do you like this? Is the movie scaring you?"

And Gabriel would shake his head, No.

He knew the world offered far more frightening things than this Disney movie. He'd look back at the other kids, and a deep void would cleave him in two. He knew in his heart that he was worth nothing. He could never laugh freely like the other kids because he didn't deserve to. What he deserved, and what the Skipper so reminded him, was to be "pounded in the ass."

He knew this was true, because his mom and dad were letting the Skipper do this to him. They were leaving the Skipper and Gilligan on their deserted island where no hope of rescue would ever come. The Skipper had finally confessed that Gabriel's parents knew all about this secret and they simply didn't care. All they would do, if Gabriel tattled, is get mad at their son for being a spoiled baby, expecting Andrew Pierce to pay for all these movies for nothing. Andrew told him he had planted a bomb in Gabriel's chest when he was sleeping. If he told anyone at all, Andrew would detonate the bomb.

"It didn't happen to me!" Gabriel said aloud, feeling his chest tighten.

It didn't happen to me. Gabriel hunched over in his chair. *My life is not that hideous.*

Dr. B had mentioned that flashbacks and memories were two different things. Memories are veiled and distant, while flashbacks put you right in the scene again. It's memory without any distance.

"Please become veiled and distant," Gabriel whispered and heard his cell phone beep once more. Gabriel sat up, determined to fight for normalcy. He picked up the phone and accessed his voicemail.

"You have four new messages," said a mechanical voice and called out the hour of the first call.

"Sergeant McRay? This is Mary Siegel from the Times. I wanted–"

Gabriel deleted the message. The mechanical voice announced the time of the next message in the queue.

"Hi, Mr. McRay, this is Gary at Gold's Gym again, and I was wondering when you were–"

Gabriel deleted the message, and waited for the next one.

"Gabriel, it's Ming. I just wanted to say how sorry I am that Miguel treats you so badly. I swear that man has no tact." Gabriel heard her recorded voice take a deep breath. "I just wanted to remind you about the theater, and make sure you're okay."

Gabriel waited for the next message.

"Gabriel, it's mother. Since you never answer my calls at home, I thought I'd try your cell. Please give me a call when you have a chance. We miss you."

The message ended with a click and the mechanical voice said, "You have no more messages."

Gabriel kept the phone warming in his hand but made no move to return any of the calls. He thought about his mother. He now knew the reason that he resented his folks so much. He'd been hurt while under their care. They were supposed to protect him. They had failed. In retrospect, he could see himself as a boy, overwhelmed at the thought that his parents knew about the abuse and permitted it. Gabriel opened his palm and gazed at the phone. Mother was a phone call away. She was waiting for him to reach out to her.

He couldn't call, not yet. He wasn't ready for that conversation. Not right now.

❧ ❧ ❧

The door bell rang around eleven-thirty at night and Ming Li walked tentatively down the staircase of her Los Feliz home. In her hand she held a can of Mace. The stairway was long and graceful, befitting her large home. Ming's bare feet descended the carpeted steps quietly. Her mind ran through all the possibilities as she approached the door. Perhaps a relative of a recent autopsy exam stood outside in the dark, upset with her findings and had come to argue with her. Perhaps the Malibu Canyon Murderer was hopping from one mountain range to another and now was poised with his knife. Ming peered through the peephole and then dropped her eyes to the ground. Gabriel McRay stood on her steps. *Should I be scared of him as well?*

"I don't want to be alone tonight," he said when she opened the door.

If Ming had considered any thoughts of intimacy related to Gabriel's midnight visit, Gabriel soon put them to rest by asking, "Could I borrow your couch?"

"I have an extra room," Ming told him and pocketed the mace in her bathrobe.

Ming led Gabriel to the guest bedroom which was tastefully decorated and never used. Gabriel sat on the edge of the big bed and stared at his feet.

Ming stood at the door. "Do you want something to eat? I can get you-"

"I remember now what I tried to forget."

Ming carefully entered the room and sat next to him on the bed. She waited.

Gabriel felt her next to him but kept his eyes on the pretty patterned rug at his feet. "I was-"

You were raped.

No, it didn't happen to me.

He turned to Ming. "I know it's late but I didn't want to go back to my place. I didn't want to be alone with it. I'm worn out. I didn't know what-"

Ming put her arms around him and pulled him close to her. She lay down with him against the pillows and he rested his face against her neck. Gabriel felt exhausted suddenly and closed his eyes. The even rhythm of her heart calmed him. The scent of her clean skin soothed him. He was eternally grateful to Ming that she didn't press him to divulge his secret. He had never needed anyone before. He was not sure he wanted to start needing someone now. Within seconds, Gabriel was sound asleep.

CHAPTER 18

On Saturday night, Ming and Gabriel took their seats in the orchestra section of the Pantages Theater. Ming was thumbing through a program while Gabriel scanned the murmuring crowd. He was looking forward to a night out. In the pretend world of the theater, he could put aside his dark recollections. He could forget thoughts of gold chains and candy; their innocent context warped by the twisted events of his childhood.

In Ming's typical assured manner, she had insisted on picking up Gabriel in her Lexus. "I asked you, after all," she told him and Gabriel had to agree his rusted Celica wasn't exactly a chariot.

Her offer to drive made Gabriel wonder why he didn't improve his lifestyle: same furniture for years, same car, despite his pay increases. Surely it had something to do with his issues. Gabriel had insisted on taking Ming out to nice dinner before the show and, thankfully, the dinner went without a hint of awkwardness.

Now Gabriel viewed his companion as she read her program. Ming wore a black pencil skirt with a red sleeveless sweater. Her hair was pinned in a French twist, which high-lighted her cheekbones and sensuous lips.

"I know you're looking at me," she stated, flipping the program pages.

He leaned close and whispered in her ear, "I don't think the show is going to top you."

"Hmmm, too much wine at dinner, huh?"

But she smiled satisfactorily and continued reading. Gabriel was grateful that Ming was keeping things low-key. He knew she must be itching with curiosity to find out Gabriel's dark secret, but she was allowing him his space. Perhaps someday he would tell her. Tonight he simply wanted to live in the moment and try to enjoy himself.

Gabriel leaned back and studied the majestic velvet curtain and the intricate carvings that adorned the walls and balconies, giving the theater the grand appearance of old Hollywood elegance. The comedy and tragedy masks, carved out of wood and painted in the colors of Mardi Gras, smiled and frowned at him from the balustrade.

The theater darkened and then the music swelled up from the orchestra pit. The curtains pulled back to reveal an elaborate set. An "Ahhh" of approval swept through the audience as they were transported into the world of "Showboat."

Gabriel admired the set, which was complete in every detail. A fabric replicating water undulated near a pier. The showboat itself, "Cotton Blossom," looked large and creakingly heavy. That, of course, was the illusion of theater. Gabriel knew everything was fake, made out of plywood and plastic.

Do you like the theater, Sergeant?

A slow realization dawned on him and he swallowed. "Ming—"

"Shhh," she whispered, watching the play, her face illuminated from the colored lights beaming from onstage.

"Ming," Gabriel pressed, "I'll be right back."

He kept his eye on the set as he moved through the seated people, banging knees and causing huffs of disapproval. He strode up the aisle and out the double doors into the lobby.

"I need to see the theater manager," Gabriel told an usher.

"Is something wrong, Sir?"

Gabriel pulled out his badge, "The manager, now!"

The usher ran off, and a minute later a young man strode up to Gabriel wearing a maroon tuxedo that bagged at the knees.

"Yes, Sir, may I help you?"

Gabriel showed him his badge, saying, "The sets. Can you tell me, how they are made?"

The manager looked at him quizzically. "Well, we have a set construction shop that we utilize to—"

"There's a machine," Gabriel said, interrupting, and snapped his fingers, trying to remember. "A machine that makes fake pillars and rocks and the detail of the boat out there."

"A vacuform machine?"

"Yes!" Gabriel blurted, "What do you use with that vacuform thing? What makes the pillars?"

"Foam casts. Sometimes we use plaster casts."

"No, no, no," Gabriel said, shaking his head, "what's the substance, the chemical used?"

The maroon tuxedo gave him a blank stare. "Lemme call our set designer."

"Hurry," Gabriel told him.

The manager moved away, dialing a number on his cell phone. Gabriel waited, nervously tapping his fingers against his pant leg.

He saw the manager end his call and Gabriel strode over to him. The manager took a subconscious step backwards.

"I believe it's called styrene," he blurted before Gabriel could reach him.

Gabriel thanked him then shot for the lobby doors. He skidded to a halt and then ran back toward the theater. He quickly made his way through the seats, aggravating more knees and stomping on women's purses.

"Ming," he said, too loudly.

A million "Shhhh's" swept through the audience.

"What is it? What's wrong?" She looked up at him worriedly.

"I've got to go."

"What? Why?"

The people behind Gabriel told him to sit down. He didn't care; his heart was racing. "I've got to go to Pepperdine."

"Now?"

"Now. Listen, you can stay – but can I take your car? Here, here's some money for a taxi." Gabriel quickly fished through his wallet and bills fell to the floor.

He bent over to retrieve them, bumping the man in the seat next to him, who cried, "Hey!"

"What are you doing?" Ming asked, watching him in amazement.

"Plastic, styrene. It's what they use to make the sets!"

"Is this a lead or something?"

Gabriel shoved the money in her hand and headed for the aisle.

"You're not leaving me!" Ming said, leaping up and following right on his tail.

On-stage, Captain Andy broke into song.

ᴥ   ᴥ   ᴥ

Gabriel drove Ming's car as they raced toward Malibu. Ming sat fidgeting in the passenger seat while Gabriel paged Dash and Ramirez. As he waited for their calls, he explained to Ming the significance of the styrene.

"Fine Arts is the one department I hadn't covered yet. I had a hunch the suspect might be a student, but I had no idea where to find him. I was concentrating on the Russian studies angle. The perp must have had styrene on his shoes at the Hall crime scene – styrene from the vacuform machine at the college."

Loose threads of disconnected thoughts quickly began knitting together, finally making sense. Gabriel remembered Dr. B's words, "He's taunting Gabriel. He's not asking for a conference."

I'm Fortunato.

He's taunting Gabriel.

I'm Fortunato. He's the one that's always taunting Montressor.

"You know," Gabriel said incredulously, looking at Ming. "I think I talked to him."

The cell phone rang shrilly causing both he and Ming to jump.

They pulled into the campus parking structure and exited the car. The mist formed halos around the yellow-lighted lamps and the university seemed to be sleeping. They could hear the waves breaking in the nearby ocean.

"It's definitely getting colder at night," Ming said, hugging her shoulders. Gabriel pulled off his jacket, removed his gun, and put the jacket gently around Ming's bare shoulders.

"I want you to get back in the car," he told her, his hands still on her shoulders.

"No way."

"This isn't the examining room, Ming. Stay here."

"Funny. You sound like Rick Frasier," she said dryly. "Now which way do we go?"

"Always to the point," Gabriel muttered and gestured for her to follow him.

As they crossed the campus, heading toward the theater department, Ming and Gabriel passed some lone students loping toward the library. Through the open doorway of a campus coffee house they saw people sipping cappuccinos and listening to a poet.

The theater building itself seemed vacant. In the hills beyond the university, a coyote howled repeatedly. Ming and Gabriel entered the deserted lobby, greeted by a flickering fluorescent light.

"Let's go see that vacuform machine first," Gabriel said, leading Ming down the hallway.

They halted in front of the property room. Gabriel tried the door, found it unlocked, and opened it.

"There," Gabriel said, turning on the light.

The vacuform machine stood poised like a quiet, hulking monster ready to pounce. Ming glanced around the room. The vacant eyes of the masks looked darkly upon her from their posts on the wall.

"There's no one in here," Gabriel said, leaving.

"What did you expect?" Ming asked him. "Look, why don't you find someone who can give you some information on the students who use this while I collect a styrene sample. I'll be right behind you."

"Good idea," Gabriel said, and strode toward the door. "Hey, keep this door locked when I leave, okay?"

Gabriel walked briskly through the darkened halls. He opened a door and found himself standing offstage in the main theater. Carefully, he stepped past a complicated-looking lighting board and moved to the dimly lit stage. Gabriel concluded that "The Cask of Amontillado" was still playing because behind him were stone caves filled with dusty wine bottles and human bones. "Mold" dripped from the cave walls.

The props were probably fashioned by the suspect himself.

I'm Fortunato.

What was his name again?

Rows of gel lights looked down on Gabriel from the front, their colors now black. From sixty feet up in the dark, where the catwalks crisscrossed, long wires swayed in the air-conditioned air.

Gabriel jumped, thinking he heard the tinkling of bells drifting down from the catwalks – did he imagine it? Gabriel squinted, trying in vain to see above. He moved to a spiral staircase off stage left. Placing his hand on the wrought iron railing, he began to climb.

The staircase shifted under his weight and Gabriel tried to peer around the bend in the stairs, but they wound too tightly for him to see ahead. The floor below stretched farther and farther away.

Finally, Gabriel reached the top and stepped onto the suspended path of the catwalk. Narrow in width, the catwalk had only a thin chain that served as a rail. The length of the catwalk extended across the stage where it met other steel paths, leading off in various directions. Gabriel couldn't see much in the dim light and he stepped warily on the catwalk, which shook under his weight.

He heard a jingling sound again and froze. Gabriel peered through the dimness, feeling dizzy with vertigo. He ventured out a few feet more and came to a stop somewhere high above the middle of the stage. A single wire, hanging ten feet ahead, gently swayed, hitting another wire.

That was the jingling sound, Gabriel assured himself, as his eyes dropped down to the darkened stage. Something bright winked at him from the floor. Curious, Gabriel returned to the spiral staircase and quickly descended the steps.

Once he was level with the stage, Gabriel could no longer make out what had winked at him. He meandered through the gloomy set, searching.

His foot hit something soft and, again, he heard the jingling. Gabriel looked down to see a dark purple jester's cap. He picked up the cap and the bells tinkled in his hand.

I'm Fortunato.

Glancing once more around the stage, Gabriel waited in the silence. He surveyed the dark, vacant audience seats before him, sure he was not alone.

"Are you there?" he asked out loud.

Above him the wires swayed but he heard no other sound.

Come forward, you bastard. Gabriel imagined he saw Andrew Pierce materialize on the main aisle and stride rapidly toward the stage.

Gabriel shook the image from his mind, turned on his heel, and exited stage left.

His next stop was the set construction room. The large space was quiet and deserted; the band saws still and the drills frozen. The blade of one table saw lay halfway embedded in a piece of plywood, bared teeth not yet finished chewing. Gabriel heard a whispering and jerked his head toward the right.

A blue plastic tarp rustled against the painting cage. Gabriel's hand moved toward his gun and carefully flipped off the safety. The tarp fluttered, a graceful move, like the flapping of angel wings.

Gabriel approached the tarp. The odor of turpentine crept into his nostrils. Streaks of pastels and primary colors confused his eyes. He reached out a tentative hand and flipped back the tarp.

A heating duct behind the tarp blew hot air. Gabriel sighed, feeling dumb, and scanned the room once more. Convinced he was alone and probably a bit high strung, he went out the doors to continue his search.

He paused in front of the costume room, listening for any sounds, and then went inside.

Gabriel made his way through the rows of silent sewing machines. Bolts of fabric leaned against the walls and assorted scissors hung on a large pegboard along with many spools of thread and assorted needle packs. A closed door beckoned him from the back of the room, and Gabriel moved toward it.

He found himself standing in a large closet, stuffed with costumes. Slowly, Gabriel began sorting through them.

Ming fashioned a crude evidence collector by dumping out her homeopathic menstrual cramp medicine and using the pill case. As she gathered some minute scraps of styrene, Ming thought about how Gabriel had reached out to her in his time of need. To feel him sleeping in her arms, knowing he found refuge there, brought her more joy than she cared to admit. For that moment he was totally and unconditionally hers; she didn't have to compete with his demons. Eventually, toward dawn, she released him, placing a blanket over his body and then retreating to her own room. The last thing she wanted was to have Gabriel resent her for being too suffocating. Perhaps someday she wouldn't have to watch her every move with him. Perhaps someday Gabriel would let her into his life and tell her the secret that he —

As Ming crouched on the floor she got the creepy sensation that she was being watched.

She stopped sweeping up the white plastic and listened to the silence for a moment. She stood up and turned her clinical eyes on the room. A large, deadly looking scythe hung on one wall, suspended between a dagger and a heavy sword.

Not heavy, Ming told herself, merely made of plastic. She fancied she saw eyes behind the grotesque masks. She took one step toward the fake bricks piled in a corner and stopped again to listen. Satisfied she was alone; Ming turned around and was immediately stunned to see the property room door wide open.

Ming walked over to the yawning door. She was certain that Gabriel had closed it on his way out, but reasoned that some doors simply didn't stay shut unless they were locked. Ming bolted the door as Gabriel had instructed.

She bent down to retrieve her pillbox under the vacuform machine and suddenly caught sight of two leather boots. Ming froze, clearly hearing her pulse beat within her ears. A full minute went by until Ming bravely ventured to raise her head above the machine. She smiled in relief. A mannequin dressed in hunter's garb, complete with shotgun and cap, stood motionless in the boots.

The door clicked. Ming tilted her head toward the sound and looked at the door.

The doorknob was slowly being turned. Ming held her breath, knowing the door was locked, but still not comforted. From the other side, someone shook the doorknob.

"Gabriel?" she called tentatively.

The doorknob froze. Swallowing nervously, Ming tucked the pillbox into her pocket, swiftly moved to the door, and rested her ear against the wood. Ming couldn't make out any sounds for a moment, and then very faintly she heard the single tap of a footstep. She pushed her body against the door in an effort to hear better.

Silence.

Ming looked down and then bravely took hold of the doorknob. Suddenly it shook violently in her grasp. She gasped and stepped back, watching the knob twist and writhe.

And then it was still.

Ming waited, standing frozen like the mannequin. She heard a key slide into the lock. Looking around wildly, Ming bolted for the suit of armor, thinking she could tuck herself behind it. She was just squeezing between the armor and the wall when the door swung wide on its hinges.

Gabriel fingered the wispy fabric of a fairy costume. A tag pinned to the sleeve read, "A Midsummer Night's Dream 2005." He moved along, sorting through period clothes and more fanciful costumes, such as a mythical bird outfit with brightly colored feathers. The tag read, "The Birds, Aristophanes 2008."

He halted midway through his search, struck by one costume in particular. Gabriel pulled it loose from the others and stared at it thoughtfully. It was a policeman's uniform.

Once again, in a never-ending movie reel, Gabriel watched the costumed cop fall toward the floor with the toy gun in his hand. Sighing, Gabriel replaced the uniform, when a thought suddenly occurred to him. He began sorting faster and faster through the costumes, rifling through the attire of Roman gods, military soldiers, hunchbacks, priests, judges, and kings. At the end of the line, Gabriel backed away, scanning the room for inventory. He found more costumes in another closet — pants, shirts, and dresses in various sizes. On pegs above the clothes, Gabriel saw wigs, hats, scarves, and gloves —too many to count.

He's dressing up, Gabriel thought, astonished. He's got access to as many costumes as he wants. Gabriel leaned against the costume of a Frankenstein monster. *That's how he's doing it. That's how he gets into their cars.*

He plays a character. He plays pretend.

Gabriel strode toward the exit of the costume shop, making a mental note to ask the head seamstress if any costumes had gone missing. He slid quietly into the hallway, closing the door behind him. When he turned around, he was staring face-to-face with a heavy-set, bearded man.

"This is Mr. Benson," Ming said, coming from behind the large gentleman. "He's the head property master and he thinks he can help us."

CHAPTER 19

"What do you want with Bill?"

"I just want to talk to him," Gabriel explained, as he hovered above Mr. Benson.

The property master, a chubby guy who sported a bald spot, a full dark beard, and a booming deep voice, sat at a computer terminal inside the registrar's office, accessing the student directory.

"What did he do, Sergeant?"

Gabriel ignored the question and asked one of his own. "You said that Bill often works in the property shop. Does he regularly use the vacuform machine?"

"He's our main guy. He's very talented."

"In all areas? How's he at putting on makeup?"

Mr. Benson paused, giving Gabriel a quizzical stare.

Ming bustled into the office, saying, "Dash is outside, Ramirez and a black and white unit are on their way. Dash said the lieutenant has something important to tell you."

Probably has a warrant for my arrest.

Ming sidled up close to him. "What if this Bill person is not the one, Gabriel?"

Gabriel didn't answer. His hunch couldn't be wrong. He couldn't afford to be wrong.

Mr. Benson, running through the list of names on the monitor, finally pointed a fat finger at the screen, and said, "Here it is, Bill Spangler, Terra Bella Apartments, number thirty-three, right off of—"

"I've got it," Gabriel said, interrupting, and headed out the door. To Ming he called, "Stay here with Mr. Benson!"

Dash was waiting in his car. Gabriel waved at him to follow and jumped into Ming's car, ignited the engine, and drove off.

Dash and Gabriel arrived at the Terra Bella apartment complex, a two story Spanish-styled affair with beige stucco and a red-tiled roof. The second story apartments had an ocean view.

"Nice," Dash said to Gabriel.

The two men first inspected the underground garage, looking to see if Bill Spangler was home. No car was parked in the space, but Dash pointed out a Yamaha dirt bike with muddy tires chained to a nearby post.

"Let's make sure to get an impression of those tires and dust it for prints," Gabriel said, relishing his sense of victory. Uniformed officers arrived on the scene and agreed to cover the garage and back entrance. Ramirez was on the radio, telling Gabriel to wait for more back up, but Gabriel, restless with anticipation, refused to wait.

The two detectives knocked on the front door of number thirty-three. Dash drew his revolver, while Gabriel hovered slightly behind. He sniffed the air, smelled gasoline, and the hairs on the back of his neck stood up and saluted.

"Bill Spangler, open up," Dash told the closed door.

Gabriel whispered to Ramirez in his radio. "We're at the front door." He studied the floor, tense, waiting; when he saw a ghostly finger of smoke poke out from under the door and then disappear back inside number thirty-three.

"Bill Spangler! Open up!" cried Dash.

Gabriel's eyes widened, and the words "back draft" were coming to his mind as he saw Dash's hand on the doorknob.

"Get back," he told Dash, who twisted the knob. "Get back!"

With a mighty crack, the door suddenly blew out, propelled by a roaring explosion, which instantly threw Gabriel and Dash backwards five feet. The radio flew from Gabriel's hand as the flames shot out the door and licked the ceiling.

Gabriel and Dash, their clothes and hair singed by the intense heat, fell to their hands and knees. Gabriel looked back toward thirty-three and was shocked to see the fire tearing a swath across the ceiling toward them.

"Go!" he yelled to Dash and the two detectives crawled like mad as the hungry flames chased them down the hallway.

They stumbled out of the building, choking on smoke, to see Ramirez staring at the building incredulously.

"It's burning?" the irate lieutenant yelled at them. "How come you didn't radio that in?"

Gabriel hunched over, gagging, catching his breath. He turned, glaring at his superior. "I was too busy getting knocked on my ass!"

Cursing in Spanish, Ramirez radioed the fire department. Gabriel walked through the chaotic crowd gathering outside the burning Terra Bella apartments and stared at the inferno in amazement.

"He didn't come out here," the officers staking out the back told Gabriel. The dirt bike had remained chained to its post and was now burning along with the rest of the apartment house.

A swat team arrived, but could do nothing. Soon the howling of the fire engines cut through the sound of crackling wood. The red and yellow engines converged on the scene, lights flashing and sirens wailing, throwing more hysteria into the already panicked souls. Other people, dressed in pajamas and robes, stared in silent shock at the blazing walls they once called home.

Gabriel scanned the street, slowly moving through the throng of people. He heard Ramirez yelling at someone and saw Dash being treated by a paramedic for a burn. His own skin felt taught and sensitive, but Gabriel didn't want to waste time treating his own wounds. The suspect could not be far.

"Where are you?" Gabriel said aloud. The suspect must have known Gabriel was going to come for him. He knew and was prepared. Gabriel studied the people around him, wondering if the killer walked among them. Dr. B had once said the fires created a dazzling display. Was he here, watching the destruction?

Gabriel felt cheated. This arrest was supposed to vindicate him.

News vans arrived and their crews were clogging the street. Gabriel heard more shouts and commands and scanned the crowd once more.

Where are you?

Frustrated, Gabriel turned his gaze down the street and immediately squinted under the glare of two headlights beaming directly on him. They came from a car parked in an unlit portion of the street. Gabriel walked toward the headlights, feeling the old anger gnawing at him. Was he still under surveillance even as he pursued a suspect? Or was it a voyeur who enjoyed spotlighting a tragedy?

Gabriel stared into the bright lights; knowing the person behind the wheel saw him all too clearly. Then suddenly the parked car jerked forward, pulling into a quick U-turn and burned rubber down the street. Gabriel stood gaping at the abrupt departure of the car, a Buick, and felt the hairs stand on end again. Fumbling for his keys, Gabriel ran back to the Lexus, pushing people out of the way. He caught Ramirez coming toward him with a determined expression, but Gabriel had no time to waste. He dove into the car and began chasing the Buick.

Gabriel reached for his radio, and then retracted his hand, realizing he was in Ming's car. The Buick blazed onto Malibu Canyon Road and Gabriel accelerated in pursuit. He scrambled for his cell phone, tried to dial, but the battery was dead.

Gabriel threw it down, cursing, and stepped on the gas. The Buick raced ahead. The two cars skidded on the twisting asphalt. The Buick passed a slow moving Volkswagen bug and cut sharply in front of it. The blaring of the bug's horn sliced the night. Gabriel was forced to pass too and received an upraised middle finger for his efforts.

Rounding a precipitous curve, Gabriel nearly lost control. The two cars were going much too fast for the winding mountain road. They entered a tunnel and then exited in seconds, the sound of their wheels a lion's roar. Outside, the moonlight threw quick shadows of trees, bushes, and boulders onto the roadway. Feeling the sweat drop on his aching skin, Gabriel pushed his foot harder on the pedal. He caught his reflection in the rearview mirror and his heart dropped. In the dim light, he looked like a charcoal ghost with two startled blue eyes.

It's just soot, he told himself, turning his gaze away. Then his eyes caught something on the passenger seat and Gabriel did a double take. Lying there was a torn page from a magazine. He knew full well the photo hadn't been there before. Gabriel flipped on the overhead light and saw a glossy photograph in bold color proudly displaying a man sodomizing a boy.

The wheel jerked in Gabriel's hands and Ming's Lexus swerved, skidding into the opposite lane. A thundering headache suddenly crashed behind Gabriel's eyes and he lost control. The car spun like a dancer on the narrow highway, the tires passing over the sheer cliff that dropped to the creek below, and then circling wildly back onto the roadway. The Lexus continued its skid, leaving black marks as testimonial, until it finally crashed into a mountain wall, which immediately showered the fossils of ancient sea creatures onto the hood of the car.

Gabriel slumped forward against the wheel, hearing the wail of an approaching siren. His head pounded and his hand limply patted his clothing for the aspirin bottle. Exhausted, his hand dropped and Gabriel closed his eyes.

When he opened them again, a Ventura County firefighter was opening the door, asking if he was all right. A paramedic was right behind him, putting his hand on Gabriel's neck, checking for damage.

Ramirez appeared at the passenger side window and rested his arms on the hood, surveying the crushed Lexus embedded in the rock wall. He flicked off a piece of shale, shook his head, and then opened the door, yanking it hard when it resisted. The lieutenant took a seat beside Gabriel and calmly pulled out a pack of Winston's.

Ramirez placed a cigarette between his lips then offered the pack to Gabriel, who was bleeding from a cut above his eyebrow. Gabriel weakly shook his head, thinking he must be in some parallel universe. Maybe he had simply died and gone to hell. He was, after all, with Ramirez.

"Well, well…" Ramirez said, lighting up and inhaling. "What a fucking mess. You're lucky to be alive, McRay."

Gabriel heard the paramedics readying a gurney and his eyes dropped to the passenger seat, sure that Ramirez was now sitting on the photo of the man and boy.

Ramirez took another casual puff, gazed into the cracked windshield, and said, "Some dude named Gary keeps calling you. I finally took the call, because he said it was important. He wants to know when you're coming in for all those clothes you've left at the gym. He says your locker is overstuffed."

Gabriel weakly lifted his head from the seat to stare at Ramirez.

"He says you've come in and worked your ass off, mostly at night, but sometimes in the day. You know a Gary at Gold's Gym?" Ramirez asked, finally looking at Gabriel.

Gabriel shook his head; then nodded. The phone messages...

Ramirez returned his gaze to the rock wall, quietly smoking, and then said, "Doesn't matter. Your name is logged into their computer and they can prove you've been coming there and working out on certain key dates and times."

Gabriel regarded Ramirez for a moment, and then leaned his head back.

"And by the way," Ramirez said, "The DNA test results came back. You're clear." Ramirez took another puff. "Man, you really fucked up this car. Can't you do anything right?"

Gabriel managed a weak smile, as they lifted him from the broken car and placed him on the stretcher.

CHAPTER 20

"**I** don't get you," Dash said to Gabriel. "Why aren't you resting at home?"

Gabriel didn't reply. He maneuvered around the wet debris that littered the floor of apartment thirty-three. Joining him to pick through the charred rubble was another team of detectives and a pair of arson investigators, one being Paul Vacher.

Gabriel stopped to pull some peeling skin from his forehead. A brown line of stitches crossed his left eyebrow.

"Cut that out," Dash said, looking at him. "You're starting to look like a monster."

Gabriel tried to smile, but his sensitive skin hurt too much. "Look who's talking," Dash sported a coat of Vaseline over his own blistered skin.

The Crime Scene Unit moved around the detectives, feverishly bagging evidence and snapping photos in the diminishing sunlight that slanted through the naked windows. A nervous firefighter hovered around the investigative group like a worried gnat. The entire complex had sustained considerable structural damage and every creaking step put more strain on the weakened building.

'You feel better, don't you?" Dash asked as he inspected a gasoline can. They had discovered many such cans hidden around the entire complex.

"I tweaked my shoulder, but other than that, I'm okay," Gabriel answered, moving into what was once the kitchen. At his feet he saw a set of knives, still stuck in their blackened wood block.

Dash trailed him into the kitchen. "I mean, aren't you relieved that, you know..."

Gabriel crouched down and examined the kitchen knives in spite of the fact none of them fit the description of the murder weapon. "You mean about working out at the gym during my – absences?" Gabriel turned his attention to the silent refrigerator.

Dash perused the burned contents of the pantry. "Well, it provides an alibi."

"All this and Bill Spangler provide me with an alibi."

"Did you get a look at him at all?"

"It was dark," Gabriel replied.

"Too bad none of us saw him."

Gabriel turned and frowned at his partner. *Do you still think it's me, Dash? Do you think I chased myself along Malibu Canyon?*

"I'll say one thing for Bill; he stored a lot of canned food." Dash changed the subject by holding up a smoldering can. He tossed it behind him and grabbed another.

"If I'd been able to radio for back up on the Buick we wouldn't have lost him," Gabriel told his partner.

"What happened out there anyhow?"

"I went too fast and lost control," Gabriel replied automatically, neglecting to mention anything about the pornographic picture. Ming's car had been taken to the repair shop and no one had mentioned the photo – yet. Gabriel figured the suspect must have watched him, possibly even followed him from the college. Had he seen Gabriel in the registrar's office? Most likely the suspect had been aware of Gabriel's ever-increasing presence on campus. The arson team had told Gabriel that while gasoline had been poured onto the hall carpet, a slower accelerant had been used to set the actual fire, which gave the suspect plenty of time to run.

Gabriel was amazed at the audacity of the killer. He had to have been walking among the crowd outside the burning building, possibly standing right next to Gabriel as the detective watched the fire.

The young ones tempt you, don't they?

Gabriel couldn't understand the meaning behind the notes and the photo. Seeing the man and boy engaged in sex reminded Gabriel of certain brutalities he didn't want to face. Reluctantly, Gabriel dragged Andrew Pierce to the surface, wondering if he could possibly be a person of interest; but soon dismissed the idea. Andrew was too old to pass for a student.

Gabriel stepped past a MCU officer taking photos. He didn't want to think about Andrew Pierce.

"How pissed off is Ming at you?" Dash asked.

"She was a little put out," Gabriel said, "but she isn't blaming me. The department will cover the expenses."

The firefighter tagged behind the MCU team and clucked like a nervous hen. "You guys better hurry up. This ceiling is going to cave and if you don't want to spend the rest of your lives in wheelchairs, I'd take what I can and get the hell out!"

Dash was hunched over a collapsed table carefully inspecting the remains of a computer. "He's got a printer here," Dash said, using his gloved hands to gently sift through the wreckage. "The lab boys will have fun picking this apart."

Gabriel paused to apply more of the antiseptic cream his doctor had prescribed for his aching face, and then stepped carefully into the dark hallway separating the kitchen from the bedroom. An ominous creaking sounded from somewhere up above his head. The stench of burn overpowered the confined space. Feeling a bit claustrophobic, Gabriel continued his trek down the hallway.

Bill Spangler's bedroom was a graveyard of splintered wood and broken glass. Here and there a spot of color surfaced, a corner of an art print, a torn piece of patterned fabric; small reminders of the life that lived before the flames.

It's not enough. There must be more about you.

Gabriel moved to the closet and pulled open two shuttered doors, rasping on their hinges. As soon as his eyes adjusted to the darkness, a gasp escaped his throat. A row of burned human heads lined the top shelf.

Gabriel rubbed the back of his hand across his damp upper lip and stepped closer, readying his nose for the putrid scent of decay; but only the smell of burned wood met his nostrils. The heads weren't human at all – just foam dummies. Gabriel pulled one off the shelf and examined it. Pinned to the foam head was a remnant of crisp netting with some hair attached. He inwardly cursed the fire's destruction. Buried in these ashes was the player's complete wardrobe. Gabriel noticed rows of pegs, similar to the ones found in the costume shop, nailed above the shelf. Searching the debris at his feet, Gabriel discovered pins, blackened buttons, and metal clips. He pulled a walking cane from a corner of the closet, along with a pair of metal crutches, contorted by the heat, and a charred, brown leg cast that unlatched like a briefcase.

I'm Fortunato.

The agitated firefighter poked his head into the bedroom. "Your two minutes are up, McRay. The demolition crew is here and I've already moved your people out."

"Okay," Gabriel told him, "I'm coming right now."

Gabriel moved to the door, but spied a broken table with a shattered mirror lying across it. Unable to resist, Gabriel walked over. Light bulb shards lay at the table's base. Gabriel bent down and saw two closed drawers. The late afternoon sun had moved away from the window, and Gabriel fished for his pocket flashlight. He opened the first drawer, shone his light, and saw the sticky debris of makeup: warped plastic cases, charred brushes, and melted tubes. He pulled out the second drawer and discovered the contents had been more protected. Gabriel steadied the flashlight in his mouth and, as drops of perspiration ran down his face, he drew out a melted bald cap, a couple of fake noses, and a beard. He opened a small metal box that contained different pairs of colored contact lenses.

A long, low creak, coming from the bowels of the building issued forth and Gabriel could swear he felt the floor shiver beneath him. He chewed on his flashlight, glancing at the table, unable to leave. Finally he let the flashlight drop into his hands and stood up in frustration. Gabriel strode to the bed, flung back the ragged blankets hoping to find something – anything of consequence, but the bed yielded nothing. As one of the blankets fell behind him, Gabriel heard a chink.

Curious, Gabriel lifted the blanket from where it fell in a corner of the room and his flashlight illuminated a large fishing tackle box. He reached down to grab it, when a harsh grating sound hit his ears and the floor beneath him suddenly collapsed with a crash.

Gabriel plummeted through the jagged hole, scraping his legs and torso on the broken floorboards, as his hands scrabbled for support. Frantic, Gabriel clutched at the bed leg and hung suspended as his own legs dangled into the apartment below. The firefighter ran over, grabbed Gabriel, and hoisted him up.

"Are you okay?" he said, hustling Gabriel back through the hallway. Somewhere above them they heard the sound of wood splitting.

"I'm okay."

"Can you walk?"

"I think so."

All at once a roaring swept through the decrepit building.

"Can you run?" The firefighter asked anxiously.

"You bet!"

Gabriel hobbled on stinging legs as they took the stairs, hearing one crash after another behind them. The two men fled the building.

Outside, the sun had turned into a vivid orange ball, floating above the blue horizon of the Pacific.

Gabriel limped over to Paul Vacher, and said, "There's a shitload of evidence in there!"

"We'll salvage anything we can," the arson investigator assured him.

Gabriel viewed the abandoned apartment house as the red light of sunset highlighted his frustration. He'd hoped for closure but the Malibu Canyon Murderer had eluded him. Gabriel was left with a mystery man, burned and demolished clues, and this last strange correspondence from the killer – child pornography; an ominous reminder that perhaps not all of Gabriel's personal mysteries were solved.

Bill Spangler had vanished. The registrar's office at Pepperdine had Bill Spangler listed as a graduate transfer from UC Berkeley. The documents were forged, however, because Berkeley had never transferred a student by that name. In fact, no Bill Spangler ever attended UC Berkeley. The DMV had no blue Buicks registered to such a person.

The Fine Arts Department at Pepperdine was able to furnish Gabriel with a copy of Bill's student ID and an all points bulletin was issued for a tallish man with blonde hair, blue eyes, and full lips.

In the meantime, Gabriel questioned every neighbor and fellow student of the suspect. He heard the same story again and again. Bill Spangler was a private man who lived alone and hung out mostly in the gothic privacy of the prop room, venturing out once in a while to perform in a play. Gabriel found the paradox interesting. Here was an individual who felt extremely shy around people, but had no reservations about performing in front of an audience.

Dr. B was able to throw some light on the paradox. He said that Bill was introverted, living in a region of fantasy, and unable to conduct healthy interactions with his peers. In costume, however, Bill was no longer an insecure misfit, but someone different; a new character. Perhaps his costume changes bolstered his nerve to carry out his death fantasies.

Gabriel talked to Mr. Benson, the property master, who was busy at the vacuform machine, pulling out a sheet of white plastic with the dimpled, rough characteristics of used brick.

"Tell me what was Bill like when the two of you were alone. What did he talk about?"

"Bill didn't much like working with other people. He preferred to work alone. He was a talented artist." Mr. Benson nodded toward the facade of a fireplace resting against one wall. "He did that."

Gabriel walked over and studied the painted "marble," the heavy-looking oak mantle, which wasn't wood at all, but rather a stretch of painted plastic, finely crafted. Bill had an eye for details, making the illusion appear real.

"He did a good job of acting as well," Mr. Benson said, scratching his ample belly.

"That's an understatement," Gabriel muttered, as he inspected the fireplace. His cell phone rang and Gabriel caught it on the second ring.

"It's Paul," the arson investigator announced. "We pulled out some interesting items from the wreckage."

Gabriel promised to come right away. He regarded the portly property master. "Did Bill ever mention to you anything about Russian military weapons?"

Mr. Benson pulled at his dark beard, thinking. "Not that I can remember."

"How about anything metaphysical?"

"What do you mean?"

"Spiritual type stuff."

"Oh, yeah," Mr. Benson said, nodding his head, his beard jutting up and down. "There was a professor here who passed away last semester, a brilliant guy really, he discovered some sort of gene. Bill thought it was a shame his soul was wasted."

Gabriel considered that for a moment, and then said, "Go on."

"Bill told me he had a great theory. He said that there were seven doors in the body through which a person could absorb energy. He said that if he'd known a smart dude like the professor was going to die, he would have made sure he'd absorbed the professor's intelligence through one of those doors. He said he had a very effective way of doing it." Benson laughed. "But you know these theater types, eccentric; right?"

The arson investigators had pulled each and every item out of their boxes and laid them out on Formica tables. Gabriel and Dash moved through the rows of tables, picking up objects and wondering if they bore relevancy to the case.

"Any military knives? Guns?" Gabriel asked, not seeing any himself.

"No," Vacher said. "Some kitchen knives."

"I saw those." Gabriel surveyed the room.

The unburned half of a book lay on one table and Gabriel gently turned the brittle pages.

"Too bad that one burned, huh?" Vacher said, looking over Gabriel's shoulder. "I think it must be pretty old."

Gabriel was sure that it was. The book was a grammar school reader from the Fifties – in the Russian language. Another singed book bore the title "The Sevenfold Journey: Reclaiming Mind, Body, and Spirit through the Chakras."

"The Yamaha dirt bike?" Gabriel asked Vacher.

Vacher shook his head. "We'll send the pieces to the lab. The parking garage sustained a lot of damage."

Vacher led Gabriel down an aisle bordered by Bill Spangler's charred possessions. He stopped in front of the tackle box Gabriel had noticed before he had fallen through the floor.

The metal box had withstood the heat and the demolition well. Gabriel opened the lid and saw a top drawer containing a penlight, a Philips screwdriver, a couple of wrenches and rolls of melted electrical and masking tape.

He lifted and pulled away the top drawer. Underneath were layers of miniature drawers that pulled out accordion style. All were filled with Bill Spangler's treasures. Paul Vacher looked on as Gabriel explored the contents.

"Be careful," Vacher told him. "We haven't photographed these yet."

Gabriel pulled out a smooth, black leather wallet, which he carefully opened. Inside were Brian Goldfield's credit cards and driver's license. Gabriel called Dash over.

Dash moved between Vacher and Gabriel. "His treasure chest," Dash observed.

Gabriel nodded and picked up a man's ring with a small diamond at its center that was weirdly tied to a couple of other gold rings by a dirty ribbon. An inscription on the inside of the band read, "Gloria loves Ted." Gloria Lusk and Ted Brody, Gabriel thought, a promise of love that would never be fulfilled.

Gabriel figured the other bands belonged to Ronald and Meredith Hall. Gabriel wondered what made someone capable of robbing another of love and life.

He reached into the tackle box and pulled out a few loose credit cards and a large, gold cross. Gabriel figured the cross came off Patrick Funston's gold chain. He set it down on the table, unwilling to think about gold chains, and withdrew a dirty blue cat's collar.

"Duffy," Gabriel said, reading the tag.

"Family pet?" Vacher asked hopefully.

"Not likely," Gabriel said, shaking the collar; hearing the jingling bell.

I'm Fortunato.

"Guys like this usually start with animals," Gabriel explained to Vacher. "They get a taste of power in dishing out fear. Problem is, they get bored and move onto bigger things."

"Son of a bitch," Dash muttered, "Look at that."

Gabriel tracked the path of Dash's eyes into the depths of the box. Tania Dankowski's earring lolled back and forth with its flag of black, dried earlobe.

A madman's treasure trove, Gabriel thought. Aloud he said, "I wonder where he went."

"Maybe he's at a friend's house," Vacher suggested.

"I don't think he has any friends," Gabriel said. "The theater people say he kept to himself."

Vacher shrugged. "You never know. Maybe he's camping in the mountains."

Gabriel wondered if the suspect was really hiding in the mountains, perhaps finding shelter in an old Chumash Indian cave etched with pictographs of jumping deer. Maybe he concealed himself in an abandoned coyote den, and slept comfortably on a twig-covered floor littered with the frail bones and puffy white tails of rabbits.

"He's gone," Gabriel said decisively.

"The airport police haven't spotted him," Dash countered. "He didn't have enough time to pack up and make a solid plan of action, Gabe. He's still around."

Gabriel didn't think so.

I'm Fortunato.

"Have you found anything else? Any notes?" Gabriel asked the arson investigator.

Vacher regarded him distastefully, saying, "I doubt any one piece of paper would have made it through. But this thing was certainly tough enough to withstand the fire." Vacher nodded at the tackle box.

Gabriel regarded the tackle box again. Why would Bill abandon his treasure chest? He could have easily carried it with him. Gabriel searched the last drawers carefully and found nothing. He then picked the box up and shook it, satisfied to hear a slight shuffling sound. He turned the box upside down and a piece of yellow paper, the size of business card, fluttered out.

On the front of the yellow card was the letter "T." On either side of the T were two masks – comic and tragic. Spelled out in the top cross of the T was the word "Thespian." The area for a signature was cut from the center of the card along with a troupe number. But the school issuing the card had been handwritten – University of California at Berkeley.

"Let's get this fingerprinted," Gabriel said, holding the card to the light.

Dash read the card as well. "What are Thespians? A secret cult?"

Gabriel had to smile. "Thespians are stage performers."

"A guild?"

"More like a club, I think." Gabriel flipped the card over and saw a pledge. Words were missing, cut out, but there was a line at the bottom of the card which read, "Act well your part; there all the honor lies."

Dash peered closer at the card. "Could be one of his fakes."

"I don't think so," Gabriel said. He hadn't forgotten the Thomas Welby murder of San Francisco. And if there were a connection between the suspect and Gabriel, it most likely had its roots in San Francisco. Gabriel was meant to find the note. The Malibu Canyon Murderer had moved north and he wanted Gabriel to follow him.

❧ ❧ ❧

Gabriel felt an odd mix of elation and fear on his drive back to Santa Monica. A full white moon hung over the freeway and the open car window let in the warm night air. He knew a return to San Francisco would dredge up bad memories for him but Gabriel could not turn back now.

At his apartment, Gabriel phoned Dr. B for an appointment. He also left a message at the UC Berkeley registrar's office asking for a list of student names, in particular, those of Thespian members from past years. That done, he collapsed on his bed.

Ming was supposed to come over. Gabriel had promised to cook for her a fabulous gourmet meal – wild duck in a Madeira sauce, as a compensation of sorts for wrecking her car. He needed to get started but he was worn out. The scabs on his legs looked like road kill and the emotional rollercoaster he'd been riding was wearing him down.

He must have fallen asleep, for suddenly Ming was there, at his bedside. Gabriel opened bleary eyes to see the gentle wave of her black hair and her quirky smile.

"The door was unlocked," she explained. "Are you okay?"

"Fine." He was surprised to hear it come out as a croak.

Ming surveyed his prostrate body and said, "I should have brought in food."

Gabriel rubbed his eyes, sitting up, "No, I'm okay. How's your car?"

"Oh, the Department rented me a nice new Volvo and the insurance company said mine isn't a total loss."

"Good."

"Should we take a rain-check on this?"

Gabriel yawned, shaking his head. "No."

Ming paused a moment and then reached into her purse. "I found this in the car when I went to clean it out." She pulled out the photo of the man and boy. "I don't usually go in for this kind of stuff. I prefer whips and chains—"

Ignoring Ming's lightheartedness, Gabriel took the photo from her, contemplating the sick mixture of pain and ecstasy. Feeling suddenly nauseous, Gabriel placed it face down on the bed. "It's his. He left it for me."

"What does this mean? What's going on?" Ming asked. "Can't you trust me?"

Gabriel took a deep breath and let it out slowly. His eyes searched Ming's for a moment and then said, "I was molested as a child by a neighbor."

Ming regarded him and Gabriel saw a galaxy of emotions evolving in the dark universe of her eyes.

Gabriel continued, finding it strangely easy to talk, "I blocked it out. I remember it now but I don't want to think about it."

"I understand," Ming whispered.

"What I can't figure out is how the suspect knows about it. Andrew Pierce, the neighbor of mine who... He couldn't be Bill Spangler. And I never told anyone else about it. I couldn't. I didn't remember the abuse myself."

Ming pondered this and said, "But those notes the killer left for you never mentioned anything specific."

"The young ones tempt you? He's knows, Ming. I mean, look at that picture. It's no coincidence."

Ming said nothing, being at a loss for words.

"And I get the feeling this guy wants to meet. He left a calling card in his 'trophy' box. He wants a one-on-one and he's gonna get it."

"Hey," Ming warned, forcing Gabriel to meet her eyes. "You are giving this guy too much credit. He made a mistake, that's all. Serial killers have a subconscious desire to get caught, remember? He doesn't know anything about what happened to you."

Gabriel shook his head, disagreeing.

"Listen to me." Ming pointed at the photo. "That is not you and you are not that. You went through a horrible experience, something no child should ever have to endure; but you are a strong and wonderful man. You have to look at who you are now. You have to see yourself the way I see you."

Ming reached out and traced a finger along the new scar on his brow. Gabriel closed his eyes, welcoming her touch which sent shivers through his tired body; waking him up.

She kissed him gently on the forehead, on the cheek, and then finally on his lips. Gabriel combed her black tresses with his fingers, his hands becoming more eager as her lips pressed his own. He finally clutched her hair, pulling her down on top of him, crushing the magazine photo. Ming flipped off her sandals, while her hungry hands rubbed Gabriel's chest, kneading his muscles. He caressed her breasts through her blouse, feeling them firm beneath his touch, until he could no longer hold back and began tearing at the buttons. Ming explored his mouth with her tongue, and he reciprocated, feeling the hardness grow in his pants. Soon, her hand was feeling it as well.

Then somebody knocked at the front door.

"Let it go," she whispered into his ear.

Gabriel nodded and dove into the softness of her breasts, allowing his impatient fingers to travel the length of her body. He pulled up her skirt and reached between her legs – under her panties.

Someone pounded incessantly on the front door. Gabriel jerked his head up, annoyed at the intensity of the knocking and then a disturbing thought crossed his mind. Maybe Bill Spangler wanted to meet <u>now</u>.

Gabriel grabbed his revolver and opened the door "Lieutenant?"

Ramirez didn't wait for an invitation; he bypassed Gabriel and stepped inside. "Why'd you make me wait out there like an asshole?" Ramirez raised his eyebrows at the gun in Gabriel's hand. "What? I'm not welcome?"

Ming walked in from the bedroom and froze upon seeing Ramirez. The short man eyed her in surprise and then grimaced at her shirt. Ming looked down to see several of her buttons still undone.

"Now this is a sick thing," Ramirez muttered as he shook a cigarette out of his pack. "Dr. Frankenstein hookin' up with Mr. Hyde."

Ming's normally mocha skin went white as she clasped her buttons. She took a prim seat on the couch and smoothed her mussed up hair.

"You've got something you wanted to tell me, Sir?" Gabriel asked tiredly.

Ramirez lit up. "Mind if I smoke?"

Gabriel was about to protest when Ramirez said, "I found out something I think you ought to know."

"What?" Gabriel asked, watching the cigarette smoke hang in the air.

"Dr. Berkowitz mentioned you'd be interested in the whereabouts of a certain individual named Andrew Pierce."

Gabriel went cold and exchanged glances with Ming.

"What did you find out?" Gabriel asked quietly.

"He's dead. He died of prostrate cancer two years ago."

Gabriel slowly sat down next to Ming. Fitting end, Gabriel thought.

"I wanted to tell you personally." Ramirez took a puff and gazed with amusement at the couple seated on the couch. "Looks like I came at the wrong time."

Ramirez smirked and opened the front door to let himself out. "Hasta mañana, Dr. Li."

The lieutenant closed the door behind him.

Ming put her head in her hands. "Oh my God; I don't believe this just happened. Of all the people..." Ming glanced at Gabriel. He was staring at a distant corner of the room. Ming put her hand gently on his arm. "Now you know for sure that your past has nothing to do with the Malibu Canyon Murderer."

Gabriel didn't reply. The fact that Andrew Pierce was dead left him strangely numb. Should he have cared one way or the other? It didn't really matter. Andrew being dead did not give Gabriel back his lost childhood. Ming seemed to be radiating strange vibes and he looked at her. She anxiously chewed on a hangnail.

"Don't worry about Ramirez," he told her.

"I'd better go," she said.

"You don't have to."

Ming could not even verbalize. She simply shook her head, grabbed her purse, and left Gabriel staring after her as she walked out.

The following day, Gabriel sat beside Dr. B and asked, "Tell me again what Figley said."

"Who?"

"And you're the guy who likes quoting people." Gabriel viewed the psychiatrist benignly. "You remember; something about turning a bad situation around."

"Oh, yes," Dr. B said, nodding. "Figley wrote that recovery from a trauma occurs when a victim is transformed into a survivor."

"A victim becomes a survivor."

"Yes, one who is able to integrate the catastrophe into his or her life history and then use it as a source of strength." Dr. B pushed his glasses up the bridge of his nose, and continued. "Figley divided the process into five stages: the catastrophe itself, relief and confusion, avoidance, which you have been familiar with, and reconsideration – which is what you are experiencing now: an ability to address the catastrophe. The last stage is adjustment and that is where we will go from here."

Gabriel gazed intensely at the wooden clock on Dr. B's desk, his fingernails absently grazing the fabric of the armchair.

"Something on your mind?" Dr. B asked softly.

"Do you think going to San Francisco would help me address the catastrophe?"

"In a controlled manner, I suppose."

Gabriel nodded thoughtfully. "And when do these fugue states stop?"

"I wouldn't be surprised if they stop altogether now that you feel safe. Any nightmares lately?"

Gabriel shook his head, rather surprised at that fact himself.

"That's good," Dr. B told him. "How about the headaches?"

"Not so frequent now."

"I'm very pleased, Gabe. And what about your trouble with anorgasmia? Are you still experiencing discomfort in sexual situations?"

Gabriel thought of the softness between Ming's thighs. "Not really."

A part of Gabriel wanted to share his feelings about Ming with Dr. B, but Ming was freaked out enough over Ramirez discovering their relationship.

Do we have a relationship?

"That is good news, don't you think?" Dr. B clasped his bony hands and brought them up to his mouth, his brown eyes glued on Gabriel's case file. "I know you've reached the point, Gabe, that you are turning things around. You are no longer willing to be victimized."

Gabriel closed his eyes. He was about to tell Dr. B about the pornographic picture left for him by the suspect when a beep sounded on the intercom and a secretary's voice cut in.

"Doctor, your next appointment is here."

CHAPTER 21

Gabriel's first instinct had been to run immediately up north, but he knew they needed something solid to go on. Since the description of the Buick did not provide any leads, Gabriel hoped that a clue would materialize in the long list of Berkeley Thespian names. The names were listed in order of the year graduated. Since "Bill Spangler" was an alleged graduate transfer student, Gabriel had asked to see the Berkeley Thespians of the last ten years. He first scanned the last names beginning with an "S."

Dash nursed a cup of coffee, watching him.

"You see a Bill Spangler?" Dash asked his partner.

"I don't expect to. Maybe something with an "S" though."

"It could be any name on that list. Let's not forget that Bill Spangler's initials are B.S."

Gabriel paused and smiled. He hadn't thought of that. "The suspect claims to know me," he reminded his partner. "If that's so, then I've got to know him."

"Long shot," Dash said, shaking his head. "Like we've said a million times, it could be some lunatic who targeted you because of your media attention."

Gabriel regarded his partner for a moment and Dash backed off.

Gabriel began with the oldest graduation dates – ten years previous. He checked off the names one by one with a pencil.

The second hand of the clock on the wall swam smoothly around, chalking up the minutes. Dash left for a refill on his coffee. He passed a pair of detectives, guns in their holsters, leaning on their desks, arguing mildly about a baseball player's trade. Someone arrived with Chinese food and the entire room filled with the fragrance of spicy shrimp.

Dash returned to his desk with a full cup, sat down, and watched Gabriel scan the list, moving from one year to the next.

"Anything?" Dash asked, blowing on his coffee.

"Nothing," Gabriel answered.

The secretaries pounded the computer keyboards. Another detective mulled over crime scene photos and talked quietly into the mini-recorder he held in his hand.

Gabriel flipped a page over and inspected the next list of names.

"You know," Dash said, grimacing into his mug. "I'm going to bring in my own coffee from now on. I think they made this coffee with used dishwater. Not fit for–"

"Oh, no…" Gabriel said, staring at the paper in his hand. He looked anxiously around his desk for a moment, reached for the phone, and then retracted his hand.

"What?" Dash asked eagerly, setting down his coffee. "What'd you find? You recognize a name?"

Gabriel ceased moving and looked at Dash with immense pain. "Yeah…"

"Who is it?"

In answer, Gabriel suddenly grabbed his jacket, his keys, pager, and cell phone and quickly jogged to the exit, punching numbers into his cell phone as he went.

Dash gaped after him, thinking there couldn't possibly be another detective with a partner as unconventional as the one he had. Sighing, Dash picked up the list of names. He fully expected to see the last name of McRay, surmising that Gabriel had seen a wayward relative listed. However, the last checked name meant nothing to Dash: Archwood, Victor.

Dash glanced at the exit, wondering who Victor Archwood was and why his name fomented such a strong reaction in Gabriel.

An hour later, Raymond Berkowitz walked briskly down the hall of headquarters in Monterey Park, fighting the urge to run. An Adlerian psychiatrist dealt with "teleology": an approach stressing that future goals or purposes mold a personality. This theory contrasted with Freud's determinism, which considered the present as a product of the past. While Gabriel certainly was a walking result of his past, his prognosis according to Dr. B, would depend upon his future goals. Right now those future goals needed to be linked with Figley's adjustment stage.

Three detectives, two male and one female, bustled by the psychiatrist, all pumped up and ready to fly. Word was out that the Malibu Canyon Murder case was about to wrap-up and the place was buzzing. The Malibu Canyon Murderer had a name and it was Victor Archwood. Dr. B already knew this of course. Gabriel had called him and told him everything.

Dr. B nervously picked up his pace and his shins cried. Gabriel was still in the reconsideration stage. True, he was addressing the molestation — memories were surfacing and he no longer avoided the unpleasant recollections; in fact, he was doing a darn good job of dealing with them, but he was not yet in the adjustment stage. He hadn't dealt with Andrew's betrayal, with his parents, with…

Dr. B stopped in the middle of the hallway and composed himself. Just ahead, more detectives poured out of the conference room.

Gabriel was not ready to face a perpetrator, Dr. B decided. No way. Not this one. Dr. B knocked heavily on the conference room door.

"Lieutenant Ramirez?" he called out.

"Just a second!"

Ramirez exited the conference room. The little man was puffed up and excited. He shook out a pack of cigarettes. "Busy time, Doc, we're alerting San Francisco PD, and they want me up there pronto. The whole team."

"That's what I needed to talk to you about, Miguel."

"Let's talk as we go." Ramirez strode down the hall with Dr. B ambling quickly at his side. Ramirez fumbled for his lighter. "Hey, didn't I tell you the suspect was somebody McRay knew?"

"Yes, he knew him from a long time ago. Listen, Miguel, I want you to pull Gabriel off the case."

"What?" Ramirez snapped and halted. "A couple of weeks ago you were begging me to keep him on."

"Yes, I know, but I think Gabriel isn't the one who should bring the suspect in."

Ramirez lit his cigarette and began moving down the hallway once more, this time at a more controlled pace. "The Feds are coming in. I've been fighting them off all summer. They'll take all the goddam credit. I need McRay. He knows this guy."

"Can you for once put your politics aside?" Dr. B asked tightly, striding down the hall, glued against Ramirez. "Can you think about a human being for Christ's sake?"

Ramirez halted once more and faced Dr. B. "I am thinking about McRay. You know how much this collar means to him. Give me a good reason why I should pull him off the case."

"It has to do with Gabriel's relationship with the suspect."

Ramirez shrugged, "It's not Andrew Pierce. That dude is fertilizer."

"It's confidential."

"Not a good enough reason." Ramirez exhaled a line of gray smoke and began walking away.

"Lieutenant!" Dr. B chased after him. "Victor Archwood is harboring a very serious vendetta against Gabriel and I don't think Gabriel is ready to handle it."

"I'm listening."

"Abused children teach themselves to endure assault. They learn they can't protect themselves. As adults, they may be blind to dangers that are obvious to others."

Ramirez dragged on his cigarette as he walked. "McRay was abused?"

Dr. B sighed, visualizing his father shaking his head, pipe in mouth; thinking that his only son was a great fool.

Ramirez grinned. "Don't worry, Doc. You can trust me."

Dr. B pushed himself in front of Ramirez, stopping the shorter man in his tracks. "What I'm trying to say is that Gabriel could freeze when faced with another – perpetrator."

"He's a seasoned cop," Ramirez told him squarely. "He'll know what to do."

"He's also a victim and this killer has got his number. Gabriel's relationship with the suspect is too emotional; too raw."

"How so?"

Dr. B looked down at the floor, wondering if he would lose his license over this. "When Gabriel was a teenager, he beat a boy entrusted to his care. That boy's name is Victor Archwood."

❧ ❧ ❧

"The thousand injuries of Fortunato I had borne as I best could, but when he ventured upon insult, I vowed revenge."

The Cask of Amontillado Edgar Allen Poe

CHAPTER 22

Gabriel stood waiting outside the lieutenant's office with his duffle bag, impatient to get to the airport. When Ramirez called him in, he knew right away something was up because Ramirez wasn't brimming with his usual cockiness; he was acting sketchy and even more frightening – he was being nice.

"Hey, you want a soda or something?" Ramirez asked, helping himself to a Coke.

"No thanks, Lieutenant." Gabriel stuck a thumb toward the door. "I should be moving along; Dash is waiting for me."

"Oh, don't worry about that," Ramirez said, pulling at his shirt, which was damp with nervous perspiration. "Did I tell you I'm really pleased with your work, McRay. You've done well, you and your partner." He gave Gabriel a brittle smile that threatened to crack open his face.

Now Gabriel was beginning to get worried. His eyes followed Ramirez as he paraded around; swinging his soda in the air. Inside Gabriel's duffle bag was the child pornography left by Archwood. Gabriel wondered if Ramirez knew about it. It was evidence, after all.

"You think you'd recognize this guy from memory?" Ramirez asked him.

"I seriously doubt it, seeing that the last time I saw him he was about seven."

Gabriel glanced at the clock on the wall. He needed to get going.

Ramirez stopped dancing and faced Gabriel. "Like I said, you've done well, McRay. You'll get the credit for breaking the case. But I'm reassigning you."

Gabriel's eyes went wide. "What?"

"It's better this way. You're too emotionally involved in this case. It's bringing up all that bad shit—"

"What do you know about it?"

"Nothing," Ramirez said, waving Gabriel away, unable to meet his eyes. "You got issues. Everyone has issues."

Gabriel studied him for a moment, gauging how much Ramirez knew, and then said, "Please don't take me off."

"Dr. Berkowitz doesn't think it's a good idea for you to confront this Archwood guy." Ramirez cleared his throat. "He mentioned this guy may try to mind-fuck you. He thinks you'll go weak in the knees."

Gabriel was stunned. "Dr. B said that?"

Ramirez nodded.

Gabriel shook his head, unbelieving. Finally, he turned to Ramirez, and said, "Do you think I'm going to freeze when I'm face-to-face with a monster?"

Ramirez didn't answer and his silence reminded Gabriel of the nightmare he'd had in which he'd laid himself down at a knife-wielding assailant's feet.

But I am not a victim anymore.

Gabriel reached into the duffle bag and pulled out the photograph of the man and boy. He handed it to Ramirez.

Ramirez looked at the picture in disgust. "What the hell is this?"

"Our friend left it for me in Ming's car the night the apartment burned. I should have turned it in, I know, but..."

Ramirez shook his head at Gabriel. "This is exactly what the doc is talking about McRay. You should have turned it in. Have you checked it for prints?"

"I did, but I couldn't find any. I hate to say it but my prints and Ming's are all over it."

"I'll enter it into evidence anyhow," Ramirez said, frowning. "He's already fucking with your mind, making you break protocol. You're off the case."

"No," Gabriel begged. "I don't know what Dr. B told you or didn't tell you about my problems. But I am telling you, Lieutenant, that I've already been face-to-face with a monster. He's been living inside me for years, feeding off every aspect of my life. But you can see I'm not frozen. I'm fully functional. You have to believe me."

Ramirez glanced again at the photo and then looked at Gabriel with what appeared to be empathy. "Go catch your plane," he said.

Gabriel nodded, grabbed his duffle bag and headed out the door.

"Don't you make me look bad, McRay!" Ramirez yelled after him in his usual manner.

✂ ✂ ✂

The Flight Attendant on the Southwest plane was wordlessly pointing toward the exit door while another female voice was heard explaining what to do in case of an emergency. Gabriel gazed out the small window into the low sun. He patted his jacket pocket, hearing the familiar shake of the aspirin bottle which comforted him.

Gabriel felt his earlier bravado slipping away with every mile that put him closer to San Francisco. He wished he could have spoken one more time to Dr. B before he had left. Leaning against the window, he closed his eyes hoping for a moment's respite; but as the plane soared into the sky, troubled images emerged, demanding his attention.

The Melody Theater, butter-flavored popcorn, butter-flavored fingers; the flapping of a gold necklace as it went up and down in the air

"What did Ramirez want to talk to you about?" Dash asked.

"Just wanted to let me know the Feds are in town," Gabriel lied, opening his eyes. He smoothed his curling black hair and straightened his tie. Anything to appear composed.

"Okay, tell me again how you know Archwood."

He knows I was raped.

"I babysat him a couple of times."

"Weird that he'd remember your name."

Gabriel didn't comment. He could barely remember Vic.

Vic. That's what I called him. Strange coincidence isn't it? A Vic is a victim.

A vague picture of a tow-headed boy with sweet, sad blue eyes surfaced in Gabriel's memory.

I remember you were a sad little kid. I remember you now.

Vic had been a boy who had carried baggage upon his thin shoulders. He'd been a boy like Gabriel, full of unfulfilled wishes, upside down smiles, and tremendous pain. Vic had adored Gabriel, hung upon his every word, told him he loved him as much as he loved his grandfather—

Gabriel furrowed his eyebrows. Something about the grandfather... Gabriel tried to nudge open that particular mental door but eventually gave up; recalling only that Vic had loved his grandpa and had lost him. Gabriel could not see a father in the picture but the mother stood out clearly. What was her name? She had surely intimidated Gabriel.

I beat him. I hurt him. How could I have done such a thing?
You're an evil, evil man.

The words wormed their way into Gabriel's brain like a parasite feeding on a crumbling host. Gabriel restlessly turned away from the window, only to find Dash staring at him.

"You okay?" Dash asked.

Gabriel nodded; mute under the hailstorm of his memories.

Rape is harder on boys, Dr. B had told Gabriel, because of the social stigmas that go along with being strong and unemotional. Gabriel's very private parts were being plundered, handled and mishandled without his consent. The very essence of his power over his own sexuality was being destroyed. He had no control over his own body. Those feelings of degradation had run along his veins like poison.

Once, Gabriel's mother had found him poking a hole in his arm with the metal point of a school compass. He was bleeding all over his math homework.

"What did you cut yourself for?" she had asked, dabbing his arm with antiseptic.

Gabriel had told her he had been trying to make a hole in himself so all the rotted stuff inside his body would drain out. Gabriel now recalled his mother's peculiar look and the sad fact that she'd considered herself too preoccupied to explore the matter further.

One day Andrew disappeared. No more chugging engine. No more knocks on Gabriel's door – knocks that filled him with dread as if the Grim Reaper himself came calling. No one ever told Gabriel where Andrew had gone or why he had moved out. The movies, the candy, and the molestations stopped as suddenly as they had started. Movie stars left indelible footprints on Hollywood Boulevard, Gabriel thought. Andrew

Pierce had left his handprints on Gabriel and there they would stay forever.

Turn the situation around. Use the catastrophe as a source of strength.

But how?

"The weather is a cool fifty-eight degrees and the sun is shining." the pilot announced. "We'll be landing momentarily, so please observe the fasten-your-seatbelt sign."

Gabriel looked out the window, viewing the orange waves of the Golden Gate Bridge over the water. Home again. Gabriel was a haunted house with empty rooms filled with ghosts. The Bay City would surely make them moan and rattle their chains.

An African-American officer with an impressive mustache met the Los Angeles detectives at the airport and introduced himself as Sergeant Krol of the San Francisco Police Department. Accompanying him was Special Agent Ralph Tenant from the FBI. The FBI agent informed them that no current residence was found for Victor Archwood, but a stakeout team was posted in front of Archwood's mother's house.

"What's her name?" Gabriel asked, sure it was on the tip of his tongue.

"Natalie Archwood," Sergeant Krol answered.

Natalie Archwood, Gabriel repeated silently. He asked Ralph Tenant, "No sign of the suspect?"

"No."

"He likes costumes," Gabriel reminded them. "Are you sure no one's been around?"

"Just the mother," Tenant said, and then quickly added, "We figured you guys would want to question her."

"You figured right," Gabriel told him and followed Tenant into Sergeant Krol's Pontiac sedan. Dash took a seat up front and perused the cold case report on Thomas Welby that Krol had provided him.

"You want to bring me up to date?" Tenant asked Gabriel.

The FBI agent was a porcine man with a chunk of gray hair on the top of his head and a stomach that bulged over his belt. His cheeks were a blotchy red and when he talked, the words wheezed out as if from a broken bellows.

"How much do you know?" Gabriel asked him.

"Just that Archwood's name was found in the Berkeley school register. You've run prints on him, right?"

Gabriel regarded the federal agent. Relations between the police and the FBI were touchy sometimes. While most other police forces welcomed the help and the technology the FBI offered, Ramirez took it personally when bigger guns crowded his investigations.

"We've got the suspect's DNA," Gabriel said. "We just don't know for sure if it belongs to Archwood. Maybe we'll find something personal we can test in his mom's house."

"Look," Tenant wheezed, "no one's going to hustle in on your investigation, if that's what you're worried about. But you guys have had an entire summer to track down this bozo and—"

"And we've tracked him down," Gabriel finished his sentence for him.

The stake-out team radioed the detectives that nobody was home at the Archwood house, so Gabriel decided to first view the site of the Thomas Welby murder.

While the other officers waited in the car, Gabriel and Dash walked the stretch of beach near the murder site. They sat on a low stone wall that bordered the sand. Unlike sunny Santa Monica Beach, Sunset Beach was continually draped in gray.

"No blood, no trace of anything found around the car?" Gabriel asked Dash as they stood looking out at the slate-colored water of the Pacific.

"Nothing was stated in the report," Dash replied. "Just a torched car."

Gabriel's finger traced a groove in the stone, remembering that as an adolescent, he had carved his own initials with a penknife in this very wall somewhere down the beach. "The accelerant was booze, correct?"

"Yep."

Gabriel glanced behind him, hearing the zooming cars on Sunset Avenue. He saw Krol's Pontiac, a row of trees planted in the street's median, and the houses beyond, stacked side- by-side.

"According to the report," Dash said, "Welby's wounds were similar in depth and width to the Malibu Canyon murders, which indicates the same knife was used. If Welby was killed with the same knife, Archwood has kept the weapon for a long time. I would guess it has some special meaning in his 'ritual.' But Welby's assault pattern was different – sloppy and random."

"Could have been his first taste of human blood," Gabriel suggested.

"I think so, too." Dash regarded Gabriel carefully. "Did you know Thomas Welby by any chance?"

Gabriel frowned at his partner. "I don't know every resident of San Francisco, Dash."

His partner shrugged, kicking up more sand. "I only thought that since you knew the suspect maybe you knew the first victim as well. This is your old neighborhood, isn't it?"

Gabriel felt a pit yawning in this stomach.

They heard a yell and turned around. Krol was waving them over.

Gabriel nodded in acknowledgement, and jumped off the wall. "Let's go. Somebody's home."

The detectives drove along Irving Street, following a trolley car and counting the miles from the Welby crime site to the Archwood house. On their way, they passed the Chinese businesses, restaurants, apartment houses, and stores, all of which characterized the Sunset District.

They pulled up in front of a light pink house. The rolling fog from the nearby beach blanketed all the houses, which were neatly stacked like pastel-colored dominos, one right next to the other. The canopy of fog crept into every crevice, eating into the car paint and laying damp hands on the residents when they stepped outside to breathe in whispers of sea salt.

While Archwood's home was a good stretch from the Welby murder site, Gabriel noted the trek could easily be made by a fit young man pumped up with adrenaline.

Gabriel and Dash exited the sedan and walked past the FBI surveillance van posted on the street. They stepped over a tiny patch of lawn and climbed the pink granite steps. Dash positioned himself slightly behind Gabriel and drew his revolver. Gabriel knocked heavily on the front door.

A moment later the door swung open to reveal an obese woman. Stringy blond hair fell unflatteringly upon the wide shoulders of a long-sleeved muumuu. "Yes?"

"Natalie Archwood?" Gabriel asked, sure that it wasn't her.

"Who wants to know?"

Gabriel displayed his badge, "Los Angeles Sheriff's Department. My name is Sergeant Gabriel McRay. We're investigating a homicide."

"You're cops?" she asked, squinting through piggy hazel eyes at the badge.

"Yes. Is Mrs. Archwood at home?"

The big woman shrunk a bit and her voice got whiny. "No, why?"

In the background something crashed, and a child screamed. The heavy woman turned her bulk toward the back. "Stop that screaming!" she screamed.

Gabriel and Dash exchanged looks.

"Cut it ouuuuuut!" she yelled behind her, and a little boy ran up. She grabbed his arm tightly. "Leave your sister alone or you'll get it, you hear me?"

The small boy broke away and ran back into the depths of the house.

To the detectives, the woman said tiredly, "Look, Ma isn't home. And I don't live here; I'm just doing my wash. What d'you need her for?"

"We'd like to ask her a few questions," Gabriel said. "You are her daughter?"

"Yeah."

"You have a brother, Victor Archwood?" Gabriel asked.

"Yes," she answered, blowing a lock of hair out of her face. "What do you want him for?"

"We'd like to talk to him. Is he home?"

"No."

The two detectives once again exchanged glances.

"Could we come in and check?" Gabriel asked, hoping they could search the premises without a warrant.

She squinted at them suspiciously, sizing them up. Gabriel withstood her scrutiny. Lady, he thought, we're nothing compared to that brother of yours.

"I think you're gonna have to talk to Ma," she told them and jumped at another crash. "God damnnnnn it!" She stomped back into the depths of the house, and the earth shook in her wake. Gabriel heard a sharp slap and then the cry of a child.

Gabriel nodded to Dash to tuck his gun away, and they peeked into the house and heard a cacophony of mewling children.

"Ma'am?" Gabriel ventured.

From the doorway, he could see a parlor brimming with antique furniture. A hallway veered to the left, from which poured the sounds of crying and a televised cartoon. The woman dragged her bulk down the hall and the two detectives stepped back.

"Look, you're going to have to talk to my mother," she said, and then halted. Grimacing, the big girl put a melodramatic hand over her heart.

Dash looked at her with concern. "Are you all right?"

Her face twisted like a pretzel. "Oooo. I've got diabetes." She leaned against the doorjamb. "My sugar sucks today."

Gabriel reached out a steadying arm. "Here, take it easy. Let me help you to the couch."

She peered at him as though she suddenly caught his scent. He sensed a primal part of her turn on like a switch. "Thanks."

She led the two officers into the parlor. The place was tidy but had a nursing home smell of old sheets and institutional food. The furniture had obviously seen better days. The fabrics were threadbare and the carved wood finishes were scuffed and dry. Gabriel, feeling claustrophobic, eased the lady onto an overstuffed couch.

The woman introduced herself as Sonia.

The two crying children ran into the room and seemed to deflate when they saw their mother languishing on the couch, obviously intent on ignoring them. Dash and Gabriel exchanged quick looks, and Dash took up the "Daddy" role, stepping over to them and speaking quietly. The children responded by whining even more, taking advantage of their paying audience.

As a last resort, Dash pulled out his badge and that seemed to interest them enough so that they took his hands and led their new friend down the hallway toward the blaring cartoon.

"Have you always been diabetic?" Gabriel asked her, watching Dash leave.

"I developed it a few years ago." Sonia grimaced again and opened one eye, directed at Gabriel. "Could you hand me that syringe on the counter?"

Gabriel's eyes searched the room. "Over—?"

"There," she said like a weak kitten. "On the buffet."

Gabriel walked slowly into a connecting dining room with a cherry wood table and matching buffet. A samovar sat on a lace doily next to some ceramic figurines. As he laid his hands on the syringe, he saw a warped color photo – a studio rendition of two blond girls in periwinkle blue dresses and a young, tow-headed boy – Victor Archwood.

Gabriel studied the photo. Archwood was pictured exactly how Gabriel remembered him, about seven or eight. He smiled the big-toothed, awkward smile of preadolescence.

Seeds of guilt sprouted in Gabriel. Staring at the faded photograph brought him back to this very house as a young man, sporting longer hair and a thinner body. Gabriel couldn't remember why he had unleashed the rage on Vic, but he could remember every detail of the beating. When Gabriel had punched the boy for the last time, he'd leaned his throbbing head against the wall, astonished that the anger was still pumping vigorously through his veins. And the boy's unusual reaction had made Gabriel feel even more like a monster.

Vic had been curled up in a ball on the floor, crying. He sat up and looked at Gabriel, hiccupping and holding his stomach. Gabriel had fully expected Vic to bolt for the door, screaming blame, but he hadn't. The little boy had looked at Gabriel with an expression of acceptance, as if he had deserved the bad treatment.

Just the way I thought I deserved bad treatment.

"This is Victor as a boy?" Gabriel asked, knowing it was.

"Huh?" Sonia looked over tiredly. "Oh, yeah, that's all of us."

"And you have a twin sister as well?"

"Fraternal twin. We look nothing alike." Sonia affected an ache somewhere in her side and she nodded, painfully. "We're not what you would call a close-knit family."

Gabriel forced a smile and walked the syringe over to her. Sonia made a great show of pulling up her sleeve and grimacing as the needle went in.

She nodded toward the back of the house. "Your partner has a great way with kids."

"Kids can be tough, can't they?" he said, playing a sympathetic advocate.

"You don't know the half of it. They drive me insane."

"You're lucky to have them." Gabriel didn't know why he said it. He felt some parents possessed such disregard for the most beautiful of creations – their own. It rang a bell too close to home for him.

"You want 'em?" she said, sniffing, and retracted the syringe. "So, what do you want with Vic?"

"We just want to talk to him. You're sure he hasn't contacted you?" Gabriel tried to sound nonchalant.

Sonia looked at him suspiciously. Gabriel wasn't worried. He doubted there was anybody Sonia trusted.

"He's not contacted me," she stated. She sniffed again and then suddenly was thrown forward by a powerful sneeze. "Oh my allergies!" She snorted like a pig and sat back against the couch pillows, winded. Gabriel caught her drift.

This one uses her illnesses like someone else uses booze or drugs.

"I think Ma said Vic called her yesterday."

Gabriel's heart thumped but he kept his manner casual. "Did your mother say where he was?"

"You'll have to ask her."

"He's been in contact with your mother though?"

She rolled her sleeve back down her meaty arm. "That's what I said. You know for a cop you're kinda dumb."

And for a woman, Gabriel thought, you're kinda repulsive. Was she protecting her brother? She seemed too caught up in her aches and pains to conceive of conspiracies. She was just another damaged being. She'd managed to push two kids out into the world, but that hadn't given her any happiness.

Sonia seemed to drift into her own world then, and it made Gabriel wonder what else was in the syringe. It was alright. He'd gotten as much as he needed for now.

Dash joined him and they left Sonia with the number to the SFPD Homicide Division.

"Will you please contact us if you hear anything more from your brother?" Gabriel requested.

She nodded, halfway into outer space.

The two detectives eyed each other and headed out the door. The kids were quiet, eyes glued to a violent cartoon rocking the television set.

272

CHAPTER

Gabriel decided to walk the old neighborhood while the other detectives waited for Natalie Archwood to return home. He was curious to see his old house again. On his way, Gabriel passed the site of the old Melody Theater, razed years ago and now home to a gas station. A chain drug store stood on the spot of the five-and-dime where Gabriel used to buy his candy. He put his hands on the glass window. Dozens of Halloween masks frowned and smiled vacantly at him from their display, reminding Gabriel of the comedy and tragedy masks. Gabriel zipped up his jacket. The cooler air and Halloween decorations signaled the change of seasons. Would it herald a change for him as well?

He walked along, feeling familiar sidewalk under his feet, remembering every crack in the cement; every tall tree lining the street. If he inhaled deeply enough, he could catch the scent of seawater and the fragrance of the distant pine trees that shaded the dirt paths of Golden Gate Park.

At last Gabriel stood in front of his house, gazing at the granite steps he used to sit on. He recalled countless days and nights, coming and going down these steps; a secret stash of holidays and birthdays celebrated behind that closed front door. After a moment, Gabriel turned to face the Pierce house.

He felt a flash of fear stab his heart, thinking suddenly that Andrew's chortling car might careen around the corner any minute; haloed in a cloud of exhaust and the fragrance of black licorice.

But Andrew was dead and the house was quiet. The garage door was closed. Somebody had painted the house another pastel color, giving it a wholesome, cared-for appearance. Still, if Gabriel tried, he could visualize the interior – the small kitchen, the living room with the rabbit ear TV, and the big couch…

Gabriel jumped as his cell phone rang.

"Yep?" he said quickly.

"It's Dash. Natalie Archwood just pulled into the driveway."

"I'm on my way." Gabriel glanced once more at Andrew's house, and then began jogging back to the Irving Street address.

"Mrs. Archwood?" Gabriel said tentatively as Dash and he stood in the doorway. Gabriel noticed that Sonia's car was gone.

"Yes?"

"We're—"

"I know who you are."

You're an evil, evil man.

Gabriel hoped he wore a poker face. He hoped Natalie Archwood didn't recognize him. He had no trouble recognizing her.

"You're the cops that came here," Natalie continued. "I spoke to my daughter over the phone a little while ago and she told me you came. She was a fool for letting you into my house."

The two detectives tried to look harmless. Dash spoke up. "We'd like to speak to your son, Mrs. Archwood. If you would be so kind as to—"

"I'll be so kind as to not tell your superiors that you came into my house under false pretenses. You didn't have a warrant, did you?"

"Excuse me, Mrs. Archwood, but Sonia asked us in. She was near to fainting—"

Natalie rolled her eyes and smiled vehemently. "She was swooning, huh? Well, that's a load of shit."

Gabriel calmly weathered the storm that was Natalie Archwood. She stood, haughty, underneath their police IDs. Her frizzy gray/blond hair fanned a face filled with angry lines and the ice blue eyes of a predator. Archwood's mother was dynamite with a burning fuse.

She had been a younger, trimmer woman back when Gabriel first met her, but still just as much of a shrew. Gabriel could see her standing before him years ago, sneering at him and calling him an evil, evil man.

"Ma'am" Dash pressed, "if we could just ask you a few questions."

"Get a warrant."

"We don't need a warrant, Mrs. Archwood," Gabriel said sternly, stemming the flow of his own emotions, "to bring you in for questioning. Your son is a person of interest in a homicide case involving six victims, possibly seven, and your daughter told us he spoke with you yesterday. If you don't cooperate with us now, we can haul you in for aiding and abetting."

Natalie blinked at Gabriel in disbelief. "Victor is a murder suspect? That's crazy. He couldn't harm a fly."

Gabriel studied her. She seemed sincere on that one. "Where is your son, Mrs. Archwood?"

She crossed her arms defensively. "I don't know where Victor is."

"But he is in town."

"I believe so."

"May we check your house?"

"You may not."

"Then we'll be back with a warrant," Gabriel told her.

"And you can speak with my attorney from now on."

Dash decided to play good cop. "Look, Mrs. Archwood, you're not in trouble. But until we can talk to Victor, we can't clear him as a suspect either. The swat team, the FBI, even the media – everyone is going to stampede this house. Do you really want all that bad publicity? I heard you own a business..."

Gabriel had to admire Dash. He didn't realize his partner had it in him.

Dash fashioned his hands in a frame in front of him. "Mother of the Malibu Canyon Murderer–'"

"What?" Natalie hissed.

"If we said you were cooperating with our end of the investigation," Dash continued, "things could go a lot quieter."

She looked genuinely worried. "Did you say he's a suspect in those mountain killings in Los Angeles?"

Dash nodded.

Natalie seemed to digest that for a moment. Gabriel could almost see the wheels in her mind turning.

"You'll keep this out of the press?" Natalie asked. "That my son is a suspect, at least."

"Of course," Dash assured her. "Look, could you tell us a little more about Victor?"

Natalie sighed impatiently. "Our conversation was all of two minutes, okay? He didn't tell me where he was staying. He just called to say he was back in town. That's all. Nothing more." She gestured curtly toward the FBI van parked across the street.

"I'm sure those apes of yours will keep a lookout for him."

Gabriel and Dash shifted uncomfortably.

"Boneheads," Natalie said to them. "You think I was born yesterday? I've seen kids all day today and I'm wiped out. I suppose you already know I run a swim school near the marina." They caught a whiff of pride from her. "I'm extremely busy. I'll deal with you tomorrow."

Dash and Gabriel looked at each other. Dash held out his card. "Tomorrow morning then. This is a number where you can contact us."

Natalie Archwood snatched the card from Dash's hand and promptly slammed the door in their faces.

Leaving the stakeout team, Gabriel and Dash checked into the Hyatt, which was straight out of <u>High Anxiety</u> with its umpteen floors that overlooked a lobby complete with water fountains and roomy couches. Looking down from his high floor, Gabriel experienced a sense of vertigo, but was relieved this was a normal sensation and not one brought on by his meeting with Natalie Archwood.

Gabriel phoned Dr. B, but learned the doctor was attending a family event. As Gabriel hung up he envied the doctor for his ability to hold a family together.

The phone company had supplied a list of outgoing calls from the Archwood residence, which the FBI had followed up with. None of them led to Victor.

The detectives decided to brainstorm their next steps over dinner, so Gabriel strolled down Market Street to the Tadich Grill, an old San Francisco landmark that specialized in crab Louis salads, tasty fish, and the best sourdough bread on the West Coast.

Gabriel found Ramirez seated in a wood paneled booth joined by Ralph Tenant, Sergeant Krol, and, to his pleasant surprise, Ming.

"Hi," he said to her.

Ming smiled and then her eyes slid to Ramirez who was watching the two of them with interest. Gabriel took her cue and sat at the seat farthest from Ming.

Ramirez explained, "Sergeant Krol requested that Dr. Li come out here to reexamine the body of Thomas Welby, which they exhumed today. She's all too familiar with the assault patterns of the L.A. victims, and I wanted to make sure the Welby homicide is connected to our boy."

"Victor Archwood," Gabriel reminded him.

"That's what you say, McRay. Remember, we don't have anything solid tying him to Bill Spangler."

"They're one and the same, trust me."

Ramirez opened his mouth to speak when Ming beat him to it.

"I've looked at the autopsy reports on Thomas Welby," she said, saving Gabriel from the wrath of Ramirez. "Although I'll feel more confident after studying the body myself, I believe the same knife was used. The assault pattern was different though. Welby was able to put up a fight. It was messy." She took a bite of crab.

"That corroborates what Gabriel told me earlier," Dash said to her. "That Welby could have been his first kill."

Ming glanced once at Gabriel, and then turned to Sergeant Krol, "Any other murders similar to Welby in recent months?"

"No." Krol broke off a piece of sourdough bread and smoothed sweet butter on top.

Ralph Tenant wiped his ample cheeks with his napkin and wheezed, "I've been checking into the Archwood family tree. The father went AWOL long ago, when the girls were wee little things. He's remarried and living in Arkansas. Wife number three, you understand. He hasn't seen or heard anything of his kids in years. Still, we've alerted our branch out there and they're keeping an eye open."

"What about the other sister?" Gabriel asked, and ordered a whiskey from the waiter.

"Katherine Archwood. She's not around." Tenant stuffed a forkful of petrale sole in his mouth, and said between chews, "I started checking on her, just in case she might know something. She was holed up in some zany religious cult in Oregon until a year ago. Then her track goes cold. I'll keep after her though."

The conversation continued. They all agreed to keep the Archwood name out of the press for as long as possible, in the hope that Victor Archwood would decide to return home. Tenant told them to follow their leads, assuring them he would stay on the sidelines.

"Uh, McRay," Ramirez whispered, leaning towards him, "About that picture you gave me."

Gabriel drained the rest of his drink and nodded.

"It came off a publication from NAMBLA – a mostly web-based organization of pedophiles."

Gabriel swallowed hard and looked at Ramirez.

"The FBI tracks these guys. They're a group of people who believe in 'uncoerced' sex with minors. Once in a while they go underground, and then pop up again like fucking gophers. They chat online, compare notes, whatever. They put out a magazine off and on. This photo came from last September's issue."

"How did you get all this?"

Ramirez nodded toward Tenant. "That fat guy can carry his weight, that's for sure." He elbowed Gabriel. "That's a joke, McRay."

Gabriel pushed his plate away in distaste and told the waiter to bring him another Maker's Mark.

"We checked the photo for prints again. It's like you said, all we found were yours and Dr. Li's. Next time don't be so sloppy, McRay. I was able to cover your ass because you had that accident."

"Thanks."

"Yeah, you owe me." Ramirez reached for another bread roll and found Ming staring at him. "¿Qué pasa, Homie?"

Ming rolled her eyes and went back to her salad.

At the end of dinner, Gabriel stood outside the restaurant with Ming. The others were busy discussing police force politics while they waited for their cars.

"I'm glad you're here," he said. Gabriel let his eyes roam her body. Just being this close to her, watching the blush in her high cheekbones, inhaling the spicy fragrance she wore, made him want to draw her close.

Dash broke away from the other men and moved alongside Gabriel, saying, "The valet is here with the car. Are you...?" His voice trailed off when he realized he had interrupted Gabriel and Ming. "Well, hey, I guess we'll see you two later—"

Ming gave Dash a polite smile and he backed away, rejoining the other men who were now waving their goodbyes.

Watching them go, Ming turned her attention to Gabriel. "Look, maybe we should lay low. It bothers me that Ramirez saw us together. It's not professional."

"How come you were willing to sabotage your career with me a few days ago?"

"That was before Ramirez knew."

"So, what does that mean?" Gabriel asked her. "I would have been your best kept secret?"

"I don't know..."

"I thought I was the one who was afraid to be vulnerable."

"Vulnerability has nothing to do with it." Ming hugged her expensive jacket tighter. "I'm not too clear on the Department's Fraternization policy, if indeed there is one and until I am—"

"Always the professional." Gabriel stuck his hands in his pockets and turned away.

"That's not fair, Gabriel!" Ming called to him.

But he ignored her and headed down the street, hoping to find a bar where he could drown his emotions in a beer.

Gabriel ended up sitting in a crowded, smoke filled bar called the Buena Vista; renown for being the birthplace of the Irish coffee. Not in the mood for whipped cream-lathered java, Gabriel settled on a Budweiser.

Ming had worn her usual mask of self-assurance to dinner. The woman who needs nobody. The busy career girl, oops, *woman.* And what mask was Gabriel wearing tonight? The "I-Couldn't-Care-Less" mask? The "It-Doesn't-Matter-To-Me" mask?

Gabriel suddenly caught the eye of a tall blonde woman leaning against the bar, watching him carefully. Through the undulating crowd, Gabriel made out that she was well-heeled, with a strange but attractive, angular face.

He gave her a weak smile, more induced by the beer than any real interest he had in her. When the blonde saw that he returned her gaze, she quickly slunk back from the bar and faded into the coffee-sipping crowd.

I'm scoring big time with the ladies tonight.

Ah, what the hell, Gabriel thought. "Salud" he said out loud and drained his glass.

CHAPTER 24

Gabriel pulled on his shoes the following morning, anchoring the phone under his chin, as he talked to Dr. B. The doctor's voice reassured him, making Gabriel feel less like a drifting boat on a churning sea.

"How are you doing up there?" Dr. B asked.

"I thought seeing Andrew's house again would knock me over, but strangely enough it didn't."

"Probably because you've addressed the issue," Dr. B said. "I suppose you'll work through some bad memories for some time, but the good news is that you are no longer afraid that the memories can hurt you. Funny thing about fear, isn't it? Once we face it, it doesn't look so scary. Facing fear, however, is altogether a different matter."

Through his hotel window, Gabriel watched the white clouds roll on a sharp blue sky. "I still can't remember everything and it's bugging me. I can't quite remember everything about Vic."

"Vic?"

"Archwood as a kid. That's what I called him."

"I don't remember everything from my teenage years. There's nothing unusual about that," Dr. B reassured him.

Gabriel wasn't so sure. "There's something about his mom. She's a real delight."

"Tell you what, Gabe," Dr. B said. "Maybe we can work something out. I'm coming to the Bay area in a couple of days. Isaac is applying to Stanford and we're going to check out the school. Maybe you and I can meet."

"You know where to find me," Gabriel told him. "Raymond?"

"Yes?"

"I appreciate you listening. I really do. Here you are with a whole other life, and I never acknowledged it. I'm a selfish bastard."

"It's not your job to ask about me." Dr. B told him. "However, asking after the welfare of someone else is a sign of growth for you. Adler says that social interest is the barometer of a child's normality. Your interest is extending beyond your-self now. You feel more community spirit with your fellow man. That's a good thing."

Gabriel was pleased to consider himself having normal inclinations.

For a pariah, that is a good thing.

Later that morning, Gabriel met Dash at the San Francisco police department. They were walking towards the courtesy desks they were given in the homicide section, when they passed a conference room and halted in their tracks.

Through the open doorway, the two L.A. detectives spied Special Agent Tenant seated at the table talking earnestly to Natalie Archwood.

"Son of a bitch," Dash said angrily.

Gabriel strode towards the open doorway but Krol blocked his path.

"Gabriel, hold your fireworks. She came in of her own accord this morning."

"So why weren't we called?" Gabriel glared at him.

"Tenant was already here, and—"

"Tenant was already here," Gabriel repeated, sarcasm ringing in his voice. "How convenient."

Dash lashed out at Krol. "This guy has the balls to tell us it's 'our investigation,' and now look at him. He called her himself, didn't he?"

Krol said nothing.

Gabriel brushed passed him. "I'm going in."

"Wait!"

"Fuck you, Krol," Gabriel said, and headed toward the conference room.

"Lieutenant Ramirez is on his way here. He said to do nothing until—"

"Fuck you, Krol," Dash echoed more loudly and followed his partner.

The two detectives entered the room, just as Natalie Archwood was standing up. Tenant quickly cleared his throat and shuffled some papers. "Uh, Mrs. Archwood, I think you've met Detectives McRay and Starkweather."

"I have." The older woman regarded them coolly. Natalie's blond frizz was pulled back in a bun and she wore an expensive peach colored suit.

Gabriel was certain the banshee lurked behind Natalie's air of calm sophistication, waiting for the right opportunity to come out shrieking.

Tenant folded a note into his suit pocket and raised his bulk from the chair. "Thank you for this information, Ma'am. We'll try to keep this quiet for as long—"

Gabriel scratched his scalp in frustration. "Mrs. Archwood—"

Tenant interrupted, addressing the older woman. "We'll let you know how it goes, Mrs. Archwood. I'll keep in touch."

Gabriel felt rage bubble inside him and had to consciously talk himself out of storming over to Ralph Tenant and throttling his throat.

Natalie moved past them to follow Tenant out the door, when she suddenly paused, turned around and looked curiously at Gabriel.

"Your name is Sergeant McRay?"

Gabriel nodded uneasily. *Face the fear.*

Natalie slithered over to Gabriel, studying him with her ice-chip eyes. "<u>Gabriel</u> McRay, am I right?"

Gabriel remained mute. Dash watched them both with a quizzical expression.

Natalie nodded. "I wouldn't have recognized you. Your hair was longer then and you didn't have your cool Southern California tan."

Gabriel felt the heat from the woman's perpetually lit fuse redden his face. He had a funny feeling Natalie was just getting warmed up. He was correct.

"How ironic that you'd become an officer of the law," she said. "Now, I guess you can abuse people legally." Natalie turned to Dash. "Do you know what your macho partner here did when he was a strapping young lad?" She guffawed, saying, "Why don't you ask him? Makes for one hell of story."

Natalie strode to the door and gave Gabriel a nasty smile. "You of all people." The smile twisted into a grimace and Gabriel found himself staring at the face of a snake-haired medusa.

"How could they put you on this case?" Natalie hissed. "How dare you involve yourself with my son again?"

Gabriel steadied himself under the cold glare of her eyes, thinking that floodlights could not have exposed him any better. Finally, the older woman pulled herself away, disappearing through the door.

Dash whistled. "What the hell was that all about?"

Gabriel leaned against the conference table and rubbed his temples, wondering if a headache would join the party. "The very last time I babysat Vic, I lost my temper." He looked at Dash miserably. "You know what I mean."

"Hey, you two," Tenant said, waving them over from the doorway. "It's show time."

The two detectives exchanged glances, and then followed Tenant as the big man stomped noisily through the department halls.

"Follow me. We can't waste any time here—"

"Yeah," Gabriel said, "you couldn't waste any time honing in on our hard work. You let us stand there like a couple of dumbshits with our dicks in our hands in front of the key to this entire investi—"

"She gave up his whereabouts," Tenant said flatly, stopping in his tracks to stare at Gabriel. "Do you want to argue or do you want to bring in your suspect?"

Natalie told Tenant that Archwood had called her that morning, notifying her he was staying at a vacant cabin in Muir Woods, a sparsely populated forested area.

"She says he seemed depressed," Tenant reported to them from the front seat of Krol's Pontiac as they drove through mountain passes to the cabin. Trailing behind them was a squadron of black-and-white support units.

"She says he sounds very despondent. Naturally, she's worried about him and didn't know what to do. I was able to talk her into working with us."

Bravo, you jerk. Gabriel stared at the back of Tenant's head. "What else did she say about Archwood?"

Tenant took a breath in and wheezed it out. "Nothing."

"Her son is wanted for murder and she's calm as pond water," Gabriel said "I would think she'd be defending him or denying his guilt or something."

"She comes off to me as a very rational woman," Tenant said. "She's willing to cooperate and, to be honest; you guys don't have a ton of hard evidence against him."

"We have items belonging to the victims," Dash told Tenant. "Items that were found in his apartment."

Tenant turned his bulk to eyeball Dash in the backseat. "You mean in the apartment of Bill Spangler. I read your report. How do you know for sure Archwood is Spangler?"

"We have his Pepperdine student I.D." Dash said. "We know what he looks like."

"You sure?" Tenant countered. "Or maybe he was in costume. You have an I.D. of Bill Spangler. What exactly does Archwood look like? Have you seen a recent picture?"

Dash exchanged glances with Gabriel.

Tenant nodded and turned to face front. "You guys don't have dick. All you've got is McRay's word that Archwood is the Malibu Canyon Murderer."

"He is," Gabriel said evenly.

A cell phone rang shrilly and Krol quickly fumbled for it, keeping one hand on the wheel. "Krol here." There was a pregnant pause as the Sergeant listened. "No shit!" He hung up and craned his neck, trying to spot something ahead in the distance. "Look!" he cried to Dash and Gabriel.

They leaned forward, staring through the windshield at a cloud of smoke.

"There's a report of a cabin burning. The fire department is already there."

"Jesus!" Dash blurted. "Is this guy full of surprises or what?"

Gabriel poked Krol on the shoulder. "Call your guys and tell them to find and detain Natalie Archwood immediately."

They arrived amid a cacophony of fire trucks and helicopters to a scene they were all too familiar with. But instead of a car, they found the smoldering hulk of a cabin. Parked nearby was an ash-covered Buick. Fortunately the moist environment did not ignite like the Southern California brush.

"I suppose this is the cabin Natalie Archwood indicated," Gabriel said, taking in the wreckage.

"Indeed it is," Krol replied, coughing from the smoke.

The officers approached the cabin, inhaling the odor of gasoline, and underneath that, the stench of charred flesh. The firefighters went in first, teamed with accelerant-detection canines. The trained dogs gave specific responses when they located the odor of ignitable liquids. Often they could find the exact spot where the fire was set.

The detectives shuffled nervously outside. Finally, a firefighter exited the cabin and strode up to them. "There's a body inside with a shotgun next to it." He sniffed then blew out a sweaty breath. "Just the one."

Gabriel leaned heavily against the scratchy bark of a tree trunk, unable to do anything until things cooled down. Nothing had turned out like he had thought. He should be like Gary Cooper in <u>High Noon,</u> facing the bad guy and bringing him home to face the music. Ming should be on his arm and together they should all be living happily ever after.

Instead, he stood in the middle of a toasted piece of forest accompanied by death, with all his questions unanswered.

He gazed at the smoldering cabin and wondered if Archwood was playing with illusions again. Gabriel began combing through the exterior brush, looking for evidence. He felt the weight of a headache coming on, but this one was due more to stress than the feasting of inner demons.

Gabriel pressed on through the trees, hoping to find closure in every fallen leaf, unwilling to accept the idea that Archwood had committed suicide. Finally, he sat down on a lichen-covered rock. The ground below him was a damp, leafy brown and filled with crawling life. Nailed to a tree opposite him was a sandwich bag containing a note.

Gabriel walked toward the bag, pulling on latex gloves, never taking his eyes off the paper visible through the plastic. He reached up, fighting the urge to swipe the bag off the tree like a tick, and angled the note toward his eyes. Under a shaft of sunlight spearing down through the treetops, Gabriel looked for his name. It wasn't there.

He found that factor strangely unsettling. All the notes had been addressed to Gabriel except this one. Through the folded paper he could make out the imprint of handwriting. The killer (*Archwood!*) didn't type this one... Why not?

Breaking protocol. Trying to mind-fuck you. He thinks you'll go weak in the knees.

After the crime scene unit swept the cabin, the charred, stiff corpse was removed and taken to the morgue. Gabriel moved through the one room cabin, inspecting the broken sticks of wood from a table and chairs, and the black skeletal ribs of a rollaway bed, the mattress burned and gone. The cabin yielded little evidence, which was fine with Gabriel. He was more interested in the corpse.

Gabriel refused to give any information to the press until the autopsy confirmed the corpse found in the cabin was indeed Victor Archwood.

"Is it a suicide note?" Ramirez quizzed Gabriel and Dash as they walked toward the lab at SFPD headquarters.

Gabriel shrugged, saying, "I didn't open it. This is the first time anyone has read it. I'm not making mistakes anymore, remember?"

Ramirez nodded. Ralph Tenant greeted them heartily as they entered the lab. Tenant wasted no time in introducing the three L.A. detectives to a handwriting expert from the FBI identification section.

"Over the years," the expert said, "handwriting can change, influenced by any number of factors, such as arthritis, age, and stress. The suspect's mother furnished us with some school essays and we were able to obtain Archwood's registration material from Berkeley. Even though these samples are a few years old, I would say that this note was written by Victor Archwood."

"But you're not one hundred percent sure," Gabriel said, stating the obvious.

The expert shook his head.

"What's it say?" Ramirez asked, indicating the note.

"Read it," the expert said, handing the paper to Gabriel.

"Don't worry," Tenant said, "They already ran it. No prints."

Gabriel's eyes dropped to the words and he read aloud, "No one knows what it's like to be the bad man. To be the sad man; behind blue eyes. But my dreams, they aren't as empty as my conscience seems to be. My love is vengeance that's never free."

The note was not signed.

"The Who," Gabriel murmured.

"What?" Ramirez asked. He was busy daydreaming about a volley of press people snapping photos of him and begging for interviews.

Gabriel pointed a finger at the writing. "These are lyrics from a Who song called Behind Blue Eyes."

"Get a copy of the song," Ramirez barked to no one in particular, and then pulled out his pack of cigarettes.

A crime scene tech entered the room and pulled Tenant aside.

"Sounds like a suicide note to me," Ramirez stated. "What do you guys think?"

"I'll take it," Tenant agreed as he walked over and slapped Gabriel on the back. "I owe you an apology. I guess Archwood really is the Malibu Canyon Murderer."

Gabriel gave the note back to the handwriting expert who bagged it once more.

"This note was cleverly crafted," Gabriel said, more to himself. "He didn't follow the killer's pattern – putting my name on it, typing it. It's a suicide note that quotes a well-known song. It's not a confession. This doesn't give us anything."

"Yeah, but this ring does." Tenant waved an evidence bag in front of Gabriel's face. "The techs just found it right outside the cabin door. It's Ronald Hall's wedding ring."

Gabriel reached out an incredulous hand and took the ring. Sure enough he saw the initials R.H. inscribed on the band. He looked at Dash.

Ramirez clapped his hands together. "That's it then! We've got him. We got the evidence and the tax-payers don't have to pay nada because the dude executed himself."

Gabriel didn't share in his lieutenant's elation. He couldn't believe the investigation was over. He chastised himself, wondering if maybe he didn't want the case to close because it coincided so deeply with his own psychological progression.

"I have no doubt that Archwood wrote this note," Gabriel said. "I just have a hard time believing he'd really do himself in."

"Hey," Ramirez said, "the dude was cornered. His own mother gave him up. Maybe she told him she wasn't gonna hide him and that was that. He broke down."

"We've got the dental records on Archwood," Krol informed them as he entered the lab. He opened a file in his hands — albiet too eagerly and a mess of papers spilled to the ground. Krol bent down to retrieve them. "Shit. Sorry. Here." Krol handed the report to Ramirez. "Archwood's got a gold inlay on the second right molar; very unusual for this day and age because they're expensive and highly visible."

Ramirez perused the dental report.

Krol received a call at that moment and answered his cell phone. He hung up and informed the team that the medical examiners were ready for them.

"Let's get to that corpse," Ramirez said, already halfway out the door, "and see if he's got something gold and shiny in his mouth."

The detectives arrived at the hospital. The autopsy was already underway. Ming had on a mask and her full scrubs. She assisted the medical examiner who was talking into a headset microphone as he worked over the burned, skeletal corpse. The body had shrunk into a near fetal position, and the two forensic pathologists attempted to stretch it out.

Although Gabriel shuddered at the sound of cracking bones, he could not take his eyes off the charred cadaver. Was this Victor Archwood? X-rays, measurements, and photographs were taken. The corpse's hair had burned off and bone broke through the black, leathery flesh at various points along the body.

Also present was a forensic odontologist who was hunched over the mouth of the corpse — or what was left of it.

The medics determined from the size of the skull and the pelvis that it was a male, roughly the same height and age as Victor Archwood.

No one knows what it's like to be the bad man.

"Periosteum still found adhering to the third and fourth ribs," said the ME.

Gabriel caught Ming's eye over her mask, but he couldn't read her expression. She dropped her eyes and concentrated on the skull and mandible. Other than the droning monotone of the Medical Examiner's words into the tape recorder and the grating of the bone saws, the place was mausoleum silent. The detectives, standing like statues in their masks and gloves, paid silent homage to the dissection unfolding before them.

"Shotgun blast – pellets found in the braincase," the ME murmured into his recorder.

Ramirez bristled with restlessness. "Is there an inlay in that stiff's mouth or what?"

"No," the forensic odontologist replied, not looking up from the mouth. "And neither are most of his teeth."

"But was it a suicide?" Ramirez pressed.

"I'll give you a more careful analysis when I'm through," the ME told him. "This appears to be a self-inflicted wound."

"The damage done to the upper plate suggests a contact entrance wound," Ming offered. "Judging from the angle of the bullet, it's feasible he could have held the shotgun in his mouth and pulled the trigger. Unfortunately, because of the fire, we can't detect any gunpowder residue on the hands. That would have been a tell-tale sign of suicide."

"Is it Archwood?" Ramirez pressed.

The ME shrugged and turned to Ming. She took his cue and said, "The corpse is in obvious bad shape. The jaws seem to match the dental chart, and the corpse is the right size."

"I want that inlay found," Gabriel demanded.

"Listen," the odontologist piped up, "if he's had any dental work in the past few years; for example, if he's replaced that inlay with porcelain, a positive ID may be impossible."

"I'm not buying this death until we know for sure," Gabriel insisted. "I want a check of recent missing persons that fit Archwood's general physical description."

Gabriel turned to Ramirez. "He's not sending me on any more wild goose chases."

CHAPTER

A leak in the department alerted the press that the L.A. Sheriff's Department was in town regarding the Malibu Canyon Murders, which unleashed a storm of fear and fury that managed to get the residents of San Francisco as worked up as their Los Angeles counterparts. Imogene Goldfield, the producer's ex-wife, appeared on one talk show after another, discussing everything from the producer himself to victim's rights. A collective shudder ran through the Bay City as the inhabitants pressed to know why the Los Angeles murder investigation had moved north.

The law enforcement agencies remained mute, keeping a tight lid on the burned body of John Doe #20123, who lay peacefully in the county morgue until his true identity could be established.

Meanwhile, Gabriel and Dash interviewed Natalie Archwood at the SFPD headquarters. She appeared her usual self; her hard face refusing to yield any clues. If losing a son to suicide had affected her in any way, Natalie did not let it show.

Dash took up his usual role of "good cop" to counter Gabriel's stern approach, but Gabriel felt a pit yawning in his third chakra that threatened to trip him up.

"What time did Victor call you?" Gabriel asked Natalie.

Natalie assumed a prim manner and turned to Dash with a sweet smile. "Is it really necessary that he's in the room?"

Dash glanced at Gabriel. "Uh, Ma'am; Detective McRay is the lead investigator on this case."

Natalie frowned and sat back. "Around seven in the morning. I came to see Agent Tenant right afterwards."

"Right," Gabriel said. "And what did Victor tell you on the phone exactly?"

"How many times do I have to tell you the same thing?" Natalie asked, exasperated. "We've been through this already."

Gabriel knew that. He was, however, hoping to catch a scrap of inconsistency in her story. "What did he say?"

She sighed curtly. "I asked him where he was. He told me he was staying at a vacant cabin. I asked him to give me directions." Studying her fingers guiltily, she added, "I thought we should meet." Natalie paused, closing her eyes. "After he gave me the directions I told him the police wanted to talk with him. I waited for him to explain himself, but he didn't. He said nothing.'"

"He said nothing?" Dash prodded gently.

"Are you deaf?" Natalie opened her eyes and daintily pulled a tissue out of her purse. She dabbed at her nose, the All-American mother once again. "But I could tell he was upset. He's my son. I could tell."

Her eyes went bright with unshed tears and Gabriel wondered if they were of the alligator variety.

Natalie continued. "And that's when I knew. I knew my boy had done something terrible. I made up my mind to go to the police." Natalie swallowed, shaking her head. "You can't imagine, what it's like to love a child and then turn them over to—" Her eyes narrowed at Gabriel. "To the <u>wolves</u>."

Gabriel felt the pit expand, but he kept a poker face.

Natalie Archwood sniffled, turned to Dash, and said, "It is Victor, isn't it?"

"We don't know for sure, Ma'am. Not yet."

Natalie pushed a strand of frizzy blond-gray hair back behind her ears and stared into space. "We had such troubles when he was a boy. His father abandoned the family and I was left a single mother. When you're young, alone, raising three children, times can be very difficult. My son is not a bad boy."

Gabriel was sure Natalie's take on the past was full of holes. He knew somehow she was as much to blame for the unhappy home life as the disappearing father, but for the life of him, Gabriel couldn't remember how. His memory was still a puzzle with pieces missing. He knocked his head lightly on the wall as Natalie continued the discourse with Dash, hoping to jar loose an important recollection. Something about the grandfather...

"Vic was close with his grandfather, right?" Gabriel asked Natalie.

Her light sapphire eyes widened for a moment with some unbidden emotion and then she composed herself. "Victor loved my father. He was a kind man. My mother was never close to the children, but my father was the best grandfather anyone could ever have. The only problem is that he died when Victor was six years old." She glared at Gabriel. "Victor yearned for a male figure in his life. That's when you came along. You're as much to blame for Victor's downfall as anybody. He was just a little boy. He trusted you. You betrayed him!"

Gabriel chewed at his lip, fighting the urge to bolt from the room. Keep on track, he commanded himself. Maybe Natalie knew what Gabriel had forgotten. He decided to test the waters.

"You're holding something back," Gabriel said. "What is it, Mrs. Archwood? What's the secret?"

"I have no idea what you're talking about!" Natalie turned to Dash with innocent eyes. "How dare this man throw his craziness at me? I read all about him. It's all over the internet. He's a psycho; a freak!" Natalie rose from her chair. "I keep asking myself how they allowed a monster like you to continue working after they had the decency to fire you! There's no justice in this world! No justice!"

Face the fear.

Gabriel stood his ground. "I got my job back because your son left personal notes to me in the mutilated bodies of his victims."

Dash shook his head at Gabriel. "Mrs. Archwood—"

"He hurt others because you hurt him!" Natalie screamed. "I never thought he would hurt anyone! I never thought he'd hurt himself!" She pointed a witch's finger in Gabriel's face. "You attacked him in life and now you want to destroy him even after he's dead! You're the monster, not Victor! You!" She headed toward the door. "I don't have to talk to a freak; not with my flesh and blood lying dead on a slab!"

She choked back a sob and Dash placed a reassuring hand on her shoulder.

"Mrs. Archwood..."

She pushed Dash away and he stumbled backwards. "Get away from me! If you have any more questions, talk to my lawyer."

Natalie stormed out of the conference room.

Dash crossed his arms, watching her go; and said to Gabriel, "Great, Atilla. What do we do now?"

Gabriel sat heavily in one of the chairs and hung his head wearily. "Something's not right."

Dash kicked the wall mildly. "Everything's right except you. Our suspect is dead, the case is pretty much closed, and we could have tied things up nicely here." Dash flopped into another chair. "What is it with you and Archwood?"

The detectives were ordered to return to the dilapidated cabin to find the missing dental inlay. The pressure was on to close the case officially and everyone was expected to put in lots of overtime. Armed with sieves, they began the arduous task of sifting every square inch of dirt through the fine mesh. Ramirez hovered over the officers doing the backbreaking work like an overseer.

They found bits of teeth and facial bones, some only the size of a pencil lead tip. Teeth could fly far from the body in the wake of a shotgun blast. If there was a gas-fueled explosion on top of that, fragments could blow even further away.

The teams of detectives worked laboriously, sifting through the charred flooring, the dirt below, and the soil around the perimeter of the cabin.

At the end of the day, Gabriel returned to his hotel room, battling fatigue and frustration. He called the hospital, asking for Ming. She wasn't there, so he called her hotel room. She answered on the second ring.

"Can I talk to you?" he asked.

"Sure," she replied.

"Can I come over?"

Ming paused. Gabriel waited.

"What's on your mind?" she asked him.

Okay, I guess I can't come over.

"I want to know if you are convinced that the dead man is Archwood."

"Gabriel, there's no real way to know for sure. You've got an unidentifiable male corpse that fits the general makeup. He's got no broken bones – neither does Archwood, according to his medical records and X-rays. The body belongs to someone who was athletic in his younger years, but less so as he got older. Archwood fits that general description. We know Archwood had dental work – a gold inlay; but the jaws of the corpse are shattered and more than half the teeth are gone."

Gabriel sighed. "Are you leaving San Francisco soon?"

"Not yet," Ming answered softly. "I'm going to work on that body a bit more. I want to take some samples. Whatever tissue I can peel off I'm going to."

"Why?"

"Didn't you hear?" Ming asked him. "Mrs. Archwood is having her son cremated."

Gabriel closed his tired eyes and melted into the hotel bed. "Hasn't he been cremated enough already?"

"The burial is her choice," Ming told him. "At any rate, you never know when the need for tissue samples is going to arise. I've still got that semen DNA from home and I'd like to compare the two. I'm playing it safe."

"Smart girl," Gabriel whispered sadly.

Ming read the emotion. "I'm sorry I was a bitch the other night. I guess you're not the only one with issues. How are you doing?"

"I'm fine."

"You don't sound fine."

"I'm tired."

"You were probably anticipating a more climactic ending to this, weren't you?"

Gabriel realized she was correct. What did it matter now anyhow?

Ming spoke again, "How can I be of help?"

That came out oh so professionally.

"I don't know. Have you checked the departmental fraternizing policy yet?" He hung up the phone. Restless and frustrated, Gabriel grabbed his car keys and vacated the room.

Ming sat with the phone in her hands, astonished that Gabriel had hung up on her. Ming slowly replaced the phone in its cradle and realized how much of an idiot she was. Her dream for months had been to get closer to Gabriel McRay and now that he was receptive to her, she worried the relationship would interfere with her job. Ming quickly redialed his room phone, but Gabriel did not answer.

Shrouded in fog and darkness, Gabriel sat in his rental car and watched the Archwood home. A 'For Sale' sign stood on the small square of lawn. Perhaps some of the neighbors had started to gossip. Perhaps Natalie felt the need to start anew somewhere else. Meanwhile, Sonia's car was parked out front.

From Sunset Beach, Gabriel heard the distant sound of a foghorn. Shouting sounded on the heels of the foghorn, and a yellow light flicked on above the pink granite steps of the home. Sonia stumbled out the door, mouth working, clutching a bundle of clothes. Behind Sonia's shouting was Natalie's banshee wail. The front door slammed and Sonia thundered down the steps. She got in her car and peeled out. Curious, Gabriel put his car into drive and followed her.

Sonia's apartment was in the middle of three identical buildings clustered together near Lake Merced. The first thing Gabriel observed was that the stakeout on Sonia's building had been called off. Gabriel guessed everyone felt the point was moot if the suspect was dead and gone.

Gabriel loitered around, hiding in the shadows for five minutes, and then knocked on Sonia's apartment door. He could hear the melodramatic music of a televised game show, and knocked again, louder this time.

The door swung open and Sonia stood in front of him, wearing white frosting on her lips and chin. Her eyes widened and Gabriel saw her draw a self-conscious hand across her mouth, wiping off the lard.

"Hi," she said warily. "What are you doin' here?"

Gabriel forced a smile, a twinkle in his own blue eyes. "Honestly, Sonia, I don't really have a good reason to be here. I wanted to hear more about your brother. It came as quite a shock to me when he took his own life." Gabriel shook his head, smile gone.

Sonia stared open-mouthed at the male on her doorstep. She wore green polyester pants and a cheap, rayon lace top that hugged her bulges. She fingered her drab blond hair reflectively, and then moved aside. "Come on in."

Gabriel entered, viewing a small two-bedroom apartment full of flea market furniture.

"Where are the kids?" he asked casually.

"With their dad." Sonia was eyeing him, licking her chops like Gabriel was a cut of prime beef. "Sit down," she told him, waving him over to the couch.

Upon the fake oak coffee table was a sheet cake with white frosting and colored roses. Half of it was gone. "Want some cake?"

Gabriel shook his head and forced another smile as he sat on the couch. "I'm sorry about the late hour."

"Oh, don't apologize!" Sonia said eagerly, sitting next to him. The springs in the couch cried in protest. She grabbed the remote control and promptly turned off the TV.

Gabriel looked down at his hands. "I guess the family is in an upheaval over all this."

Sonia gave him a blank stare which Gabriel took as disinterest. After a moment, she stuck a fork in the cake, gathering together a huge bite. "When I heard Vic killed those people in L.A., I was shocked. But then, Vic always was a bit distant, hard to understand. I guess it's not his fault."

"How so?"

"Some folks are mean to their kids," Sonia said, focusing on the cake. "My mom and dad were downright criminal."

Gabriel gazed at the heavy girl as she stabbed the cake again. She pushed a purple frosted rose next to a group of other flowers, obviously saving them for last. Watching such a childlike move made Gabriel instantly feel sorry for Sonia, and he regretted having made mental quips about her weight.

"I had some problems myself when I was younger," Gabriel told her gently. "So maybe I can relate. What went on?"

She shrugged her big shoulders. "Oh, I don't want to bore you with ugly old stuff. It's ancient history."

"It may shed light on a part of Vic the world doesn't know."

"He's dead. Why do you care?"

Because he single-handedly unlocked all my closets and the skeletons are still falling out.

"People think your brother is a monster," Gabriel said. "Is that your story as well?"

Sonia gaped stupidly at Gabriel for a moment, and then took another bite of cake.

"Dad was a machinist," Sonia began, "He was very good with his hands. According to Mom, he had been beaten regularly as a kid and didn't see anything wrong with handling discipline problems the same way. Only thing was Vic didn't have to misbehave to get a beating. I only know this 'cause Mom told me so. Dad left when Katherine and I were only three."

"What else did your mom tell you?" Gabriel said, prompting her.

"She didn't want Vic," Sonia said, half-smiling at Gabriel. "Her goal was to be an Olympic swimmer. She was of strong Russian stock, and she had great technique–"

"Natalie, I mean your mom is Russian?"

"Yeah. She never made it past the high school girl's swim team because her one- night stand with my dad got her pregnant. She didn't mind being pregnant. She says everyone opened doors for her and her friends threw her a big shower. Even Grandma, a stick-figured, apple-faced old lady – that's Mom's description, seemed happy for a change. But when Vic was born, I guess reality set in. Her friends were still single and out having a good time and Mom had to stay home."

"Pity," Gabriel muttered.

Sonia gave him a sideways smile. "One time Mom was drunk and told me she never smiled at Vic, even though he was a cute baby. He would look up at her from his changing table and smile, but she never smiled back. She said she hated changing his diapers. She hated feeding him. She hated the fact that she was saddled with him while Dad got to go to work. She says Gramps helped her out some, but his help wasn't enough."

Gabriel watched Sonia devour another piece of cake.

"Once Katherine and I asked why our dad left." Crumbs fell from her lips as she spoke. "We blamed Mom for chasing him away."

"What did she say?"

"She said, 'you miss your daddy? Let me tell you what kind of daddy your daddy was.'" Sonia chewed thoughtfully for a moment, and then said, "Dad would come home from work and yell at her. He'd tell her she was a crummy wife and an even worse mother. She'd yell back. One time Vic started crying during their fight and Dad socked him and screamed, 'Shut up, you little shit machine. Shut up!' I guess after a while, even Vic got the message, because Mom said every time Dad would come in the room, Vic would toddle the hell away. And Dad called Vic shit machine from then on."

Being on familiar footing with child abuse himself, Gabriel felt a pang of sympathy for Vic. "And what was your mom doing during all this?"

Sonia's expression soured and Gabriel knew he had caught her at a good time. She was angry at Natalie and there would be no sugarcoated words tonight. Gabriel readied himself for some good information on Natalie Archwood.

But Sonia said nothing. Instead, she put the purple frosted flower in her mouth and closed her eyes, savoring the sweetness and the comfort it brought.

Gabriel suddenly realized the cake was more than three-quarters gone. Sonia opened her eyes, caught him looking at her, and smiled seductively through purple-tinged teeth.

Gabriel quickly made his departure.

CHAPTER 26

It was on the second day of searching that an officer with the SFPD CSU held the small glinting piece of gold up to the light.

"I think I've found it," he said, wiping the sweat from his brow onto his shirtsleeve, "Either that or I've just discovered another Sutter's Mill."

The fragment of gold was still attached to the molar. They ran it back to the lab and gave it to the experts. It matched the tooth and inlay shown on Victor Archwood's dental records perfectly.

An announcement was made to the press that very day. A press conference was scheduled in Los Angeles and Ramirez and Chief Kemper flew back home to join the District Attorney on the podium in front of a jungle of microphones.

Dash went home to Eve, and Gabriel, who was now viewed as a hero, was told to stay and tie up any loose ends. Gabriel thought he might take some vacation time and Ramirez gave his blessing to the idea.

Ming called him on his cell phone to congratulate him on a closed case.

"You should be in front of the cameras," she told him. "You're the one who lived and breathed this case, day in and day out."

Gabriel didn't seem to be bothered by the hoopla. "Actually, Archwood ran this whole investigation from the start. He closed it himself, too."

"That's right." Ming told him over the phone. "Don't take any credit for yourself. After all, you did nothing."

Gabriel smiled. "Sorry I hung up on you."

"Sorry I didn't take the chance when I had it," Ming said.

Gabriel was about to suggest that she take another chance when Ming spoke again.

"Are you staying here for much longer?

"For a couple of days," Gabriel replied. "Ramirez says I need a vacation."

"I think Miguel respects you, seeing what this case brought out in you and how you stayed to fight."

"I think Ramirez is happy that I've exonerated myself. That way he comes out smelling like a rose."

Ming laughed. "Very true."

Gabriel weighed the option of asking her to spend a vacation day with him but then decided not to push her, especially since they were on the subject of Ramirez. They ended their phone dialogue – friends again. No one mentioned the future.

The funeral for Victor Archwood was scheduled on that Tuesday and Gabriel planned on attending. Since the body was cremated, it was really a memorial of sorts and took place at the family church. The name Victor Archwood had made every paper in the country, but inside the small building, the mood was solemn.

Natalie Archwood wore customary black with her blond-gray hair pulled back severely in a clip. Victor Archwood Sr. was too ill to make the plane flight from Arkansas, but nobody seemed to miss him. Natalie was joined by her daughter, Sonia, and the two grandchildren. Sonia seemed to lack a husband.

One daughter gone back to Mommy Dearest and the other daughter, simply gone. All of them burying a brother that made his mark on society with slashes, blood, and fire.

The Archwood's put the fun in dysfunction.

Gabriel scrutinized Natalie Archwood as she sat in her pew. She primly wiped at the tears as they came into her eyes, but to Gabriel, Natalie resembled steel wool. Fuzzy in appearance but something even rats couldn't chew through.

There were a handful of kids present, accompanied by their parents. Clients from the swim school, Gabriel supposed, come to pay their respects to Natalie. Other than that, there was only the tide of reporters, held back by a bevy of policemen outside the church.

After the service, Gabriel felt some trepidation when Natalie approached him.

"I was wondering, Detective McRay, if you would like to come back to the wake at my house."

Gabriel searched her eyes, trying to find a trap in her invitation but Natalie seemed sincere. He could not resist.

"Thank you," Gabriel murmured and watched her depart among a group of supporters.

When he pulled up to the Archwood home in his car, Gabriel kept a low profile against the throng of reporters, armed with cameras and mikes; fighting with the patrolmen intent on keeping them from the house. Gabriel was in no mood for public relations so he inserted himself into a group of mourners and avoided the press.

An unappetizing spread of cheap bakery cookies, small white bread sandwiches, coffee and sodas lay on the dining room buffet. Gabriel walked over and popped a bite-size sandwich into his mouth, tasting dry tuna. Natalie approached him with two other women at her side.

"This is the detective who let me know what had happened." Natalie shook her head and one of the women, a redhead, put her arm around Natalie.

The other woman reached out a hand to Gabriel. Surprised, he took it and she shook hands with him heartily.

"Thank you for bringing a close to this nightmare. We're so devastated for Natalie. She does not deserve this."

Now Gabriel understood why he had been invited to the wake. Natalie wanted to show the world how she had cooperated with the law enforcement agencies. She was distancing herself as much as possible from her murderous son. The ladies hugged Natalie and moved off.

Natalie affected the wronged woman by sighing deeply. Looking after them she said to Gabriel, "The red-headed one has a daughter who was a former student of mine. The girl is top of her league. Going to state finals."

Gabriel responded by shoving another tea sandwich into his mouth. Natalie was not getting off the hook so easily.

"You're moving?" he asked her, dabbing his mouth with a paper napkin.

She seemed to deflate in front of him. "Yes."

Natalie absently pulled at the sleeves of her black silk blouse. "I'm afraid this house has too many memories for me. Not all of them good." She nodded and smiled sadly at a guest across the room and then looked back at the detective. "Time to move on."

"To where?" Gabriel asked gently.

Her eyes turned mean. "The investigation is over, Detective. I mean, my son –" She sniffed suddenly and tears sprang into her eyes. She flung a hand over one side of her face as if she were afraid it would fall off and held it there.

"I'm sorry, Mrs. Archwood." Gabriel offered.

"No." She glared at him. "Don't pretend to pity me. I know how you feel. You think I failed as a parent and raised a monster."

The thought had crossed my mind. "What I feel isn't important."

"Damn right." she said with venom. "It isn't important. 'Let he among you, who is without sin, cast the first stone!'" Natalie glared at him, challenging him to cross her.

Since when do you quote the bible? Gabriel figured this was part of the new and improved Natalie Archwood. She certainly had no intention of defining herself as the mother of a serial killer. Again, Gabriel was struck by how truly unlikable Natalie was. He wanted to tell her he thought she was a tacky bitch and it must have been hell on earth to be her child, but he was afraid she would start speaking in tongues.

"I wasn't blaming you, Mrs. Archwood." Gabriel held back and then couldn't resist. "Why are you blaming yourself?"

In response, Natalie Archwood abruptly turned and strode away from him. Gabriel hid his smile behind a drink of soda.

Let's see how long dynamite-lady can act her part before her fuse blows.

On the coffee table, lay a small chest, around which some kids and Sonia were gathered, examining Victor's collection of World War II medals and knives. Gabriel walked over and picked through them as well.

"Where did Vic acquire all of these?" he asked Sonia.

"They were our grandfather's. He fought in the Second World War." She beamed up at him. Gabriel ignored the spotlight.

He fingered a Soviet medal. It was a solid piece of work, with the profile of Stalin at its center and the date "1945" on the back. The striped red ribbon was old and faded. There were other medals, designed with ships, tanks and planes.

"How did your grandfather get these American ones?" Gabriel waved a hand over a part of the collection.

"Oh," Sonia was hunched over a rusted knife. "He used to trade with other soldiers after the war. American, English, it didn't matter."

So, that's how he got the American-made Camillus trench knife, Gabriel thought. Gabriel took a seat close to her, which Sonia instantly appreciated. "Tell me about your grandfather," Gabriel said. "Tell me everything."

As a young man, Mr. Sokolov lived with his wife in Leningrad. They had a two-year-old boy who was their pride and joy – Natalie's older brother.

During World War Two, Mr. Sokolov fought for Stalin. While he was gone, the Hero City went under siege by Hitler's army. Leningrad was completely cut off from the rest of the country, and its three million residents began living day and night with falling bombs, starvation, and snow.

Mrs. Sokolov watched her family members die one by one. She fought desperately for food for her baby boy. One day there was no more bread in the bread lines. Mrs. Sokolov tried to feed the baby a mixture of flour, glue and sawdust, which was what most of the inhabitants were reduced to eating. Then one day, Mrs. Sokolov stumbled and could not get up. A passerby helped her to her feet, taking her little boy as Mrs. Sokolov found her footing.

"He's stiff and cold," the passerby remarked.

"Give him to me. I'll warm him," Mrs. Sokolov said weakly, reaching for him.

"The child is dead."

Mrs. Sokolov and the Good Samaritan began struggling. Others walking by who knew Mrs. Sokolov, assured her they would bury the boy so the starving dogs would not get at him. But Mrs. Sokolov would have none of it. First his coat was torn from him as they pulled the child away, and then his little jumper. The sympathetic hearts finally let her hold him in the snow, and Mrs. Sokolov sat there, felled by exhaustion and hunger. She must have fallen asleep for when she awoke, her friends had made good on their promise. Her son was gone; taken away for proper burial. All she had of her pride and joy was the empty jumper she still held in her hand.

Mr. Sokolov was captured and suffered at the hands of the Germans. He survived, only to return to a half-demented wife who refused to part with the torn jumper she kept at her breast.

Later, when Mr. Sokolov managed to defect to the United States, he took his wife, now pregnant with Natalie. In her new home, Mrs. Sokolov would sit and rock the jumper for hours. She would search the jumper for any tiny hairs or stains – anything that might have been a part of the little boy. She would cry because she was intimate with the finality of death, and it made her exceedingly afraid to love anyone or anything that much again. The fear of another loss hardened her heart so completely, that when Natalie was born, Mrs. Sokolov distanced herself emotionally from her daughter. Only at night, when she fingered the jumper, would she let out all the pain and love she had stowed in her heart and pay a tearful tribute to the child that died.

"We were poisoned against our grandmother from birth," Sonia told Gabriel. "Mom couldn't stand Grandma. Grandma was insane. She always thought she could capture the soul of her lost baby through the jumper and bring him back to her."

Gabriel's interest piqued. "Did Vic know about that?"

"Sure! After Grandpa died, Grandma lived with us. She was a total nutcase. But she had the money." Sonia paused, giggling. "You know what Grandma bequeathed to Mom when she died?"

"No, what?"

"She told Mom she was going to give her the most valuable treasure she owned, and Mom was never to part with it."

"What was it?"

"The jumper. She gave Mom the baby's raggedy jumper."

Gabriel glanced at Natalie across the room where she held court. Some families are marked for discord right from the start, Gabriel thought pensively. To Sonia he said, "What did your mom do with the jumper?"

Sonia leaned conspiratorially toward Gabriel and spoke in a hushed tone. "She ripped it up and burned it. The way Grandma used to worship the jumper; we thought for sure Mom would be hit by lightning."

"Then what happened?"

"Nothing much. Mom got the courts to declare Grandma incompetent. Mom got power of attorney and then she got all the money."

Sonia, still leaning close to Gabriel, smiled demurely and cocked her head flirtatiously. Gabriel took that as his cue to make a quick exit.

In the early evening, Gabriel strolled through Golden Gate Park and sat, looking at the ducks in the pond, trying to get a sense of what went into creating someone like Victor Archwood. Gabriel knew deep down that he wanted to clear himself of any culpability. Could the beating he gave Vic—

You are an evil, evil man!

Could it have caused Archwood to become a killer? Obtaining any further clues into Archwood's personality from his family seemed impossible. Sister Sonia lived in a fantasy world and Natalie was intent on redefining herself as another of her son's victims.

Gabriel had to admit he didn't know much at all about the man. How did Victor Archwood know so much about him? And then there was that little matter regarding the child pornography. Gabriel shivered involuntarily. The rug had been ripped out from under him. That's what happened. Archwood had killed himself and left Gabriel with a million unanswered questions.

*"It is easier to fight for one's principles
than to live up to them."*

Alfred Adler

CHAPTER 27

Although Gabriel was officially on vacation, he couldn't keep away from the Archwood home. After months of being haunted by a ghostly suspect, Gabriel craved to learn as much about Vic as he could. In doing so, perhaps he could manage to unearth the missing links in his memory as well.

Gabriel spied a waving flag that said "Open House" and a Jaguar parked out front, probably belonging to a realtor. Gabriel pulled his car to the curb. Perhaps Vic had managed to hide his grandfather's weapons somewhere in the house before he took his life.

The real estate agent, a slim brunette in a smart tan pantsuit, greeted Gabriel warmly as he climbed up the pink granite steps. "Hello! Welcome home!"

Gabriel smiled genially and gestured toward the inside of the house. "Can I browse through?"

"Oh, certainly. This is such a wonderful location, isn't it?" She began trailing him. "So close to the beach and to the park."

"A very good location," Gabriel murmured, surveying the room. "Owners are here?"

"Oh, no, not during the open house. Did you know that trolley access is right outside?"

"No kidding," Gabriel said absently and wandered down the hall.

"Well," she said uncomfortably, watching him go, "I can take you on a tour. Are you looking for a bachelor pad or–"

"I'm a bachelor."

"Well, this will really allow you to stretch your legs–"

Gabriel was relieved to see a young Chinese couple enter the front door.

"Oh, will you excuse me for a moment?" the brunette said to Gabriel, as she hastily moved toward the couple.

Gabriel moved down a hallway that smelled of old sheets. He entered the first of the three bedrooms, which consisted of two twin beds, a dresser, and a tiny vanity table with an oval mirror. The bedspreads were frilly, old-fashioned things, which matched the faded wallpaper. Gabriel saw no dolls or other girly effects, but figured the room had belonged to the twin sisters. He opened the closet, fully expecting to see Sonia's muumuus, but other than a couple of rain parkas, the closet was empty.

The decor of the master bedroom was distinctly feminine as well. Swimming trophies lined a long shelf, some dating back to the sixties. Gabriel inspected a black and white photograph hanging on the wall that depicted a coltish, teenage Natalie Sokolov, hair tucked under a tight swimmer's cap, wearing medals and an open smile that would never be that genuine again.

Gabriel left Natalie's room and crossed the narrow hall to the last bedroom. The wood floorboards creaked under a worn carpet. This room consisted of a faded gray couch and a squat, particleboard coffee table. Dull colors. This had been Vic's room, but nothing existed of the little boy who once lived here. Gabriel walked inside and shut his eyes, trying to recall the details.

On the left had been a bureau with a picture of Vic's grandfather in his Red Army uniform. Gabriel opened his eyes to find a single floor lamp in the space. To the right, Gabriel remembered a toy chest; a robot lay on top that was supposed to walk, but never seemed to have batteries – and an assortment of stuffed animals. Gabriel turned around. Vic's twin bed had been against that back wall and –

How could you do that to a child? You're an evil, evil, man!

Guilty feelings arose inside Gabriel along with nausea.

The realtor's voice drifted toward Gabriel and he quickly retreated from the drab room and ducked through a door that led to the backyard.

As Gabriel stood composing himself under the puffy white clouds, he caught sight of a dilapidated woodshed tucked behind a group of overgrown hedges. He walked over to it.

The door scraped loudly against a warped plank floor as Gabriel opened it. A hole in the ceiling flushed the small hut with welcomed sunlight, but Gabriel saw nothing except broken shelves and shards of glass. Bending down, he picked through the debris that littered the floor, and found nothing of interest. Low clouds descended with the afternoon, bringing shade and moist cool air. In the dimming light the shed took on a more ominous appearance and Gabriel felt the hairs stand up on the back of his neck.

This was Archwood's secret lair.

Tucked away from the rest of the household, dark and private – the budding killer had practiced his art. Gabriel surveyed the small interior and pulled at some fractured shelving.

He lightly kicked at a few pieces of wood with his foot. A black widow quickly scuttled into the crack of loose floorboard. Gabriel watched as a millipede crept out of the same crevice. Breaking out his Swiss army knife, Gabriel lifted the board easily from the floor. He had uncovered a deep hole, pitch black, and smelling of damp earth.

"The house is perfect for children..."

The real estate agent had come outside. Gabriel reached into the hole. His heart skipped a beat as his hand glanced against something hard rolling around in the darkness. He pulled the object up to the light.

A brass egg shined in his hand. Gabriel shook off a large black ant and gently cleaned the egg with his sleeve. He could make out Russian lettering and an Easter type design etched on the surface.

Gabriel glanced once at the shed's door, and then turned his attention back to the egg, which was very delicate and finely crafted. A tiny clasp on one side opened the egg and Gabriel flicked it with his thumbnail, half expecting to see something sinister inside, but the egg was empty. Gabriel sniffed the inside and ran his finger gently around, hoping to uncover some residue or powder, but the egg gave away no secret.

He pocketed the egg and reached into the hole once more, groping in the dark. Gabriel managed to grasp two more items, pulling out a small brass box with two entwined hearts and an ornamental Christmas tree box. He quickly buffed the dirt to reveal more beautiful designs and Russian inscriptions.

"There's room enough here for a swing set or possibly a spa!"

Gabriel quickly tucked the brass boxes inside his jacket, clumsily pushing the floorboard back in place with his foot. He trudged through the weeds, passing the Chinese couple and the realtor without a word.

"Oh, that's coming down!" the realtor said to Gabriel pleadingly. "Don't let the shed worry you." Ignored by Gabriel, she turned manically back to the couple. "The current owners are paying to have it removed. Imagine how much larger the backyard will be without it. There's plenty of room for play equipment!"

Gabriel entered the house, quickly strode down the hall, and headed out the front door. On his way down the pink granite steps, he bumped into a tall, blonde woman.

"Pardon me," Gabriel mumbled as the woman pivoted around to stare after him from her perch on the stairs.

Gabriel laid the brass boxes on the table in his hotel room and sat looking at them. The Russian word "дедушка" was inscribed in one heart of the valentine box, joined by another heart that contained the word "внук." The Easter egg contained the word "дорогой."

After emailing the webmaster at the language translation website, Gabriel learned that the engraved words were "grandfather," "grandson," and "dear one."

Now Gabriel inspected each box carefully. Apparently, Archwood's grandfather had given him more than knives and war mementos. But why had Archwood buried his grandfather's gifts in a long-forgotten shed? While Dr. B was surely more equipped to answer such a question, Gabriel was willing to give it the old college try.

Perhaps he buried his grandfather's gifts like a pirate buries treasure – hoping to retrieve them at a later date. Perhaps he was forced to quickly hide them from Natalie's prying eyes, and then he forgot about them. Or maybe, Gabriel mused, Archwood's memory of his grandfather eventually warped like the old photograph in the dining room; and the knife and gun had more appeal to his violent fantasies than these creations fabricated out of love.

His cell phone rang and Gabriel figured it was Ming. That was good, he thought, because he wanted to share his find and get her take on Grandpa's gifts. He reached for his cell phone and saw the caller identified as Sergeant Krol.

"This is McRay."

"Gabriel? How're you doing? How's your vacation?"

Gabriel fingered the brass items lying before him. *How's my obsession...?*

"Nearly over."

"Sorry to bother you, but a strange phone call came in over the desk for you today."

Gabriel's ears piqued. "Yeah?"

"I don't know if you want to pursue this," Krol said, "but it came from a girl who claims to be Victor Archwood's sister."

Gabriel smiled sympathetically. "That would be Sonia."

"No." Krol said, "She said her name was Katherine."

Gabriel's brows furrowed. He thought that the other sister had disappeared into thin air.

"Give me her number." Gabriel tucked the phone under his chin and reached for a pad of paper. "I do want to talk to her."

"Sorry. She told the desk she couldn't be reached. But she wants to meet you in person, tonight, eight on the dot at Fisherman's Wharf, Pier 39."

Gabriel took down the information and chewed his lower lip, wondering what Archwood's sister wanted with him.

"You want a tail?" Krol asked. "Cause she could be as wacky as her brother."

"Nah, I'll be okay. You have anything on her at all?"

"To tell you the truth, I gave up following her trail when the case closed. She was living in Oregon as of about ten months ago."

Gabriel whistled. Not much there. "That's okay. Thanks for passing this along."

"A pleasure." Krol stated. "If you change your mind; I'm on call."

Gabriel thanked him again and hung up.

Gabriel took a cable car to Fisherman's Wharf, comforted by the familiar clanking sound and the rush of fresh, salty air. He arrived well before the appointed time and browsed through a few tourist shops. He ended up among a row of restaurants, their storefronts boasting refrigerated cases filled with fresh crab, lobster, and shrimp. The place teemed with people. Gabriel bought a beer and took a seat at an outside table that afforded him a view of the wharf.

Strands of miniature lights hung over the awnings of the cafés, giving the place a magical aura. Gabriel was watching the fey, twinkling lights, when he noticed the angular-faced blonde observing him from between a case of iced, bug-eyed fish and another filled with headless shrimp.

He recognized her as the woman from the Buena Vista and realized he had passed her on the Archwood steps that very morning. It was not eight o'clock yet. Apparently the mysterious blonde woman had the same idea as Gabriel: come early and stakeout the location. Gabriel stood up at his table and looked directly at her. After a moment, the blonde slowly approached him.

"Katherine?" He asked when she was within earshot.

The woman nodded. She stood nearly a head taller than Gabriel and through her glasses; he made out Kelly green eyes. Her thick blond hair hung in a style reminiscent of a Sixties starlet. She was long and trim; like a model.

"Can I buy you something to drink? A beer maybe?"

"A beer would be nice." Her voice was sensual; throaty and low.

"I'll be right back." Gabriel moved to a cafe, bought a beer, and then returned to the table. She was sitting now; arms and legs crossed.

"I've seen you before." Gabriel set the beer and a glass down in front of her. "I saw you today. Why are you following me?"

"I've wanted to speak with you about Vic," she answered plainly. "But I just didn't know how to approach you without setting off the family alarm." Katherine surveyed Gabriel for a moment. "Why were you at our house this morning, Sergeant McRay? Why are you interested in my brother after he's dead?"

Gabriel could feel the brass boxes in his jacket pocket, pressing against his skin. He looked up at the night sky and said nonchalantly, "Because I was assigned to the case, Miss Archwood – or is it missus now?"

"It's Katherine."

Gabriel could feel her green eyes studying him and wondered what she was looking for. "Naturally, I'm interested in your brother."

"I know you want to know more about Vic. I don't blame you for that."

Gabriel tried not to be obvious in his inspection of Archwood's wayward sister. He wished he could have seen her in the daylight. The twinkling lights barely illuminated her.

"Tell me about Vic," Gabriel said as he sat across from her.

She poured her beer into the glass. "I was very close to my brother. He and I often teamed up together."

"That's funny; Sonia told me he was pretty distant."

"Of course he was distant from Sonia," Katherine snapped. "She was always a whiny, pathetic oaf and Mom's spying little kiss-ass besides."

"That's a bit harsh, don't you think?"

"Could you live with Sonia?"

Gabriel didn't answer.

Katherine guffawed and took a swallow of the beer. "I thought not."

"Do you speak to your father at all, Katherine?" Gabriel asked.

"No, I don't even know where he is."

"He's in Arkansas," Gabriel told her bluntly. "He's seriously ill."

"What a pity," Katherine said dryly and then met Gabriel's eyes. "Sergeant McRay. Well, well, well."

"Tell me about your brother," Gabriel reminded her.

Katherine paused, sat back, and smiled. "Ah, stick to the facts, Ma'am. The hero of the investigation needs only the facts. You are a hero now, aren't you?"

Gabriel narrowed his eyes at her and said, "What exactly do you know about the murders, Miss Archwood?"

"Katherine."

"Katherine," Gabriel repeated and felt the hairs on the back of his neck stand at attention. "Were you aware that your brother wrote notes to me?"

"Of course," she replied.

Gabriel was surprised by her blunt answer and wondered how to tackle Katherine Archwood. "Then you and Victor were talking. You knew he was committing murder."

"Wrong, Sergeant McRay," Katherine said. "I'm no accessory to Vic's crimes. When Vic returned to San Francisco, he called me. I had no clue where he was."

"And where did he reach you?"

"Let's stay on the subject, shall we? Vic called me and told me everything he had done."

"And what did you do?"

"I was aghast, of course," Katherine said calmly and took a swallow of beer.

Gabriel gazed at her, shaking his head. She was definitely as bizarre as the rest of her family. He was beginning to tire of the crowd, the twinkling lights, and Archwood's sister.

"Do you know why he wrote to you?" Katherine asked Gabriel. Gabriel shook his head.

"He wanted you."

"He wanted me?"

"He wanted your detective skills. He felt that was the very least you owed him after what you'd done to him."

Gabriel took a nervous draught of beer and then set the bottle down a bit too hard on the table.

"Okay, so you know too. I lost control of myself and beat him. It was a terrible thing to do and I'm not proud of it. But it has no bearing on this case."

"What else did you do to him?"

Perplexed, Gabriel met her eyes. "What do you mean?"

"You heard me."

"I told you what I did."

"You touched him, that's what you did. You abused him sexually."

Gabriel's jaw dropped as his eyes widened. "I did no such thing."

The young ones tempt you, don't they?

"That's a lie," Gabriel told her firmly. "I never touched him like that. Not ever." Gabriel lifted his beer, saw his hand shaking, and set the beer down again.

Katherine observed him coolly. "You did. That's why you beat him up. You were ashamed that you had touched him."

"Is that what Vic told you?"

"It's what my mother told me."

Gabriel looked beseechingly at the water beyond. "My God. Why would she say that? I never did that to Vic." Gabriel closed his eyes. *How could you do that to a child? You're an evil, evil man!* "I wouldn't have done that."

The young ones tempt you, don't they?

Gabriel shook his head. "No, I know that didn't happen."

"It happened. You ruined his life because of it," Katherine said.

"No." Gabriel opened his eyes and looked right at Katherine. "I would never do what was done to me." Gabriel shut his mouth then; shocked that a stranger had successfully fished out his secret.

"You were molested as a child?" Katherine honed in on Gabriel like a hawk.

Gabriel felt a dull ache behind his eyes. The miniature lights – they were going to drive him crazy. What was Dr. B talking about when he mentioned "perpetration issues?" Had Gabriel touched Vic? Was that another suppressed memory?

Katherine took a thoughtful sip of beer. "You yourself were abused. By whom, may I ask?"

Gabriel paused, feeling a hole in his gut and wishing badly that he had never divulged his secret to this peculiar stranger. Too late; the damage was done.

"A neighbor," he admitted.

Katherine nodded, studying Gabriel through her glasses. "Well, there goes the neighborhood. Do you think it was something in the water, Sergeant?"

Gabriel stared at her. Was she making a joke?

"I didn't touch your brother in that way. I want you to know that."

Katherine fell silent for a moment and then rose like a spirit, never taking her eyes off Gabriel. "But we're not sure now, are we?" she said demurely. "Vic may have died a murderer, but you're living as a disgusting pedophile. Thanks for the beer, Sergeant."

She walked away, disappearing beyond the lights of the wharf. She left Gabriel sitting frozen under the spell of her words.

~ ~ ~

CHAPTER

"Gabriel, listen to me—"

"What about what she said?" Gabriel asked Dr. B as they sat in the Hyatt lobby. Dr. B was on a Stanford University tour with his son but took a side trip to meet Gabriel at his hotel.

"You said it yourself," Gabriel told him. "Perpetration issues. People who were molested as kids become molesters themselves."

"That's not true; not in all cases." Dr. B balanced a cup of coffee on his knee. "My goodness, Gabe; first you think you are a killer and now a pedophile. Is that truly what you think of yourself?"

Dr. B watched his patient reflect on it. Finally Gabriel shook his head. "I don't remember doing anything like that. I swear to God."

"Why don't you trust your own memory then?"

"My memory sucks, you of all people know that! I could have just blocked it out like I did with − my own thing. I might have done it in a fugue state."

"You told me the fugue states happened later in your life. Were you suffering from them as a teenager?"

"No."

"Do the young ones tempt you, Gabe?"

Gabriel focused on Dr. B, amazed to hear those words spoken out loud and so calmly.

"Absolutely not," Gabriel answered. He looked across the lobby, surveying the tourists. He had been getting used to feeling normal; looking forward to experiencing the everyday triumphs and failures of the Average Joe. And then Katherine Archwood came along with yet another way the killer could torment Gabriel.

"I wish I could remember clearly that day with Vic," Gabriel said. "I only remember hitting him then feeling terrible afterwards."

"From what you've told me about the Archwood family, I'd say you are relying on a highly unstable source to assist you in your goals of personal well-being."

"Christ, they are weird. All of them," Gabriel muttered. "But being around them brings it back. I guess that's why I can't leave them alone. I never kept friends from here. I don't speak with my own family. Andrew's dead; I can't confront him. It's like I want them to give me something of my past."

"Please do not depend on them," Dr. B said. "If you want to make peace with your past then I suggest you reach out to your parents."

Gabriel was not listening. "I think I can get something out of Katherine. Then I can put this thing to rest and get on with my life."

"Gabe," Dr. B said. "The Archwood's are prejudiced against you. You represent the law, for God's sake – the cop that nailed their son, their brother. They won't do anything to benefit you and it's dangerous for you to depend on them."

Gabriel seemed to digest that for a moment and then turned to his psychiatrist. "You're right. I do represent the law."

Dr. B could tell something had occurred to Gabriel and was about to ask his patient what was up when Gabriel stood, shook Dr. B's hand and thanked him for coming to see him. Their meeting was over.

In the silence of the SFPD forensic offices, Ming finished off the last of her paperwork. Taylor, the Haitian janitor, quietly mopped the floor nearby. Ming was filing away her report on the Thomas Welby exam, possibly Archwood's first victim. She scanned through her work one last time with a proud eye, knowing it would be forever archived. As she had previously discussed with the detectives, the Welby murder had been haphazard. Obviously Archwood had not developed his chakra murder pattern yet.

He almost made it.

He'd had only one chakra left to go – the crown chakra; the spiritual portal of all consciousness. The level of the soul...

Ming glanced at her wristwatch, noting the time as 8:30 p.m. She could have called it a day except that she was expecting a fax from Anthony Hamilton in Los Angeles. Anthony had received the dental DNA a week ago and, succumbing to her urgings, promised Ming she would get the comparisons tonight.

"You gonna be here much longer, Doctor?" Taylor asked in his Caribbean accent.

"Not much longer," Ming replied. "I'm waiting for a fax."

"You don't mind bein' alone with dead folk? My granny used to scare us kids wid' talk of dead folk comin' alive."

Ming smiled and said, "Nice Grandma. Well, I don't believe in voodoo and I guess I'm not the squeamish type."

"I kinnot say dat for myself, no way. You hav' a good night, now. I'll be catching da end of da ballgame."

"You have a good night too, Taylor."

The janitor collected his cleaning supplies and left the room. Ming welcomed the silence. She neatly stacked the report on the desk and looked wistfully toward the fax machine. Ming planned on calling Gabriel with the results and then asking if he would be interested in accompanying her on her last night in San Francisco. She promised herself there would be no more awkwardness between them. Gabriel was right. If Ramirez wanted to cause trouble because he thought her and Gabriel –

Oh, will you shut up?

Ming rolled her eyes at her own stupidity. Just go with it. Let the world go to hell if it must. She smiled at the thought of living on a wild side.

A door creaked outside, and curious, Ming rose from the desk and went to the door. She stuck her head out and looked down both sides of the empty hall.

"Hello?"

She listened for a moment but the hallway was quiet. Suddenly a high-pitched ring caused Ming to jump, and she swiveled her gaze toward the fax machine coming to life behind her. Ming walked over, crossed her arms, and waited. The machine purred genially, moved a sheet of paper through its body, and dumped the fax in the receiving tray. Ming inspected the report as another page came through. She felt her face falling as she snatched the following page for more details.

Chilled, Ming quickly called Gabriel's cell phone to leave a message.

"Hi, it's Ming. I've got the DNA results from the body at the cabin. Something weird. The tooth matches the DNA from the semen sample back in L.A. But the DNA from John Doe does not match the tooth. Understand? We have two sets of

DNA from the cabin. Gabriel, that cremated body is not Victor Archwood! Please call me right away."

Unable to do or say more, Ming replaced the receiver back in its cradle and stared at the report. Archwood must have extracted his own molar, knowing it would identify him. He's unbelievable, Ming thought.

And he's still alive! Struggling to keep calm, Ming dialed the Hyatt.

"Gabriel McRay's room, please."

She heard a pronounced swishing sound coming from outside in the hall but Ming ignored it. She waited anxiously as the phone rang. Ultimately, she was transferred back to the operator.

"Can I leave a voicemail?"

The swishing sound was more apparent, obviously moving closer to her. Ming held the phone as she walked to the door. "Gabriel, I left a message on your cell..." Ming bumped right into the janitor who was mopping the floor directly outside the doorway. "Oh, Taylor; I didn't know you were still—"

The janitor turned around with a grin and Ming instantly saw that he was not Haitian at all, but a lean blonde male.

Gabriel stood outside the Archwood door, shrouded in fog. He rapped once on the door, loudly. In the unseen distance, Gabriel heard the ding-ding of the trolley car rolling past. A single beep on his cell phone signaled he had messages. They would have to wait. Gabriel raised his hand again to knock, but the door swung open.

Natalie stood before him, holding an empty tumbler. Gabriel caught a whiff of liquor on her breath.

"What do you want?" Natalie said tipsily.

"I want to talk," Gabriel told her. "May I come in?"

Gabriel was sure the answer would be "no," but surprisingly Natalie stepped back, allowing him into the house. Gabriel followed her into the dining room, where the older woman picked up a bottle of vodka from the buffet and refilled her glass.

"You want a drink, Detective?"

"No, thanks."

Natalie thrust the bottle down and then moved to the kitchen. Gabriel was right at her heels.

"Well?" she said, as she opened the freezer for ice. "You have something to say?"

"I do. Your daughter told me some interesting news. She's been following me, you know."

Natalie whirled the ice around in her glass, watching the vodka with hungry eyes. "I'm not surprised."

"I want to know exactly what you told your kids about me."

"The truth," Natalie said and tossed back some of her drink. "You hurt my boy. You betrayed him."

"Your daughter says you told Vic I molested him."

Natalie gazed at Gabriel for a while through reddening eyes; then took another drink. "That's right; and you're damn lucky I didn't call the cops on you."

Gabriel stared her down. "I've been wondering why you didn't."

Natalie's eyes found the window and she walked over to straighten the curtains. "I didn't want to make things worse by putting my boy through a long court case and prying eyes. He'd already been through too much. Consider yourself blessed." She knocked back another swallow.

"You've accused me of something very serious, Mrs. Archwood. It wasn't very responsible of you as a parent not to press charges."

"Would you like me to press the issue now?" Natalie said smartly, turning to Gabriel as the ice clinked in the glass.

"I know I didn't molest Vic. You would have had me arrested in a heartbeat."

Natalie leaned against the kitchen sink and raised the glass to her lips again. "What else did Sonia tell you?"

"I didn't hear it from Sonia. Katherine told me."

Natalie nearly choked on the vodka. "What?"

"Katherine told me what you said I did."

"You saw Katherine?"

"I did. We met at Fisherman's Wharf."

Natalie stood like a statue, drink poised in mid-air. "Katherine is dead."

"She's very much alive, Mrs. Archwood. She's just avoiding you."

Gabriel suddenly ducked as the glass whizzed by his head and crashed against the oven. The smell of spilled vodka quickly permeated the small room. Gabriel stared at Natalie in astonishment.

"She died five months ago in that lunatic commune of blood poisoning, you stupid asshole!" Natalie screamed at him. "She's buried up there in their compound."

Shaken, Gabriel said, "That's impossible."

"Really? Then whose body did I identify in Oregon? Get the fuck out of my house!"

Gabriel gaped at Natalie for a cold moment, and then turned like a lost man to the family photograph in the dining room. Both young, smiling sisters wore periwinkle dresses that matched their blue eyes. The Katherine he drank beer with had green eyes.

I'm Fortunato.

Gabriel recoiled from the buffet, suddenly remembering the burned contact lens cases found in the Pepperdine apartment – all assorted colors; the Theater Arts student who could get into character anytime; even that of his own dead sister. Cold rippled through Gabriel's body, freezing every muscle in its path.

I'm Fortunato. Oh my Lord...

Archwood had been sitting directly across from him hiding behind another mask, mocking Gabriel. Gabriel realized he hadn't even gotten a good look at him.

Because you thought you were looking at a woman.

Gabriel flew down the pink granite steps of the Archwood house, quickly paging Ramirez. His phone beeped once more and Gabriel quickly retrieved his messages as he drove toward the Embarcadero Hyatt. He had only one message.

"Hi, it's Ming. I've got the DNA results back from the body at the cabin..."

Gabriel flew into his room in the Hyatt and saw the red message light beeping. He pressed the button for retrieval, hearing Ming's voice again, "Gabriel, I left a message on your cell..." Gabriel heard a pause, and then the moment of fright in her voice, "Oh, Taylor! I didn't know you were still –"

Gabriel listened intently, made out some sort of shuffling sound, and then he winced at Ming's sudden, panicky – "Oh! Oh, no!"

Heart pounding, Gabriel replayed the message and then phoned the San Francisco police. Grabbing his revolver, he ran to the elevator.

As his car sped toward the hospital, Gabriel's mind raced as fast as the wheels under him. *What does Archwood want? He wants souls.*

Gabriel fought to keep calm. *He wants to perform his ritual on the seventh and final chakra.* A flash of panic flared in his gut at the thought of Ming alone with the Malibu Canyon Murderer. *Keep calm! Get into Archwood's mindset.*

Ming's a doctor, Gabriel thought, a pathologist. Archwood's twisted ideas might include "absorbing" the intellect of a doctor, but that's not what Katherine (*Archwood!*) had told him. He wanted Gabriel.

The cell phone rang and Gabriel grabbed it. Sergeant Krol told him the police were on the way to the hospital and Lieutenant Ramirez was flying up immediately.

Gabriel's tires screeched on the damp pavement of the near-empty parking lot.

He bounded up the stairs to the lab and halted in his tracks, seeing a fallen mop in the middle of the hall. Positioning his gun in front of him, Gabriel slowly skirted around the mop, scanning the floor tiles and relieved at finding no traces of blood. Ming had to be okay, right? How else would Archwood lure Gabriel to him?

Gabriel heard a distant commotion and pivoted around, pointing the revolver down the hall. Sergeant Krol turned the corner accompanied by a team of uniformed officers, also bearing weapons. Sighing, Gabriel lowered his gun.

"We just phoned the janitor at home. He said Dr. Li told him she was waiting for a fax. He claims he put everything away and left around eight-thirty."

Gabriel wandered into the lab and looked around. He saw the fax on the floor, read the report, and then dismally handed it over to Krol.

"Jesus," Krol muttered as he read the report.

A uniformed officer stepped into the room. "Excuse me, but I think you two ought to see what's up in the morgue."

"Dr. Li?" Gabriel asked worriedly, already heading out the door.

"No," answered the officer, following behind. "You gotta see it for yourself."

Gabriel pushed open the door to the morgue. Along a row of body compartments, the men saw two gaping doors. The occupants had been moved to a center examination table.

The disintegrating body of an old man lay prone on the back of a recently examined teenaged gang member. A note stuck out of the shriveled buttocks of the dead man.

"Jesus," Krol repeated.

Steadying himself, Gabriel walked forward across the sterile floor. He stopped and absently searched his pockets for gloves, unable to free his gaze from the macabre display in front of him.

Krol quickly obliged Gabriel by handing him a pair of latex gloves he pulled from a nearby container. "Looks like our friend had a little time on his hands."

"For setting the scene," Gabriel mumbled as he drew on the gloves, and the other men looked at him strangely.

Grimacing, Gabriel carefully withdrew the note and unfolded it.

"Better remember where we played the day you attacked me," the note read. "The doctor is depending on it."

A hail of black and white units stood guard over the Archwood home and the revolving red and blue bar lights from the cars shone through the dusty lace curtains of the parlor, where Gabriel hovered over Natalie Archwood.

"I don't know where Victor is," the older woman exclaimed, sitting fretfully on her overstuffed couch. "I thought he was dead!"

"He's holding a woman hostage!" Gabriel yelled at her. "Who knows if he's killed her already?"

"What do you want me to say?" Natalie pleaded, and for the first time, Gabriel saw true fear in her eyes.

He put his hands on her shoulders and brought his face close to hers. "Now you listen to me. You've lied about me for years to Vic. Why? Why did you lie?"

She stared wide-eyed at Gabriel; nervously licked her lips, and said, "I had to."

"What do you mean?"

"I had to lie about you to Victor. You never touched Vic, not in that way."

Gabriel felt his grip loosening.

Natalie searched Gabriel's eyes. "My father did."

Gabriel released her and backed up. He found his way to an armchair and slowly sat down as Natalie begged a uniformed officer for some aspirin. Gabriel's eyes found the parlor window, and he looked through the glass at the hypnotic red and blue lights circling on the patrol cars outside. In a gentle rush, all he had forgotten floated to the surface of his memory.

Vic was sitting on Gabriel's lap after they had returned home from one of their excursions. The two of them were talking in Vic's room about how much Vic missed his grandfather, when the little boy gently pushed back Gabriel's long, curling black hair and whispered, "My grandpa and I had a special game. Want to know what it was?"

The little boy confided to Gabriel about the games they used to play, how sometimes it hurt and sometimes it didn't. Gabriel had felt the breath choke up in his throat. He did not want to conjure up the images from Vic's story. He pushed Vic away as if the boy was a stinging wasp and he told him to shut up; to keep quiet. Vic had stared at Gabriel for a moment, and then he unzipped his pants. The little boy asked why Gabriel was angry. He didn't want Gabriel to be angry with him. Perhaps if they played the game, Gabriel would be happy again. Playing the game had always pleased his grandfather and the old man had given Vic presents.

But all Gabriel wanted was for Vic to stop talking – stop talking of things that stirred up the black sludge in his own soul. He did not want to go there. He would turn his mind away. Vic would not stop talking – he took Gabriel's hand. He placed it on his body. Gabriel's chest filled with unremitting rage and he lashed out...

Gabriel jerked his eyes away from the whirling alarm lights. He placed his head in his hands and heard Natalie speaking again.

"Oh how Victor loved his grandfather. I wanted nothing except for him to cherish his memory. Do you know how his pig of a father used to greet him? By pushing him away!" Natalie began crying.

Gabriel watched the tears gush from her eyes. He remembered that Natalie had returned home and seen the bruises on her son; the dried tears on his face. Although Vic kept quiet, Natalie could guess what had happened. Gabriel had stayed, feeling terrible and willing to be reprimanded. Gabriel had expected her to call the police, his parents, anybody. But Natalie hadn't. She simply held Vic's hand and yelled at Gabriel.

How could you do that to a child? You're an evil, evil man.

"At first Victor didn't believe me," Natalie said. "He admired you so much. Eventually though, I was able to convince him that you were the one who had hurt him in that way, not his grandfather who loved him. Children forget. Children can be taught."

Children can be twisted. Gabriel glared at her in anger.

Natalie sniffled and said with shaky, ethereal confidence. "I teach, you know; I run a swim school for children. I trained for the Olympics." Natalie Archwood drifted into a dream for a moment, and then she turned to Gabriel with trembling lips. "You can't blame me, can you? I mean, you hurt him – you beat him up. Wasn't it better that he continued to love his grandfather? The one man in this family he could depend on?"

Gabriel stood, unable to form words; unable to find pity for the wretched woman before him. How could a family become that wasted?

I suggest you reach out to your parents...

Ming...

Where did I take Vic that afternoon? Where did we go?

"Gabriel?" Sergeant Krol asked warily.

Wracking his brain, Gabriel headed to the front door.

"You can't blame me!" Natalie cried after him. "I was a single mother with three kids to raise! I did the best job I could! He loved his grandfather!"

Vic had liked the park, Gabriel thought, jogging down the granite steps. He liked feeding the ducks at the pond. But Golden Gate Park did not ring a bell. Not for that day.

Where did I take him?

"Gabriel!" Krol called after him from the doorway. "Where are you going? Wait for us!"

In his mind, he heard a little boy laughing carelessly. The sun had been out. There were sodas and a packed picnic lunch.

Gabriel got in his car and peeled out onto Lincoln Avenue, searching the green treetops of the park, smelling the nearby ocean – trying to remember.

Where would Vic take Ming? The park had a million hiding places. Archwood would have gone somewhere secret, yet quick and easily accessible.

There were sodas and a packed picnic lunch – sandwiches, peanut butter sandwiches. Vic said those were his favorite kind.

Gabriel slowed the car in front of the charming, nineteenth century Cliff House; a restaurant perched above the Pacific.

He could visualize the black and white reprints hanging on the papered walls that depicted the Victorian edifice at various stages of its historic life.

A little boy's laughter bubbled up from the pool of Gabriel's memory and –

He could feel the sun warming his face as he watched Vic scramble...

Gabriel drove slowly and then stopped the car at a stone wall just beyond the Cliff House.

He could feel the sun warming his face as he watched Vic scramble along the ruins of the public swimming pool.

On the other side of the stone wall, down a winding trail, lay the ruins of Sutro baths.

Gabriel pulled a flashlight from the glove compartment, grabbed his gun, and exited the car. He leaned over the low cinderblock wall and searched the sea-swept ruins from his vantage point, looking for Ming.

Sutro Baths got its name from Adolf Sutro, who had the vision of making a bathing resort by the crashing waves of the ocean. The multi-pool structure, which used the available saltwater, fell into disrepair and was eventually closed due to lack of interest and polio. Only the stone foundations remained. Gabriel listened to the restless pounding of the Pacific against the old walls. Bordering the ruins were steep cliffs perforated with caves. Vic had liked to hide in those caves.

The lights from Louie's, a diner squatting on a hill above the site, shed weak light upon the weathered stones; but other than that, Gabriel had only his flashlight and a blanketed moon to illuminate his way.

Following the cinderblock wall, Gabriel found the footpath and began his descent. He stumbled once and cursed as his ankle fired in pain.

Gabriel paused, resting his foot, and tried imagining where Archwood would hide Ming. His eyes settled on a large cave near the water's edge. He made his way toward the mouth of the cave which yawned open, threatening to swallow Gabriel in darkness.

The tide had already begun to rise and Gabriel's shoes sloshed through water as he shined his light inside the cave's interior. He saw nothing except a piece of white PVC piping sticking up like a leg bone through the rising water.

Keeping the beam of light trained on the pipe, Gabriel slowly advanced, aware that Archwood might jump at him from the darkness. As he neared the pipe, he could see it jutted from a long mound just visible below the moving surface of the water.

"Oh, my God…" Gabriel dropped the flashlight and ran to the mound. He plunged his hands into the icy water and began digging frantically.

"Oh, my God," he repeated as the flashlight bobbed on the water, tossing light erratically on the cave walls before it died. Gabriel uncovered Ming's face; he could see her gorgeous hair now free and swaying gently below the water. The PVC pipe was wedged between her teeth. "No…"

Gabriel gripped her body tightly and hauled her up from her makeshift grave, relieved to feel Ming shudder. The pipe fell from between her lips and she gagged, coughed up dirt then took a deep, rasping breath. Gabriel held her to him as she convulsed into hacking coughs. She was so cold. "Ming…"

He felt tape at her wrists and his own hands fiercely ripped at it. Ming continued to cough as Gabriel leaned her against the cave wall, pushed his hands in the water again to free her ankles from their bonds.

Ming wailed and flung herself at Gabriel. "Help me! Help me!" The sand and mud blinded her and Gabriel steadied her arms as she pawed at him.

"I'm here," he told her.

"Help me!" she sobbed in her soaking clothes.

Gabriel quickly pulled off his jacket; wrapped it around Ming as she struggled in panic.

"I'm here. I'm not letting you go," Gabriel assured her and looked around the cave warily. "Let's get out of here."

The water was already up to their knees.

"I can't see!" she cried, clutching him, threatening to pull them both down into the muck again.

"I know. I know." Gabriel used his sleeve to gently wipe at her eyes. Ming began crying hard and Gabriel put his arm about her and maneuvered them both toward the mouth of the cave as the water continued to rise. Gabriel urged Ming up the footpath, keeping her shivering body close to his, while the dark caves mocked them and the fog masked the trail. Gabriel glanced furtively around him; sure that Archwood was close by. Without hesitation he walked them over to Louie's diner. He pushed open the glass door and waved the manager over.

"Call the police; tell them to send an ambulance for this lady. You got some hot coffee?"

The manager was too busy staring at the mud-covered, shivering mess before him. Gabriel jabbed at his shoulder. "Bring her to the restroom, help her clean up, and give her some coffee! Now!"

The manager nodded wildly.

To Ming, Gabriel said, "Go inside, you'll be warm and safe here."

Ming stared at him wide-eyed and shook her head wildly. "You can't go! You can't leave me here!"

She threw her arms around his neck, clinging to him and burying her face so hard into his neck it seemed as if the two of them might fuse together. "Don't leave me!"

Despite the cold, despite the wet, despite the fact a murderer waited in the mist, Gabriel felt an alien sense of well-being.

Ming needed him and he knew he was capable of protecting her. He felt her body shuddering against him and realized he was no longer a victim. He kissed the top of her head.

"You need to warm up. I'll be right back."

Ming clutched at him tighter. "Don't go! You can't go!"

"You'll be okay." Gabriel nodded to the manager who took Ming by the arm.

"Nooooo! He's going kill me! He's going to kill me!" She broke into hysterical sobs.

Gabriel didn't know what to do. He held her a moment longer and then pushed his gun into her hand. "Keep this. No one will hurt you."

Ming stared trance-like at the weapon in her hand as the manager led her into the warm glow of the diner. Gabriel made a cursory inspection of the remaining two patrons sitting at the counter, who stared wide-eyed at Ming, the gun, and her dirty, wet clothes. Convinced Archwood was not one of them, Gabriel exited the diner.

He made his way through the fog toward the lights of the Cliff House. Gabriel could barely see two feet in front of him. His car suddenly appeared like a phantom before him.

The Russian words were scrawled in the condensation forming on his car windows. Gabriel shivered and looked around.

"Vic!" Gabriel called. "I'm here, Vic!"

Gabriel walked passed the closed gift shop that catered to tourists, selling them "canned San Francisco fog" and photos of old Nob Hill mansions. "Where are you?"

From the fog, Gabriel heard a voice say, "It's time to unmask!"

Gabriel followed the voice and peered around the corner behind the restaurant. A balcony running the full length of the building was unoccupied.

"Vic?" Gabriel moved to the railing, glancing down at an angry ocean filled with riptides. Gabriel remembered warning Vic to keep away from the water here, despite Natalie's swim school lessons.

"The curtains have parted," said a voice directly behind him.

Gabriel turned around to face a deceptively good-looking blonde man. Archwood held the Nagant at point blank range. Catching his own sweaty reflection in Vic's amused blue eyes; Gabriel compared himself to a rabbit caught in the jaws of a coyote.

Gabriel spoke. He had to. "Hello, Vic. It's been a long time."

He had seen the man in disguise, but for Gabriel, seeing Vic unmasked bordered on the freakish. Imprinted on the adult face was clearly the boy Gabriel once knew and it wrenched him.

The gun shifted merrily as Archwood said, "Not so long. You remember my sister, of course."

"How could I forget?"

"I did do a good job on that one, didn't I? Although I doubt my hippie sister ever dressed so fashionably."

"You're very good with playing characters, I'll give you that."

Archwood pushed the gun closer to Gabriel's face. "I simply make costume changes. But you, you're the best actor of all. You've been masquerading as a cop all these years; pretending to be an upstanding guy when you're as warped as me."

"I never molested you, Vic. I hit you but I didn't touch you like that."

"You touched me alright, Sergeant. What do you say? Wanna give it another go?"

Gabriel wondered what he should do. Archwood waved the gun around when he talked. Perhaps if Gabriel could jump him—

"By the way," Archwood said, "how did you like the set design at the morgue?"

Gabriel's flesh was crawling. "What was I supposed to like about it?"

Archwood guffawed as if Gabriel had asked the most ridiculous question on earth. "I thought it was pretty self-explanatory. I thought you would enjoy it. What I find most interesting is that you yourself were abused. Now that makes for interesting character development, wouldn't you say?"

He's got the control, Gabriel thought tensely. If Gabriel didn't turn the tables soon, things were going to escalate rapidly into Gabriel either getting a hole carved into his head or becoming a target for the Nagant.

"Are you hungry for dick now that you've had it?" Archwood poked the gun at Gabriel's neck. "Are you a faggot now?"

Gabriel ignored the inner demons, now awakening afresh to stomp and chew at him. He had to remember everything he knew about being a detective. He had to get Vic on a different track. Gabriel tried to keep his voice steady. "If I were gay, Vic, would that bother you?"

Again the shrug. "I don't care if you like guys, Sergeant. I like them too once in a while. Doesn't make a damn bit of difference to me."

"So what now, Vic?"

"Now we become Blood Brothers. Brothers in blood. " Vic smiled. "Only, I get to live and you get to live through me."

"Is that so?" Gabriel asked, peering through the fog, waiting for his backup.

"That's right. You will become part of me. You'll become stronger."

"The seventh chakra."

"Exactly." Vic pulled out the knife from his boot. "The final chakra had to be you. It was going to be you all along. You're going to come with me now. We're gonna take a drive in your car. And then everything you are will become part of me."

Gabriel nearly laughed. "Everything I am, huh? You sure you're making the right decision?"

Archwood wasn't amused. "You've got a lot to offer, being a detective and all; someone with a sharp wit and a strategic mind. Do you know why I was always one step ahead of you, Sergeant? Because so many souls have helped me along."

Vic's senseless, egotistical banter was melting Gabriel's fear. The melting fear was like oil running into a thirsty engine, giving his muscles back their movement, returning the color to his face. Gabriel wondered where the rage had gone. He had always depended on his anger to see him through threatening situations and now, he had no such crutch to lean on.

"Put away the gun," Gabriel told Archwood gently. "Let me try to help you."

"Oh, you'll help me, don't worry about that."

"I know what happened," Gabriel continued. "Put away the gun, Vic, and let's talk about it."

Archwood paused. For a moment they were back in time and Gabriel saw the tow-headed boy who had worshipped him. Both the knife and the gun faltered slightly.

The wail of approaching sirens ripped through the fog. The gun raised and Archwood's face tightened. "Right. You'd do anything to postpone the inevitable."

"It wasn't me, Vic," Gabriel said. "Your mother lied to you. God, I would do anything to turn back the clock and help you, but I couldn't help anyone back then. I had too much baggage myself. We were both hurt. I know what you went through and –"

"How dare you compare yourself to me?" Vic asked.

"You're right, Vic," Gabriel said, "There is no comparison. I took responsibility for what I did in my life and what happened to me, and I've tried to become a better man. All you did from your lot in life was to become a murderer. That's all you are, Vic, and that's all you'll be remembered for."

The howls of the police cars drew closer. Gabriel suddenly grabbed the gun in Archwood's hand. They struggled and Gabriel repeatedly slammed Archwood's hand against the railing, until the gun dropped. Gabriel bent to retrieve it when he felt a burning pain shoot through his arm – he'd forgotten all about the knife, which was now buried to the hilt in his bicep. Archwood threw himself on Gabriel and they bumped against the railing. Archwood, younger and more agile, managed to pull the blade out and shove it again in Gabriel's side.

A whoosh of air escaped Gabriel's lungs and he knew he'd been sliced badly. Blood flowed like a river onto the cement balcony as the two men danced, shoes slipping in the redness. Down below, the ocean riptides swirled and the sea lions barked crazily.

Gabriel, charged with adrenaline, savagely pushed Archwood back from him and punched him in the face. The blonde man lost his footing and fell. Gabriel felt his side and grimaced, closing his fist around the trench knife. With a grunt, he pulled out the blade. Bent like an old man, Gabriel staunched the flow of blood with one hand, and held the knife with the other.

"Don't do this, Vic. I don't want to hurt you," he gasped. "Can't you remember? You told me yourself your grandfather was touching you in places –"

Archwood wiped blood from his mouth from where he lay on the ground. "Don't talk about him! Don't you say another word about my grandfather!"

"He abused you, Vic! Your mother told you it was me, but she lied. She wanted to protect his memory. She didn't want you to think he could..." Gabriel winced in pain, "do something like that to you."

Archwood slowly rose to his feet like a phantom, holding the gun.

"You told me about it," Gabriel said, watching him. "I had a terrible reaction. I'm sorry. Please let me try to make it up to you –"

Archwood raised the Nagant once more, saying, "I'm sick of your lies. I thought you'd be an asset to me, but you're just a liar. I'm going to rid myself of you and take the doctor instead. You're not worth it. You've ruined your opportunity and now your miserable life is over."

Blood poured between Gabriel's fingers as he held the wound on his side. His other hand weakly reached into his pocket and he pulled out the Valentine and Christmas tree boxes the grandfather had made. He held them out to Archwood and whispered. "And when you buried these, you ended your life as well."

Archwood's eyes widened at the sight of them, and he yelled, "Give them to me!"

"You want them so bad? Go get them!" Gabriel chucked the boxes as far out to sea as he could.

"Nooooo!" Archwood cried and lunged over the railing, nearly falling. He stared through the fog at the churning water. Cold fury swept across his face and he turned to Gabriel, teeth clenched. "Just wait until they find what's left of you—" Archwood rushed Gabriel, and they slammed together against the railing. The knife slipped from Gabriel's hands as he struggled to hold Archwood's arm away, the gun trembling in air. Gabriel was weakening from the loss of blood – he knew Archwood would shoot him. He glanced over the side of the balcony. There was only one possible way he could make it, and it was a desperate chance to take.

Once more, Gabriel fell heavily against the railing with Archwood in tow, and in an instant, they both toppled over the side. Archwood yelled in surprise and the gun discharged, sounding like a firecracker.

The first thing that hit Gabriel was the shock of the water. So freezing cold, his breath stopped in his lungs. Archwood was a dark form, struggling near him, but they were both caught in a violent undertow that immediately tore them apart and swept them out toward sea. The roiling, black water dragged them along the coast, dangerously close to the rocks. Gabriel's tired body was no match for the riptides. He didn't think it would end like this, being pounded to death against the rocks in his own Pacific ocean.

Gabriel lost sight of Archwood, but he didn't care. His own life was ebbing away. The cold, the fight – he needed to cease struggling and go under.

The next thing he knew, bright lights were in his eyes, blinding him. Gabriel thought he had been yanked heavenward, sailing to the stars, but he was still in the freezing water... and the lights, the lights above him were loud.

Helicopters, he thought.

His last vision was someone coming out from the fog, down from the sky, like an avenging angel. Gabriel attempted to reach up his hand, but his muscles rebelled and he couldn't move. Then, there was only darkness.

Noise again... A loud rapid tattoo of noise. Gabriel's body shook uncontrollably. He was in the noise, a part of the whirring. Gabriel opened his eyes and focused on the face of Miguel Ramirez.

"You think I'd let you take all the credit, McRay?"

Gabriel rolled his eyes. Ramirez smiled and nodded to someone just out of Gabriel's vision. "He's gonna be fine."

Then the darkness fell once again.

"Be cheerful. Strive to be happy."

Desiderata, Attributed to Max Ehrmann 1872-1945

CHAPTER 29

The Pacific Ocean lolled gently against the beach. Gabriel lay on his back, feet toward the water, head toward the highway. He adjusted the bundle under his head, getting comfortable. The sand was cold, but he wasn't, not with his jacket and Levis. Above him, white clouds moved along an azure sky. Moving faster, he mused, chased by the promise of rain due to come later in the week. On Gabriel's left, the Ferris wheel turned lazily on the Santa Monica Pier. On the right, he viewed the sloping Santa Monica Mountains.

The beach was practically deserted, but in the distance, backed by the hills, a woman was making slow progress along the sand toward him.

Gabriel raised his hand in greeting and winced. His arm was still sore. His side nagged him as well, where his kidney had been pierced. No matter, Gabriel thought, he would recover.

Gabriel reached into his jeans and pulled out Vic's Easter egg box. He flicked it open, half-expecting a genie to appear. Holding it against the sky, Gabriel could clearly see why Archwood had buried his grandfather's gifts of love. No matter what Natalie had told him, somewhere deep inside, Archwood had known the truth. He had battled with his own suppressed memory, Gabriel supposed; never wanting to accept the knowledge that his relationship with his grandfather had been anything less than wholesome.

Twisted family dynamics made Gabriel think about his own parents living in Seattle. He only now realized how much he blamed them. He had never been able to express it clearly; he'd just blown them off, wanting them to know they were not important to him. When they gave up and moved to Seattle to be near his sister Janet, the action only further cemented what Gabriel considered to be their absolute negligence toward him.

He had called them. He didn't want his funeral to be the next time they saw him. His family had given him a hero's welcome over the phone. He could feel a wall of ice rising as he heard the emotion in their words, but Gabriel was getting pretty adept at cracking through his cold defenses.

Perhaps now, Gabriel thought, he could put to rest that aching little boy ghost who had been haunting him.

Both little boy ghosts.

Gabriel returned the Easter egg to his pocket.

We are one.

No, but perhaps Victor Archwood and he shared a few things in common. Despite whatever similar abuses they had endured in the past, the two boys had developed into two entirely different people. Gabriel would never know exactly what turned the wistful, tow-headed boy who once worshiped him into a homicidal monster. Perhaps Archwood had been born with a proclivity toward mental illness, which had only been exacerbated by his childhood abuse. Perhaps murdering people had been built into his DNA right from the start – although Gabriel didn't buy that one.

Gabriel gazed up at the white clouds again and their steady movement gave him a tranquil feeling.

Archwood was alive but he had no disguises to hide behind now. The only costume available was a prison uniform. Natalie Archwood, however, had developed the new character role of doting mother. She was trying to make up for the past by standing by her boy with furious determination. She was busy putting together the best defense team in the country and whenever Gabriel thought about that, the stab wound on his side hurt a bit more. But the case was out of the detective's hands. The next performance belonged to the District Attorney's office. Gabriel understood they were going for the death penalty.

A little boy ran by, rushing toward the waves, running when they chased him back, and screaming with the sheer joy of being alive and present.

Gabriel watched him. Andrew Pierce had stolen that exuberance from Gabriel long ago. He knew he would never forget Andrew Pierce and the wrong that was done to him. Although Andrew had stolen his childhood, Gabriel had no intention of allowing Andrew to steal his adulthood.

Ming nodded a greeting and took a seat next to him on the sand, wearing jeans and a sweatshirt. Gabriel noticed a new worry line stamped between her eyebrows as she stared pensively at the rolling waves, her fingers digging into the sand.

She's under the water again, Gabriel thought. Bound, unable to move, with a pipe wedged between her teeth and wondering all the while – how did this happen? The tight control she had on her environment had been blown to bits and she was suffering from the fallout.

Ming had epitomized self-assurance, comforted in the knowledge that she was only a clinical observer of the catastrophes that were wheeled into her examination room. How things had changed...

Gabriel smoothed her raven tresses with his hand. "Talk to me," he said gently.

Ming stared at the seaweed rolling in the green waves. "I was just thinking that it's November and still a beautiful day for a picnic."

She wasn't exactly being to the point, mused Gabriel. She was mincing words. That was okay. He was willing to help her survival in whatever way he could.

"Speaking of picnics..." Grimacing a little from the stitches pulling, Gabriel sat up and proudly displayed the picnic basket he'd been using as a pillow. Ming smiled like a birthday girl, opened the lid, and then looked up at him in astonishment.

"Nothing fancy," Gabriel joked. "Just homemade pheasant pate, brie cheese with caramelized pecan sauce, assorted homemade rolls, fruit, and sparkling grape cider."

Ming leaned over and kissed him. "You made good on your promise."

Gabriel caught her before she could sit back and returned the kiss – a bit more emphatically. He brought her body close to his with determined hands.

An inch from his lips, Ming said, "The beach isn't <u>that</u> deserted."

Gabriel traced a hand along her back. "Whatever we can't finish here, we can continue at my place."

Further words were unnecessary. As he allowed himself to drift into her scented hair, Gabriel decided this was going to be a good day; and he tossed any unpleasant thoughts out into the realm of the wide Pacific.

Behind Blue Eyes
Words and Music by Peter Townshend
Copyright © 1971 Towser Tunes, Inc. Fabulous Music Ltd. and
ABKCO Music, Inc.

Copyright Renewed
All Rights for Towser Tunes, Inc. Administered by Universal
Music Publishing International MGB Ltd.
All Rights for Universal Music Publishing International MGB
Ltd. In the U.S. Administered by Universal Music - Careers
International Copyright Secured. All Rights Reserved.
Reprinted by permission of Hal Leonard Corporation

My Last Affair
Words and Music by Skip Heller
Copyright © Skip Heller Music, BMI

Look for these upcoming novels in the Gabriel McRay series

Deep into Dusk
The Mask of Midnight
In Twilight's Hush

Visit us at www.facebook.com/thedarkbeforedawn

12042886R00212

Made in the USA
Lexington, KY
20 November 2011